CULTU

By Cindy L. Hull

Mission Point Press
2554 Chandler Road
Traverse City, Michigan 49696
www.MissionPointPress.com

Printed in the United States of America
ISBN: 978-1-954786-85-1
Library of Congress Control Number: 2022904220

Artwork: Jim DeWildt
Photograph: Keith Vandenbergh
Book design: Sarah Meiers

Visit the author's website at www.cindylhull.com.

CULTURE SHOCK

A Claire Aguila Mystery

Cindy L. Hull

MISSION POINT PRESS

Still and always to my husband, my children, and grandchildren. And to baby boomers everywhere, whether retired from city to the country, from country to the city, or to retirement communities anywhere: Rock On!

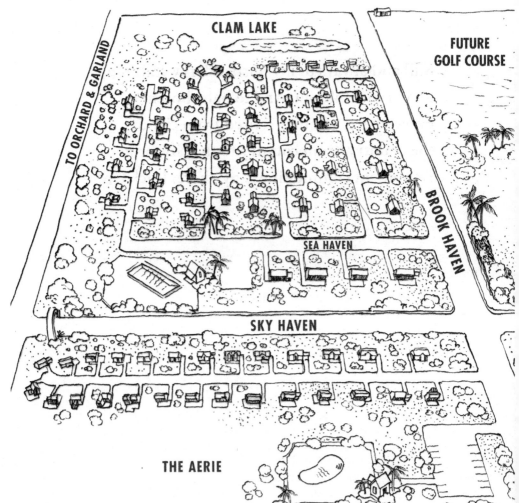

THE HAVENS

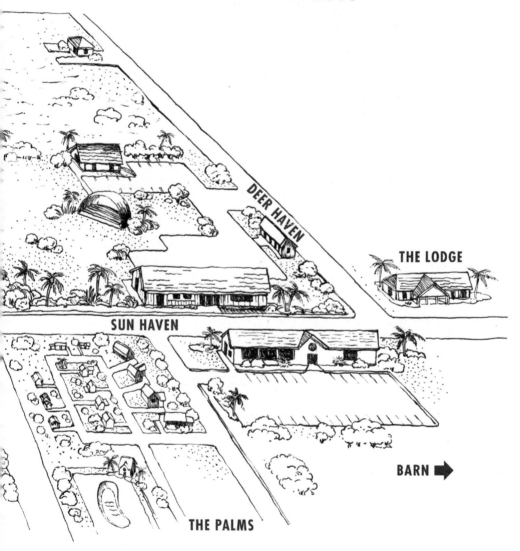

DEER HAVEN

THE LODGE

SUN HAVEN

BARN ➡

THE PALMS

PROLOGUE

Sunday Morning: Orchard, Florida

Julio Gonzalez ended his call and stuffed his flip phone into his pocket. *This could work out,* he thought. *Just be calm.*

"*¿Que pasa, Daddy?*"

"*Nada,* Billy." Julio caressed his stepson's black curls. "Eat your breakfast."

"Dada." Julio turned as his two-year-old daughter, Mary, tipped over her bowl of oatmeal.

"*¿Que haciste, mija?*" Julio plucked Mary from the high chair, carried her to the living room, and sat her on the frayed carpet to play with her secondhand doll. Mary smiled, petting her doll's snarled hair. Julio worried about Mary, who still struggled to walk on her own. Her surgery had helped, but her progress and the expenses weighed on him.

He left Mary on the floor, took a sack lunch from the refrigerator, and stuffed it into Billy's battered backpack. The six-year-old grabbed the pack, kissed his father, and ran out to the street where he joined the neighborhood kids, a collection of immigrant children and descendants of freed slaves who had settled in Orchard since the Civil War.

Julio watched the bus pull away, then carried Mary, still clinging to her doll, into the bedroom. He situated her on the unmade bed while he rummaged in the closet for the cardboard box his wife, Paula, had filled with Billy's outgrown clothes. He reached into the box and extracted a smaller box, pouring its contents onto the bed. Mary immediately shifted her attention from the doll to the knick-knacks, shiny bracelets, and jewelry

1

that tumbled out. *I'll have to do something with these soon,* he thought.

He then lifted a small metal cash box from the larger box and unlocked it with a key he had hidden from Paula. He knew exactly how much money he had stashed there. Returning to the closet he took a thick wad of money from another hiding place. His hands shook as he added it to the cash box.

Over five thousand dollars. That's good, he thought, *but now what?*

He looked at his frail daughter and thought about his family in Mexico, expecting him to save them from poverty. Too many obligations. *Gracias a Diós* that his cousin, Carlos, had taken him under his wing. But he himself had failed them all, and now he had broken an agreement.

Julio also worried about his plan. His next step could threaten everything and everyone he loved. If he were caught, his citizenship would be the least of his worries, but he had no choice. Resolved, he replaced the boxes into the larger one, piling Billy's clothes on top. He prayed that Paula didn't sort through the clothes box any time soon.

He carried Mary to the living room and read to her from her favorite animal book, then chose another book, this one in Spanish, and read it to her. He looked at his watch. He had hoped to hear from Carlos about a lawn job. Carlos knew he needed notice, so he could call his sister-in-law to watch Mary. Perhaps the job hadn't come through.

Later, after Julio had given Mary a snack and put her into her crib for a nap, he tidied the kitchen and washed the dishes. Paula worked thirty hours a week at the Dollar Queen in Garland. Julio tried to do as much as he could for Paula during the day, so when she came home, she could concentrate on the kids while he worked the night shift at Havens Gas & Grocery. Sometimes he cooked supper, but he wasn't a good cook and Billy always complained about his meals.

Julio looked through the cupboard and pulled out a can of black beans. He found a hamburger patty in the refrigerator left over from supper the night before along with a few tomatoes and a *jalapeña* pepper. He decided to take Mary for a walk to Maria's Mercado to buy tortillas and rice. He would surprise Paula with supper. As he and Mary left the house, his cellphone rang. When he hung up, he had forgotten any plans to shop for dinner.

CHAPTER 1

Sunday morning: The Havens, Florida

Alice Van Dee wiped her face with a gloved hand, leaving a smudge of dirt on her forehead. Nine o'clock in the morning and the heat already threatened to send her indoors for the day. She adjusted her hat and aimed her gardening shears at her unruly red bougainvillea, which threatened to block her view of the neighbor's driveway.

Gardening in Michigan had been much easier. Everything died in the winter, and one could start fresh every spring, a new beginning. In Florida, flowers exploded at unexpected times—brilliant reds, pinks, and yellows—then, just as suddenly, disappeared. Her husband wanted to be the gardener, but he had failed her, dying within the first year of their retirement in their dream community, The Havens.

Alice had carefully placed her shears just above a bud, poised to cut the thickened branch, when her neighbor's car pulled into the driveway next door. She dropped her shears on the crushed-shell landscaping, pulled off her gloves, and fished in the pocket of her gardening pants for her phone. She lunged through the fragrant hedge, stumbling over a bag of mulch next to the driveway.

"Todd! Wait!"

Todd Vogel's shoulders slumped as he waited for his car trunk to automatically open. He watched Alice crash through the hedge, her short gray hair sticking out from her wide-brimmed gardening hat in unruly tufts. She glanced into the trunk as Todd moved his golf bag aside and removed his suitcase. She waved her cellphone in front of his face. *Not now,* he thought.

"Good morning, Alice." He pushed a button and watched the trunk close.

Alice brushed her hands against her baggy pants. "You should take care of that mulch. It's likely to rain. It's rained every afternoon this week." She cast a swift look at Todd's silver Lexus and the Prius next to it. "Barbara's not with you?" She took off her hat, tossing it onto Todd's car, specks of dirt falling onto the trunk.

Todd glanced at the two bags of mulch, then at the offensive hat, resisting the urge to knock it onto the ground. Instead, he said, "No. Why?"

"I've been calling her all morning," Alice said, holding up her phone. "It's the mulch. I wanted to tell her I could help her spread it. I rang the bell, but no one answered. I thought you two might have gone away for a few days."

"I've been at a convention." Todd turned away from her and pulled his suitcase toward the connecting door between the garage and the house. "Barbara should be home."

"She's not," Alice declared. "And I also wondered if you could help me with my phone. My voicemail is filled up and I can't empty it out. Ray used to do it for me, and my son hasn't been down since Christmas." She looked up at Todd with her most imploring smile, holding her phone out to him.

Todd leveled his eyes on Alice. "I can help you later, okay? I'm tired."

He opened the door, leveraging his suitcase up the step. Alice took five determined strides to join him there. "How long have you been gone?" she asked.

"Four days, and I'm beat, Alice." He pulled the suitcase into the entranceway that separated the kitchen and dining area.

"I'll make coffee," she offered, following him into the kitchen.

Damn woman, Todd thought. "Barbara will have coffee

ready," he said. But there was no aroma of coffee. The coffee maker sat empty on the counter, and the house was quiet. He turned to Alice. "I'll come over later and fix your phone."

But Alice walked past him, leaving a trail of dirt in her wake. She surveyed the bright aqua-colored walls, granite countertops, and stainless-steel appliances. Her eyes followed Todd's as he looked down at the floor by his feet.

"Oh, I'm sorry, Todd." She returned to the door and kicked off her crocs, shedding even more dirt on the tile floor. "I wonder where she went," Alice said, looking around. "Did she take the golf cart?"

Todd left his suitcase in the kitchen, and Alice followed him through the dining area that separated the kitchen from the living room. A white-leather sofa divided dining and living areas. Micro-blinds were still drawn over the sliding glass doors that separated the living room from the lanai. The room smelled stale, the air conditioner not yet adjusted for the warm day ahead.

"Barbara?" Todd called into the quiet house.

"Maybe she's sleeping," Alice suggested as she hesitated behind Todd, who stood transfixed several steps ahead of her.

He saw his wife just beyond the sofa. She lay on the Oriental area rug in the living room, her long kimono crumpled around her legs, her eyes staring and lifeless. He gasped and turned back to Alice. When their eyes met, something changed in Alice's face.

"What?" Alice asked, straining to see beyond him.

Todd patted his pockets. He had left his phone in his car. "Call 911."

"What happened?" she asked, coming closer.

"Stay back," Todd said, holding up his hand.

Alice backed into the kitchen and scrolled her frequent contacts. She often called The Havens Department of Public Safety to report transgressions of community rules: visiting grandchildren swimming in the resident-only pools, speeding golf carts, or people of color in Founder's Plaza.

"Hello, Patsy? This is Alice Van Dee in Sea Haven. Is Judy there—or Danny?"

Patsy Burton, the desk clerk for The Havens DPS, put Alice on hold and pushed a button. "Judy, it's Alice Van Dee again."

Judy Barnaby, a retired bookkeeper and currently the chief public safety officer in The Havens, grumbled, "What is it this time? Some animal poop on her lawn?"

Judy punched the blinking button on the office phone and sighed into the receiver. "Alice? This is Judy. What's the problem?"

"I don't know!" Alice said. She didn't like the tone of Judy's voice, as if she was too busy to answer the phone. "I'm at Todd Vogel's house, and I think something's wrong with Barbara."

Judy sat up. "Did you call 911? We're not the ambulance service, you know."

"Can I do that on a cellphone?" Alice's voice raised in agitation.

"Never mind. We'll be right there."

Judy turned to Danny McKay. The retired shop teacher and football coach had been listening to Judy's side of the conversation.

"The Vogels," Judy said as she punched the extension for the EMS office, located in the building between theirs and the fire department. Then Danny and Judy hopped into their official golf cart, attached the blue flashing light to the top, and headed to Sea Haven.

CHAPTER 2

Todd heard Alice's voice in the distance, but he couldn't take his eyes off his wife's body. Blood had drained from a bullet hole that pierced her silk kimono-style robe. Her hands were bound in front of her with the sash from her robe. Her makeup was intact, and her short blonde-gray hair lay neatly behind her ears, as if she had lain down on the floor to take a nap. Except for the blood. Somehow, in his mental haze, he thought not of the horror of Barbara's death, but that she had died on *that* rug wearing *the* kimono they had purchased on their China vacation.

Their marriage had been, in his mind, divided into two phases: before and after their 40th-anniversary trip to China, several years after they moved to Florida to take over the family business. Since China, everything began to fall apart.

He heard Alice moving around in the kitchen. He roused himself and intercepted her in the dining room.

"Is she okay?" Alice asked, her eyes wide with curiosity. She peered around Todd's chest to see past him.

Todd wiped his eyes and stood to block her view. "No, she's not okay." He ran his fingers through his graying hair, a gesture that rumpled his waves rather than bringing them under control. He looked down at the diminutive woman and led her back toward the kitchen. "Did you call 911?"

"I called Judy."

"Judy?"

"Judy Barnaby at DPS. She's taking care of it." As she said this, they saw the flashing lights of the EMS ambulance as it pulled into the driveway. "I'll show them in," Alice said, turning toward the garage door.

Todd didn't stop her. He resisted the urge to look out the kitchen window. Instead, he studied the countertop. Three Waterford glasses sat upside down on a draining board next to a half-full bottle of single-malt scotch. *Three glasses*, he thought. He heard a vehicle door open and shut, then another door. Alice's shrill voice carried through the closed kitchen window as she reported her version of the event.

Two paramedics entered through the garage door. A balding middle-aged man led the way, and a younger man, with a military haircut, followed with a medical bag.

They didn't introduce themselves but paused briefly upon entering the kitchen. The older man asked, "Your wife?"

Todd nodded and pointed to the living room. The paramedics hurried past him. The younger man looked back at Todd before squatting down to the floor. Todd could see their two heads bobbing just above the sofa, already knowing their services wouldn't be necessary.

Minutes later, the front doorbell rang. Todd frowned as he invited Judy Barnaby and Danny McKay into the house. He didn't know Judy well but had seen her driving around The Havens in her official golf cart. She and Barbara were of similar age, but where Barbara had been petite, Judy was tall and sturdy with shoulder-length gray hair that matched her eyes. Danny McKay's football physique had softened over the years. Todd and Danny played golf together from time to time, but for Danny, golf was more about the 19th hole beverage than the game itself. Both DPS officers wore blue uniform shirts and capri shorts. Todd directed them to the living room. Unable to look at his wife's body again, he returned to the kitchen, contemplating the scotch and the three glasses.

In the living room, Danny peered over the older paramedic's shoulder. "Is she dead, Bud?"

Startled, the older paramedic looked up at Danny and saw Alice creeping into the living room. "Ma'am, you shouldn't be here." Bud stood and positioned himself between Alice and the body. "You and Judy shouldn't be here either," he told Danny, who reluctantly stepped back.

"Alice called us," Judy said, from behind the sofa. "We're waiting for the police to come."

"Wait outside please," Bud said, "and call them again." He looked at Alice, who still lingered in the dining room. "Mrs....?"

"Alice Van Dee."

"Mrs. Van Dee, you need to leave the house."

"But I'm a witness," she said.

"Someone will talk to you later, ma'am."

Danny led Alice to the kitchen, where she fussed as she slipped into her crocs. Outside, Judy sat in the DPS golf cart, making her call. Danny and Alice sat on a small iron decorative bench near the garage, one clearly not meant for human weight. He asked Alice how she came to be at the Vogels' house, and she related her story of the mulch and her cellphone woes.

"I've never seen a dead body before..." Alice said when she had finished her story, "except my husband." She blushed as she made this addendum, lowering her voice. "But he had a heart attack—died in his sleep."

Danny paled at her story. "I'm sorry, Alice."

Judy approached, placing her phone into her belt. "I've seen bodies," she said. "I worked Neighborhood Watch. Lots of bodies in Chicago," she added, watching the crowd begin to gather in the street.

"I thought you lived in Norwood Park," Danny said, his eyes scanning the neighbors loitering along the road.

"Same thing," Judy shrugged as she pulled Alice up from the bench. "You can go home, Alice. Thanks for your help."

"But the police are coming. I should stay," she protested.

"I'll send them over." Judy urged Alice toward the hedge, using her sternest tone, not the sympathetic voice she employed when Alice complained about trash pickup or rowdy seniors on *Fiesta* Night.

Resigned, Alice retrieved her hat from Todd's car and disappeared through the hedge. Danny and Judy reentered the house quietly, going through the garage and into the kitchen, where Todd still stared at the glasses on the draining board.

"Todd, I'm really sorry," Danny said.

Todd jerked his head toward Danny, and for a moment Danny was shaken by the look of fear on Todd's face. "Someone murdered my wife!" Todd said through teared eyes. "Who would do this?"

Todd slumped onto one of the high stools along the breakfast bar that separated the kitchen from the dining area. Through reddened eyes, he watched the paramedics approach from the living room.

"I'm very sorry, Mr. Vogel," the older man said. They both removed their plastic gloves and stuffed them into their coveralls. "I'm Bud Anderson, by the way, and this is John Gleason." They shook hands. "I'll call in the Gardenia County Coroner." Bud then turned to Judy. "Are the police coming?"

"A Detective Sergeant Davenport from the Sheriff's Department is coming. It may take a few minutes," Judy said. "Should we stay?"

Bud nodded. "Yes, but stay outside. Keep the cars and people away and watch for the detective."

Todd followed the EMS team and the DPS officers into the garage, collecting his phone from the car. He brushed the dirt from Alice's hat off the trunk and returned to his kitchen stool, where a window afforded him a view of the commotion outside. Dismayed, he watched his neighbors congregate in their front yards or stare out from windows. While Danny made unsuccessful motions to keep people away, Bud sat in the ambulance, talking into his cellphone.

CHAPTER 3

An hour later, after Todd had been asked to move to the dining table, his kitchen had finally been cleared, the glasses and scotch bottle taken away, and appliances dusted. Back at the counter, Todd stared out the kitchen window in his attempt to ignore the detective and medical examiner speaking quietly in the next room, and the evidence team, led by a Deputy Hughes, leaving a trail of fingerprint dust over everything.

His home had been invaded by strangers, and he imagined all of them suspected him of murdering his wife. The uniformed photographer, who looked too young to be a cop, followed Deputy Hughes as he studied the scene. The detective had permitted him to brew a pot of coffee. He drank it as he thought about his wife.

He and Barbara Denton met in graduate school. After earning their master's degrees in management and finance, Barbara worked at her family's large-equipment business in suburban Chicago while he worked at his father's firm. He joined Denton Equipment and Sales when he and Barbara married, and they took over the company when the elder Dentons expanded their business to Garland, Florida, anticipating their retirement. When they passed away, he and Barbara took over the Florida store while their twin children managed the Chicago company. Now, he mused, he and the twins would inherit the businesses.

Todd looked at his shaking hands, swabbed for gunpowder residue, barely able to hold his coffee mug. He left his stool and crept into the dining room. The detective, who had insulted him with his "it's just procedure" indignity, knelt next to the medical examiner, who sat on the floor next to Barbara's body. He could just see their heads above the sofa.

Assuring himself that the detective was occupied, Todd returned to the kitchen and took a whiskey bottle from a cupboard. He quickly poured a generous portion into his coffee and replaced the bottle, his attention turned again to the kitchen window. He cringed at the growing crowd outside his house, stepping back a few steps when he noticed several neighbors aiming their cellphone cameras in his direction. He took a large gulp of his spiked coffee as a brown and tan sheriff's cruiser pulled into the driveway. The driver, a female deputy, proceeded up the walkway to the front door while a second deputy stayed behind. Todd heard her enter and speak with the detective.

Returning his gaze to the window, he groaned as he noticed Danny talking with Joe Collins, a retired small-town journalist from Indiana, now a reporter for *The Havens Gazette*. The newly arrived officer shooed him away. Todd sipped his coffee to calm his nerves. *What are they doing? Why don't they talk to me?* he thought.

As if to answer his question, the female officer entered the kitchen with Detective Davenport, who introduced her as Deputy Pamela Stokes. Davenport identified Stokes's partner, Deputy Mike Powers, who stood outdoors, staring down Judy, who was taking photographs with her cellphone.

Todd watched Deputy Stokes with interest as she removed her hat and pulled sweat-dampened strands of brown hair back to the ponytail at the nape of her neck. He turned his attention to the detective's stern face, narrow with deep-set blue eyes behind wire-rimmed glasses.

"The whole town is out there—not to mention the entire Sheriff's Department," Todd complained, his eyes pleading. "Can't you get rid of them?" He pointed at the collection of vehicles crowded in his driveway and along the curb: the ambulance, the sheriff's cruiser, the medical examiner's black SUV, the detective's Equinox, and the Department of Public Safety golf cart with the blue bubble on top. "Couldn't you be a little more discrete?" he croaked.

"Mr. Vogel, I know this is difficult," Davenport said. "Your DPS officers have been asked to keep the onlookers at bay, and Deputy Powers will interview your neighbors. As for the vehicles—and the invasion of your privacy—your wife has been murdered."

Todd leaned back against the kitchen island, narrowing his reddened eyes. "I know that."

"I understand your pain and concern," Davenport reasoned, "but the sooner we can do our job, the sooner we will be out of your way."

"Oh, God, Channel 9 is here!" Todd gripped his cup, watching the news van pull into an opening along the curb. "How do they know already?"

"Police scanners." Davenport gave him a sympathetic smile. "Let's move to the dining room table."

Todd nodded and followed Davenport and Stokes to the dining area.

Once settled, Davenport said, "Deputy Stokes is working with me today. My interim deputy detective, Scott Malloy, is on assignment, but will be joining our team tomorrow." Davenport gave a quick glance at Stokes, noting her tightened jaw.

"I know that you may have already provided information to the public safety officers, but I need to ask again," Davenport continued. "It's important for us to establish time of death and determine a possible motive for your wife's murder. Do you understand?"

Todd nodded and sipped his tepid coffee.

"I understand that you've been away?" Davenport asked.

"At an equipment convention in Orlando. I left on Wednesday

and returned home this morning."

"What time did you return?"

"About nine o'clock. My neighbor, Alice Van Dee, came into the house with me and called the DPS." Todd watched as Stokes wrote Alice's name in her notebook.

"When did you see your wife last?" Davenport asked.

"Wednesday morning when I left, but we talked on the phone just after six last night. I called again at around ten-thirty and early this morning, but she didn't answer."

"Is there anyone who might want to harm your wife?"

"Harm Barbara? No! She's...was...perfect. Everyone loved her."

Deputy Stokes thought Vogel's word choice—perfect—contained a tinge of sarcasm, but Davenport didn't hesitate. "Did she have a job?" he asked.

"We own Denton's Equipment in Garland. We work...worked...together."

"Is there anyone at the business who might be unhappy?"

"Unhappy enough to kill her? Absolutely not!" He clenched his fists on the table. "I assumed it was a robbery, and she caught the thief in the act."

"Why would you say that?" Davenport asked.

"Because of the other robberies," Todd said. "There have been several in the past few months...mostly when people are away."

"Have they been reported to the Sheriff's Department?"

Todd straightened in his chair and looked from Stokes to Davenport. "They've been reported to the DPS. In fact, there's a group planning a neighborhood watch program, and I think they're looking at the Mexican workers. They seem to come and go at will." He examined his empty coffee cup.

"Do you know any of these workers?" Stokes asked.

"Not really." Todd pointed to the coffee pot. Davenport nodded, and Todd rose to fill his cup. Davenport's eyes scanned the kitchen as he waited for Todd to return to the table.

"What time was my wife killed?" Todd asked as he sat down.

"Doctor Carlisle will have an estimate for me soon," the detective answered. "When you talked to your wife, how did she seem?"

"Fine. She had planned dinner with her friends."

"Do you know which friends?"

"Probably her bridge club. I don't know…"

"Do you know if anything has been taken?" Davenport asked.

"How would I know? I haven't left this room, except to use the bathroom."

"Did you see anything unusual in your bathroom?" the detective asked.

Todd pressed his hands on the table, his voice quivering in frustration. "I didn't see anything. I looked at my wife's things on the bathroom counter—her makeup, lotions, toothbrush—I can't believe I'll never see her use them again." He choked. "I didn't think to look at anything else."

"I understand," Davenport said. "The evidence team hasn't found any sign of forced entry, but we'll have a better idea when we have fingerprints. Unfortunately, there's been a lot of traffic through the house already." He skimmed his notes. "When deputies arrived, the door from the pool area to the backyard was locked, as was the door connecting the garage to the backyard. The sliding doors leading from the living room to the lanai and from the garage to the kitchen were unlocked. The local DPS officers don't remember if the front door was locked when they opened it from the inside. Are those doors usually locked?"

Todd rubbed his forehead. "We're casual about the slider because we go in and out all day. We lock the outside doors every night…but I wasn't home, so I don't know if Barbara locked them."

"When you came home this morning, you came in through

the garage?" Davenport asked.

Todd nodded.

"Was the entrance door from the garage locked or unlocked?"

Todd sat back, thinking. "Unlocked, I think. I remember coming in without using my key, but Alice distracted me. I don't remember."

Davenport leveled his eyes on Todd. "Where do you keep your valuables?"

"We have a metal storage box in the bedroom closet—mainly for cash, but Barbara had a few expensive pieces of jewelry there."

"How much cash?" Davenport asked.

"Several hundred dollars, maybe three-hundred. It's pocket money and petty cash for paying the lawn maintenance men."

Davenport nodded and turned to Stokes. "Deputy, can you take Mr. Vogel into his bedroom to see if anything is missing?"

When they left, Davenport sniffed Todd's coffee cup and raised his eyebrows. He walked past Doctor Carlisle and the body toward the large sliding-glass door that opened into the birdcage, the name for the protective enclosures that protect Florida pools and lanais against birds, reptiles, bugs, and uninvited guests. Beyond the birdcage, and behind all the homes on Marlin Lane, a large reservoir, euphemistically named Clam Lake, extended to his left and right. A vast open area lay beyond the lake, prime real estate for another haven, he thought.

Davenport turned to see the photographer staring at a gigantic Chinese painting on the wall. The rookie, Ken Griffin, hadn't been given a permanent assignment yet, so for now his unofficial title was 'evidence photographer.' So far, Griffin, tall, lanky with red hair and green eyes, had shown promise—eager to learn, and accepting the chiding that comes with his rookie status.

"Griffin," Davenport said, "see if Stokes needs anything photographed in the master bedroom and bath, then go around the outside of the house and check for footprints. Let Hughes know if you find anything." Griffin nodded and slung his camera over his shoulder. Davenport rejoined the medical examiner, Doctor Jennifer Carlisle, in the living room.

"He's a good kid," Doctor Carlisle said as the detective hovered over her shoulder. "He turned green when he photographed Mrs. Vogel. It's his first murder."

"This case will give him a taste of the job, for sure," Davenport said as he watched Carlisle examine the bullet hole in the victim's chest, carefully adjusting her night clothing. Barbara Vogel had been a beautiful woman who had aged gracefully. Her face had character, gently lined and clear, even without makeup. Her arms and legs, as they extended from her silk robe, were well-shaped.

"She was shot at close range," Doctor Carlisle said. "There's residue on her robe and negligee. The bullet is likely lodged inside her. They have the casing, but there is something else—a bloody one-hundred-dollar bill underneath her body. Craig Hughes has it."

"Interesting," Davenport said, scanning the room. "Have they found the gun?"

"No sign of it yet but look at this." She lightly lifted the victim's arms, sheathed in the sleeves of her kimono, her wrists bound with the silk sash from her robe. "There might be a problem here." She pointed at the blood stains on the robe and sash.

Davenport looked at the belt and nodded. "And her ears," he said. "Did you notice the blood smears?"

"On both ears," she commented, raising her eyebrows. "Robbery?"

"It looks like it," Davenport said. "What about time of death?"

"I would guess she died sometime between nine o'clock last night and two o'clock this morning."

Davenport considered. "She may have been dead when the husband called her last night." He pulled gloves from his pocket and examined the area around her body. "Have we found her phone?"

"I'm not sure anyone has looked for it," Doctor Carlisle answered.

When Judy Barnaby wandered in from the dining room, Davenport put his fingers to his lips. The doctor nodded.

CHAPTER 4

Davenport intercepted Judy as she approached them. "Please stay back, Mrs. Barnaby."

"Call me Judy." She moved to within inches of the detective, who took a step back.

"Of course," Davenport said. "Can you tell me about the security gates at the entrance of each of The Havens' neighborhoods?"

"Each of the three neighborhoods—Sun, Sky, and Sea Havens—has two gates, one for residents and one for guests," Judy said.

Davenport nodded. "I entered through the guest gate and noticed two cameras, one in the call-box and one aimed at my license plate."

"Exactly," Judy said, lowering her voice at Davenport's prompt, "but the photos are blurred, and the cameras aren't always triggered. Residents have a code card, but many people know the code and can punch it in. Residents tell their guests, and the workers who live outside all know it."

"So, there's no way to trace who comes in using the resident button?"

Judy shuffled her feet. "Not really. Danny and I have been begging corporate to fix that, but they claim the gates are a deterrent. There aren't any gates at the main entrances because all residential roads are public."

"Thank you," Davenport said. He adjusted his eyeglasses. "How is everything going out front?" he asked.

"Deputy Powers is going door-to-door, and Danny is holding

back the neighbors," Judy answered. She tried to peer over the sofa where Doctor Carlisle still sat on the floor, blocking the victim with her body. "What do we know so far?" she asked, taking on the tone of a television police officer.

"We don't really know anything yet," he said, taking her arm lightly and moving her back toward the kitchen. "But there is something you can do for us." Judy stiffened, but allowed him to turn her away. "Can you set up an incident room at the DPS? We'll want to work from here as much as possible."

Judy stood straight. "We can do that."

"Thank you, Judy. Mr. Vogel will go to your office later today to meet with me. Please, let us know when he arrives."

"Do you suspect him?" Judy said, eyes wide. "I know he couldn't do it!"

He gave her a warning glance. "We don't know anything yet."

"But we know him," she said, her mouth set.

Davenport lowered his voice. "Is this going to be a problem?" he asked.

"No. It's just that..."

"Do you and Danny know how to take fingerprints?" Davenport asked.

"Of course," Judy said. "We've both had training."

Davenport, increasingly worried about this arrangement, said, "When Mr. Vogel arrives at your office, please take his fingerprints...and, of course, we'll need yours and Mr. McKay's prints from your employment files."

"Well, I..."

"Elimination prints in case you touched something before we arrived."

Judy crossed her arms, ready to argue, but at that moment Stokes, Griffin, and Todd emerged from the hallway and entered the kitchen.

"Judy," Davenport asked in his calmest voice, "can you show

Deputy Griffin to the backyard? He needs to photograph the periphery." He paused, then continued. "It rained in Garland yesterday afternoon. Did it rain here?"

"Yes, our usual spring afternoon downfall," Judy said importantly, "around four o'clock."

"Thank you."

When Griffin and Judy departed through the lanai, Davenport asked Stokes about their findings in the bedroom.

"The money box is empty," Stokes reported. "It had been opened but didn't look forced. It also appears that several pieces of jewelry are missing."

Davenport turned to Todd. "Was the jewelry valuable?"

"It was a matching ruby necklace and bracelet," Todd said. "She has...had a gold watch and a pair of diamond earrings that she wore regularly. I didn't see them on the dresser...I didn't notice...was she wearing them?"

"It looks like someone took earrings from her ears," Davenport said.

"Oh, my God." Todd pressed his lips together and rubbed his face.

"Have you seen your wife's phone?"

"Phone?" Todd blinked and glanced at a charging station on the kitchen counter. "It's not here—maybe it's in the bedroom? I didn't notice."

"I didn't see it," Stokes said. "I'll check with the team." She turned to find Hughes.

Davenport looked at Todd. "Mr. Vogel, do you own a gun?"

"Yes, but...you don't think...?"

"Do you know where it is?"

"It's in the sideboard," Todd said, pointing to the teak buffet table along the wall where Stokes conversed with Deputy Hughes.

"Any luck on the phone?" Davenport asked Hughes as he and Todd approached the sideboard.

"Not yet," Hughes said. He turned toward Griffin, who was waving wildly from a spot along the birdcage, "Excuse me, sir."

Davenport nodded as Hughes hurried toward the lanai.

"In which drawer do you keep your gun, Mr. Vogel?" Davenport asked.

"The top right-hand drawer—way in back." He moved toward it as he spoke, but Davenport stopped him and motioned to Stokes, who slid the drawer open and reached inside, shuffling around pens and miscellaneous items with gloved hands.

"It's not here," she said after a few moments.

"What kind of gun do you have?" Davenport asked Todd.

"A Ruger 9mm...oh, no. What kind of gun killed her?"

"We don't know yet, Mr. Vogel. Did your wife know how to use the gun?"

"She knew how, but she resisted the idea." He looked around the room as if he expected to find the gun lying on the floor.

"Would she use it if she had to?" Davenport asked. "I mean, would she think about the gun and look for it if she had a chance?"

"I...I really don't know. If she had time, she might. She knew how to squeeze the trigger."

"Did she know how to load it?"

"I taught her, but I'm not sure she would think of it. Besides, I kept it loaded, just in case."

"Mr. Vogel, did you come home at any time during your convention?"

"No."

"I do need your help," Davenport said. "I'd like you to make a list of your wife's friends...those she would most likely have gone to dinner with. I also need a list of everyone you socialized with in Orlando last night, for dinner, meetings, whatever, as well as the times." Davenport noticed the twitch at Vogel's eye. "What, Mr. Vogel?"

"I'm a suspect, then?" His lips quivered as he spoke.

"Just routine, Mr. Vogel. We need to check everyone's where-abouts, including yours."

"I…I couldn't…wouldn't kill her." Todd swallowed, and tears came to his eyes. "Besides, it will be impossible to make a list."

"Why is that?"

"I moved around, and the groups kept changing. Some people had drinks but didn't go to dinner. Others joined us at dinner, but not for drinks at the hotel after…I can't possibly remember everyone. I hardly know most of them, or just their first names." He ran his fingers through his hair again, as if trying to construct the list in his head.

Davenport nodded. "I do understand. I just returned from a conference in Orlando myself, but I need you to do your best."

Todd glanced at his wife's body, now enclosed in a black body bag. He blinked back tears. "What happens now?"

Davenport directed Todd back into the dining room. "The evidence team still has work to do. It might be better if you leave for awhile, or even overnight. Do you have a place to go?"

Todd paused, considering. "I haven't eaten since early this morning or showered since yesterday. I could go to the country club to shower, eat, and write up my lists." He looked at his suit-case, sitting where he left it when he entered the house. "Can I take my suitcase?"

"Do you mind if I take a look first?"

Todd pressed his lips together. "Why not? You're already going through my entire house."

Davenport searched through the suitcase, noting a binder from the convention he had attended. "Thank you," he said. "When you have your lists, please take them to The Havens Department of Public Safety. We'll be setting up a temporary office there. When you submit your lists, Judy or Danny will fin-gerprint you."

"Fingerprints? It's my house!"

"That's why we need them—to compare with others we might find."

"Then what?"

"We do our job and find your wife's killer."

CHAPTER 5

Deputy Mike Powers, perspiring through his uniform, stood in Alice Van Dee's driveway. He took off his hat and wiped his forehead as he skimmed his notes. Judy Barnaby reported that Mrs. Van Dee had been with Mr. Vogel when he found his wife's body. He watched Judy now, moving along the street, smiling and waving like a candidate for office.

He approached the front door and rang the bell. He didn't understand these lavish retirement homes. What did empty-nesters do with such large houses? And worse, aside from construction crews, Powers had not seen anyone who looked like him on any of his official visits to The Havens.

"Hello?"

Powers replaced his hat and looked down at an elderly woman wearing loose-fitting pants and a sleeveless blouse. "Mrs. Van Dee?"

"Are you a policeman?" She tilted her head back to take in the tall, muscular deputy.

Powers sighed. "I'm Deputy Powers of the Gardenia County Sheriff's Department, ma'am."

She frowned, her eyes still skeptical. "I've been waiting to be interviewed," she huffed. "No one seems to care what I saw."

"That's why I'm here, ma'am. May I come in?"

With some reluctance, Alice opened the door. She scooped up a tabby cat and ushered Powers into the house, which was conspicuously clean and white-carpeted, with oversized furniture and drapes.

"Did Judy tell you I saw Todd come home this morning? And

that I told him I tried to call Barbara all morning? I even rang her doorbell, but she didn't answer."

"Not exactly," Powers said, removing his hat again. "Can I sit down?"

She frowned but offered him an overstuffed chair. She settled herself onto the sofa, and her cat cuddled in her lap.

Powers turned to a fresh page in his notebook. "Do you remember what time Mr. Vogel arrived home this morning?"

"Around nine o'clock. He said he was at a convention—for his job."

"Did he invite you into his house?"

"Well," she hesitated, "he struggled to pull his suitcase out from behind the golf bag in his trunk…I don't get golf…anyway, I asked him to fix my phone, but he seemed frustrated, so I…I just followed him in."

"What happened inside?"

"He called his wife's name, but she didn't answer, so he went into the living room."

"Did you see Mrs. Vogel yourself?"

"No, she was behind the sofa. I thought she was sick or something. Todd asked me to call 911, but I called Judy and she called the EMS guys."

"How did Mr. Vogel act when he found his wife? Did he call her name? Run to her?"

"No! He was in shock." She narrowed her eyes at the deputy.

"How well do you know Mr. and Mrs. Vogel?"

"Well," she said. "I knew Barbara best. I liked her, but we didn't socialize, really."

"And Mr. Vogel?"

"He's friendly, but busy. Sometimes he helps me with things around the house. Sometimes he calls maintenance for me when my TV doesn't work or the cable goes out…I'm a widow," she explained.

"What time did you call Barbara this morning?"

She thought. "Around eight o'clock. I...I saw the mulch bags. I didn't know when they were delivered, but with the rain we had yesterday, I thought I'd offer to help her spread it in her garden. Those lawn people aren't supposed to just drop mulch bags in the yard like that."

"Did she usually work on the lawn?"

"It's always her or the lawn people, never him," Alice answered.

"Did you suspect that something might be wrong with Mrs. Vogel?"

"There *was* something wrong." Alice pressed her lips together. "I wondered why she didn't answer the phone. And I was right, wasn't I? Those EMS men should've thanked me for checking up on her. Instead, they kicked me out."

"I'm sure Mr. Vogel appreciated your help," Powers said, hoping his tone was grateful, "but once the paramedics arrived, they had to follow procedures."

"Hmph," she snorted.

"Did you see anything or anyone unusual last night? Strange cars, people?"

Alice pursed her lips in concentration. "Well, I can't see much from my house, that hedge being there and all...but I was outside looking for Puffy, my cat, last night and I saw a car pull into her driveway."

"About what time?"

"Around seven. The news had just ended. I realized Puffy wasn't around. She always lays with me to watch television. I went to the window and saw her in the front yard. I ran outside to grab her. I don't usually let her out...alligators...but I saw the car pull into Todd's garage. I thought it was Todd. It looked like his silver car."

"But you're not sure?"

"He told me this morning that he was gone all week, so, it

must have been someone else."

"Was the garage door open, or did the driver open it from the car?"

"Open, I think, but I don't remember."

"Did it close behind him?"

"Yes, I think so. It must have been Todd." She paused, her face scrunched inward like an overripe apple. "But if it wasn't Todd, who was at the birdcage late last night?"

"You saw someone in the house last night?" Powers asked, startled.

"No," she answered impatiently, "outside."

Powers stood. "Can you show me?"

Alice lay the cat on the sofa and led Powers to her lanai. Her home didn't have a pool, but did have a screened-in lanai that gave her a partial view through the hedge into the Vogels' backyard.

"He stood outside the birdcage," she said, pointing. "It was dark, and he wore one of those dark-colored hooded sweatshirts."

"What time was this?"

Alice pursed her lips. "I was watching a crime show on television and I heard a noise. I guess I dozed, because I thought it came from the TV—it must have been around ten. I looked out the back door and saw the guy, but by the time I went back to the sofa to get my glasses, I heard a car. I went to the front door and saw the headlights just pulling out of Todd's driveway."

Powers studied the yard and the area between the Vogel garage and Alice's hedge. Someone could have run through easily. "Let me get this straight, Mrs. Van Dee. You saw a car that looked like Todd's come into the garage around seven, then you saw a man in the backyard around ten, and then someone driving away from the house a few minutes later?"

"It had to be Todd, right?" Alice said, frowning. "Who else could it be?"

Powers looked down at the woman. As silly as she seemed, Alice had locked onto the implications of that possibility. He gave Alice his card and led her back to the front door. "Is this where you stood and saw the car pull out?"

"Yes."

Powers could barely see the driveway, but noted that Alice might have seen car lights through gaps in the hedge.

"Did you see any other cars around, or any strangers?"

Alice sighed impatiently. "The only people I see around are the lawn guys. There's a lot of them around," she said, raising her eyebrows mysteriously.

"Them?" Powers asked, taking the bait.

"You know…Mexicans."

"Are they hired by The Havens?"

"I think so. One of them came to fix my kitchen faucet once. They do odd jobs, and residents hire them to do their lawns."

"Do you know who the Vogels hired?"

"I don't know any names," she said. "The one I've seen at the Vogels wears a funny straw hat…kind of like my gardening hat," she said, smiling. Alice paused and adjusted her glasses. "In fact," she confided, "now that I think of it, I did see the guy with the hat last evening."

Powers studied the angle from the house. "Can you show me where you stood?" She nodded and led him to the front yard.

"Is this where you also stood when you saw the silver car go into the garage?" Powers asked, again looking at the angle.

"Yes, but…well…I didn't exactly see the Mexican man leave the house, but I saw him get into his truck—it was parked in the driveway—and he drove away. It's a red pickup."

"What time was this, do you think?" he asked doubtfully.

Alice thought. "Just before the six-thirty news started. I remembered I hadn't gotten the mail and I went out to the mailbox. I think that's when Puffy escaped."

"And it was the same man who usually mows their lawn."

Alice nodded vigorously. Her mouth opened, and she reached out to touch his arm. "I just remembered," she said, putting a finger to her lips, "he had a plastic grocery bag."

"Could you tell what was in it?"

"No," she scoffed. "I don't have x-ray vision—but it seemed bulky."

"Can you remember anything else about him?"

"I just know he works for The Havens. His truck is beat-up, very old, with a Mexican flag sticker in the back window."

"Who do you hire for your lawn work or maintenance?"

She shrugged. "I call the maintenance building—The Barn— and I get whoever can come, sometimes the man with the hat, sometimes someone else."

"How do you pay them?"

"Only cash," she sighed. "They don't want to pay taxes, I guess. Or they're illegals."

Powers cringed. "Thank you, Mrs. Van Dee. You've been very helpful." Powers wrote down her address and phone number and asked her, dubiously, not to talk to the neighbors. "I'll bring a statement for you to sign." Powers gave her a card. "If you remember anything else, please contact us."

"Yes, sir." She nodded and watched as he retreated down her driveway.

CHAPTER 6

Deputy Pamela Stokes rang the doorbell at the home across from the Vogels, a beige stucco ranch with a two-and-a-half stall garage. Ground seashell covered the front yard, interrupted by several tri-palms erupting from a large patch of ivy encased in a brick border. A decorative wrought-iron post near the driveway identified the owners as the Davises from Grosse Pointe, Michigan. No one answered the door, but a voice caused her to turn around. A tall, impossibly thin woman jogged toward her, wearing spandex capris and a sleeveless tank top. Stokes doubted this woman was older than fifty-five, but the lean, steel-gray-haired, bearded man coming up behind her with the labradoodle dog, definitely was.

"Officer?" the woman asked, making a slight bounce at the end of her effortless jog to the front door. Up close, Stokes recognized the telltale signs of injected youth masking the facial lines which would indicate she had laughed or frowned at some point during her life. She removed her visor and shook her head, loosening blonde curls from her perspiring scalp.

"Mrs. Davis?" Stokes asked.

"Amanda Davis," the woman replied, "and Jordan, my husband." She nodded toward the older man, who struggled to keep control of the dog as he caught up with her. "Is this about Barbara?"

"I'm afraid it is," Stokes said, introducing herself.

"I can't believe it…I talked with her yesterday," Amanda said.

"Can I take a few minutes of your time?"

Amanda deferred to her husband, who fumbled with the

door key.

"Of course," Jordan Davis said, scanning up and down the street. "Can we go inside?"

Stokes followed the couple into their home. It resembled the Vogels' house, with a high, vaulted ceiling and painted in light peach tones. Jordan released the dog, who ran to a water dish and then to a dog bed. Stokes noticed that the Davises had a clear view of the Vogel home from their living room window.

Amanda directed Stokes to a plush Italian leather chair. "Can you tell us what happened?" she asked, perching on the edge of a matching chair.

"I'm sorry, but I can only tell you that Mrs. Vogel died some-time last night or early this morning." Stokes settled her note-book on her lap.

Jordan collapsed onto the sofa. "We heard there was a rob-bery—that maybe Barbara caught one of the workers stealing from her."

"Who told you that?" Stokes asked.

"Well, people are just talking. We all know about the robber-ies," Jordan said defensively as he rubbed his chin, pressing his finger into his deep cleft.

Amanda added, "Judy mentioned it."

"Judy Barnaby?" Stokes asked with poorly disguised scorn.

Amanda nodded, throwing a furtive glance at her husband.

"Were you both home last night?" Stokes asked.

"What time?" Amanda asked.

"Let's say after six o'clock and into the evening?"

Amanda examined her professionally lacquered nails. "I went to supper with friends around six-fifteen." She looked up at Stokes, her brown eyes meeting the deputy's. "Barbara had planned to go, too."

Stokes's eyes flashed to Jordan and back to Amanda. "You and Barbara were friends?"

Amanda's cool façade cracked, and tears came to her eyes. "Yes."

"Please tell me what happened last night," Stokes pressed.

Amanda swallowed, then spoke with a soft, airy voice, almost a whisper. Stokes leaned forward to listen.

"Our bridge group had a reservation for six-thirty. Barbara and I planned to leave together around six-fifteen, but she called and said she would meet us there, that she might be a few minutes late."

"What time was this?"

Amanda looked at her husband as if he had the answer. "I guess about five-forty-five."

"Did she say why she'd be late?"

"She said Carlos was stopping by to get paid, and that Todd hadn't called yet from Orlando. She said that she'd come as soon as she could." Amanda pulled a tissue from a box on her end table and dabbed her eyes.

"Who's Carlos?"

"The gardener. I think his last name is Chavez."

"She never came?"

"Well, no. She called again before six-thirty—we were already at the restaurant. We ordered drinks and thought we'd wait a few minutes for her, but she said that something came up and she couldn't make it."

"She didn't say why?"

"No."

"Did she seem upset, angry, happy?"

Amanda paused and peered briefly at her husband again. "She seemed fine, not angry."

"Did you talk to her again, after dinner?"

"No," Amanda answered.

"You didn't call her to see if she was okay?" Stokes asked.

"I wish I had." Amanda wiped tears from her eyes with the

damp tissue.

"What about you, Mr. Davis? Did you see Mrs. Vogel or anyone else come and go from her house last night?" When he hesitated, Stokes added, "You have a good view of the Vogels' driveway and garage."

Jordan shifted in his chair. "I saw no one."

"Did either of you see any cars parked at the house?"

Amanda opened her mouth to speak, but Jordan turned his dark eyes on her, and she pressed her lips together, sitting back in her chair. *Damn*, Stokes thought as she jotted in her notebook.

Jordan cleared his throat as if beginning a prepared speech. "I saw a gray or light-colored sedan in the driveway around nine-thirty. I couldn't tell the make, and it didn't look unusual. It was gone when I closed up the house around ten-thirty."

"Had you seen this car before, or have any idea who owns it?"

"No."

"You saw no other vehicles or pedestrians?"

"No, we were having cocktails by the pool after Amanda returned from dinner. I noticed the car when I came into the kitchen to replenish our drinks." Jordan's jaw set and his eyes narrowed. "I thought you would be looking for the workers... like that Carlos guy. No one else would be robbing houses."

"We're more concerned about a murder right now," Stokes said. "Mr. Davis, how well do you know Todd Vogel?"

"Todd and I play golf together, but we aren't really close friends. Amanda and I are retired, but Barbara and Todd have a business and don't socialize much."

Stokes studied Amanda. "But Barbara was in your bridge group?" she asked.

"Yes," Amanda said, ignoring Jordan's warning glance.

"Is there anything else you would like to tell me about the Vogels? Any reason why someone would want to harm Mrs. Vogel?"

Amanda seemed to hesitate for a moment, but her husband said brusquely, "No, nothing."

Stokes thanked them for their time and requested that they report to The Havens DPS to sign statements. "The DPS office isn't set up for us yet, but please, later this afternoon, we would like a formal statement." She paused, closing her notebook. "If you think of anything else—either of you—please include it in your statements."

Jordan and Amanda walked Stokes to the door. They both looked up and down the street to see who had witnessed her visit. Stokes returned to the Vogel house, where Judy Barnaby held court with a television reporter.

CHAPTER 7

Sunday afternoon

Gwen Estes carried her newly groomed Shih Tzu dog, Precious, from The Pet Palace. She placed Precious in the back seat of her pink Cadillac, her reward for years of selling Mary Kay Cosmetics in Ohio. She carefully backed out of the parking lot and aimed her car toward Sea Haven, only to brake sharply in front of The Barn maintenance building. She stared at the two vehicles parked there. She knew the red pickup belonged to Carlos, the maintenance man, but it took her a few minutes to remember where she had seen the blue Ford. As she considered what to do, someone honked at her from behind. She recognized Sheila Cavanaugh in her newly customized golf cart—a fake Cadillac. Gwen waved Sheila by, purring apologetic words to Precious as she detoured off the main road.

At The Havens DPS, Gwen scooped Precious from the back seat, debating whether to leash her or carry her. *Carry,* she thought, wary of her pet getting her paws dirty on the questionable DPS floors. She pushed through the front door, greeting Patsy at the information desk as Precious whimpered to be put down.

"Patsy," she said, breathlessly, "where's Judy?"

Patsy looked up at Gwen, whose streaked and coiffed hair resembled that of her dog. "She's with the uppity cops. Is it important?"

"Yes! Tell her to hurry!"

◆ ◆ ◆ ◆ ◆

Martín Aguila, new resident in The Havens, parked his blue Ford SUV in front of The Barn. He worked his lame leg from the car and limped toward the barn-red maintenance building. In his view, everything in The Havens was merely a cheerful façade hiding the ordinary, with a costly price tag. He opened the front door, embedded in fake barn-sized double-doors, and entered the huge building.

Inside, Carlos Chavez stared at the air-conditioning unit he was repairing for a home in Sun Haven. He found it hard to concentrate, the audio tape in his head continuously replaying his encounter with Mrs. Vogel the night before.

He prepared an alibi in his head, imagining an interrogation. He had arrived home late because he had stopped at Mrs. Vogel's house. He had supper with his wife, Sofia, and their two daughters, then went to the bar with his friends. He wished that his cousin, Julio, had been there to vouch for him. Would the police believe a bunch of Mexican workers? But Martín had been there. They might believe him. Carlos couldn't stop the chaos of thoughts bumping around his brain. He picked up his pliers and aimed them at a loose connection.

"Hey, Carlos."

Carlos jumped and turned to see Martín Aguila approaching.

"What are you doing here?" Carlos asked. "I thought your family was visiting."

Martín sat on a high stool next to Carlos. "They'll be here soon, but I wanted to find out what happened at the end of Manatee Street this morning. I thought you'd know about it."

Pete Morales, the manager of The Barn, emerged from his office and joined them.

"Martín, what are you doing here on Sunday? Carlos offered to work on Mr. Stryck's air conditioner. Don't you have any friends?"

Martín laughed. "You guys are my friends. How pathetic is

that?"

Carlos remained quiet, fingering his pliers and staring at his project. "Martín wants to know about the murder," he said.

"Murder?" Martín said, his gaze shifting from Carlos to Pete.

Pete pulled up another stool and sat. "Can you believe it?"

Carlos frowned and lay his pliers down. "It's awful," he said as he rubbed his eyes, wondering when he could afford to buy glasses, "and strange."

"Hell, yes," said Pete. "A woman murdered in The Havens? I don't think it's ever happened."

"It's worse than that," Carlos said, stammering. "I saw her yesterday. I…in fact, I went to her house." He tapped his fingers nervously on the table.

Pete's eyebrows furrowed. "Why were you there?"

"She owed me money for lawn mowing, so I stopped on my way home."

"She was there?"

"Yes, and alive," Carlos said defensively. "She paid me and gave me some kids' books she bought at a library sale. She's always doing nice things like that."

"Mrs. Vogel?" Martín sat back on the stool. "On Marlin Lane?" He leaned his elbows on the worktable and ran his fingers through his thinning gray hair. "I was there last night, too."

"What?" said Pete.

"That mulch. I forgot to deliver it on my way home like I promised." He turned to Carlos. "I remembered it at the bar and dropped it off on my way home."

"Did you see her?" Pete asked.

"It was late, and the house was dark. I put the bags next to the garage."

"So, both of you were at Mrs. Vogel's house the night she was murdered?" Pete groaned.

"What do we do?" Carlos asked, his eyes wide. "Should we go

to the police?"

As the men stared at each other, the front door opened and Judy Barnaby entered, followed by two uniformed deputies. A male deputy stood near the door, but the female deputy and Judy approached the three men.

Carlos stared in dismay, his eyes darting from his boss to the new arrivals. He stood, nearly knocking his stool over in his haste. Pete, fearing Carlos might flee the room, placed his hand on his employee's arm. Martín stood calmly, his face a mask, giving Pete the impression that the newcomer had experienced this before.

"Hey, Judy," Pete said.

"Hi, Pete." Judy introduced Deputies Stokes and Powers, then identified Pete and Carlos.

Carlos stared at the deputies, afraid to speak. Although he often saw Judy issuing tickets to cars and golf carts on main street, she rarely acknowledged him. He didn't realize she knew his name.

Judy turned to Martín. "I don't know you."

"Martín Aguila, of 1275 Urchin Court."

"Is that your Ford outside, with the Michigan plates?"

"Yes, ma'am."

Deputy Stokes moved between Judy and the men. "What's your position here, Mr. Morales?" she asked Pete.

"I'm the supervisor of the maintenance department."

"You're Carlos's boss?" Deputy Stokes asked.

"Yes, and he's a good worker—the best."

"That's good to hear," Stokes said, smiling slightly. She turned to Martín. "And what do you do here?"

"I work part-time, mainly doing lawn work."

Stokes addressed Pete again. "We need to speak to Mr. Chavez and Mr. Aguila at the DPS office."

Martín stood and positioned himself close to Carlos. "What's this about?"

"Both of your vehicles were reported at the scene of a murder last night. We have a few questions."

"I didn't do anything," Carlos protested. He could feel the perspiration form under his shirt. "*Nada*," he reverted to Spanish, wiping his hand over his brow.

Judy stepped forward and started to take Carlos's arm. "Come on, Carlos, you were seen."

Martín reached out and pulled Carlos back as Stokes turned angry eyes on Judy. "We'll take it from here, Judy," Stokes said.

"I'm in charge of the DPS," Judy said, glaring at Stokes. "Detective Davenport isn't here yet."

"Please," Stokes said, smiling and softening her voice, "the Gardenia County Sheriff's Department is in charge of the investigation."

Judy pressed her lips together and turned to leave. She walked past Deputy Powers, who struggled to suppress a grin.

Stokes waited until Judy left the building, then turned to Carlos and Martín. "We're developing a timeline for the death of Mrs. Vogel, and we need to talk to anyone who was seen in the area or who might have visited her that day. It's just routine. We can't force you to come with us, but it's better if you come voluntarily."

"Can I come in after work?" Carlos asked. "I can't afford to lose any hours." He threw a pleading glance toward Pete.

"It won't take long," Stokes reasoned. "You can drive over. We might want to look at your car, also, if that's okay with you."

Pete nodded toward Carlos. "It's okay, man."

Martín patted Carlos on the back. "We should go, my friend."

As Carlos and Martín followed the deputies to the door, Carlos turned back toward his boss.

"Pete, call Sofia…"

"And my wife, Theresa," Martín added.

CHAPTER 8

"Are we there yet?" Cristina Aguila laughed as her mother's red Prius crept down Highway 27, past citrus groves, fruit stands, and a continuous stream of retirement communities, mobile home parks, and RV dealerships. She was far beyond the years of tormenting parents on long trips, but memories of past family vacations brought out her mischievous nature.

"Almost." Claire Aguila Carson rolled her eyes as a thirty-foot RV pulled out in front of her from a fast-food restaurant, a Jeep Cherokee weaving from behind. She slammed on her brakes. "If the Happy Wanderers from Topeka, Kansas, don't kill us first," she added, reading the colorful spare-tire cover in front of her.

Claire smiled at Cristina, so grateful to have her daughter on this journey. Although a well-traveled anthropologist herself, Claire had worried when Cristina joined a graduate school research trip to Malawi, East Africa. Now safely home, her only child had agreed to join Claire on a road trip to another alien culture—a retirement community in central Florida.

Their adventure had started days after Claire's department-chair duties and Cristina's graduate classes ended for the summer. Their destination was The Havens, where Claire's parents had been invited to stay at a winter home belonging to the Carsons, the parents of Claire's deceased husband—Cristina's father. Claire's former in-laws were traveling elsewhere for the winter. Taking advantage of the Carsons' generosity, Claire and Cristina decided to drive to Florida together to visit Martín and Theresa. Both mother and daughter wondered how Martín, the child of migrant farm workers, was fitting into the world of affluent white retirees. They couldn't wait to find out.

Claire's GPS, dubbed "Dolores," directed them to turn left onto Highway 301, but construction signs detoured them onto a secondary road. They bounced over abandoned railroad tracks and passed a sign welcoming them to the town of Orchard, a misnomer, since there were no fruit trees in sight. They crept along a potholed road past dilapidated stores. Maria's Mercado, splattered with faded advertising posters in English and Spanish, stood squeezed between Bubba's BBQ and Pham's Laundry. Across the intersection, *Los Hermanos'* gas station and car repair leaned into the Dollar Queen, which in turn threatened to tumble into Mama's *Taqueria*. Mother and daughter resisted the temptation of Carlita's *Panadería y Pastelería* on the corner.

Beyond the stores, clapboard homes, painted years ago in bright pastels, lined the street and narrow asphalt roads that led off from it. A scattering of live oaks, draped with Spanish moss, provided the only shade where children, a miniature United Nations, played among battered pickup trucks.

Cristina opened the car window to take in the sounds of children playing and the mingled aromas of BBQ and tacos emanating from outdoor smokers and open windows.

Eventually, Dolores directed them back to the highway, a three-lane thoroughfare that skirted Orchard. Here, big-box stores and franchise restaurants replaced small family businesses. This was Garland, the governmental center for Gardenia County. Several miles down the highway, the GPS directed them to Haven Boulevard, a wide road divided by a median landscaped with palm trees and a brilliant array of colorful tropical flowers. A brightly colored arch welcomed them into the cocoon of southern retirement—The Havens.

In the median, a statue of the founding father, arms raised to the heavens, stood on a pedestal surrounded by a koi pond, like a miniature Statue of Liberty.

Cristina laughed out loud. "Bring me your tired, your old…
your retired masses yearning to play golf…"

"Be nice, Cris," Claire warned. "You'll be old one day."

"Not here."

On the left, they passed a collection of immense single-storied homes on generous lots. Claire slowed at a sign directing them to turn left on Brook Haven Road for Sea Haven. "Sea Haven is the newest and most exclusive of the three communities. It is also where your grandparents are staying."

"You're kidding! They're living here?" Cristina raised her eyebrows.

"Let me give you a quick tour before we settle in. I spent more time in The Havens than I wanted when I moved them into the house last fall."

Claire ignored Dolores and reluctantly, it seemed, the GPS agreed to "reroute." They continued down Haven Boulevard, passing the other two havens, Sun Haven and Sky Haven, on their right. Located closer to the town center, these neighborhoods contained less extravagant homes on smaller lots.

Cristina looked out her window at the front yards, either manicured lawns or seashells bleached by the sun. She watched as a woman with short, bobbed gray hair stood patiently, blue plastic bag in hand, waiting for her Yorkie to do its business on a lawn.

A mile down the boulevard, they approached the town center, called The Hub. Contiguous businesses lined both sides of the boulevard, each with its distinctive small-town façade: Glamour Boutique, Pauline's Salon, The Ashram, and the New You Fitness Center. A small group of couples, dressed in senior chic—capris and decorative shirts for women and cargo shorts and faded T-shirts for men—ate lunch at the outdoor tables of Betty's Café. A visiting family, wearing baseball caps and Disney garb, studied a map at Starbucks, and a lively collection of teens, likely surviving their annual visit to grandparents, formed a spontaneous gang, simultaneously texting and laughing, at the Five Guys Burgers and Fries.

Golf carts impeded their progress, following mysterious traffic regulations that resulted in a cacophony of horns, from 'ka-doo-ka' to 'I Can't Get No Satisfaction,' whenever Claire violated an unknown infraction. Each golf cart could be identified by its owners, 'John and Joyce' or 'The Coopers,' and by souvenir plates proclaiming their state of origin.

"I bet Papa's hating this," Cristina said through a laugh.

Claire smiled. "Welcome to Paradise."

They passed The Barn on the right, then a mile further until the boulevard emptied into the Glen Haven Golf Course and Country Club. The road opened into a wide circular drive with signs directing traffic to the clubhouse, various small bars, and the fine-dining restaurant, The Oasis. Claire drove around the circle as Cristina stared at the sprawling golf course. A golf cart modified to look like a Rolls Royce swerved from the road leading to The Oasis. Their tipsy demeanor hinted that both 'Horace and Helen' had spent more time at the bar than on the greens, but their golf bags bounced merrily on the cart behind them as they honked "Let it Be."

Claire headed back toward The Hub, turning right on Deer Haven Drive. She pointed out The Lodge, a massive structure, replicating a plantation manor, that served as the visitor center, real estate offices, and community center. An impressive sports complex spread out behind The Lodge, with a baseball diamond, tennis and pickle ball courts, community pool, and playground.

"Playground?" Cristina asked. "Where are the kids?"

"They visit on vacation and holidays—and they are registered and tagged so their parents can't leave them here," Claire said, winking.

Down the road to the left, off the main road, Claire pointed out Founder's Plaza, a large grassy park surrounded by a narrow avenue for golf cart parking only. Paths, benches, kiosks, and a rest area sat among huge live oak trees covered with Spanish moss, and a central gazebo that offered a shaded stage area.

Beyond the plaza, they turned around in the parking lot of the Department of Public Safety, Fire, and EMS. They returned to Havens Boulevard, then right onto Brook Haven Road, where Dolores directed them into Sea Haven.

As they turned into the entrance to Sea Haven, Cristina pointed to an extensive construction site just beyond the gate on the other side of the road. "What's that?"

Claire laughed. "That will be another golf course, an 'executive' course, whatever that means. It will take up the entire section between Brook Haven and Deer Haven Roads, and all the way to the county road at the back entrance to The Havens."

Claire pressed the guest button at the entrance gate, and the security arm rose obediently.

"Awesome security," Cristina said, rolling her eyes.

"Did you notice the cameras?" Claire said. "These places are obsessed with security. People who live here are afraid."

"Of what?"

"Outsiders," Claire said with some bitterness. "Have you seen anyone who looks like your grandfather?" She looked over at her daughter and raised her eyebrows.

Just beyond the gate, the scene became anything but bucolic. A barricade blocked one lane of the first road, Manatee Street. Claire paused to look.

"Something's going on at the end of the street," Cristina said, her finger pressing on the closed window. "I see another barricade and lots of cars…looks like police."

"Someone probably jaywalked and got hit by a golf cart," Claire quipped, as she strained to see.

A heavy-set man, wearing a blue uniform shirt and cargo

shorts, hurried toward them, panting from the exertion. Claire and Cristina opened their car windows to the blistering heat. The officer came around to Claire's side of the car and leaned in. A shoulder patch identified him as The Havens Public Safety, and a name tag identified him as Daniel McKay.

"The road is closed to non-residents, ma'am," Danny said. "Where are you headed?"

"Urchin Court."

"You live here?" he asked, studying her carefully, then turning to the younger, lighter-skinned woman.

"My parents are staying at the Carsons' house. The Aguilas?"

"Oh, them. Okay. Go ahead."

They closed their windows.

"Any questions?" Claire asked Cristina.

"Not one," Cristina said.

They passed the next street, Dolphin, where a uniformed deputy guarded another partial barricade. They turned right on the next street, Urchin Court.

"Can you believe this?" Cristina asked her mother as they passed enormous homes with carefully manicured lawns and professional landscaping.

Claire laughed. "I suspect that Mom is in suburban Heaven and Dad is in the Mexican version of Hell."

"I can't believe that Papa agreed to live here for a week, let alone months."

"I doubt he had a choice. Your nana gave him the evil eye and the 'I spent forty years in your world, it's time to spend some time in mine' line. I don't think your papa dared refuse her request."

Claire spotted the pale green stucco home with light-colored brick at the curve of the cul-de-sac where narrow front yards opened into large rear living areas. The Carsons' front yard did not allow for the circular driveways that adorned other houses along the street, but their flower garden, with tropical flowers and a tri-palm centered in a large coral island, compensated for the inconvenience.

The two women unloaded their suitcases from the car. Both the May heat and the aromas emanating from the garden reminded Claire of Yucatán, Mexico, where she had conducted her doctoral research many years before. But her thoughts returned specifically to the previous May, when she had attended an anthropological conference in Merida, became reacquainted with an old friend, now a detective, and helped him solve a murder mystery.

"What's that look for, Mom?" Cristina asked as she pushed the doorbell. "Are you okay?"

"I'll let you answer that question later," Claire said, throwing her daughter a cryptic smile.

The door opened, and Theresa Aguila appeared in the doorway, her blue eyes wide with worry. "I've been calling you! Your father's in jail!"

CHAPTER 9

Martín, in his car, and Carlos, in his pickup, followed the squad car to the Department of Public Safety. The deputies led them into the reception area where Judy Barnaby stood ominously over the receptionist, Patsy Burton, pointing at the computer screen in front of them. Carlos stood close to Martín, who seemed to grow in stature as he entered the building.

"The detective's not here yet," Judy said as they entered.

"He'll be in soon," Stokes reassured her. She paused, afraid to ask the next question. "Is there a second room available? We'd like to interview Mr. Aguila and Mr. Chavez individually."

"Just the one room," Judy responded curtly.

"Are you sure?" Stokes asked.

"That's asking a bit much," Judy said, crossing her arms.

"We could wait for Detective Davenport to return," Powers shrugged.

Judy sighed. "I guess you can use Danny's cubicle." Judy turned toward the back offices. As Powers and Martín followed Judy, Martín turned to Carlos and said, "Read the statement carefully before you sign it."

Stokes led Carlos to the newly designated incident room, spacious with two large desks and a window view of the sports complex across the street. She regretted giving Judy a hard time about a second room. Stokes sat behind the larger desk near the window and set up a digital recorder that had been furnished. She invited Carlos to sit in a folding chair across from her, and started the recorder. Carlos removed his straw hat, twisting it in his fists.

"Do you understand that this interview is voluntary, and that you are not accused of any crime?" Stokes asked.

Carlos looked at his hands. "I understand," he said, slumping in his chair.

Stokes identified herself for the recording, indicating Carlos as the witness, followed by the date and time.

"Do you know that Mrs. Barbara Vogel was murdered last night?" Stokes asked.

"Everyone knows about it," Carlos responded, giving his hat another twist.

"Yes," Stokes said, "but you and Martín Aguila were both at the Vogel house last night."

"I didn't do anything!" Carlos placed his hand on his leg, which had begun to twitch.

"Why were you there?"

Carlos's voice shook and his hands nervously twisted his hat as he struggled for the words. "She owed me money for mowing her lawn."

"What time?"

Carlos paused to collect his thoughts. "I…I left The Barn after six. I usually leave around five-thirty, but I needed to finish a project. I talked to a friend in the parking lot, you can ask him—Jorge Sanchez—I think I got to her house around six-thirty." He watched Stokes write in a notepad. "I called her to tell her I'd be late."

"Did you go into her house?"

"Just inside the front door."

"And she paid you?"

"Yes."

"Did you argue with her?"

"Why would I argue with her? She paid me."

"Someone saw you carrying a bag from the house." Stokes paused, her hazel eyes piercing his.

A sob escaped from Carlos's mouth. "I didn't steal anything. She gave me some books for my kids. I can show you. They're in my car. I didn't steal anything."

"How long were you there?"

"It...it took her awhile to collect the books. She took the money from her purse...maybe five minutes total."

"How much did she give you?"

"A hundred dollars. I charge forty-five for mowing. She owed me for two times, and she gave me an extra ten."

"How did she act?"

"She seemed in a hurry," Carlos said, "but she apologized for paying me late."

"Did you go back to her house later last night?"

"No."

"Is there anyone who can vouch for your actions last night?"

"My wife...and...Martín," Carlos said, wiping perspiration from his forehead. "Martín and I were at Jonah's Bar in Orchard together."

"You two were there together last night?"

"After I got paid, I went home, and then to the bar after supper, a little before eight. My wife and Jonah can vouch for me, too. I left around ten-thirty and went home."

"And stayed home?" Stokes asked.

Carlos nodded. "Yes."

"When did Mr. Aguila leave?"

"He left about fifteen minutes before me." Carlos pressed his hands down on his thighs, flattening his hat. "Can I go now?"

Stokes called Powers and asked him to bring Martín and the fingerprint scanner to their office. "Powers, could you check out Mr. Chavez's car? He gave us permission to examine the bag he got from Mrs. Vogel—and, please, thank Judy for setting up our office."

"Fingerprints?" Carlos asked, when she had finished her call.

"Do you mind if we take your prints?" Stokes asked. "For comparison purposes?"

"It's okay," Carlos said, then blanched. "What if I touched her door?"

"If that's the only place we find your prints, you'll be fine."

"Okay," Carlos agreed.

"Thank you," Stokes said. "After we take your fingerprints, Deputy Powers will take you to your car. Then we'll have you come back in to sign a statement." Stokes paused. "One more question, Mr. Chavez. Do you own a gun?"

◆ ◆ ◆ ◆ ◆

Deputy Powers and Carlos—who claimed he didn't own a gun—left the office. Martín entered and took his friend's seat. He waited quietly while Stokes read the notes Powers had left with her.

"Do you understand that this interview is voluntary?" Stokes asked when she had finished reading. Martín said yes, and she entered the preliminary information in the recorder.

"I see you've lived in The Havens since last fall, right?" Stokes asked.

"Yes. It's likely we'll leave by the end of June." He explained the invitation from Claire's former in-laws.

"You seem to have settled in nicely," Stokes suggested. "You have a part-time job and friends already."

"My wife likes it here," Martín said simply.

"And you're involved with the employees at The Barn."

"Involved?" Martín asked, his voice raised. "I work with them, and I've made some friends."

"Mr. Aguila, you're being defensive. I wonder why."

Martín folded his hands in his lap. "I apologize. I hired many Hispanic workers at my business. I also spent too much of my time in offices like this, protecting them against false accusations."

"What kind of business?"

"Home and business electrical. Often, whenever something went missing…a wife couldn't find her bracelet or some other misplaced item, the first to be accused was the Hispanic electrician who happened to work for her the week before."

"So, you don't think we have the right to question those at the scene, just because they're Hispanic?"

"Not at all," Martín said. "It's just striking a chord, that's all."

"Tell me then," Stokes asked, "why did you go to the Vogel home last night?"

Martín sat back in his chair, folding his arms. "Pete asked me to take two bags of mulch to the Vogel house on my way home. We live two streets behind them. I put the mulch in the trunk of my car and forgot about it until I met with Carlos at the bar. He asked if I had delivered it, and I remembered that I hadn't. I left the bar around ten-fifteen and arrived at the Vogels a little after eleven. The house was dark, so I didn't ring the bell. I unloaded the bags next to the garage and went home."

Stokes paused, then asked, "Did you see anyone at or in the house?"

"No one. Nothing."

◆ ◆ ◆ ◆ ◆

Stokes led Martín to the parking lot where Powers was talking to Griffin, who carried his camera case slung over his shoulder.

"Did you get Carlos's statement?" Stokes asked Powers as they passed.

"Read and signed," Powers said. "I sent him back to work."

Griffin held up a large envelope. "I have the photographs Davenport ordered."

Stokes gave a thumbs up and led Martín to his car. "Are you sure you're not a lawyer?" Stokes asked as Martín fished his keys from his pants pocket.

"Just a retired businessman," Martín repeated, rubbing his stiff leg.

They both looked up as a red Prius screeched into the parking lot. The passenger and rear doors opened before the car came to a complete stop next to Martín's SUV, and Theresa and Cristina jumped out. Parking askew, Claire flew from the driver's seat.

"Oh, no," said Martín as he aimed his remote key toward the trunk.

"We thought you were in jail!" Theresa said, panting as she approached her husband.

"I'm not in jail, Theresa. It was just an interview."

"But Pete...he said the police took you and Carlos away," she said, looking askance at Stokes who stood by stiffly, assessing the women.

"I wanted you to know where we went," Martín said. He pushed the remote and the trunk door eased upward. "I see that was a mistake," he added, frowning.

"What are you doing?" Claire demanded, as she jumped forward and grabbed the trunk remote, initiating its slow-motion closure.

Stokes stared at the women, whose ages spanned at least five decades, as if unsure how to proceed. "Who are you?" she finally asked.

"This is my daughter, Claire Aguila Carson, my wife, Theresa, and my granddaughter, Cristina."

Claire said, "Dad, you don't have to say a word to them."

Stokes sighed. "So, you're the lawyer?"

Claire's forehead furrowed. "No. I'm an anthropologist."

"Great," Stokes said.

"I'm okay with this," Martín said. "I have nothing to hide. It seems I was in the wrong place at the wrong time, and the deputy has asked me some questions."

"It's not fair," Theresa said, her hands on her hips. "There's no reason to suspect you of anything." She turned to Stokes. "You have no idea what kind of man you are accusing!"

Martín took his wife's arm. "I'm not accused of anything, *amor*. They're interviewing witnesses."

"You're a witness?" Theresa said, her voice rising again.

"I'll explain later."

Martín took the remote from Claire and opened the trunk again. The pungent odor of wood mulch escaped into the air. He turned to his daughter, her eyes wide with anger. "Claire, please go back to the house. I'll be home after I sign the statement. Don't worry about me, I'm fine."

Claire gave Stokes a questioning look, but the three women returned to the Prius and pulled out of the driveway. Powers and Griffin joined Stokes and Martín as Stokes put on her gloves. Powers smiled, and Griffin watched the car as it sped from the parking lot.

"You have strong womenfolk there," Powers said, laughing.

"You have no idea," Martín said.

CHAPTER 10

Pete Morales stood in the doorway of his office, arms folded, listening to the argument between Carlos and his wife, Sofia. He loved speaking and hearing the Spanish language, so much more passionate—in anger or in love—than English.

"And my sister had to bring me all the way here *and* watch the kids…" Sofia said.

"You didn't have to come," Carlos said. "I just wanted you to know I might be home late."

"Well, I'm here now," she said, looking over her husband's shoulder and catching the look of amusement on Pete's face.

"And you went to Mrs. Vogel's house last night?" Sofia asked, switching to English. "Then to the bar last night? *Dios Mío!*"

"I told you, *amor*, Martín was with me at the bar. I'm sure he vouched for me."

"But you said he left first…" she said, her voice strained. "You have no one but the bartender to say when you left."

Carlos brought his hands palms-up facing the ceiling, as if in church. "*Esposa,* my wife, there were several people there who can tell the police when I left, and you can tell them when I got home. *No hay problema.*"

"You think they'll believe *me*?"

Reluctantly, Pete left the couple to their argument. He closed up his office, locked the back door, and joined them at the worktable. "I gotta lock up. You can finish your discussion at home." He chuckled, but neither Sofia nor Carlos laughed. Pete watched them leave, Sofia in the lead and Carlos following in her wake.

At the truck, Carlos said, "We need to stop to see Julio on the way."

Sofia looked at her watch. "No, Carlos. I can't ask Susanna to stay with the kids any longer."

"Just for a minute. He wants to see me. And I have something to give him."

Sofia clenched her jaw and pressed her lips together. "*Vamos.*" She opened the passenger door and climbed into the truck, lifting a plastic bag from the seat. Carlos pulled out of the parking lot as Sofia peeked into the bag.

"What's with the books?" Sofía asked. She held her hair off her neck, allowing the slight breeze from the open window to cool her. The afternoon clouds had failed to produce rain; it was five-thirty, stifling hot, and the truck's air-conditioning had quit working six months ago.

Carlos stopped at the light and glanced at his wife, noting the set of her mouth and the slight twitch of her eyes that indicated either fear or anger. "Mrs. Vogel gave them to me when she paid me. I want to give them to Julio. They're too young for our kids."

Sofia sighed. "So, to understand, you went to her house, she paid you and gave you books, then she was murdered? *Dios Mío,* Carlos."

"I told you this," Carlos pleaded as he turned onto Brook Haven Road, heading past the future golf course and toward the back entrance to The Havens. "But she died much later, maybe while Martín and I were at the bar. Otherwise, I'd probably be in jail." He patted her knee. "Besides, Martín went there after me."

"Are you saying he was involved?"

"No, *amor.* I'm just saying, I was there early."

Sofia pulled her knee away as Carlos turned into Havens Gas & Grocery.

The G&G sat at the intersection of Brook Haven and the county road that led from The Havens to Garland and Orchard. Locals preferred this route to the main highway, traveled primarily by tourists heading south to Orlando.

Carlos parked next to Julio's dented sedan and grabbed the bag. They entered the air-conditioned comfort of the store, where Julio was stocking the cigarette shelves with one bandaged hand.

Julio turned from his chore when the door opened. "Hey, *primo*!" He noticed Sofia hesitating at the door. "*Hola,* Sofi."

"What happened to your hand?" Carlos asked after greeting his cousin.

"Box cutter," Julio said. He looked toward one of the far shelves and yelled to an invisible employee, "Ryan, can you take the counter? I need a break."

A young man, with blond hair tied back in a ponytail, poked his head up from behind the cookie aisle and nodded. He took Julio's place behind the counter and picked up the cigarette cartons to finish Julio's job. Julio led them to the back door of the store. Sofia followed behind, staring at Ryan as he reached up to fill the shelves, mesmerized by the colorful swirling tattoos covering his arms and ending abruptly at his wrists.

Outside, they settled at the workers' picnic table. Carlos held the book bag in his lap. He noticed that Julio's hands shook slightly as he extracted a cigarette from a pack and lit up.

"I had to go to the cops today, about Mrs. Vogel's murder," Carlos said. "Did you hear about it?"

"Yeah, sure, everyone's talking about it," Julio said, taking a long puff, and turning his head to blow the smoke away from Carlos and Sofia. "Why did they talk to you?"

Carlos told him and explained how Martín became involved. "They took my fingerprints," he added.

Julio ran his injured hand through his dark curls as he inhaled again. "What time was the lady killed?"

"They didn't tell me, but it had to be late, because they asked me for an alibi for the nighttime."

"When did you leave the bar?" Julio asked.

"Around ten-thirty," Carlos said, "but I went straight home. Martín delivered the mulch to Mrs. Vogel later."

Julio's hands shook as he took another puff on his cigarette. "Did Martín see Mrs. Vogel?"

"No, he just dropped off the mulch and left," Carlos said, frowning. "Why the questions?"

"It's weird, don't you think?" Julio said. "That you were both at her house the night she was killed?"

"No shit," Carlos said. "That's why they hauled us in. I don't think they believe our story."

Julio threw his cigarette stub on the gravel and ground it with the heel of his tennis shoe. He looked briefly at Sofia, then spoke quietly. "I just missed you," he said. "I was at Jonah's around eleven."

"Jesus, Julio! You left work early?" Carlos said.

Julio lifted his hand. "I went to the ER, but I didn't stay… crowded…you know…I don't like the hospital…too many questions."

"Who closed the store?"

"Ryan did," Julio said, avoiding eye contact. "I had already planned to leave early."

"Is everything okay, Julio?" Carlos asked. "You can't just take off work whenever you want."

"I needed some time off, okay? What's the big deal?"

"So, you went to the ER, then to the bar?"

"So what?"

Sofia pressed her lips together, a movement that emphasized her high cheekbones, supporting her claim of Native American ancestry. "After what Carlos has done for you, you can't screw up, Julio," she said. "If you lose this job, don't come to Carlos to find you another one."

Carlos looked closely at his cousin. "Do you need an alibi?"

Julio shrugged, feigning indifference. "They're looking for a

Mexican, no?"

"How do you know?"

"Who else are they questioning?" Julio looked from Carlos to Sofía.

"¿*Qué pasa*, Julio?" Carlos asked. "Are you in trouble?"

"No, *primo, nada*."

Ryan stuck his head out the back door. "Julio, it's my turn for break."

"Just a minute, man," Julio said.

Carlos balanced the book bag in his lap and covered Julio's shaking hands with his own. "You need to be careful, *primo*. You do anything wrong, and you'll be deported. Then what will happen to your family?"

"I didn't do anything," Julio insisted. He pointed to the bag. "What's that?"

Carlos placed it on the table. "Some books for Mary and Billy—from Mrs. Vogel."

Julio reached out to open the bag, but quickly pulled his hand back. "You're giving me books that a dead lady gave you? Are you kidding?"

"I didn't steal them, Julio," Carlos said. "And I didn't kill Mrs. Vogel. She gave them to me. The cops have already seen them and didn't take them from me—they're good."

Julio opened the bag and peeked inside. "*Gracias,*" he said. He glanced at Sofía, then asked Carlos, "Can we meet tonight? When I get out of work? I'll buy you a beer."

"Sorry, man, I gotta work early in the morning," Carlos said. "I'll call you tomorrow."

Julio sighed and nodded. "*Bueno.*"

CHAPTER 11

After Stokes searched his car, Martín returned with her to the DPS office to sign his statement. As he passed through the reception area he smiled at Patsy, who responded with a skeptical glare. He held the front door open for two men who approached from outside. The older man wore a lightweight blue suit with striped tie, while the other man wore beige khakis, light-blue shirt, and a tie displaying manatees swimming in a blue sea. The men glanced at Martín briefly, paused in their conversation, nodded, and entered the building.

It took Martín a few minutes to straighten his car after Stokes had rummaged through it. He settled himself into the seat, lifting his weak leg carefully, and headed home. After going through the Sea Haven gate, he paused at the corner of Manatee Street. The roadblock was down, but he could see several official-looking vehicles parked at the end of the street where it met Marlin Lane—where he had dropped off the mulch. He continued to Urchin Court and parked next to Claire's car in the driveway. His leg felt stiff, and his head ached. He entered his beautiful stucco prison.

"We're out back!" Theresa called. Martín followed the voices to the lanai at the rear of the house where his family lounged on cushioned terrace furniture, enjoying pre-dinner cocktails. Despite their forced casualness, the faces of his family were somber and drawn.

Theresa jumped up and hugged her husband. "What happened?" she asked. "Why did they search your car?"

He removed her hands from around his neck and kissed

them gently. "It's a long story, deserving of a drink."

"Gin and tonic coming up. Don't start without me," Theresa said as she left the room.

Martín turned to his daughter and granddaughter, spreading out his arms. "Can I get some hugs?" he asked. "Or are you afraid I'm a murderer?"

"We worried about you," Cristina said as she and Claire took turns hugging him.

"We didn't expect to find you in the hands of the police," Claire said, holding tightly onto her father's arm, assisting him into a lounge chair.

"I'll tell you everything I know when Theresa returns." Martín settled into the chair and straightened out his leg. "What do you think of our digs?" He waved his arm around the room.

"Papa," Cristina said, looking out at the artificial lake behind the lanai, "if I had known you lived like this, I would've come sooner!"

"We're just squatters, *amor*."

"The Carsons are happy you're here, enjoying it," Claire said, her comment causing a brief look of unease to cross her father's face. "But you're not?" she added.

"Let's say, it has been an experience," he said. Then, gazing at his daughter's worried face, he smiled suddenly. "I've waited months to see you both." He turned to his granddaughter. "Cris, I worried about you every day you were in Malawi. I'm so glad to see you."

"I was fine," Cristina insisted. "You needn't have worried."

"We're dying to know how you are adjusting to retirement in the land of Oz," Claire said.

Martín shook his head. "These people are strange. They do nothing all day except play golf, shop, and eat out. They don't mow their own lawns, tend gardens, maintain their pools, or even clean their own houses." He smiled as Theresa entered the lanai with his drink.

"So, what happened?" Theresa asked. "Tell us about the murder and why we had to come to your rescue."

Martín smiled. "You didn't have to come."

"Well, according to Pete, you were in shackles," Claire said.

"Hah, don't believe Pete," he said, then sipped his drink and frowned. "A woman who lives here, in Sea Haven, was murdered—Barbara Vogel."

"Barbara?" Theresa said, bringing her hands to her face. "How awful."

"Did you know her?" Martín asked.

"Not very well but I liked her."

"Cris and I saw the barricades," Claire said. "Some rent-a-cop stopped us."

Martín shook his head. "Danny McKay. He stopped me this morning, too, and he should know me by now. I've been in the DPS multiple times, filling out papers...ID cards for us and for my truck, and employment forms for my job..." He paused and smiled at his daughter. "Maintenance worker."

Theresa shifted impatiently in her wicker chair. "Why did they want to talk to you?"

"Carlos and I both went to her house last night...wrong place, wrong time."

"That's where you delivered the mulch?" Theresa asked. "I didn't know."

"And we were together at Jonah's Bar. I knew I shouldn't have gone out with Carlos, but he wanted me to meet his friends in Orchard." Martín sighed. "I hope Carlos gave the deputy the same story I did."

"Isn't the husband the first suspect?" Cristina said.

Martín shrugged. "They didn't tell us anything. I only know there have been robberies here. Perhaps they think she caught a thief in the act."

"And Hispanics are thieves, of course," Claire grumbled.

"That's the assumption," Martín said with a tinge of sarcasm. "Workers don't live here, but they come and go and have the codes, so they're the first to be accused. I'm more worried about Carlos than myself. He's afraid he might have been the last to see her alive."

"Where was Mr. Vogel?" asked Cristina, her thoughts moving in another direction.

"I don't know. I suppose we'll learn the details sooner or later."

"How awful," Theresa repeated, her hands folded around her glass.

Martín shifted his position, looking from his daughter to his granddaughter. "I've been waiting to see you both, and here we are, discussing a murder."

A silence ensued as Claire checked her phone. It was time to share her news. "You might have more company than you imagined." Three faces looked at her curiously.

Claire placed her glass on the table and set her gaze on her father. "I told you all about the anthropology conference I attended in Merida last May…"

"How could we forget—three deaths and you in the middle of it," Theresa said, shaking her head.

Claire sighed. "The deaths were connected to the selling and smuggling of Mayan artifacts pillaged from archaeological sites. The detective investigating the case asked me and my colleagues, George and Madge, to assist him because it involved anthropologists and archaeology. I guess we were the only people in our group he trusted."

She tried a smile, but the faces gazing at her morphed into frowns. "The detective was Roberto Salinas, someone I knew from my internship in Merida—where Aaron and I met," she added unnecessarily. "When I taught English at the American School, one of my classes included a group of rookie police officers. Roberto was one of my students."

Claire paused here, feeling like a teenager concocting a lie. "We had a few dates, but nothing serious—dating locals was discouraged—but anyway, I met Aaron. Roberto and I never communicated after I left." She added this last as her daughter's eyes narrowed and she began to nibble at her lower lip.

"So, what happened at the conference?" Martín asked, eyebrows raised.

Claire reached across from her chair toward Cristina, taking her daughter's hand. "Nothing happened at the conference, Dad, but we decided to keep in touch. We've been communicating via email, and it turns out that he's in Orlando this week for an international conference on smuggling antiquities. Madge is there, too."

"He's in Orlando now?" Theresa asked, leaning forward, her gaze settling on her granddaughter, who took in a deep breath at the news.

Claire stammered, "Yes, and I invited him to visit us this week."

She looked at Cristina, who pulled her hand away and began to fidget with her glass.

"We drove a thousand miles together this week, and you never mentioned this?" Cristina asked, accusation in her voice.

Claire studied her daughter. Always close, they had found strength together as they watched Aaron—her husband and Cristina's father—succumb to cancer. Was this new friendship a betrayal of her husband? Her daughter?

"I'm sorry," Claire said, her voice almost a whisper, "but I didn't know for sure he would come. I still don't know for sure." Claire reached for her daughter's hand again. "I know how you must feel. I should have talked to you about it."

"Is this serious?" Theresa asked.

"We have a lot in common, and I like him."

Theresa sat back in her chair, her face lined with concern. "Is he divorced?"

"Widowed. Like I said, we have a lot in common."

"He's a cop?" Martín said.

"A detective," Claire blurted, "and he has a daughter who attends the University of Yucatán…and his mother lives with them." Claire felt her heart racing as she absorbed the looks of concern and surprise on the faces of her daughter and parents.

"I'm sorry," she repeated. "I knew this would be hard, and perhaps it's too soon to put this on you. The timing—all of us together in Florida—seemed like a good time for him to meet you and for us to see each other. We might find that there is nothing between us at all. I have no idea what he is thinking… as a detective, he's not very forthcoming in the emotion department." Claire watched as the facial expressions around her morphed from surprise to curiosity.

Finally, her mother said, "This is a good time to meet your friend."

"That is, if I'm not arrested for murder before he gets here," Martín said.

CHAPTER 12

Deputies Pamela Stokes and Mike Powers shared a large wooden desk in their incident room at the DPS. Davenport's desk sat next to the window, now awash in the rays of the setting sun. The office had been outfitted with a computer, printer, and landline. Air-conditioning blasted frigid air into the room, and they hadn't yet found the controls to moderate the temperature. Stokes studied her notes as Powers leaned back in his chair, his feet propped up on the table. The door opened and Detective Davenport strode into the office, holding his phone to his ear. Stokes jumped and Powers nearly fell over trying to lower his chair legs to the floor. Davenport placed his briefcase on his desk and settled into his swivel chair.

"Good evening, sir," Stokes said.

The detective held up his finger as he began to speak into his phone. Behind Davenport, a tall, sandy-haired man entered, wearing pressed khakis, a pale shirt, and manatee tie. He also held a cellphone to his ear.

Stokes's face tightened as Scott Malloy glanced at her and winked. He sat in the chair opposite Davenport and continued his conversation.

Stokes leaned close to Powers. "It's Mr. Interim Deputy Detective," she whispered, but not softly enough. Malloy glared at her and turned toward the window as he spoke on the phone.

Click-click. Stokes's jaw clenched as she tapped her pen rhythmically on the table, *click-click.*

Davenport ended his call and waited for Malloy to finish his conversation. A quick look from Davenport caught Stokes's attention and the clicking ceased.

Malloy ended his call and said, "Hughes is sending a preliminary lab report over."

"Good," Davenport said. "Doctor Carlisle is finishing up her report."

Malloy cleared his throat loudly.

"Sorry, Malloy," Davenport said. Turning to Stokes and Powers, he said, "You both know Scott is acting as deputy detective until Sara returns from maternity leave. I'm bringing him in from the Miller case in Garland."

Malloy straightened his tie, grinning. "I appreciate the opportunity to work this case, sir." He threw a quick glance at Stokes.

"Congratulations," Powers said, fumbling with his own pen.

"Congratulations," Stokes mumbled, fuming under her calm —she hoped—façade.

Stokes was certain Davenport knew she and Malloy had been involved when they both took the detective's exam. Davenport also knew she had scored higher, yet he had chosen Malloy to fill the temporary slot. Her frustration at Malloy's thinly veiled self-satisfaction, and, she admitted, her jealousy, had eroded their relationship. And here he was, with his sun-bleached hair, khakis and ridiculous tie, following Davenport around like a puppy dog…and she still in uniform.

Davenport opened his notebook. "Let's go over what we have so far, so Malloy can catch up. Powers, what did you learn from Alice Van Dee, the next-door neighbor?"

Powers sighed heavily. "Our Mrs. Van Dee wouldn't believe I'm a deputy. The uniform didn't convince her." He rolled his eyes. "She was first on the scene—came through the hedge and over the mulch bags when she saw Vogel drive into the garage. She watched him pull his suitcase from the trunk, gave a commentary on his golf clubs, and entered the house with him. She said he was shocked at finding his wife's body, and told her to call

911. She called the DPS instead."

Powers reviewed his notes. "Alice—who, by the way, seems to wander around her yard a lot—gave us several leads. Chronologically, she saw Carlos Chavez leave the Vogel house with a plastic grocery bag around six-thirty last evening."

"Was the grocery bag in his truck when you searched it?" Stokes asked.

"Yup, with six kids' books inside, in Spanish and English," Powers said.

"If Carlos is involved, he must have returned later," Stokes mused.

Powers nodded. "Unless Alice is completely delusional, she later saw a car resembling Mr. Vogel's pull into the garage around seven-thirty p.m. The garage door closed behind it. She thought it was Vogel, but he told her this morning that he had been gone all week."

"A busy lady," Malloy interjected.

"I'm not done yet." Powers smiled. "Alice also saw someone behind the Vogel house late that night, around ten—someone in a hoodie...*and*," Powers continued, "she *also* saw car headlights backing out of the driveway a few minutes later."

"Busy, indeed," Davenport agreed. "Hopefully the photos Griffin took around the birdcage will help us out." He turned to Stokes. "What do you have for us?"

Stokes cleared her throat. "I interviewed Jordan and Amanda Davis, the neighbors across the street. Mr. Davis saw a light-colored, maybe gray, car in the driveway around nine-thirty, but it had gone when he closed up the house for the night around ten-thirty. That might be the same car Alice saw." She tapped the table with her fingernail, then addressed Davenport. "Sir, you should talk to Mrs. Davis without her husband around. There's something there."

Davenport jotted on his pad. "Who was that Mexican guy

Malloy and I saw leaving when we arrived?"

"Mr. Aguila, yet another person at the Vogel house last night," Stokes said. "He dropped off a load of mulch around eleven. He signed a statement and provided an alibi for the gardener, Carlos Chavez, for part of the evening."

"Which part?" Malloy asked, waiting for Stokes to meet his gaze.

"From approximately eight o'clock to ten-thirty in the evening, when they were both at Jonah's Bar in Orchard. Mr. Aguila left first, around ten-fifteen. I interviewed them separately and their stories match. I called Jonah, the owner of the bar, and he confirmed that Carlos left around ten-thirty."

"But Carlos could have returned to the Vogel house within the time frame of her murder," Davenport said.

"Possibly," Stokes agreed, "but no one has reported seeing his truck there after six-thirty, and he claims he went straight home from the bar. His wife will likely confirm that."

Malloy shrugged. "She could lie."

"Who is this Mr. Aguila?" Davenport asked. "And why was he at the Vogels last night?"

"He works part-time at The Barn," Stokes said. "That's how he knows Carlos, and it explains the late-night mulch delivery. A Mrs. Estes recognized his car at The Barn. She saw it at the Vogel house around eleven o'clock last night. Powers and I brought them both in."

"He lives here?"

"He's currently living in the same neighborhood as the Vogels, on Urchin Court," Stokes said.

"Did he talk to Mrs. Vogel? See anything?" Davenport asked.

Stokes shook her head. "The house was dark, and he didn't ring the bell because of the time. He claimed he went home from there. He could have killed her, but somehow I don't think so," she reasoned. "He hasn't lived here long, and didn't seem to know

Mrs. Vogel. Besides, when he opened his trunk, we could smell the mulch."

"Who's we?" asked Davenport.

"Griffin and Powers were there. And strangely enough, his wife, daughter, and granddaughter arrived as we checked out his trunk. They're fierce ladies. It's a long story...but he signed the statement."

"Did Carlos sign a statement?" Davenport asked.

Powers passed the statement to Davenport. "Something interesting there," Powers said. "Aguila warned Carlos to read his statement carefully before signing, like he's an attorney or something."

"Is he?" Davenport asked.

"No," Stokes said, "but he owned some kind of company that hired Mexican workers. He was a bit sensitive about how he and Carlos were brought in."

Davenport leaned forward. "Was there a problem there?" he asked.

"No, sir," Stokes said. "They both understood the meeting was voluntary."

Davenport looked out the window, then turned to Stokes. "Tell us about the Davises. What did they tell you, and why do I need to re-interview them?"

"Amanda Davis was a friend of Barbara's, and the two couples socialized from time to time." Stokes explained the sequence of events that resulted in Barbara canceling out of the dinner. "The Davises claimed they didn't see either Carlos or the silver car. The light-colored car Mr. Davis saw at nine-thirty was the third car, and Mr. Aguila's was the fourth."

Malloy interrupted her. "So, what's the problem?"

Stokes glared at Malloy, but turned to Davenport again. "It concerns what Mrs. Davis started to say...twice...and how her husband kept her from speaking. He gave her a warning glance when I asked questions about Barbara. Then, when I asked if either of them had seen other cars in the driveway, he interrupted her."

Malloy frowned. "If Davis saw a light-colored car in the driveway around nine-thirty and gone by ten-thirty, and Mrs. Van Dee saw a silver car arrive at seven and also saw a car leave around ten, it can't be Todd Vogel's car."

"Mrs. Van Dee didn't see the color, but you're right," Stokes admitted, "unless there were two cars, one in the garage and one in the driveway."

The conference room door opened, and Judy Barnaby entered with the reports, handing them to Davenport. "It's shift change," Judy said. "Danny and I are leaving soon, and the night dispatcher, Dick Broden, will be coming in."

Davenport looked at his watch. "Thank you, Judy. Could you arrange for someone to bring us some sandwiches and coffee? We'll be here awhile longer."

"Now?" She looked around the room.

"That would be great, thank you," Davenport said sympathetically.

Judy tore a sheet from a legal pad and wrote down orders. "Who's going to pay?" she asked, narrowing her eyes at the detective.

Davenport reached for his wallet and pulled out two twenty-dollar bills. "I'll need a receipt."

Judy stiffened, took the bills, and left the room.

Davenport glanced at the reports Judy had delivered. "There's a preliminary lab report, crime scene report, and autopsy." He skimmed the autopsy report. "Only sketchy results so far. Toxicology will be back in a few days." He paused, moving his fingers along the page as he skimmed. "Doctor Carlisle refined her earlier estimate. Mrs. Vogel died sometime between nine p.m. and one in the morning. The bullet lodged near her heart. She died fairly quickly, but not immediately."

Davenport turned a page. "Doctor Carlisle noticed that the sash used to tie her hands had an unusual pattern of blood stain. She sent that along to the lab, along with the negligee, kimono-style robe, and the hundred-dollar bill found under the body."

"Money?" Stokes asked.

"Carlisle found a blood-soaked hundred-dollar bill under her robe," Davenport said. "It was nearly dry, but had a partial fingerprint."

"Botched robbery," Malloy suggested.

Davenport adjusted his glasses. "The bed was unmade, and the comforter had been thrown carelessly over the bed sheets…" Davenport raised his eyebrows as he continued, "…suspicious stains on the sheets…sheets and pillowcases removed for analysis."

"Interesting," Stokes said. "When I took Mr. Vogel into the bedroom to check the security box, he stared at the bed. Before I could stop him, he reached down and straightened it a little, like it bothered him that it hadn't been made."

"That doesn't mean anything, does it?" Malloy said. "Not everyone is neat about making beds."

"But the house looked like a museum, not a magazine out of place," Stokes said. "It's unlikely she left the bed unmade in the morning. An early evening unmade bed can have an entirely different meaning." She bit her lip, thinking. "Another thing, the closet was spotless—huge, with his and hers sides, clothes all folded or on hangers, and the shoes in cubbies."

"What about fingerprints?" Malloy asked.

Davenport skimmed again. "Good news. They found her cellphone just under the sofa—looks like it might have been taken from her, hastily wiped off, and thrown—no blood or discernible prints. It hasn't been dumped yet." Davenport scanned further. "Mostly Mrs. Vogel's prints around the furniture and doors."

"Mostly?" asked Stokes.

Davenport shrugged. "We won't be able to verify until we get Mr. Vogel's prints and analyze any stray prints. He should be coming in soon."

"Did they find any gun residue on his hands?" Malloy asked.

Davenport shook his head. "No, and we didn't really expect to find anything, even if he did kill her. He had hours to clean up and dispose of clothing." Davenport looked at Stokes and said, "What you observed about the condition of the house is correct, it was very tidy." He scanned the report, turning to the second page. "Ah, the three glasses and the scotch bottle were clean with no prints, which is interesting."

"Barbara could have washed them all," Stokes said, "but why wipe off the bottle?"

"Do you think Todd cleaned up the kitchen?" Powers asked.

"It doesn't seem likely he would wipe the bottle and glasses," Malloy said. "Wouldn't he want us to get the prints?"

"Besides," Stokes said, "he didn't have time to wash them between the time he returned home and our arrival. Either Mrs. Van Dee or Judy was with him."

Davenport nodded. "We took the glasses and bottle away first thing. The three glasses rattled him, though."

"What if she was having an affair?" Stokes suggested. "Perhaps her lover killed her and wiped the glasses and bottle clean."

"A lover," mused Davenport. "But three glasses?"

"Would she be drinking scotch with the lawn worker?" Powers said, smiling.

"We'll have to ask him," Davenport raised his eyebrows and tapped his finger on the desk. "I smelled alcohol on Todd's breath, and in his coffee cup. I checked the cupboard and saw a bottle of whiskey. Seems he poured a little courage into his coffee. There may be an alcohol problem there."

He paused, looking over another document. "Mrs. Vogel's

car is at the police garage for analysis. So far, nothing suspicious in contents, and specifically, no gun has been found anywhere in the house or car." He stroked his chin. "Odder and odder," he said, as he shuffled papers on his desk. "Did you say Griffin brought photo enlargements?"

Stokes handed him the envelope.

"Good," Davenport said as he sifted through the stack. "I'm looking for outdoor prints," he said. "Yes, here we go—footprints along the birdcage and the side of the house—both back doors were locked. Unfortunately, we don't know about the front door or side door from the garage to the kitchen. There's no sign of a break-in."

"So, Alice did see someone outside the house," Powers said. "I apologize for dissing her."

Davenport read on. "...blood splotches on the birdcage...and here's the mulch." He sat back. "Judy said it rained around four o'clock. Kudos to Griffin. He took a photo of the ground around the bags—a little damp under the bags from the afternoon rain, but dry on top. It seems to support Aguila's story of a late-night delivery."

A knock on the door interrupted their conversation. Danny McKay entered, balancing two paper bags in one arm as he pushed the door open. "Supper," he said, depositing the bags in front of Stokes and handing a receipt and change to Davenport. "By the way, Mr. Vogel arrived. Should I send him in?"

"Give us ten minutes," Davenport said. "Has he provided fingerprints yet?"

Danny shrugged. "Don't think so."

"Take his prints, then send him in."

"Yes, sir," Danny said, and turned to leave.

"Wait," Davenport said. "When is trash pick-up?"

"Tuesdays and Thursdays for the three residences, and Friday for the businesses." Danny pointed out toward the back of their building. "We have two dumpsters here…" he paused. "Oh, man, you're not going to make us go through the trash, are you?"

"I'll let you know," the detective said.

"Sure." Danny left the room, his shoulders sagging.

CHAPTER 13

While they ate, Malloy called Craig Hughes, the evidence technician, who reported that his team had found nothing of importance in the Vogels' trash. Malloy requested that the team come to The Havens in the morning to go through the business and residential trash bins before they were collected. Hanging up, he said, "They're not happy campers, but they'll be here early in the morning."

"What are they looking for?" Powers asked.

"The gun, for one thing," Davenport said. "And whoever killed Mrs. Vogel had bloody clothes or shoes."

Stokes stood and cleared the supper detritus from the table. "What about the lake behind the Vogel house?" she asked. Her companions groaned collectively. "That's easier than finding a trash bin in Gardenia County," she argued, "and just a few yards from the back door."

Davenport said, "Let's do the likely trash locations first." He turned to Powers. "I'd like you to supervise the search tomorrow morning."

"Yes, sir," Powers said, stifling a sigh.

Judy Barnaby knocked briefly and entered the room. "Are you ready for Todd Vogel?"

"Yes," Davenport said. "Send him in."

Judy led Todd in and directed him to a chair. She turned to Davenport. "We're leaving now. Broden just arrived." She turned on her heel and exited.

Todd had clearly found someplace to shower and change clothes. He now wore wrinkled khakis, a blue polo shirt, and the same soft leather loafers he'd had on that morning, without socks. His hair lay in soft waves around his ears. He collapsed into the chair, gripping two sheets of paper.

"Thank you for coming in, Mr. Vogel," Davenport said after Judy had left. "I think you know everyone here, except Detective Malloy."

Todd nodded toward Malloy and handed his lists to Davenport, who placed them on the desk. Todd sat at the edge of the chair, tipping it forward with his weight. He clasped his hands tightly in his lap. His eyes scanned the faces before him.

"Mr. Vogel," Davenport said, "I hope you've had time to rest."

"Not rest, but I showered at Glen Haven and ate. I have a reservation at The Havens Inn tonight." He looked down at his clothes, as if embarrassed. "These were in my suitcase, but they're dirty. Can I go home to get clean clothes?"

"Your wife's body has been removed for autopsy, but the evidence team is conducting a final sweep of the house and yard," Davenport said. "It's a good idea to stay elsewhere tonight."

Malloy spoke up, saying, "Deputy Powers can go with you to get your things, if you wish." Powers gave Malloy a quick glance but did not argue.

"Do you mind if we record your comments?" Davenport asked, his hand hovering over the button.

Todd bit his lower lip. "I guess not."

After Davenport recorded Vogel's name into the machine, alongside the date and time, Todd pointed to the lists he had compiled. "I think the names are accurate, but as I said before, people came and went all evening. I don't have phone numbers or addresses."

"That's fine, Mr. Vogel. We can find those." Davenport paused, his hand on the list of Barbara's friends. "In fact, we know that Barbara planned to have dinner with friends last night, but changed her mind."

"She didn't go?" Todd asked, surprised. He stared blankly at Davenport. "When I called her at six last night, she didn't say anything about that."

"How did she seem?" Davenport asked.

"Normal. She said nothing about dinner."

"It seems she had arranged for Carlos Chavez to come by," Stokes said. "She owed him some money for lawn work."

Todd struggled to compute the information. "Why did that conflict with her dinner? She could have paid him anytime."

"You know Carlos?" asked Stokes. She looked to Davenport, who nodded for her to continue.

"I know who he is." Todd looked from Stokes to Davenport. "I don't really know the workers. Is he a suspect?"

"A witness saw him at your house around six-thirty," Powers said.

"That must have been Alice," Todd scoffed. "She should have been a war-time spy…maybe she was."

"Do you know a maintenance man named Martín?" Stokes asked.

"I don't know. I might recognize his face…my wife took care of those things."

"You might have seen him at the country club," Stokes said. "He mows the golf course, but he is also staying in Sea Haven."

Todd shook his head. "I…I don't know him, but I heard that a Mexican and his wife were living here. Is he a criminal or something?" Todd asked.

"Not that we know of," Davenport responded. "Did you order a delivery of mulch?"

Todd shrugged. "Perhaps Barbara did. As I said, she took care of the lawn and garden." He paused, then said, "I do remember bags of mulch next to the garage this morning."

"Do you know if this Martín and Carlos are friends?" Malloy asked.

Todd shifted in his chair. "I told you, I don't know the work-ers, but they must know each other. They all stick together, don't they?" Todd glanced briefly at Powers and turned away.

Like us Black folks, Powers thought bitterly.

Davenport asked, "Did you call your wife at any other time besides your six o'clock call?"

"I called her again around ten-thirty last night, and twice early this morning, with no answer."

"We found your wife's phone," Davenport reported. "The team is checking phone calls and texts."

Todd's eyes hardened. "That will confirm my calls," he said.

"And the length of calls, and where they were made from," Davenport said evenly.

Todd looked at the detective, resigned. "Can you tell me what you know…about my wife's murder?"

"There is not much to tell yet, Mr. Vogel. The crime scene team has taken fingerprints, and several items have been taken to the lab."

"What items?"

"I can't tell you specifically at this time, Mr. Vogel," Davenport said, "but I do have a few questions." Davenport straightened his glasses again. "Did you clean the glasses and Glenlivet bottle on your counter before the crime team took them away?"

"No. I just made coffee."

Davenport watched Todd's face carefully, noting his set jaw, how his eyes jerked from deputy to deputy.

"I also have a question about the security box," Davenport said. "Was the stolen money of any particular denomination? Fifties? Hundreds?"

"Mainly fifties and twenties for small expenses, like paying the workers, or entertainment at the plaza. Why do you ask?"

"We found a one-hundred-dollar bill near your wife. We wondered if it came from your box."

Todd shrugged. "We probably had some hundred-dollar bills in there." He paused and took a deep breath. "Have you found the gun?"

"Not yet." Davenport leaned forward, watching Todd's face carefully. "You noticed that the evidence team took the sheets and pillowcases from your bed?"

"Yes. Why?"

Davenport folded his hands and placed them on top of the lists Todd had provided. "To determine if there had been…foul play." He paused as Todd's face altered from questioning to horror. "We have no suspicions," Davenport added quickly, "but we didn't want any evidence destroyed."

Todd brought his hands to his face. "Oh, my God," he said.

Stokes spoke, and Todd pulled his face from Davenport's to hers. "Several of your neighbors saw cars in your driveway last night—a silver car, like yours, and a light-colored sedan. Do you recognize either of these cars?"

"My car is silver, but I wasn't home last night." He bit his lip again. "It's Florida. Lots of people have light-colored cars. What time were they seen?"

"Between seven-thirty and around ten o'clock," Stokes replied.

Todd ran his hands through his hair. "That lawn guy could have returned later," he said.

Davenport folded his hands and leaned forward. "Yes, that's true, but no one reported his truck there later that night."

"What about the mulch?"

"A third vehicle has been identified," Stokes said. "Does anyone else have your garage door opener?"

"Only Barbara, why?"

"One of the cars pulled into your garage."

The four deputies watched as Todd deflated in front of them. He sank back in the chair.

"Is there anything else you can think of that might help us?"

Davenport asked.

Todd shook his head. "I'm too tired and upset to think."

"I understand," Davenport assured him. "That's all for now. Thank you."

◆ ◆ ◆ ◆ ◆

Once again, Todd pulled his suitcase from his Lexus, this time with Deputy Powers following behind. They switched on lights as they moved through the hallway and into the living room. The Oriental rug had been taken away, and the area looked bare. He tried to conjure up the image of his wife…alive and well, but he could only remember her as he had seen her this morning, crumpled on the floor.

Powers tapped Todd's shoulder and directed him into the master bedroom. Dusting powder covered every surface. Anxiety built up in Todd as his obsessive-compulsive tendencies arose within him, and he resisted the urge to wipe the powder off the furniture with his hands. The bed had been stripped. Not only the sheets, but the mattress pad and the lightweight comforter had also been taken. Todd tried not to think of what had happened in that bed.

He looked at the deputy. "Can I clean the room?" Powers noticed the agitation in the husband as he circled the bedroom like a caged animal. "My children are coming tomorrow. I don't want them to see the house like this."

"You can clean it tomorrow morning." Powers turned his attention to the backyard and Clam Lake, giving Vogel a modicum of privacy as he packed.

Todd placed his suitcase on the bed and passed through the bathroom, where he wiped his fingers over the powder that covered the granite countertop. Barbara's hairbrush and toothbrush were missing. He wondered what else they had taken.

Todd closed his eyes to calm himself before entering the large walk-in closet. Barbara's clothing had been tampered with, her silk scarves and sweaters shifted around only slightly, but he could tell. He pulled a small duffel bag from the top shelf. He wondered if the police needed a search warrant for the house of a murder victim, then dismissed the thought. No good would come from asking—it would only pique their interest more than it already was. He unzipped the duffel and laid it next to the suitcase, opening both. He took his shaving kit and a zippered portfolio case from the suitcase and placed them into the duffel, along with some clean clothes.

"Do you have everything?" Powers asked, turning his attention back to Todd.

Todd nodded, and Powers followed him into the hallway. He paused at the kitchen, glanced at the empty counter, and turned off the light.

"You're sure I can come back early in the morning to clean before my children arrive?" he asked Powers.

"Yes." Powers pulled a card from his pocket. "Detective Davenport will visit you sometime tomorrow with an update."

Powers got into his patrol car and pulled out of the driveway. Todd looked at his phone. He had received several text messages from Jordan Davis. He tapped the phone to call his friend, not sure he wanted to hear what Jordan had to say.

CHAPTER 14

Detective Davenport drove away from the DPS, leaving Stokes and Malloy glaring at each other. He accepted some responsibility for their animosity, having chosen Malloy over Stokes to replace his deputy detective during her family leave. After today, he wondered if he had chosen wisely. Had he mistaken Stokes's thoughtfulness for indecisiveness and Malloy's assertiveness for good judgment?

Dusk had descended, and Davenport yearned to go home, but he had no one there to greet him. That pleasure had ended five years ago when he and his wife divorced. Instead, he decided to drive through the neighborhood where the murder had been committed.

He turned into Sea Haven, pressed the button for the guest entrance and wondered if a camera recorded his entrance. He turned right onto Manatee Street, followed it to Marlin Lane, and turned left. He drove past Alice Van Dee's house, dark except for a dim light coming from a back room. He imagined the elderly woman watching television. Beyond Alice's house, the Vogel house was steeped in darkness.

He checked his notes for the Davis's address, remembering Stokes's suggestion. As he located the house, across from the Vogels, the garage door opened and a car pulled out, driven by a man with gray hair. The garage door closed, and the man drove past him. Davenport pulled into the driveway.

At first glance, the woman who answered the door looked too young to be a resident, her age disguised by careful makeup. On closer inspection, though, he realized her youthful appearance had likely been artificially enhanced.

"Mrs. Davis?"

"Yes?" She looked past him into the street.

He showed his identification. "I am Detective Davenport. Could I have a few minutes of your time?"

"We've already talked to the female deputy...and my husband isn't here."

"I'm sorry to bother you. I know you spoke with Deputy Stokes, but I'd like to follow up on some of the information you gave her." He paused, easing a step back. "I'll only take a few minutes."

She let him in and offered him the Italian leather chair. She sat on the matching sofa, her eyes darting from Davenport to the window. "My husband will be home in an hour or so. Can't we do this tomorrow?"

"I'd like you both to come to the DPS tomorrow to sign a statement. We expected to see you today."

"We told the deputy everything we knew. I guess we forgot to go in."

"Well, I'd like to clear up a few things, and then you can both come in tomorrow." Davenport paused to focus on her face as she settled herself onto her sofa, and bit on her lower lip. "Where is your husband?"

"He's visiting a friend." She sat back and curled her shapely legs underneath her skirt. "What do you want to know?"

"I want to ask about the car you saw in the driveway last night."

"I didn't see it. My husband saw a light-colored sedan."

"And he saw no other cars there...or trucks."

"He said he didn't."

"And you saw nothing unusual?"

Amanda glanced at the Vogel's house across the street. "N... no," she said hesitating. "I didn't see anyone."

Stokes had been correct. There was something amiss here. Amanda's attempt to emit a calm demeanor was defeated by incessant adjustments of her clothing and nervous glances out the window.

"You told Deputy Stokes that Mrs. Vogel had planned to go to dinner with you, but changed her mind. Is that correct?"

Amanda nodded.

"When you returned home from dinner, did you see any cars in the driveway?"

"No." Her voice rose in agitation. "I already said that."

"Did you call her to ask why she changed her mind?"

"No, I just thought she decided not to join us. It wasn't a big deal. We go out weekly. Not everyone attends every dinner."

Davenport adjusted his glasses. "Several witnesses suggested that Mrs. Vogel might have interrupted a robbery—that perhaps someone knew Mr. Vogel went out of town and that Mrs. Vogel might be out. Do you think it's possible that a thief might have felt safe entering her home?"

Amanda nodded in assent. "Yes. We think it must be one of the Mexican workers."

"They have house keys?"

She shrugged. "They might, or they know how to get in. We're sometimes lax about locking doors. We lock the front door, but, with high fences and multiple doors, someone could enter through the back and not be seen."

"Let's assume, just for the moment, that it wasn't a stranger or a gardener. Do you know of anyone who disliked Mrs. Vogel, or who might want to harm her?"

"No, of course not," Amanda said. "She wanted to help everyone. We often warned her about being too friendly with Carlos, letting him into the house to do repairs when Mr. Vogel wasn't home." She shook her head in disapproval.

"Do you know anything about their business? Anything

going on there that you know of?"

Amanda opened her mouth to speak, but closed it again. She bit her lip, and her gaze went back to the window. "Not that I know of."

"What about their personal life—their marriage?"

Amanda pulled her legs from under her and stretched them out, examining her red toenails. "Their marriage was no different than any others."

"She never talked about marital problems? I suspect women dining together every week would talk about their husbands."

She smiled. "Of course, we do. Don't men talk about their wives?" She wriggled her toes and crossed her ankles. "It's not easy being married and working together every day."

"Yes, I think you're right." Davenport stood to leave. "Thank you very much, Mrs. Davis. And please remember to come in tomorrow. You can give your statement to any of the deputies who might be in the office: Deputies Stokes or Powers, Detective Malloy, or myself. If none of us are there, Judy or Danny can tell you when we'll return." He handed her his card.

Davenport returned to his car, turned left onto Brook Haven Road toward the county road. Mrs. Davis had lied to him. He would have to send Stokes in again to ruffle the female feathers.

He looked at his gas gauge and pulled into Havens Gas & Grocery. After filling his tank, he went inside, grabbing milk and a large coffee to go. He added two pods of cream, assuming the brew was hours old. A Hispanic man and a young man with blond ponytail and tattoos sat together on stools near the cash register. The older man, his hand wrapped in gauze and duct tape, was reading a local Spanish-language newspaper, and the young man studied what looked like a college textbook. Davenport paid for his purchases and left.

CHAPTER 15

Two hours after the last customer bought gas, milk, and coffee—and six hours after his cousin, Carlos, had dropped off the books—Julio Gonzalez kicked the large rolling mop bucket with his foot, sending a wave of soapy water over the lip and onto the floor. He pushed the bucket into the next aisle, dipped his mop into it, and squeezed out the excess water, attempting to keep his bandaged hand dry.

Since the murder, Julio's moods had swung wildly between fear and anger. Fear because Mr. Patterson found out he'd been cutting work early and leaving Ryan to close up, and anger because Ryan had promised he wouldn't tell their boss. Now, Mr. P wanted to talk to him. *Not good,* he thought. But something worse than work scared him. *That conejo will betray me!* he thought.

Putting his mop away, Julio's mind wandered in another direction. He thought about what he had seen the night before— that man. If he worked this right, it might be good for him, and his daughter. He pulled the trash bag from the wastebasket and tore off a new liner from the roll underneath. He glanced at his flip phone. No calls. A plan formed in his mind.

He took the trash and the bucket out back, emptied the bucket into the drain, and threw the trash into the dumpster. Back inside, he signed out, tested the automatic door lock, and left. A car sat empty at the edge of the parking lot, away from the streetlights. *A car-share or lovers meeting,* Julio thought as he unlocked his car. The bag of books lay on his passenger seat. As he reached for it, a figure emerged from the shadows and pulled on the passenger side door.

◆ ◆ ◆ ◆ ◆

The Aguila women abandoned Martín to his foul mood and drove into Garland for the latest chick flick. Garland, the county seat of Gardenia County, had a small governmental sector and business district. After the film, Cristina pointed to a small restaurant next to the theater, and they entered, not ready to return to The Havens.

It had been several years since all three of them had been together, and much had happened in their lives during that time. Over dessert and coffee, Cristina expounded on her research trip to Malawi, where she had studied malaria and malnutrition.

"And here we sit eating hot fudge sundaes," Claire said. "I feel guilty."

"About the starving children in Malawi, or the calorie count?" her daughter asked.

"Both," Claire laughed. "Tell your grandmother about Kyle."

Cristina dipped her tall spoon into the bowl, collecting the perfect proportions of ice cream, hot fudge, and whipped topping. "Well, yes, I am seriously dating a medical student, Kyle," she said, and, between spoonsful, she told her grandmother about how they met. "And while I told Mom all about Kyle, and while she went on and on about the Mayanist program and the travails of Madge and George, she said nothing to me about her detective." She rolled her eyes as she finished off her dessert.

Claire sighed. For the past week, she had attempted to conceal her anxiety from her daughter. "You're right. I'm very sorry," she said, avoiding eye contact as she scraped the last of her dessert onto her spoon. "I was afraid he wouldn't come, and I would be embarrassed. The conference ended today. He might come tomorrow, but I haven't heard from him. His plans might have changed."

"Tomorrow?" Theresa asked.

The waitress appeared, replenished their coffee, and removed the dishes. Claire pulled her phone from her purse and looked again, seeking the missed call notification and regretting having told her family about him. *What if he didn't come at all?*

"Mom, it really is okay. I want you to be happy," Cristina reassured her.

Claire covered her daughter's hand with her own. "I know that."

Theresa fiddled with her coffee cup. "Claire, remember when I asked if I could invite you to speak at my book group?"

"I forgot about that, Mom. I thought you changed your mind. When is it?"

"Well, Doris, the president of our group, asked if we could do it tomorrow."

Claire sat back. "Tomorrow?"

"I didn't know your friend was coming," Theresa said. "I'm sorry I didn't confirm it with you."

"Mom, that's fine," Claire assured her. "Of course, I'll do it." Claire finished her coffee. "In fact, I'm beginning to think he changed his mind. I'd love to meet your friends," she said, checking her phone again. "Oh, I got a text from Dad. We'd better get home before he calls 911."

"So how do you—did you—know Mrs. Vogel?" Cristina asked Theresa as Claire drove down the darkened county road that linked Garland and Orchard to The Havens.

Theresa, in the front seat, turned her head toward Cristina. "I worked with Barbara once. The bridge and euchre clubs worked together in the fall to raise money and collect toys for the children of the workers here—for the community Christmas party. She collected a carload of toys from employees at their dealership."

"Dealership?" asked Claire.

"Denton's Equipment in Garland—lawn equipment, tractors, things like that."

Claire slowed as she approached the Havens G&G. As she started her right-hand turn onto Brook Haven Road, a car made a sharp left-hand turn from Brook Haven and sped into her lane. She stomped on the brake. "What the…!"

A car braked behind Claire, and she pulled quickly around the corner and onto the gravel shoulder to catch her breath. "Did you see that?"

Theresa had grabbed the dashboard. "In a hurry, no doubt," she said.

From the back seat, Cristina said, "That was close! Good driving, Mom."

Claire turned to her mother. "Did you see the driver?"

"No, dear, I was bracing for the collision," Theresa said in a shaky voice.

Christina slid down in her seat. "It was a man in a silver car," she said. "Only a million or so of those around," she added, laughing uneasily. As another car turned the corner and paused behind her, Claire waved the driver on with her left hand, then pulled out, past the G&G, and into Sea Haven.

CHAPTER 16

Monday Morning

Pamela Stokes leaned against the sheriff's cruiser, jotting notes. Perspiration already seeped through her uniform, the morning sun threatening another hot and humid spring day. She lifted her coffee cup from the hood of the squad car and groaned as Scott Malloy turned into the G&G parking lot. She could hear the music emanating from the radio in his red Mustang convertible. Her mood darkened as she compared her mode of transportation—the county squad car—to Scott's.

She used to love the Mustang, cruising along the Atlantic shoreline with him, seeking out the beaches that tourists didn't know about and staying overnight in small beachfront hotels. Now she wished she could slash his tires and get away with it.

Malloy parked next to the squad car, as if to twist the knife into her wounded ego. Today he wore black slacks, a yellow button-down shirt, and a tie with multi-colored circles. Clutching his coffee, he leaned against the cruiser, next to her. He motioned to the collection of vehicles congregated along the edge of the rear parking lot—ambulance, squad cars, and the coroner's SUV. "A murder?"

"What's your first clue?" Stokes retorted.

"Whoa," Malloy said. "That's a lot of hostility for a Monday morning."

Stokes sipped her coffee, not looking at him. "Actually, it's a suspicious death at this point," she admitted. "An employee of the store—Julio Gonzalez. Doctor Carlisle is examining him, and Ken Griffin is taking photos. Davenport's on his way."

"Where's your partner?" he asked.

She smiled briefly. "He's at The Havens' dumpsters, with the evidence team."

Malloy snorted. "Rank has its privileges."

Stokes knew he meant to be humorous, but it rankled her. She threw him an angry glance and moved away.

Malloy followed her, nudging her arm. "By the way, you look great, Pam."

She glared at him. "Did you expect me to gain fifty pounds and age twenty years because we broke up?"

"It's a compliment."

She considered her next retort as Detective Davenport's Equinox pulled into the lot and parked next to Malloy's Mustang. Davenport looked up and down Brook Haven Road, where gawkers had parked to watch the drama. He joined Stokes and Malloy. "We need backup," he said.

"I called the department," Stokes replied. "They're sending deputies over for crowd control."

"Good," Davenport said. As he spoke, a brown and tan county car pulled into the lot. Two deputies emerged from the cruiser, both nodding to Davenport before going along the line of cars, directing the onlookers to disperse.

"What have you learned, Malloy?" Davenport asked.

"Just got here, sir," Malloy said.

Stokes cleared her throat. "Julio Gonzalez, an employee, found dead in his car."

Davenport thought about the Hispanic man with the bandaged hand. "Who found him?"

"The owner. He's inside, shaking like a leaf."

Davenport turned to Malloy. "Have you interviewed him?"

"Just got here, sir," he repeated.

"I talked to him, sir," Stokes said. "His name is Mark Patterson. He arrived at six this morning, his usual time. He saw

Mr. Gonzalez's car and wondered why it was still here. When he approached the car, he saw blood on the driver-side window and called us around six-ten."

"He identified the body?"

"Yes," Stokes said, "with Doctor Carlisle. He wants to know if he can open the store. His employees will be arriving soon. I told him to wait until the evidence techs are done. They're in the store now."

Davenport assessed Stokes. "Good." He looked up to see Judy Barnaby approaching from the direction of the scene. "You can't be here, Judy," he said as she joined them. "It's not your jurisdiction."

"I heard the scanner…thought I'd check it out…it's a bloody mess. Who is it?"

"Not a resident of The Havens. Not your jurisdiction," Davenport repeated.

"It looks like a suicide, huh?"

"It's too early to say, Judy. It's suspicious…that's all we know now." Davenport cleared his throat. "Perhaps the deputies could use some help clearing traffic."

"If that's an order," Judy huffed, turning abruptly toward the road.

Davenport sighed heavily. *Disaster.* He turned his attention to Ken Griffin, who was approaching from the scene, his face pale, camera slung over one shoulder.

"Doctor Carlisle said you can see the body, sir."

"Thanks, Ken," Davenport said. He turned back to Malloy. "I stopped here last night and saw Mr. Gonzalez with a young man in the store. I'd like you to find him. Ask about his relationship with Mr. Gonzalez and find out if Mr. Gonzalez worked the Saturday night shift."

"I'll get his address from the owner," Malloy said.

Stokes ripped a page from her pad and handed it to Malloy.

"His name is Ryan Cunningham. He lives in Garland."

"Okay," Davenport said. "Let's meet at Nick's at…" he looked at his watch, "…around one o'clock. Call if you can't make it." Malloy nodded and headed for his car.

Davenport addressed Stokes, saying, "Stay here and intercept any employees as they arrive. Tell them only that Mr. Gonzalez has died. If they have information to share, have them stay. Otherwise get their contact information and send them home. Mr. Patterson will contact them later. I know you can be tactful."

"Yes, sir."

Davenport walked with Griffin toward the scene. The rookie was silent, his jaw clenched.

"Are you okay?" Davenport asked.

"My first month on the job and I've photographed two gunshot deaths," he said, tucking his red hair behind his ears. "The lady was bad, but…this guy…" He shook his head and sighed deeply.

"Go to the store and ask the owner, Mr. Patterson, for water," Davenport said, patting him on the shoulder. "And please, don't mess up the crime scene." He smiled and added, "I'll come get you when I'm through."

Griffin didn't argue. He turned back toward the store, and Davenport joined Doctor Carlisle, who was speaking into her recorder.

"We have to stop meeting like this," Carlisle said, clicking off her recorder and forcing a smile.

Davenport peered at the body sprawled on the car seat, its head lolling to the left. He recognized the man he had seen in the store the night before.

"I had to move him away from the door to open it," Carlisle said. "I've tried not to move anything else. He probably died between midnight and two o'clock this morning."

"I saw him around ten o'clock," Davenport said. He leaned

into the car to examine the gaping wound at the right side of the victim's head. "Could it be suicide?"

"It's possible." She picked up her flashlight and aimed it onto the floor between the two front seats. "There's the gun."

Davenport took her flashlight and examined the blood-splattered gun. It resembled the type of gun Mr. Vogel had claimed to own. "Could this be a remorseful suicide?"

"That would certainly make your job easier." She stood and stretched her back. "Can we take him out of the car?"

Davenport nodded. "I'll send Griffin back for photos. He's taking a breather."

"Poor kid," Doctor Carlisle said. She motioned to the ambulance drivers who stood in the shadows, talking quietly.

Davenport moved to the passenger side and looked in at the body, noting the bandaged left hand and a spray of blood on the passenger window and seat. "There's a shopping bag here."

"Yes," Carlisle said. "I left that for you and the evidence team."

Davenport watched as the ambulance drivers maneuvered the body from the car and into the body bag. He returned to the store, where Stokes stood speaking with a middle-aged woman whose mass of unnatural red hair had been tied up with a huge clip. She wore tennis shoes, baggy black slacks, and an oversized lavender blouse under a sleeveless vest with her name tag on it. The two women looked up as Davenport approached.

Stokes said, "Detective Davenport, this is Helen Suarez, the day manager."

Davenport shook her hand. "Has Deputy Stokes explained the situation to you?"

"Yes, but I want to talk to Mr. P. She won't let me."

"I understand, Mrs. Suarez, but we need to follow procedures, and we haven't finished in the store yet."

"Have you talked to Ryan?" Helen asked.

"Someone's talking to him now, ma'am," Davenport said.

"But we need your cooperation. Mr. Patterson will call you later. It might be this afternoon."

Mrs. Suarez sighed heavily, adjusted her huge purse over her shoulder, and left.

As Davenport watched Mrs. Suarez depart, he asked Stokes, "How many employees have you talked with?"

"Only one other employee arrived, a young man, Will, who stocks the shelves and cleans for the day shift. He never worked with Julio."

"But Mrs. Suarez knows Ryan?" Davenport asked.

Stokes nodded. "Ryan's shift starts one hour before Mrs. Suarez leaves. Mr. Gonzalez—Julio—arrives later. He and his wife work separate shifts to watch the kids and share the car. So, Ryan is here from four to ten or eleven, and Julio worked until midnight and closed the store. There's also a weekend schedule that's more flexible."

"Did Julio work Saturday night when Mrs. Vogel was murdered?" he asked.

"I'm not sure."

"Let's find out." Davenport opened the side door to the store, allowing Stokes to enter first. The evidence team leader, Craig Hughes, stood with Griffin, who leaned against the front window drinking a soda.

"Your turn," Davenport said to Hughes. He turned to Griffin. "Are you okay?"

Griffin nodded. "I'm good." He hoisted his camera and followed Deputy Hughes back to the scene.

CHAPTER 17

Mark Patterson sat in his small office at the rear of the store, his head in his hands. His wife had warned him about hiring Mexican workers, but he'd never had reason to distrust his employees. Julio had been a good worker. *What happened to him?*

Patterson looked up to see the female deputy standing at his door beside a tall, lean man with graying hair. Patterson invited them in.

"Mr. Patterson? I am Detective Sergeant Davenport. You've met Deputy Stokes?"

Patterson stood and shook hands, then nervously removed a bundle of unsold newspapers off one chair and a pile of invoice vouchers off the other as the deputies waited. Stokes studied the work schedule tacked to a bulletin board, along with a collection of notices and messages.

"I'm sorry," Patterson said at last. "Please, sit."

Davenport and Stokes settled into the chairs and pulled out their notepads. "I'm sorry about Mr. Gonzalez," Davenport said. "Had he been working for you long?"

"About a year."

"How did you come to hire him?"

"His cousin, Carlos Chavez, worked for me before getting his job at The Havens. He brought Julio in about a year ago. I guess— though I don't remember for sure—they didn't have any openings at The Havens, so Carlos brought him here to see if I needed help. I trusted Carlos, so I hired Julio on his recommendation."

"Did you like Julio?" Davenport asked.

"Yes. He married a local woman—Paula—and they had two

kids…actually, she had one child—the older boy—and they had the baby girl."

Davenport looked quickly at Stokes. "Can you call the department and see if anyone has talked to Mrs. Gonzalez?"

Stokes left the room, pulling her phone from her pocket.

Davenport turned back to Patterson. "Was Julio a good employee?"

"Yes, very good…until recently."

"What do you mean?" Davenport pushed.

"Helen—Mrs. Suarez—learned that Julio sometimes came in late for his shift. When I asked him about it, he admitted he had a second job at The Havens. He apologized but said that a half hour or hour lawn job would get him thirty to forty dollars, more than he earns here. I checked with Ryan, and he said he didn't mind if Julio came in a little late some days…as long as it wasn't too busy."

He smoothed his already highly gelled black hair and adjusted his glasses. "I knew he needed the extra income because his daughter has some kind of disability, and they don't have much money."

"Had anything else changed in his work habits lately?"

Patterson nodded. "I didn't think much more about it, until Ryan's mother called Helen and complained that she was making Ryan work until midnight. But the sign-out sheets indicated that he left at eleven, and Julio left at midnight as scheduled."

"What was going on?" Davenport asked.

"Helen didn't want to tell me—she liked Julio—but Ryan admitted that Julio had started leaving work in the evenings, sometimes taking long breaks and acting nervous when he returned. Sometimes he left early, leaving Ryan to close up. Ryan didn't care at first, because Julio had promised to pay him for the difference, but I guess he didn't always follow through. He didn't want to get Julio into trouble by complaining, but then his mother called Helen and it all came out."

"Did Julio tell Ryan why he had to leave early?"

"He always had an excuse—said he had to go home to watch the kids for an hour or do a quick job for Carlos."

"Do you know if Mr. Gonzalez worked on Saturday night?"

"When Mrs. Vogel was killed?" Patterson shuffled through a pile of schedule and sign-out cards. "Julio closed as usual at midnight." He pulled another card. "Ryan left early, at ten-thirty."

Davenport pursed his lips. "Perhaps Ryan worked, and Mr. Gonzalez left early?"

Patterson slumped back in his chair. "Maybe."

"Did Julio take care of the cash box when he closed up?"

"Yes," Patterson responded, "and I never had a shortage."

"Was Mr. Gonzalez at risk of being fired?" Davenport asked.

Patterson sighed. "I called him last night and asked him to come in to see me today. Do you think…?"

Stokes returned to the office. "Mrs. Gonzalez called the Sheriff's Department at five o'clock this morning when she awoke and realized her husband didn't come home last night. They told her it was too soon to make a report, and that he would probably show up. No one followed up until Mr. Patterson reported the death. The department sent a deputy to her house to break the news, but she's heard nothing since. It's been three hours."

Davenport sighed. "Do you have her phone number and address?" Stokes nodded and gave it to him. He turned to Mr. Patterson. "Thank you, sir. We'll let you know when you can open your store."

Davenport turned to Stokes. "Walk me to the car." Outside, he said, "Stay with the evidence team and record whatever they find in and around the car. There's a bag in the front seat along with the gun. That will give us a start. When they've finished with the store, you can let Mr. Patterson open up. Meet us at Nick's at one o'clock."

Davenport started to walk away. "Wait…I forgot to ask about a store video."

"I'm on it, sir."

"Good. And one more thing," he said as he opened his car door. "Have the team check the dumpster out back. It's beginning to look like there might be a link between the two deaths."

◆ ◆ ◆ ◆ ◆

In Orchard, Detective Davenport parked his car in front of a single-story clapboard house, now a faded pink. The house resembled the others wedged together along Seminole Street, each with a different pastel color competing for prominence, with the bare wood beneath it. A narrow walkway led from the road to the house. Tufts of weeds erupted from the loose gravel and coral that dominated the front yards up and down the street. Ixora and hibiscus plants provided decorative color.

Davenport knocked on the screen door and waited. A young woman appeared, holding a small child; a young boy huddled behind her legs.

"Mrs. Gonzalez?"

Blinking away tears, Paula Gonzalez opened the screen door after Davenport introduced himself.

"Mrs. Gonzalez, I have news about your husband."

She wiped her eyes with the back of her hand and led him into the small living room.

"I'm very sorry," he said. He looked at the young boy, now clinging to her legs. "What are your children's names?"

"Billy and Mary."

"Perhaps they could play in another room?"

"Where's Daddy?" Billy asked, glancing at Davenport as Mary started to squirm in Paula's arms.

Paula excused herself and led her son into the kitchen. She

took two cookies from a chipped Mickey Mouse cookie jar and took the children into their bedroom. When she returned, she sat on a chair with frayed upholstery in a pink-and-orange floral design. Davenport sank deeply into the matching well-worn sofa across from her. He guessed that she was in her thirties, but she looked older. Her prematurely creased face was framed by graying uncombed hair that fell in curls around her shoulders.

"Can you tell me what happened to my husband?" she asked. "The person who called wouldn't say anything."

"I am sorry no one followed up," Davenport said.

"Are you sure it's him?"

"Mr. Patterson identified him."

"When did it happen? How...?" Her words stuck in her mouth, tears flowing from her dark eyes to her neck and onto her faded T-shirt. She reached over to the end table and pulled a baby wipe from a plastic container, using it on her face.

"We think it happened after work. He had signed out and was found in his car." Davenport paused to let the information sink in. "Does your husband have a gun?"

"No," she sniffled. "He wouldn't have one. He applied for citizenship and wouldn't do anything to ruin that."

"Your husband died by a gunshot wound that might have been self-inflicted."

Her eyes turned to him in a questioning look, her eyebrows knitting together. "No! He wouldn't do that to us. We're Catholic—that's a sin!"

Davenport sat quietly as her sobs renewed and she wiped her face again with the wet wipe. Hearing his mother, Billy sprinted into the living room, his eyes wide. Mary toddled behind him, fussing.

"Mommy, why are you crying?" Billy asked.

"It's nothing, *mijo.*" Paula lifted Mary onto her lap. Billy stood next to her, staring at the detective, his young face marked by fear.

"Is your daughter ill, Mrs. Gonzalez?"

"Mary has a heart defect."

"Do you have insurance for her care?"

"Medicaid, but that doesn't pay for everything. We miss work for appointments, and she needs special food..." She broke down into tears again.

Davenport thought about this. "Is it possible that your husband obtained money for Mary in illegal ways?"

Her head shot up. "No! I told you he wouldn't do anything to ruin his citizenship application."

Billy gave a warning glance to the stranger, and Davenport decided he liked the boy. He would be the rock his mother needed.

Paula placed her hand on Billy's cheek. "Go play, *mijo*."

After Billy left the room again, Davenport said, "But the baby needs special care. Perhaps he had been stealing? There have been robberies in The Havens lately." He paused again, watching Paula's face as it transitioned from anger to fear. "Perhaps he was caught stealing and he...hurt...someone? Then felt remorse? Is that possible?"

She stood so rapidly that Mary rolled off her lap onto the sofa. Paula picked her up and comforted her, tears rolling down both faces. "No, it's not possible! He couldn't hurt anyone. He wouldn't do anything to hurt us."

CHAPTER 18

Malloy pulled into the small subdivision of Gull View. Far from the ocean or gulf coast mansions, most Floridians live in communities like this one, where narrow streets meander past stucco bungalows in muted tropical colors. Malloy's parents had lived in a community like this one, but his family had moved into one of the more affluent subdivisions with larger lots, more spacious homes, and, often, swimming pools.

Malloy's GPS directed him to a small, faded-blue bungalow with a crushed-stone yard, which, nonetheless, had not prevented a dollar weed invasion. A Honda 350 motorcycle was parked in a detached garage—more a lean-to than a formal structure—next to an old-model Chevy Impala. Malloy frowned as he turned his spotless convertible into the unpaved driveway, past the plastic dolphin-encased mailbox with "Cunningham" painted on the side.

A woman, perhaps in her fifties, answered his knock. Her gray eyes examined him carefully, but her nose drew his attention, long and thin, following the oval shape of her face. Small barrettes held her chin-length gray-streaked hair from her face.

"Mrs. Cunningham?"

"Yes?" she said, eyes moving from Malloy to his car.

"I'm Detective Malloy from the Gardenia County Sheriff's Department. Is Ryan here?"

Her mouth tightened. "Is this about Julio?"

"I'm afraid it is. Is Ryan your son?"

"Yes, but he's getting ready to leave for school."

"It shouldn't take long. I need to ask him a few questions."

Mrs. Cunningham opened the screen door. "I knew there was something going on with Julio—making Ryan work his hours—I told Helen it wasn't right." She dropped her voice to a whisper as she led Malloy through a compact living room with well-worn furniture and a small flat-screen television sitting on a wooden hutch.

Malloy followed her into the kitchen, where a young man sat on a stool at a high kitchen counter eating a bowl of cereal. He had long blond hair tied back in a ponytail at the nape of his neck, and sleeve tattoos with swirling waves and surfboards running down each arm. Ryan turned deep blue eyes toward the deputy.

"Ryan, this is Detective Malloy. He wants to talk to you about Julio."

Malloy said, "It'll just take a few minutes, Ryan."

Ryan pushed his bowl away, saying in a shaky voice, "So it's true? Julio's dead?"

"Who told you?"

"People are saying…maybe he committed suicide?" Ryan swiveled his stool to look at Malloy.

"It's too early to say." Malloy noticed Ryan's mother standing worriedly by the kitchen sink. "Can we talk…outside perhaps?"

Ryan grabbed his orange juice from the counter and led Malloy through the kitchen door into a narrow backyard enclosed by an eight-foot wooden fence, long since stripped of its original color. They sat on deck chairs with faded floral upholstery that took up most of the cement patio. The remaining space contained a round patio table and a dilapidated, and probably dangerous, gas grill.

"Ryan, what was it like, working with Julio?"

"I liked him," Ryan said, pulling on his ponytail. "My dad left us when I was young. Julio was like an uncle…listening to me talk about my friends and dating and stuff." He smiled. "He gave me advice, but it was funny, old-fashioned, Mexican stuff—like asking the father's permission to go on a date, having chaperones at parties—real last-century."

Ryan sat back, remembering. "He asked me how to pronounce things in English or name items in the store so he could help the customers. Like bagels—he didn't know what they were. He wanted to learn so he could pass his citizenship." He paused, pressing his lips together, then smiled. "He helped me with my Spanish class, too."

"How did you learn that Julio had died?"

"Mr. Patterson called me. He wanted to know if Julio was there when I left last night. I said, it was like usual…or at least like it used to be."

"Tell me about that," Malloy said. "I heard that you and Julio switched hours?"

Ryan nodded and gulped his juice. "He seemed worried about something. He started taking long breaks. Later, started leaving early, and I stayed and closed up."

"Was that a problem?"

"Only later. He didn't want Mr. Patterson to know he was leaving early, so we signed each other out, and he paid me back from his paycheck." Ryan looked over his shoulder toward the kitchen door. "But sometimes he didn't, and I didn't tell Helen, because I thought he would make it good, but then my mother complained to her."

"Why would you talk to Helen and not Mr. Patterson?"

"Because she's the day manager. She does the schedule."

"Did anything else happen that made you distrust Julio?"

Ryan sighed deeply. "I felt sorry for him because of his daughter. When he needed to go home and watch the kids, I told him it was okay…"

"But?"

"Once, his wife called after he left, and she seemed confused when I told her he went home, so I knew he'd lied. So, when Helen came to me about my mother's call, I asked her not to tell Mr. Patterson. I didn't want to get him fired, but I didn't want to work for free either."

Ryan's words came out in a torrent, his emotions ripped between loyalty to Julio and his boss. "Helen said she would figure out a way to tell Julio…and explain to him that I couldn't do that for him… but I think she told Mr. Patterson." Tears began to form at the corners of Ryan's eyes. "I'm afraid he killed himself because of me!" His shoulders heaved as he sobbed, shaky hands gripping his juice glass.

Malloy sat back. "Listen, Ryan. Whatever happened, it's not your fault."

Mrs. Cunningham opened the door and looked out. "Ryan, you'll be late for class…" She looked at Ryan's reddened eyes. "What happened?"

Malloy stood quickly. "It's nothing, ma'am. He's fine."

Ryan wiped his face with his hands. "I'm okay, Mom." He turned to Malloy. "I gotta go."

"Just one more question," Malloy said. "Did you and Julio work together Saturday night?"

Ryan turned from the door, tears welling in his eyes again. "He asked me if I would close for him. He said something came up at home, and he asked if he could leave around nine o'clock." He lowered his voice and focused his eyes on Malloy. "I told him I would, but it had to be the last time."

"What did Julio say?"

"He promised it would be the last time," Ryan sighed. "But all evening he acted nervous, his hands shaking, even slicing himself with the box cutter. Blood spurted all over. It was nearly nine, so I told him to go to the ER. I had already offered to close the store, so it wasn't a big deal."

"He didn't come back to work?" Malloy asked.

"No, I didn't expect him to…I gotta go."

They reentered the house together. Ryan grabbed his helmet and backpack from the living room sofa. He kissed his mother, who stared at Malloy with disdain. "Really, Mom, I'm okay."

Malloy followed Ryan to the front yard. The young man forced a smile as he pulled on his helmet. "Mom insists I wear this. I feel like a dork. But if she catches me without it, she'll kill me."

Malloy held the motorcycle while Ryan settled himself and the backpack onto the bike. "Ryan, you were a friend. You didn't cause his death."

"He promised me it would be his last time—and it was."

He maneuvered his bike around Malloy, who considered the truth of Ryan's statement.

"Mr. Patterson will call you with more information," Malloy said.

The young man nodded, revved the engine, and drove past him down the driveway.

CHAPTER 19

Pamela Stokes sat at a corner booth at Nick's, a local diner and bar near the courthouse and Sheriff's Department. It was popular with county employees and attorneys during the day, and alive with locals in the evening. Nick, a northern transport, wanted to bring the rustic Midwest feel to the Florida swamps. But in reality the knotty-pine paneling, wooden floors, and vinyl booths portrayed central Florida regional culture, embedded in horse farms and agriculture. Stokes stirred her iced tea as she spoke into her phone. "Okay. See you soon."

Malloy slid next to her into the booth. "Was that Powers?"

Stokes nodded. "He spent the morning dumpster-diving. Said he'll meet us here in a few minutes."

Malloy laughed and moved a little closer to Stokes. He scoffed at her iced tea, but when the waitress approached, he ordered a Coke.

"If the boss wasn't coming, I'd be ordering a beer," Malloy said after the waitress left.

Stokes moved away from him. "What did you find out from Ryan?"

"He's a nice kid…thinks he caused Julio to commit suicide."

"Why did he think that?"

Malloy explained the complicated work relationship between Ryan and Julio. "Ryan's afraid that Patterson fired Julio, and that he killed himself because of it."

"Who's spouting this suicide theory?" Stokes asked, then slumped in her seat. "I only need one guess—Judy. I hope you told him that his fear is unjustified."

"Of course, I did." Malloy sat back in the booth, crossing his arms. "But suicide is not an unreasonable possibility." The waitress returned with his drink and left for another table. "What's your problem, anyway?" he asked Stokes.

"You know what the problem is." Stokes straightened her uniform shirt self-consciously.

He waved his hand in a flourish. "That's not my fault. If he'd hired you, I wouldn't be whining, and we'd still be together."

Stokes snorted. "I had a higher score on my exam, and I had more time clocked on the job."

"More hours, but I was hired two months before you." Malloy looked toward the entrance and spoke. "Listen, I heard from some of the guys that Davenport got some heat for taking Sara under his wing. They called her the Affirmative Action Hire— and worse—but you don't want to know what guys say."

"That's bullshit. She's more than qualified."

"Yeah, but I think it got back to him, so he was reluctant to hire another woman, even temporarily." He leaned toward Stokes again. "Besides, I have other qualifications. My father is a lieutenant in Tampa…policing runs in my blood."

"That's not a qualification," Stokes sneered, looking toward the door. "He's here."

Davenport slid in across from them. "Long morning, eh?" He pulled his notebook from his pocket. "Did you hear from Powers?"

"He went home to shower and eat lunch after his morning at the dumpsters," Stokes said. "He'll be here soon but said to order without him."

The waitress returned, and they ordered. "What can you two report?" Davenport asked when his coffee arrived.

Malloy sat forward and reported on his interview with Ryan Cunningham.

"Ryan's information confirms what we learned from the

owner, Mark Patterson," Stokes added. "He actually asked Julio to meet with him today."

"What did Ryan say about working Saturday night?" Davenport asked.

"Ah, yes." Malloy explained Julio's plan to leave early Saturday night, and how Julio cut his hand and went to the ER around nine. "Ryan closed for him, but that's not all." Malloy paused for effect. "He told Ryan he wouldn't ask him to do it again."

"And he won't," Davenport said, sitting back in his seat. "Julio's hand was bandaged last night when I saw him, but it didn't look professionally wrapped." He turned to Stokes. "What about the employees?"

"None of the day-shift employees—other than Mrs. Suarez—really knew Julio," Stokes said. "Those who worked with him said he was quiet and worked hard." She paused to sip her drink. "By the way, the store has security cameras, but none of them are working." She raised her eyebrows. "Why bother?"

Malloy gulped his drink and asked Davenport, "What did Julio's wife say?"

They all looked up as Mike Powers dropped onto the bench next to Davenport, who slid over to make room.

Davenport answered Malloy's question. "Mrs. Gonzalez claimed her husband would never kill himself or do anything to hurt his family." He paused as the waitress brought their food and asked Powers for his order.

"Just a Coke," he said.

"What did Hughes and the evidence techs find?" Davenport asked Stokes, who quickly swallowed a bite of burger.

"Hughes said the gun is likely the one taken from the Vogel home. He'll compare the serial numbers with those on Todd's registration, if he has one."

"At least we don't have to dredge that lake," Malloy said.

"True that," Powers agreed.

Stokes sipped her tea. "Hughes found several interesting items in the car. First, the plastic bag on the floor of the passenger seat held six children's books…sound familiar?"

"Should it?" asked Malloy.

Powers answered, pausing as the waitress brought his drink. "Carlos said that Mrs. Vogel gave him some books, and Mrs. Van Dee saw Carlos carrying a bulky plastic bag."

"How did the books get into Julio's car?" Malloy asked.

"That's not the only mystery," Stokes said. She drew out the drama as she sipped her tea. "The bag also contained jewelry: a matching necklace and bracelet, an expensive watch, and one bloody diamond earring."

Powers held his drink in mid-air. Davenport put his burger on his plate.

"One earring?" Malloy asked. "In the book bag?"

"Wait!" Powers said. "There was no jewelry in the bag when Carlos showed it to me at the DPS."

"What if Carlos added the jewelry to the bag later and planted it in Julio's car?" Malloy said.

Stokes shook her head. "When did Carlos steal the jewelry? He was at the Vogels for five minutes early Saturday evening. If Julio was there later that night, and if he somehow committed this horrible murder and stole jewelry—without leaving one fingerprint—he already had the jewelry in his possession when Carlos dropped off the book bag Sunday evening."

"Did Julio put the jewelry in the bag after Carlos dropped it off?" Malloy suggested. "To do something with it later?"

"In with books for his kids?" Stokes asked. "Before killing himself? I don't see it."

"Me either," agreed Davenport.

"So, who's the community thief?" Powers asked. "Julio or Carlos?"

"Unfortunately, it was likely Julio," Stokes sighed. "Hughes found a keychain filled with house keys and a small key-lock set in Julio's trunk, along with a black hoodie."

"Mrs. Van Dee's mystery man wore a hoodie," Powers remembered.

"Maybe they planned it together," Malloy said. "Maybe Julio killed Mrs. Vogel, then killed himself out of remorse…not thinking about the books, or maybe Carlos killed his cousin."

"Stop," Davenport warned, "we're getting way ahead of ourselves here."

The younger deputies sat back. Stokes flushed and concentrated on her drink, and Powers ran his fingers through his black hair.

"I interviewed Carlos yesterday," Stokes said tentatively. "Somehow, I don't see him as a thief, or a murderer. And I don't see why Carlos would implicate his cousin in a terrible crime after getting him a job. He was genuinely terrified, but not in a guilty way, if you know what I mean. It was more about family."

Conversation paused as the team finished their meals, Powers chewing on his straw in concentration. Davenport looked to Powers. "What did you find in the dumpsters?"

"The team hadn't finished when I left the G&G," Powers said. "But they finished at The Lodge…interesting findings there… bingo cards, plastic bottles, diapers…the adult kind…and, get this, condoms." Powers smiled.

"Condoms?" Malloy groaned. "I heard the STD rates in these places were the highest in the state."

Stokes glared at both men, then turned to Davenport. "I talked to Hughes. He said the lab is comparing Julio's shoes with the photos Griffin took of the footprints in the Vogel yard."

"Good," Davenport said. "Anything else interesting?"

"Yes," Stokes said. "The blood tech noticed something very intriguing about Mrs. Vogel's kimono sash—something about blood stains not matching up. His report will be ready soon."

"Doctor Carlisle saw that also," Davenport said.

"Where do we go from here?" Malloy asked.

Davenport scanned his notes. "I also talked with Mr. Chavez, briefly, this morning at The Barn. We need to talk to him again, ask him how the bag of books got into Mr. Gonzalez's car and what he knows about the jewelry." He paused as the waitress brought their checks, then turned to Powers. "I'd like you to check on Mr. Vogel's contacts from the conference."

Malloy frowned. "You don't really think he was involved, do you, sir?"

Davenport studied his new detective. "We check everyone, especially the husband."

"My assignment, sir?" asked Stokes.

"Go back to the G&G and talk to Mr. Patterson and Mrs. Suarez, if you can find her." He paused to calculate the tip on his credit card. "And talk to anyone else at the store who might have known Mr. Gonzalez. Let's meet back at the Sheriff's Department around six o'clock."

Davenport stood to leave. "I haven't reported on my less-than-successful conversation with Mrs. Davis, the neighbor." He looked to Stokes. "It might require a woman's touch."

Stokes pulled bills from her wallet. "I already failed with her, sir. Perhaps Detective Malloy should give it a try."

CHAPTER 20

Mark Patterson stood outside the G&G, staring at the officers perched on ladders, rummaging through his dumpster. They had already searched the store, but had not given him permission to open up. He tensed when he watched Deputy Stokes pull into the lot and talk to another deputy, who was directing the load-up of Julio's car onto a hauler. The deputy handed Stokes a clear plastic bag. When she approached Patterson, he saw it contained a cellphone.

"Good afternoon, Mr. Patterson," Stokes said. "Have you contacted Mrs. Suarez?"

"She's on her way," he said as he led her into the store. "And Ryan's coming in also." When they had settled back into the office, Patterson asked, "Will this take long? I have to open up."

"No, sir. You've already given us most of what we need." She skimmed several pages in her notepad. "We've confirmed the unusual work agreement between Julio and Ryan. We understand you had planned to talk to him about it today?"

"Do you think that's why he killed himself?" Patterson asked, his hands shaking.

"We haven't established it as a suicide yet."

"Not suicide?" Patterson asked. "That's what Judy Barnaby said…and it looked like…you know."

"It's too early to say, sir." Stokes pushed the evidence bag toward him. "Is this Julio's phone?"

"It could be. Where was it?"

"Under his car seat."

Patterson shrugged. "It's probably his."

The coffee room door slammed against the wall, and Helen Suarez sailed into the room. She wore the same clothing as before, and her hair had not been improved upon. "Sorry I'm late," she said as she plopped down on a chair. "My fool of a husband didn't tell me you called." Patterson had worked with her long enough to know that she and her husband of fifty years practiced a life-long commitment to mutual harassment.

"What are they looking for in the bins?" Helen asked, without taking a breath. She pointed out the small office window at the officers crawling out of the dumpster.

"I can't say, ma'am," Stokes said, following her gaze toward the men brushing themselves off and laughing among themselves. "Thank you for coming to talk with me again."

"Can I open the store?" Patterson asked, edging out of his chair.

"Yes, thank you," Stokes said. She turned her attention to the day manager, who un-self-consciously adjusted her ample bosoms through her blouse and vest. She placed her purple-framed glasses, that hung from a rhinestone chain, on her nose.

Reaching toward the bagged phone, Helen asked, "Is this Julio's phone?"

"Do you think so?" Stokes asked.

"I don't know," Helen responded. She turned her blue eye-shadowed eyes toward the deputy. "What can you tell me?"

Stokes stifled a smile. "That's my question, Mrs. Suarez."

"You can't tell me what happened to Julio?"

"We don't know what happened yet. That's why we're interviewing everyone who knew him."

"Poor Julio," Helen said. "I didn't know him well, you know. He usually arrived after I left, but the store was always clean when Mr. P and I arrived in the morning. He did a good job."

"When did you learn that Ryan and Julio were switching

hours?"

"Not until Ryan's mother called to complain."

"About the schedule?"

"About everything, bless her heart." Helen adjusted her clothing again and leaned forward. "She complained that Ryan had been working until midnight on class nights and missing his morning classes. And she didn't like him on his motorcycle late at night… drunks are pickin' off motorcyclists like ducks in a pond, I tell you. I don't blame her." She paused to think. "But she was really hoppin' when she found one of Ryan's pay stubs in a drawer—I guess he hid them—and no wonder, because he was only getting paid for working until eleven, not midnight."

"You talked to Ryan first, before going to Mr. Patterson?"

"I wanted to hear what Ryan had to say. He confirmed the arrangement, but said he didn't want to get Julio into trouble. So, in the end, Ryan got screwed…excuse my French."

"Did you believe Ryan's story?"

"I had no reason not to. He's a nice kid," she said, then lowering her voice continued, "Don't judge him on the tattoos. Why do people do that to themselves?"

Stokes looked at the woman with cerulean blue eyeshadow and fire-engine red hair, wondering the same thing.

◆ ◆ ◆ ◆ ◆

Ryan closed his Spanish textbook and shoved it into his backpack. *Who's going to help me with Spanish now?* he wondered as he shuffled down the hallway of the Liberal Arts Building. *Damn,* he thought as tears erupted unexpectedly. *Poor Julio.* He checked his phone and opened a voicemail from Mr. Patterson asking him to come into work early. Ryan looked at his watch. His history class would start in an hour. No problem. He hated history. He called Mr. Patterson, ran to the parking lot, and hopped on his motorcycle.

Ryan had never seen the parking lot at the G&G this crowded, and more cars lined up at the gas pumps. He suspected people were more interested in Julio's death than buying gas. Inside, Mr. Patterson stood at the check-out counter as customers lined up to pay. This was the first time Ryan had seen his boss actually working the counter.

"Thank God," Mr. Patterson said as Ryan entered.

"I'll be right back." Ryan strode past the counter to the office, where Helen sat with a female officer. They both looked up as Ryan entered. The deputy stared at his tats, and Helen blushed as if she'd been caught smoking in the bathroom.

"Thanks for coming in, Ryan," Helen said. Mr. P is in a panic."

"Ryan Cunningham?" Stokes asked.

"I already talked to Detective Malloy."

"I'm Deputy Stokes," she said. "Thank you for talking to Deputy Detective Malloy. Mrs. Suarez and I need a few more minutes."

"I just need to take care of my stuff." Ryan held up his helmet and backpack, then stuffed them into his personal cubby. As he left the room, Helen grabbed the evidence bag before Stokes could take it back from her.

"Hon, the deputy wants to know if this is Julio's phone." She waved it in front of his face.

"Yeah, it looks like it," Ryan said as he turned to leave.

Helen resettled herself in her chair and said to Ryan, "Tell Mr. P I'll be back shortly."

◆ ◆ ◆ ◆ ◆

That night, Ryan slapped the mop over the floor. He liked the closing shift. It was quiet with few customers, but a little sad without Julio. He wished his mother would let him work this shift all the time, but she had told Mr. P, in no uncertain terms, that he had to find another closer. Ryan's music blared into his ears, but his mind wandered, thinking of Julio, who talked to him like a friend, asking about college and his future plans—unlike his mom, who gave him the third degree about where he went on the weekends with his friends. Did she really think he would tell her?

He squeezed the mop in the huge bucket one last time and took the bucket outside to empty it, admitting that he couldn't really blame her. He knew she worried that he would pick up his father's bad habits. But he resented the fact that she always went through his stuff. He could tell because his drawers were always neater than he left them, his computer incorrectly turned off, and his phone never where he thought he left it.

Then there was the motorcycle. *You're gonna get killed, and then what will I do? I'll be all alone! You'll be sorry if you're dead or in a wheelchair...honestly!* But Julio had been fascinated by his bike, and Ryan had promised he would give him a ride someday. He regretted that he never got around to taking him out for a spin. Even more, he felt the heavy burden of guilt because his mother had reported Julio to Helen, and now he was dead.

Ryan plodded through the rest of his chores. He finished by emptying the wastebaskets, which weren't full because the cops had gone through them earlier. In the lunchroom, he pulled the plastic liner from the wastebasket and dropped it into the larger black trash bag. It was empty except for a mess of coffee grounds and several of Mr. P's nicotine gum packets...hilarious, because everyone knew he still smoked secretly behind the store.

It was store practice to keep a roll of plastic bags at the bottom of the basket so fresh bags were handy. He pulled the roll out of the basket to tear off the next bag. It felt different, though, heavier. Usually the bundles were tightly rolled, but now he felt a bulge at the core of the bundle; it looked like someone had tried to take a bag out from the center. He thought perhaps the police had fiddled with it, but when he pushed the loose bags back into place, his fingers felt something hard. He reached into the roll and pulled out a small flip phone, like those they sell at department stores.

He took the phone over to the lunch table and sat down. Opening it, he saw only one contact, a local exchange with no name. Ryan scratched his head and stared at it. *What the hell?* He turned it around, wondering whose it was. It couldn't be Julio's. The cops already had his cell. Then his mind worked along more creative lines. Who might miss it? Mom wouldn't even know about this one. If someone asked about it, he'd give it back, really. He shoved the phone into his jeans pocket.

CHAPTER 21

The flurry of preparations started immediately after Roberto Salinas had finally confirmed his visit to The Havens. Claire intercepted her mother as she rearranged the furniture in the office-sewing room and opened up the sofa bed.

"He has a hotel reservation," Claire said.

"Absolutely not," her mother said. "He'll stay here. Tell him to check out of his hotel."

All morning, Claire, her mother, and her daughter cleaned the already-spotless house, and now the kitchen was the focus of activity.

"What kind of appetizers does he eat?" her mother had asked earlier, as they stood in the deli section of the Publix grocery store.

"Mexican cops don't eat appetizers, Mom," she had pleaded, even then remembering their first non-date when they had shared appetizers at El Caracol, a small bar in Merida.

"Would sandwiches be better? Help me, Claire."

Now, Theresa scurried around the kitchen preparing lunch. Cristina and Claire were making sun tea and fresh lemonade.

"Are you sure we can't have margaritas?" Cristina asked as she squeezed the last of the lemons into the pitcher.

"I'm sure," Claire said. "Besides we can't show up at the book club drunk…on second thought that would probably be better," she said, laughing.

"What if he doesn't like us?" Theresa asked.

"He'll love you, Mom. Mexican men love mothers." She cringed, hearing herself spout another stereotype. "He and Dad will circle each other a few times, then hug, and all will be well."

Claire knew her mother was perturbed because her father had disappeared an hour ago, ostensibly to do a quick mowing job, but Claire suspected that the poor man had to escape before he became swallowed up in the estrogen vortex.

"It's one o'clock," Theresa said, looking at her watch. "Where's Martín? He promised he'd be back by now."

Claire shook her head. "Don't worry. He'll be back soon."

When the doorbell rang, all three women jumped and looked toward the door. "He's here!" Theresa said, rushing to clean the countertop.

Claire led her mother toward the door, both tense with anticipation. Cristina stayed back, her heart pounding for reasons she could not quite understand. Claire's eyes widened as she opened the door.

"Damn! You're hard to find," said a plump woman as she dropped two large travel bags on the stoop. "You'd think it'd be easy to locate the only Hispanic family in the whole place!"

Theresa stared at the woman, of similar age but from another cultural decade. Cristina, expecting to hear a male voice, joined them at the door and gaped at the woman with the unruly gray curls, wearing an ankle-length Mexican skirt and oversized peasant blouse.

"Madge?" Claire said, as if she had no idea who had just landed on the porch.

"We had to go to the visitor's center to find you."

"We?" Claire asked as Roberto appeared at the door, raising his eyebrows as he shrugged.

"Roberto and I met up at the conference in Orlando," Madge said. "He told me he was coming to meet your family—you shouldn't keep secrets from me, Claire."

Claire felt faint. "Mom, Cristina, this is Madge Carmichael, my colleague and friend." Claire struggled to control her pounding heart. "And this is Roberto Salinas."

Cristina grabbed the two bags and moved them into the hall-way so Roberto could enter. She reached out to shake his hand. "I'm so glad to meet you, Detective Salinas."

"It's Roberto, please. And I am pleased to meet you. I've heard so much about you."

Cristina turned to Madge. "Welcome, Doctor Carmichael. I feel I know you from Mom's stories."

"It's Madge to you." She pulled Cristina into a hug. "We met once, when you were a toddler. I don't expect you to remember, but I've been following your career. Your mother is shy about everything except your accomplishments."

Cristina blushed as Madge moved into the living room, kick-ing her bags ahead of her with her Birkenstock sandals.

Stepping around Madge's bags, Theresa took Roberto's hand. "*Bienvenidos, Señor Salinas.*"

"*Muchas gracias*, Mrs. Aguila. I am very glad to meet you, but you must call me Roberto."

Theresa quickly assessed the confident smile of the stranger at the door, dressed in a pale blue shirt with vertical pleats and embroidered with tropical birds. "If you call me Theresa."

Claire stood back as her mother and daughter greeted Roberto. Finally, their eyes met, and Claire couldn't find the words to speak. She and Roberto stared at each other, neither knowing how to handle the moment—a handshake, too formal between people who had worked together and shared their life stories—or a hug, too intimate for friends?

Roberto acted first, and in true Mexican fashion. "Ah, Claire, my comrade in crime." He approached and hugged her tightly. She breathed in, alarmed at her own reaction to his closeness. "I have missed you, my friend," he said, releasing her slowly.

"This is a beautiful house!" Madge said, assessing the living room. "I hope you don't mind me dropping in. Roberto offered me a ride here—he insisted."

Claire looked up at Roberto, who shrugged again, smiling wryly.

Claire knew Madge well enough to know Roberto had no choice but to bring her along.

"We're happy you came," Theresa said. "It's nice to meet both of you, finally."

"You know, Theresa," Madge said, "that I consider Claire the daughter I never had. She was a fresh-faced graduate student in my archaeology seminar, and now we work together." She smiled her sweet Madge smile. "I hope you don't mind sharing her."

"Not at all," Theresa sighed, glancing quickly at Claire's stunned face. "Please, both of you, come and sit." She led the way to the lanai, where Madge collapsed into the largest patio chair. Claire led Roberto to the sofa.

Theresa and Cristina excused themselves and retreated to the kitchen. They smiled at each other as they placed glasses on a tray. "Well, this will be interesting," Cristina whispered, as Claire joined them in the kitchen.

"Interesting isn't the word I'd choose," Claire said. "I can't believe Madge weaseled her way into an invitation—on second thought, it's exactly like Madge."

"Roberto was very kind to bring her here," Theresa said as the women placed glasses and pitchers on two trays.

"Poor Roberto," Claire said. "He didn't have a chance."

"Didn't George come with you to the conference?" Claire asked as she offered tea and lemonade to their guests. "I thought this might be a nice getaway for you…getting back together and all."

Madge snorted. "Why do you think I came without him? Working it out is killing us both. Besides," she added, "he's working on those artifacts coming in from the field school." She gulped her lemonade. "I heard someone was murdered here."

"How did you know?" Claire asked Madge, a little more

sharply than she meant. She poured herself a glass of tea and settled next to Roberto.

Madge laughed. "Well, this isn't Guatemala—we went to the visitor's center for a map and directions, and I grabbed a copy of your high-class newspaper, *The Havens Gazette*. It's on the front page. Tell me all about it!"

Claire glanced nervously at Roberto, who had accepted lemonade from Theresa. "A woman was murdered, and they're questioning some of the Mexican workers."

"That's horrible!" Madge said, then turned to Roberto. "You could help with the investigation."

"That's my day job—I'm on vacation," Roberto said, "but that's a terrible thing to happen here...or anywhere."

Madge fingered her near-empty glass. "By the way, I saw that you're giving a presentation at the Book Lovers Group today. That'll be a blast."

"Madge!" Claire said, stunned. "I didn't even know about it until last night!" She shot her mother a pleading glance.

Madge pulled her copy of *The Havens Gazette* from her oversized cloth bag and opened it to the weekly event section. She read aloud:

"The Book Lovers Group will have a special guest at their Monday afternoon meeting. Doctor Claire Aguila Carson, a famous anthropologist, will discuss her two books and her life with the Maya Indians."

"Did you write this, Mother?" Claire asked, horrified.

"No, I promise," Theresa grimaced. "Our president, Doris, did. But it's exciting for us to have a guest author. Everyone's anxious to meet you."

"But they're expecting Margaret Mead!" Claire turned to Roberto. "I'm sorry about the book group."

"The guys will have to hang out together," Madge said, shrugging.

"Where *is* Mr. Aguila?" Roberto asked.

"Martín had a mowing job," Theresa said, glancing at her watch. "He'll be back soon."

"Tell us about the murder," Madge prodded.

Theresa sipped her tea then placed her glass on the table. "Oh, it's terrible," she said.

Claire sat quietly as Theresa related the story of the murder, including how Martín knew the workers who had been questioned. Claire watched Roberto absorb the story. His dark eyes gazed intently at her mother, his eyebrows rising and lowering as he took in her narrative. His gestures and bearing had become familiar to her in Merida the year before when she'd been his cultural mediator, not only between Anglo and Mayan culture, but as an insider into the strange world of anthropology.

"And that's not the worst of it," Cristina added. Claire and Teresa both shook their heads in warning to Cristina. Neither wanted Roberto to start his visit thinking Martín was involved in a murder, but Cristina blurted, "The police interviewed Papa yesterday."

"*¿Que?*" asked Roberto, falling quickly into his native language.

Theresa's hands fluttered and rested on her neck, a gesture that Roberto noted was shared by her daughter. A year ago, he had been both enthralled and unnerved by the gesture, because Claire's left hand still bore a wedding ring. He glanced quickly at Claire now and, though she too held her hands to her neck, the ring was no longer there.

"It was a coincidence," said Theresa. She explained Martín's errand at the Vogels' home as the Mexican detective made sympathetic noises.

"He went to her house?" Madge exclaimed. "This is serious."

"Not serious, Madge," Claire retorted. Noticing Roberto's attention to her hands, she placed them in her lap. "The police suspect that Mexican workers were involved, and they're not sure what to think of a Mexican-American man who lives here."

The room became silent as the door leading from the garage to the kitchen opened and closed. Martín entered the lanai. A look of confusion crossed his face as he noticed not one, but two new guests.

"Sorry I'm late," Martín said, "my job took longer than I thought." He approached Roberto, who rose to shake his hand. "I'm very pleased to finally meet you, Mr. Salinas."

"It's Roberto, and I am enjoying the company of your family." He returned to his seat, and Martín's attention turned to Madge.

"Dad, this is Madge Carmichael." Claire said. "I'm sure you remember me telling you about her."

"Of course. I'm pleased to meet you," Martín said, throwing quick glances at Claire and Theresa.

"Madge and Roberto attended the same conference and they met up," Claire explained. "She wanted to visit us, and Roberto brought her."

"Wonderful," Martín said, with some hesitancy. He then settled into a chair, stretching his stiff leg as Theresa, Cristina, and Claire excused themselves. They disappeared into the kitchen with the drink tray, leaving Madge with the men.

"Madge and I are learning that your community is not as quiet as you anticipated, and that you had an interesting day yesterday," Roberto said after the Aguila women left the lanai. "I hope you don't mind that your family has…how do you say… thrown you from the bus?"

"That's throwing me *under* the bus, but the result can be much the same," Martín laughed. "I'm learning once again that, in America, when in doubt, the guilty person is always the one with the darkest skin."

"As strange as it may seem, that's often the case in Mexico too."

"Is this your first time in the United States?" Martín asked.

"Yes. I was invited to the international conference by your government to give a Mexican perspective on smuggling from the many archaeological sites in Mexico, in my case, the Mayan sites…"

"And that's how Roberto and I met up," Madge interrupted, fluffing her hair. "I attended to learn more about the new international laws, for our own museum acquisitions—it was exciting helping Roberto solve the murders last year…"

"No, Madge," Claire interrupted as she returned to the lanai with an ice bucket. Theresa and Cristina followed with freshened pitchers of tea and lemonade. Claire poured an iced tea for her father. "We didn't help the police solve the case."

"Yes, actually, you both did help," Roberto said, accepting a lemonade refill from Theresa. "Especially with your connections and knowledge of archaeology."

"That's Claire, being humble," Madge said as Cristina refreshed her drink. "Anyway, Roberto and I sat with a group of Florida cops—police officers—at the conference and had drinks. They liked Roberto's paper, and a Miami detective suggested a possible police exchange…"

"They were being polite," Roberto interrupted.

"No, really," Madge said, "anyway, Roberto mentioned he was coming here—so here I am. I thought I'd stop by for a few days."

Days? Claire thought. She asked, "Where are you staying?"

Madge shrugged. "I haven't made a reservation yet…Roberto said he's staying here…?"

Claire gave her mother and daughter a desperate look.

"My guest room has twin beds," Cristina said. "I'd love to share."

"That would be lovely," Theresa said.

CHAPTER 22

Roberto's first day in The Havens didn't turn out as Claire hoped, even less so with Madge there. She had expected quality time with her family and Roberto. Instead, after lunch, the two men set off to visit Carlos. Roberto and her father had immediately hit it off, and, as Claire thought about it, she understood that they might like some male-bonding time. Claire offered to drive to the Book Lovers Club at The Lodge while Roberto and her father climbed into Martín's car.

Claire drove through The Hub, concentrating on the traffic as sidewalks and golf cart paths crisscrossed the road, posing multiple opportunities for disaster. Her mind wandered to this book group meeting, which she hadn't thought about since her mother mentioned it months ago. What would she say to these women about Mexico?

Claire turned into The Lodge's huge parking lot that served the many community, social, and sporting activities. She parked among numerous cars and golf carts, the latter of which were adorned with personal items, stuffed animals, Christmas lights, and personalized license plates.

"This is exciting, Claire!" Madge said from the back seat. "I didn't know you were so famous!"

"Shut up, Madge. This is embarrassing," Claire said. "You're the one they'd love to have as a guest—a famous Mayanist archaeologist." She smiled at her friend as they locked the car and approached the building.

"I'll save that for when George and I live here." Madge winked at Cristina.

"Besides, Mom," Cristina said, nudging Madge, "you're the only anthropologist they've met."

"Stop it, you two," Theresa laughed. "Don't worry, Claire. They'll love you."

They entered The Lodge, where a spacious lounge area opened up before them. Middle-aged couples rested in wing-back chairs and sofas, reading newspapers or brochures, or strolled around the room, studying the photographs and maps along the walls.

"This is the visitor's center, where potential buyers meet with salespeople," Theresa explained. "The sales pitch starts here, then they take the bus tour."

They passed through the lounge, where a large sign pointed to the real-estate offices on the right and the social areas on the left. They turned left and passed a large event room with tables and chairs arranged in groupings for games or dining. Stepping inside, they explored the game and supply cabinets along the side wall, then the community kitchen.

A diminutive Hispanic woman moved around in the kitchen, cleaning counters. When she turned to them, they noticed that her eyes were red, her smile forced.

"Hello, Elena," Theresa said.

"Hello, Mrs. Aguila," Elena said. "I've taken coffee and tea to the library for your group."

"Thank you." Theresa introduced Elena Huerta to her family and Madge.

"Very nice to meet you," Elena said. "If you need anything, please let me know." She smiled, but her mouth quivered.

"Are you okay?" Theresa asked.

Elena sniffled into her sleeve. "I just heard that someone I know has died."

"Mrs. Vogel?" Claire asked.

"After Mrs. Vogel," Elena said. "I'm sad about Mrs. V. I cleaned house for her. But someone else died, too—Julio Gonzalez." Elena wiped her eyes. "He was a nice man."

"I'm so sorry for the loss of your friend," Theresa said, the others joining in with condolences.

"Thank you." Elena sniffled and tried to smile again, then turned back to her work.

◆ ◆ ◆ ◆ ◆

"Two deaths," Theresa said as they left the event room. "How terrible."

"Do employees of The Havens often work for residents on the side?" Cristina asked as they proceeded down the hallway, past a pool room, puzzle room, and several game or meeting rooms.

"Sometimes," Theresa said. "The men do yard work or handy-man jobs on the side, and women clean houses. It gives them extra income."

They entered the library, where book group members busied themselves pouring coffee or making tea. Copies of Claire's two ethnographies lay scattered over a coffee table.

A woman, wearing a faded pink 'Favorite Great Grandma' shirt and blue-jean skirt, greeted them.

"I'm sorry we're late, Doris," Theresa said. "Elena just told us about the death of her friend."

"Yes, we heard," Doris said, ushering them into the room. "It's a horrible thing…but who knows?"

Members of the book group glanced at each other and bus-ied themselves with coffee and choosing their seats. They had already discussed this news.

"Theresa, please introduce our guests," Doris said quickly, directing Claire to a special chair set up for her.

Theresa introduced her entourage. "This is my daughter, Claire, a cultural anthropologist and our guest speaker; Cristina, her daughter, a graduate student in bio-medical anthropology;

and Doctor Madge Carmichael, a specialist in Mayan archaeology."

When Theresa's group had settled in with refreshments, Theresa introduced her family and Madge to the members of the Book Lovers Group—Doris, their president; Louise, whose wire-rimmed glasses and short bobbed hair marked her as the most likely to be a librarian; Beverly, whose long, frizzed hair formed a halo around her face; and Rose, a stout woman whose electric blue bangs stopped just above her eyebrows.

Rose flipped her bangs and asked, "What's the difference between anthropology and archaeology? And what is bio-medical?"

"Do tell us," Louise said. "I thought anthropology and archaeology were the same."

Claire smiled. "Cultural anthropologists study living societies; archaeologists, like Madge, excavate ancient sites and study past cultures; and Cristina studies cross-cultural concepts about health...indigenous medicines, healing, etcetera."

The door opened and Doris waved to another woman who rushed into the room, carrying a large book bag. "You're late, Gail," Doris admonished.

After Gail poured a cup of coffee and joined the group, Doris reintroduced the guests.

Gail considered them through large, black-rimmed glasses. "Did you hear about Julio Gonzalez?" she asked after sipping her coffee. "They say he was the thief and might have murdered Barbara, then killed himself."

"Thief? Murderer?" Theresa asked. "Elena's friend?"

"The police questioned Carlos Chavez, his cousin," Gail said. "Maybe they were in on it together."

The women turned to Theresa, Doris asking the question on everyone's minds. "Does your husband know Carlos?"

Theresa sipped her coffee, steadying herself. "We all know

Carlos, don't we?" she said quietly. "But I guess Martín knows him better than most of us," she admitted.

"I know Carlos," Rose said. "He wouldn't steal or hurt a fly. I don't know why they automatically blame the workers."

"It's because of the robberies," Gail said.

Claire looked down at her books, *Yaxpec: A Village in Search of an Identity* and *Yaxpec: Then and Now,* lying on the table, ignored.

Doris followed Claire's gaze. "Let's talk about something uplifting," she said. "Any questions for Claire?"

Louise, who had sat quietly during the exchange, started. "You discuss culture shock in your books. I'm wondering why you had culture shock when you are Mexican-American?"

The room turned quiet, a collective breath taken.

"I'm glad you asked that," Claire said. "I am Mexican-American and bilingual, but I was born and raised in the United States. When my husband and I arrived in Yaxpec, we suffered that feeling of displacement. Very few homes had indoor plumbing, there were no telephones in the village, and many people—especially the elders—spoke Mayan. Local customs differed from ours: marriage ceremonies, funerals, and religious practices. However, the people accepted us into their community, and we have a godchild.

"Then," Claire continued, "when we returned to Michigan, we went through culture shock again—department stores, modern homes, speaking English—in fact, I'm going through culture shock here, in The Havens."

"Here?" the women all giggled together.

Claire shrugged. "The lack of children, the Disney-esque quality of it all?"

Louise, who it turned out *was* a retired librarian, mused, "There are different cultures here in The Havens too."

"Yes!" Rose said. "The Sun and Sky Havens are different from

Sea Haven."

"Sea Haven is the preferred community—the upper class," Beverly agreed.

"Why is that?" asked Madge, her interest piqued.

Rose wrinkled her nose. "It's how The Havens developed. The corporation built the Sun and Sky Havens first, for northern retirees. The houses are very nice, but smaller. But they designed Sea Haven as a custom community, and more affluent retirees built the mega-houses, especially at the edges of the community. The corporation built the golf course and country club to lure rich people here. And, now they're building a nine-hole course, closer to Sea Haven and the future community across Clam Lake."

"It's not only that," Louise said, "I think most of the women in Sea Haven are second or third wives…you notice the age differences. Most of us have been married to the same boring men for years."

"Yes," Rose agreed, nodding her head. "And we look like it. No Botox or liposuction here!" She laughed as she playfully pushed on her thighs and middle. "You know the theory of the third wife. First wife gets the kids and the debts, second wife gets to travel, and the third wife retires in The Havens."

Most everyone laughed, but Doris fidgeted uncomfortably and cleared her throat. "Not your in-laws, Claire. The Carsons came a little earlier. They aren't like the new bunch coming in."

Undeterred, her mind clearly set on her social class theory, Rose said, "It's like every few years, someone blows a whistle and everyone in Sea Haven changes partners."

Madge smiled. "My second husband, after George, tried to civilize me—taught me bridge and golf—but neither one took." She laughed. "I married three times, and none of my marriages took either." She smiled, clearly enjoying the curious looks she received from the Book Lovers.

Recovering, Beverly gave Rose a stern look, but couldn't help shaking her head and smiling. "It seems true," she admitted.

"Even the Vogels," Gail added.

"What?" asked Theresa.

Claire, Cristina, and Madge shared glances.

"I saw Barbara with an older man, very distinguished-looking, at the Sky Haven Aerie," Louise said. "I don't think he lives here though."

"My neighbor saw her in the Sun Haven Palms with Melanie Cook's husband," Gail said.

"Affairs with two men?" Beverly asked, shaking her frizzled curls. "I don't believe it—not Barbara."

"Well, Todd is having an affair too, with Julie Barnes," Rose said. "Everyone knows. I saw them at The Aerie. It's amazing that these people don't run into one another," she added with a stifled snort.

"Why are these people seen at the other bars, not the Sand Bar?" Theresa asked, confused.

All the women looked at Theresa as if she were a child.

Gail explained, "Because they're as naïve as you, Theresa. They think no one knows them in the other neighborhoods."

Theresa flushed, and Doris patted her on the shoulder. "Never mind Gail. You're new here, and hardly aware that this is Peyton Place South."

"Really?" said Madge. She turned to Claire and whispered, "This place is an anthropological gold mine!"

"Peyton Place?" said Cristina, confused.

"Hah," Madge smiled, "for you, it's the Senior Housewives of Central Florida."

Claire, suspecting that her books had not impressed this group, ignored Madge and asked, "Are the Hispanic workers at the bottom of the class system, then? Is that why they are suspected of the crimes?"

Louise sat forward. "It's like what you wrote about, the idea of stereotypes and prejudice. Obviously, not everyone in Sea Haven thinks they're better than others," she said. "People here come from all over the country and all careers. Most everyone just wants to meet new friends. Like Doris said, the Carsons are wonderful people, and so was Barbara. She did a lot for the community."

"But we stereotype the Mexican culture and the workers as poor and unintelligent, and that's unfair," Rose said, "like you describe in your books."

"They don't live here," Beverly explained. "We can't imagine any resident stealing from neighbors or murdering people."

"Yet white people murder people all the time," Madge said.

"Just not here," Gail said.

CHAPTER 23

Martín drove through Sea Haven to show Roberto where Barbara Vogel lived and died. "These homes all look the same to me," he admitted, as he paused at the Vogel house. "The mulch bags are still there."

"Do you like it here?" Roberto asked, as they passed the massive homes and well-tended yards.

"I'm in a beige Hell," Martín said, smiling. "I can't explain it…everything is…too clean."

"You don't have to explain," Roberto said, smiling. "What does your daughter think of it?"

Martín looked knowingly at the detective. "You'll have to ask her," he grinned, "but I think you're safe." He pulled through the gate and turned onto Brook Haven, toward The Hub. "Theresa and I wanted her to be a lawyer, so she could help her people with legal troubles. Instead, her dream was to teach."

"I'm glad she chose anthropology," Roberto said, "or I might not have met her in Merida all those years ago. And if not for the murder-artifact smuggling case in Merida last year, I might not have reconnected with her, or been invited to Orlando for the international conference. Of course," he confessed, "when I heard Claire planned to come to Florida this spring, I persuaded her to come at the same time."

"Ah, *así es*. That explains it, then," Martín laughed. "She seemed quite insistent that she and Cristina come this week."

Passing through The Hub, Martín pointed out The Lodge where the women were meeting. Further down, they parked in front of a vibrant red building.

"This is The Barn," Martín explained, unnecessarily. Roberto followed him up the walkway to the maintenance building, noticing the older man's limp. "How did you injure yourself?"

"I fell from an apple tree when I was young," Martín said as he opened the front door and held it for Roberto. "My parents and grandparents were migrant workers."

"How does the descendant of migrant workers become a business owner?" Roberto asked.

Martín smiled. "My family settled in Grand Rapids, Michigan. After high school, I got a job at a small electrical business. The owner encouraged me to train as an electrician. When he retired, I took over the company. I owe a lot to him for taking in an immigrant kid with little experience but a lot of enthusiasm. And I wouldn't have achieved any of this had I not married the beautiful nurse who cared for my parents at the community health clinic."

Inside The Barn, Roberto took in the large, well-organized room. Two long tables spanned the central area, with various projects set out. Floor-to-ceiling cabinets lined half of the long wall to their right. Opened cabinets displayed tools and miscellaneous supplies. A variety of table saws and workbenches lined the back wall. A middle-aged man with a graying mustache sat at one of these tables, removing hinges from a window shutter.

"Hey, Pete," Martín called out.

The man started, deep in concentration on his project. "Martín, it's you. I'm getting jumpy, the police coming in and out like they live here."

Pete studied the new man, recognizing someone who, like Martín, strode into a room confident and observant of his surroundings, a contrast to those who lived in fear of authority, hesitant and suspicious of strangers. It had taken his own family several generations before they felt comfortable looking people in the eyes.

This stranger had a distinctly Mexican appearance, with dark eyes and black hair, graying at the temples and lying loosely around his ears and onto his neck. He wore a light-blue pleated shirt with tropical birds embroidered on it, and, instead of tennis shoes or work boots, he wore loafers and black slacks.

Martín introduced Roberto as a friend of the family, then asked, "Is Carlos here?"

"He's out back, on break," Pete said. "He had bad news about his cousin."

"Julio?" Martín asked. "What happened?"

"I'll let him tell you. It's not good."

Martín led Roberto past Pete's office and the restroom. An apartment-sized refrigerator, microwave, and coffee maker sat on a long table between the two rooms. A donut box, nearly empty, sat on the table, along with a collection of foam cups, plastic spoons, and packets of sugar and cream.

They exited onto a brick patio, covered with a slatted pergola. Carlos sat at a picnic table, eating from a plastic container. The comforting aroma of warm beans and rice met the two men as they sat across from him.

A quick look of fear crossed Carlos's face when Martín introduced Roberto.

"Don't worry, my friend," Roberto assured him. "I'm here for a social visit. But Martín told me about the murder."

"You mean murders, don't you?" Carlos dipped his plastic fork into his bowl.

"Murders?" Martín asked.

"You didn't hear?" Carlos wiped tears from his eyes and moved his dish away. "Julio's dead, Martín. Paula called…she was frantic. People are saying he killed Mrs. Vogel and then himself."

"That's impossible," Martín said.

"That's what Paula told the detective."

"Did the detective talk to you?" Roberto asked.

Carlos nodded. "He was here this morning. They're calling it a suspicious death." Carlos looked at Martín with tear-filled eyes. "Julio wouldn't kill himself!"

Roberto lowered his voice. "I am very sorry about your cousin."

Carlos looked to Martín, then to his cooling food.

"Please eat, Carlos," Roberto said apologetically. "We're disturbing your break."

Carlos took a half-hearted bite, followed by a drink of his soda. "It's okay," he said. "I can't eat anyway."

"Does the detective think Julio was involved with Mrs. Vogel's murder?" Martín asked. "Or something else?"

"He didn't say that, but you know how it is."

"I do," Martín said. "What do you think?"

Carlos glanced quickly at Martín. "I...I don't know, but something was worrying him," he said hesitantly. "I helped him get his work visa. I wanted to get him away from his friends in our Mexican town—they drank a lot and sometimes stole small things—nothing major. Now, here, he has a job. He's married and has a family. Anything like that would disqualify him for citizenship."

"Do you think he's doing the robberies?" Martín asked, startled.

Carlos pressed his fingers against his eyes to hold back his tears. "Julio needed money for his daughter, and for his family in Mexico," he explained. "I'd been giving him mowing jobs. If I couldn't do a job, I'd give it to him."

"And you noticed that perhaps things went missing from the homes where he worked?" Roberto probed.

Carlos pushed his food away and finished his soda. "I suspected it. I recommended him for the job at the G&G so he wouldn't be working in The Havens as often, and he'd have a regular paycheck."

"This doesn't explain who would kill him or why, but it does explain how he might have killed himself out of guilt," Roberto reasoned.

"Perhaps he stole for someone else?" Carlos suggested hopefully. "And they had an argument?"

"Is that likely?" Roberto asked.

"It's the only thing that makes sense to me," Carlos said, tearing up again.

Roberto sat back, his fingers tented. "I'm afraid the only possibility that makes sense is the robbery-murder angle and a distraught, guilty man."

"It can't be!" Carlos said, covering his face with his hands.

Roberto paused, regretting he had pushed so hard. "Did he ever mow the lawn for the Vogels?"

Carlos sighed and nodded. "Mrs. Vogel usually asked for me. I think she trusted me because I did maintenance work for her from time to time." He turned to Martín. "You must understand that Julio would never kill a lady—or anyone."

Martín put his hand on Carlos's arm. "Would he steal for his family? What if Mrs. Vogel caught him?"

Carlos reddened and pulled his arm away. "I thought you wanted to help me, Martín. This is sounding like the police all over again."

Roberto answered for Martín. "Let me ask just a few more questions before I let you go back to work. Is that okay?" Carlos nodded. "Did Julio have the code to get into the three neighborhoods?"

Both Carlos and Martín snorted simultaneously.

"Those gates are a joke. It took me about a week to figure it out," Martín explained. "The cameras are on the guest gate, so if someone comes from the outside without a passcode, the camera takes a photograph. I have no idea if anyone looks at these photos, or if the cameras are even working. In any case, the resident gates don't have cameras, just passcodes. It doesn't take much for the residents, workers, and frequent visitors to get the passcodes."

"Most of us use the passcodes," Carlos said, "and Julio probably did too."

"Interesting," Roberto said. "I came through the guest gate, so there will be a photograph of me somewhere?"

"Or not," Martín mused.

Roberto leaned forward, his elbows on the picnic table. "How well do you know Julio's wife?" he asked Carlos.

"Fairly well, but my wife, Sofia, knows Paula better."

"What would Paula do if she thought Julio was stealing?" Roberto asked. "Would she confront him?" When Carlos paused, Roberto warned, "Paula can get into serious trouble if she knows her husband has stolen, or if she is hiding evidence. The police can arrest her, and then what would happen to the children?"

Carlos put his face in his hands again and leaned his elbows on the picnic table. "I think she knows something. She called me once to ask if I could give Julio more jobs. When I told her I had stopped giving him jobs when he started at the G&G, she seemed confused…she told me he was taking off time from work for extra jobs. I told her maybe he'd gotten work on his own, but I think she was worried about something." He clenched his fists. "I had to keep Julio away from private homes, for his own good… and mine. I'd get in serious trouble if Pete learned that my cousin might be a thief, and I didn't say anything—I'd lose my job."

"Pete's a reasonable man," Martín said. "You did the right thing. Pete should know that about you."

"This is important," Roberto said. "The detective is probably looking at these deaths as connected. If he thinks Julio murdered Mrs. Vogel and killed himself, he will need strong evidence that someone had killed him and why. This will be hard, but you need to convince Paula to talk to the detective. She might know something that will explain Julio's death as something other than a guilty suicide. Can you do that?"

Carlos nodded, then wiped his eyes again. "Last night, when Sofia and I went to the G&G, Julio asked me to meet him after his work…he seemed scared…but I told him I had to work early this morning. I know he wanted to tell me something…I should have said yes…he might still be alive…"

Carlos paused when his cellphone rang. He answered, blanching as he listened. After ending the call, he bowed his head and said, "The officers want to talk to me…again."

CHAPTER 24

"Go with me, please!" Carlos pleaded. "I don't want to go back there alone!"

"I'll go, but I doubt they'll let me sit in with you," Martín said, sympathizing with his friend.

Carlos turned to Roberto. "Will you go?"

Roberto paused, considering how he would react if a foreign detective intruded into his investigation. He sighed heavily. "Unofficially, and only as a special request from you," he said.

After explaining to Pete that he had been called to the DPS, Carlos, Martín, and Roberto climbed into Martín's car. "I can't understand why they're concentrating on the workers and not the family," Carlos complained as they pulled into the DPS lot.

"Can't you?" Roberto asked. "You and Martín were both seen at the Vogel house, and a Mexican has died. In their minds, the crimes are connected."

"In your mind too?" Martín asked cautiously.

"In my mind too, as a cop," Roberto agreed. *Why is this becoming another day on the job?*

Roberto's self-pity dissipated as he contemplated the DPS building. He could accept the idea of a maintenance building designed as a barn, but he took offense to a public safety building with shutters and flower boxes. "This is the DPS?" Roberto asked.

"Just like Disney," Martín smiled, opening the door for Roberto. "Have you been to Disney World?"

"No, but I get the idea."

Carlos hesitated at the doorway, but Martín placed his hand on Carlos's back and led him to Patsy. "Deputy Powers asked

Carlos to come in to see Detective Davenport," Martín explained. Patsy frowned, disappeared into an office behind the reception desk, and returned with Judy Barnaby.

"Detective Davenport's not here yet." Judy looked at Martín and squinted. "Did Detective Powers ask for you, too?" she asked.

"No," Martín said curtly.

Judy raised her eyebrows and looked at Roberto. "Who are you?"

"This is Roberto Salinas," Martín said. "He's visiting my family."

Roberto held his hand out, and Judy shook it, her hand limp. "Are you a lawyer?" Judy asked.

"I'm a detective."

"This isn't your jurisdiction."

"I understand," Roberto said, smiling.

"Well then," Judy said, catching loose strands of hair from her ponytail and arranging them behind her ears, "you can't go in with Carlos. I'll tell Detective Davenport you both came in." She handed Martín a pad of paper. "Your name and number."

"You have this already," Martín said as he wrote on the pad and handed it back. Judy glanced at it, then turned quickly as Detective Davenport entered the building. She opened her mouth to speak, stopping short when Roberto and Davenport looked at each other and smiled.

Davenport reached out his hand. "Detective Salinas, welcome to The Havens. We discussed a police exchange, but I didn't expect it to happen so soon."

"I had no idea you worked here," Roberto said, embarrassed.

"I am assigned to the Gardenia County Sheriff's Department, but we are here on a case." He turned to Carlos, "Thank you for coming in, Mr. Chavez."

A confused look crossed Davenport's face as his gaze moved from Carlos to Martín. "Have we met?"

"I'm Martín Aguila. I work with Carlos in The Barn, and I made a statement with your deputies yesterday."

"Ah, yes. Mr. Aguila. I planned to speak with you," Davenport said, "but I didn't expect to see you here today."

Roberto cleared his throat. "I'm sure this seems very strange, but we were talking with Carlos when Deputy Powers called. Carlos asked us to come with him. He's upset about his cousin's death—Julio Gonzalez."

Judy interrupted by saying, "I told Mr.—Detective—Salinas this isn't his jurisdiction."

"Let me explain," Roberto said, casting a glance at Judy. "I know I overstepped my jurisdiction, but..." he lowered his voice, realizing the DPS employees had congregated at the front desk. "Martín asked that I talk to his friend."

Martín took a deep breath and spoke. "Carlos has some information that might be important. He'd like to have us with him for the interview."

Davenport looked from Martín to Roberto. "Detective Salinas, you may come with me as a professional courtesy and as a native speaker." He turned to Martín, "I'm sorry, Mr. Aguila, but I can't include you."

"It's okay," Martín said, stepping back.

Davenport turned to Judy. "Please call Deputy Stokes and have her meet the team at the Sheriff's Department at six tonight, with her report."

"Sure," Judy said shortly.

"Oh," Davenport added, "can Powers use your office to make some calls?"

Judy bristled. "I have to sit out here?" She indicated the reception area.

"If you don't mind, unless you have official work to do in town?" he said.

"Whatever," she said as she grabbed the golf cart keys from a hook near the desk.

"Thank you," he said to her back as she pushed through the front door.

"She's a little testy about us taking over her building," Davenport explained as he led Roberto and Carlos down the hall. Roberto felt embarrassed for Davenport but followed him silently to the office, his hand resting lightly on Carlos's arm in case he decided to turn and run.

Martín settled into a reception chair and picked up a copy of *The Havens Gazette*, chuckling out loud at the masthead: "All the News You Need."

◆ ◆ ◆ ◆ ◆

Davenport, Roberto, and Carlos entered the cluttered office, where Deputy Mike Powers was sorting documents into piles.

Davenport introduced Roberto. "Detective Salinas and I met at the conference in Orlando. He's visiting friends in The Havens."

Powers reached out to shake Roberto's hand. "Welcome to the United States, sir."

"Thank you," Roberto said.

Powers turned to Davenport. "This is Mr. Chavez's statement from yesterday, sir."

"Good." Davenport took the statement and sat in his chair, inviting Roberto to sit next to Carlos.

"Powers," Davenport said, "you can use Judy's office to make your calls until we're through here."

Powers's jaw clenched. "Does she know, or do I have to tell her?"

Davenport smiled. "No worries, I told her. She'll stay out of your way."

"Thank you, sir." He handed several reports to the detective, took his notebook and left the room.

Davenport paused for a few moments to review Carlos's statement, then started the recorder. "Mr. Chavez, I understand you have spoken to Detective Salinas. Is it okay with you if he sits in on our conversation?"

Carlos nodded.

"Please answer for the record."

"Yes, I understand," Carlos said. "Do I need a lawyer?"

"If you want one, that's your right," Davenport said, "but Detective Salinas has asked to witness our conversation, and I am interested only in what you can tell me about your cousin."

"I understand," Carlos said again, but his hands began to shake, and he shuffled his feet.

"Mr. Chavez," Davenport started, "I'm in charge of investigating both Mrs. Vogel's murder and the death of your cousin. I'm very sorry for your loss. I'm also sorry we called you in today, but I have a few matters to discuss. Do you understand that the deputies asked you to come, and that you are not being accused of anything?"

"Yes," Carlos said.

Davenport turned to Roberto. "Detective Salinas, for the record, do you understand that your presence is unofficial and a courtesy?"

"I understand," Salinas said. "Can you tell Mr. Chavez how his cousin died?"

Davenport folded his hands and turned to Carlos. "As of now, we suspect suicide."

Carlos blurted out, "Julio wouldn't kill himself! He wouldn't do that to his family."

"Not even if he did something horrible, like murder?" Davenport asked.

"He didn't kill Mrs. Vogel," Carlos pleaded. "I know he wouldn't."

"Would he steal from her?"

Carlos sat still, his eyes darting between the two detectives. "I don't know."

Davenport scribbled on his pad. "Tell me about the bag of books Mrs. Vogel gave you Saturday evening."

Carlos looked confused. "I told Deputy Powers about that. He saw it in my car."

"We need to know how the bag came to be in your cousin's car."

Carlos sat back, relieved. "My wife, Sofia, and I dropped the bag off at the G&G yesterday around five o'clock, after I showed it to Deputy Powers."

Davenport said, "What would you say if I told you that the bag you gave Julio also held Mrs. Vogel's stolen jewelry?"

Carlos jolted upright, as did Roberto.

"What jewelry?" Carlos asked.

"You tell me," Davenport said, his voice even.

"How can I tell you? I don't know about any jewelry!" Carlos said, his voice trembling. "Ask Deputy Powers. He looked in the bag."

"Are you saying that Julio put the jewelry in the bag himself?" Davenport reasoned.

"No...I can't explain it." Carlos lowered his voice. "I know my cousin, Detective. He wouldn't kill anyone. And I don't know how the jewelry got there."

Davenport adjusted his glasses. "Your friends told me you have something to tell me?"

His hands shaking, Carlos looked at Roberto, who nodded. Carlos stammered, "Detective Salinas said that if Julio didn't commit suicide, then you need to know who might want to kill him."

"Do you have evidence that someone wanted to harm Julio?" Davenport asked.

Carlos pressed his hands together. "Julio's wife, Paula, called me a few weeks ago, asking why I hadn't been giving Julio many jobs. She also wanted to know if I knew where Julio went at night, because she found out that he'd been leaving work early, but not going home."

"What did you tell her?" Davenport asked, leaning forward.

"I told her I didn't know anything about that," Carlos pleaded.

"What about her first question? Why haven't you been giving him jobs?"

Carlos swallowed. "I knew about the robberies in The Havens. Officer Barnaby came to The Barn to question Pete, my boss, about the workers. When I heard this, I thought of Julio."

"Why did you think of him?" Davenport asked.

Carlos looked at Roberto, then Davenport. "I…I don't know," Carlos admitted. "Maybe he got involved with someone who made him steal for them. Maybe someone who used him to find empty houses…maybe he was just an accomplice…maybe they argued…"

"That's a lot of maybes," Davenport said. "Do you have any evidence he was involved in something out of his control?"

"No, but something changed in him if he missed work without telling Paula." Tears welled in his eyes as he looked at Roberto again. "Julio wanted me to meet him last night after he left work…I told him I couldn't be up that late…he wanted to talk to me about something."

Carlos gulped and wiped his eyes. "I *know* he wouldn't murder anyone, but I can't swear he didn't get involved in something. He…he needed money to care for his daughter, and he had promised his mother in Mexico he would save money so his younger brother could come here. He was under a lot of pressure."

"Do you think his wife knows something about his?" Davenport asked.

"I don't know."

Davenport turned to Roberto. "Is this your understanding of

his conversation earlier today?"

"Yes," Roberto said.

Davenport turned to Carlos. "Would you be willing to call her for me?"

CHAPTER 25

Detective Scott Malloy parked in front of the Vogel home. *Julio Gonzalez committed the murder.* Malloy knew it in his bones. He didn't understand why Davenport was so interested in Todd Vogel. He wasn't even home. It had to be the Mexicans—they were all around the house that night—and now Judy told him there was a Mexican cop hanging around, too.

He sat, summoning his nerve for what he had to do now—show Mr. Vogel the jewelry and give him the information he wouldn't want to hear. At least Davenport gave the assignment to him and not to Stokes—*I was the first one here, sir*—and Davenport eating it all up—*nice job, Stokes.*

He grabbed a leather satchel, locked his Mustang, and rang the doorbell. As he waited, he looked up and down the street. He had not been involved in the initial investigation and was uncertain of the logistics. He knew that Mrs. Van Dee lived in the house next to the Vogel garage, since she had seen Todd return home. He also knew that the Davises lived in one of the large homes across the street. The neighborhood seemed eerily quiet, residents apparently enjoying the seclusion of their private backyards and pools.

Todd Vogel opened the door. His neutral face turned to a frown when he saw Malloy. "I thought Detective Davenport would come."

"He sent me," Malloy said. "We've met. I'm Detective Malloy."

"Yes, I remember." He moved aside to let Malloy enter. "I heard that you had the guy, and he killed himself."

"That's not yet determined," Malloy said, though it wasn't

what he believed. "I'm sorry, but I have a few more questions. Can we sit?"

"I'm expecting my children in a few hours. I...I can't seem to concentrate on anything." Todd directed Malloy to the living room.

"We can sit in the kitchen if that's more comfortable," Malloy said.

Vogel shook his head and motioned for him to sit on the sofa. Malloy sat and placed the satchel next to him. The bare tile floor loomed between them.

"This is my house, and I can't let it become a shrine," Todd said. "I'm forcing myself to use it—for me and for my children." He sat in a leather chair, looked around the room, and ran his fingers through his hair. "Can you tell me when you will release her body to the mortuary for cremation?"

"I'm sure you understand why we have to finish our investigation first." Malloy removed his notebook and pen from a pocket. "That's why I'm here."

Malloy sat back on the sofa and examined his surroundings. The house had a feel of sterile elegance. Other than several family photographs on the sideboard the home lacked any personal touches, no grandchildren's artwork on the refrigerator, not even any bookshelves.

"First, Mr. Vogel," Malloy said when Todd settled into a chair, "I know you've called Judy Barnaby several times and she has told you what she could, but..."

"She told me damn little."

"She's not authorized to give out information. You'll get updates from Detective Davenport or me." Malloy flipped a page in his notebook. "We found some footprints behind the birdcage, so we believe someone stood there at some point after Saturday's rain."

"Someone could have looked in?"

"It's possible," Malloy said. "We also found a gun, registered to you, with Mr. Gonzalez in his car. We suspect it's the same gun used to murder your wife, but the bullet casings associated with each body are still being compared." He reached into his satchel and retrieved a small stack of photographs. He shuffled through them. "Is this your missing Ruger 9mm?"

"It looks like mine."

"And you kept this in your sideboard drawer?"

Todd nodded. Malloy chose another photo from his stack. "This matching necklace and bracelet were found in Mr. Gonzalez's car. Are these the pieces your wife kept in the security box?"

"Yes, and that proves it was him, doesn't it?"

"It is compelling evidence," Malloy agreed as he chose another photograph. "What about this earring and watch?"

Todd frowned. "Earring?" he asked.

"He must have lost the other one," Malloy said, shrugging. "Are these the items she might have been wearing when she died?"

"I have no idea what earrings she wore, but it looks like hers, and so does the watch. If they have her blood on them, it seems obvious."

"We're sending them to the lab for DNA testing, but the results might take awhile."

Todd leaned back. "So, what else do you need? Why can't you just close the case?"

Malloy returned the photographs to his satchel. "I do have additional information from the coroner and crime scene techs that I can report." He paused to calm himself, noticing that Todd's hands shook. "We found traces of semen in your wife's underwear and on the bed sheets," Malloy said, sitting forward on the sofa. He felt his own heart rate increasing as he watched Mr. Vogel's eyes dart around the room to settle on the bare area on the floor.

"You mean he raped her, too?"

"That's not yet determined."

"Why do you need to determine anything? He was here. He robbed us and killed her with our gun…why do you need to humiliate her in death?"

"Again…"

"A loose end?" Todd's voice cracked in emotion and he stood, placing his hands on his hips. "So, take a sample from that man and see if it matches."

"Please sit, Mr. Vogel," Malloy said. "We have a sample, and it's being tested. Are you sure you weren't home with your wife that night?"

Todd sat and crossed his arms. "Of course, I'm sure."

"If you don't object, I'll need a DNA sample from you today, for comparison." Malloy paused. "It's just that—the way your wife was dressed—it didn't look like rape. It looked…more intimate."

"You make sure that you don't destroy my wife's good name! Believe me, I'm talking to your boss about this. It's impertinent to even suggest that I might be responsible in some way…or imply that she might have…" He stopped short. "Never mind."

"I have no such intention," Malloy insisted, his own heart racing. "It's just routine. Did you know Julio Gonzalez?"

"No," Todd spat. "My wife is…was…a do-gooder, friendly to everyone. I warned her about letting those people into the house."

"Did she have any regular Saturday activities?"

"Sometimes she golfed or did yoga at The Ashram." Todd squirmed in his chair. "And I thought she'd have gone to dinner with her friends…but I guess she didn't go."

"We're looking for a date book or planner. Did your wife have one?"

"She had a planner that she took back and forth from the dealership."

Malloy watched as Todd rose and went to the kitchen, where

he opened several drawers. "It's not here. Your people must have taken it."

"Could it be anywhere else?" Malloy asked. "We have her phone, but we're also interested in her business contacts."

"Perhaps she left it at work on Friday," Todd suggested.

"Does she have a computer?"

"At work, but she doesn't bring it home often. It's our business computer, not for personal use."

"If you find her planner, please contact us."

Todd nodded. "Is that all?"

"Just one more thing," Malloy said as he retrieved the DNA swab kit from his satchel, "then I'll leave you for now. We'll keep in touch."

When Todd closed the door on the detective, he poured himself a healthy shot of single malt scotch from a fresh bottle and gulped greedily. He wished he could leave, but he had nowhere to go without well-meaning friends bombarding him, hugging, and assuring him it would be okay. It would never be okay again. His cellphone rang out a Paul Simon tune, and Todd pulled it from his pocket.

"I can't see you now," he said. "My kids will be here soon." He listened for a few moments and said, "Later, I promise." He watched a rental car pull into his driveway. "I have to go."

CHAPTER 26

Todd observed his children, Drew and Diana, glare at each other over their suitcases in the driveway. Their childhood had not been like twins Todd had read about, always taking care of each other, united against the parents. In their family, at home and at the businesses, it had always been Drew and Todd against Diana and Barbara. The twins had been competitive since childhood, in school, sports, friendships, and even now as business partners.

Todd recognized the moods and gestures they had developed as children, and now, as adults, he could read them clearly. Drew stood over Diana, who stared up at him defiantly, her fists clenched at her sides. Drew reached up and closed the trunk of the car.

Todd sighed and finished his scotch as he watched them approach, rearranging their faces as they neared the front door. Looking past his children, through the shrubbery, he saw Alice Van Dee in her front yard, peeking through the bougainvillea.

Drew followed his father's gaze and looked over his shoulder, then followed Diana into the house. Diana pecked her father on the cheek, but Drew averted his eyes as he maneuvered his suitcase through the door. Diana pulled her suitcase behind her and stopped in the space between the dining and living room. She stared at the open area in the center of the room where the Oriental rug had lain.

"Is that…?" Diana half-asked.

Todd nodded but directed his children toward the hallway and the guest bedrooms. "Let's get you settled first," he said, dreading the conversation.

159

They found their father in the kitchen, pouring his second drink. Drew asked for the same, but Diana shook her head. "I'll wait for dinner."

"There's iced tea in the fridge. Barb…your mother made it. I'm sure it's still fresh…"

"That's fine, Dad. Thanks."

She poured tea into a glass of ice cubes and joined her father and brother at the teakwood dining-room table.

Todd looked to Drew whose chair faced the living room and whose blue eyes finally settled on the bare area of the floor. "Thanks for picking Diana up at the airport."

Drew shrugged, avoiding his father's eyes. "No problem. I was coming from Orlando anyway."

Todd looked from one twin to the other, both with light curly hair, like their mother and grandmother. "I expected a little more emotion from you two. Your mother has been brutally murdered, and you sit here as if waiting for her to come into the room."

"Maybe we are," Diana said, blinking away tears. "I've done nothing but cry for the last thirty-six hours. Carl and I are struggling to explain to our children how their grandmother was murdered, and Penny is a wreck without Drew there to help with their kids." She sniffled. "I've been useless at work. Imagine having to explain to our employees, most of whom were Mom's long-time friends, how she was murdered in a Florida retirement community."

"Well, it's horrible for me too," Todd said, twirling his glass and watching the ice cubes pensively. "I went into the dealership today—the women crying and the men standing around, not knowing what to say."

"Everybody loved her," Diana said.

"Have they found the guy?" Drew asked, gulping his drink.

"Judy Barnaby says a Mexican worker committed suicide. My gun and your mother's jewelry were in his car."

"My God!" exclaimed Diana.

"So, it's over?" asked Drew.

"Well, I would think so, but the police keep coming around with more questions...tying up loose ends, as the cliché goes."

"What loose ends?" Drew asked.

"They're trying to identify some footprints in the backyard. They have her phone, the security box, three glasses, and a bottle of scotch." Todd's jaw tightened. "I hope they enjoy it."

"What about the security box?" Drew asked.

"Whoever killed her took the earrings and watch from her body, and her ruby jewelry and money from the security box."

"How much money?" Diana asked.

"I don't know."

"How did they know she was wearing the earrings and watch?" Drew asked.

"The cops found them in the Mexican's car with blood on them...with the gun and the stolen jewelry."

Drew emptied his glass. "Who would do that?"

Todd stood unsteadily, taking his glass and Drew's back to the kitchen. "They also found evidence of...well...bodily fluids."

"He raped her?" Diana said, her hands flying to her face.

Drew stared at his father. "What?"

Todd took a few moments in the kitchen to calm himself as he refilled the glasses with ice and scotch. "They don't know. She was...well...dressed in her negligee and kimono." Todd handed Drew his drink and settled back into his chair. Diana stared, shocked, as her father and brother nervously attacked their drinks. "They took my fingerprints and DNA swab for comparison," Todd added.

Diana sat back, biting her lip. She looked from her brother to her father. "Could she have been with someone?"

Todd regarded his daughter with angry eyes. "It's your mother you're talking about, Diana."

"I'm sorry, Dad, but…it seems bizarre."

"What's more bizarre, a thief breaking in to rob her, then deciding to rape and kill her? Or being intimate with someone who then robs and kills her?" Todd gulped his drink. "Well?" he demanded.

"You're right, Dad," Diana said.

"Of course, he is," Drew said, with a glare.

"This guy who killed himself—Julio—has a cousin who came here that night," Todd added. "He's the maintenance guy, Carlos. Alice from next door saw him leave the house earlier in the evening, carrying a grocery bag."

"Well, that's something," Drew said. "Perhaps they were in on it together."

Todd shrugged. "Except that several cars were seen here Saturday night."

"My God," Drew said. "How many?"

"It seems nosy Alice is our personal neighborhood watch. She told the cops she saw a silver car and thought it was me." He looked at his son and daughter. "It wasn't." He sipped his drink. "Jordan Davis, from across the street, called me, and we had drinks at the Inn last night. He told the cops he saw a light-colored, maybe gray, car here late at night."

"Everyone has either a light-colored, white, or silver car in Florida," Diana said.

"That's the problem," Todd said. "He couldn't tell the make or color in the dark."

Drew frowned. "What kind of car did the Mexican have?"

"How the hell would I know?" Todd said, his voice rising. "All I know is they found her jewelry and my gun in his car—the gun used to kill your mother and himself."

Drew stared into his glass. "When did you talk to Mom last?"

Todd sighed and slouched back in his chair. "Around six o'clock Saturday night. She said she was going out with friends. I called her at ten-thirty and got no answer."

"Have the police checked this out?" Diana asked.

"The detective said she didn't go to dinner after all." He placed his glass on the table. "They don't have any lab results yet. I don't remember everything he said…I can only think about what I saw."

"When you called her and she didn't answer, did you worry?" Diana asked.

"I thought she was sleeping, or still with her friends—she was probably already dead." He finished his drink. "I called her early Sunday morning—still no answer, and she didn't return my call—so I checked out and arrived home around nine o'clock… and found her."

Diana rose from her chair, walked into the living area and stood staring at the floor where the Oriental rug had been. "Have you been sleeping here?"

"No," Todd said. "I stayed at The Havens Inn, but I'll be able to sleep here tonight, with you both here."

They walked together through the sliding doors to the enclosed birdcage. The men reclined on lounge chairs. Diana sat on the edge of the pool, took off her sandals, and dipped her feet into the water. Clouds gathered overhead as they watched a great blue heron standing statue-still on the bank of Clam Lake. Two squirrels scampered up and down a palm tree that stood along the lake. As if on cue, the afternoon showers began, big plops of rain sending the squirrels scattering.

"I can't believe I'll never see her again," Diana said.

CHAPTER 27

Monday evening

One by one, Malloy, Stokes, and Powers hung dripping raincoats on hooks along the entrance to the squad room. They were exhausted from their daily round trips from their homes and Sheriff's Department in Garland to the DPS in The Havens. They joined Davenport in the incident room where a large whiteboard hung on the wall, and documents filled the conference table.

"Sorry to call you in this late," Davenport said, "but it's important that we digest all the information coming to us." He spread documents and photographs on the table between them.

"It's nice to have a conversation without Judy around," Stokes said. "Everyone in The Havens seems to know the details about the case."

"Keep an eye on her," Davenport said. "She's talking, but she doesn't know what she's talking about."

"She's just a busybody," Malloy said.

Davenport looked at Malloy over his glasses, then turned to Stokes. "What did you find out about Mrs. Gonzalez?"

Stokes flipped a page in her notebook. "Paula's employer at the Dollar Queen confirmed that she worked Sunday and seemed fine. This morning, however, Paula called her boss when she woke up and realized her husband hadn't come home. Her boss told her to call the police and stay home."

Stokes scanned her notes. "I also called Carlos's wife, Sofia. She confirmed his story of how he obtained the books, and that she was with him when he delivered them to Julio. She claimed that Carlos arrived home before eleven Saturday night, the timeframe of Mrs. Vogel's murder."

"What about Carlos's alibi for earlier Saturday evening?" Davenport asked Powers. "What did you find out at Jonah's Bar?"

"The bartender and another regular customer confirmed that Carlos left around ten-thirty Saturday night," Powers said. "Martín Aguila left after ten."

"What about Julio?" Stokes asked. "Was he there that night?"

Powers reported, "His friends said they didn't expect him to come that night, something about being sick, but he showed up anyway, around eleven o'clock. They said Julio looked ill, and only stayed for one beer."

"Wait a minute," Malloy said. "Ryan told me that Julio cut himself with a box cutter and blood splattered all over him. He said Julio left work to go to the ER. His shirt should've had blood on it, unless he changed it."

"Why didn't his friends mention a bloody shirt or a cut hand?" Stokes asked.

"That *is* interesting," Davenport said. He made a note, then moved on. "The team reported that the footprints fit the size and pattern of Julio's shoes, so it's likely he was the hooded man Mrs. Van Dee saw." He stroked his chin. "We'll let the friends stew awhile and get back with them when we have more information."

"Who's this Aguila guy?" Malloy asked. "How's he connected with Carlos, and why is he hanging around with a Mexican detective?"

"The Aguilas are staying in the house of his daughter's former in-laws," Powers said, "and Mr. Aguila works at The Barn part-time."

"He's living here and working at The Barn?" Malloy said.

"I guess he's bored with the gringo culture," Powers said. "I can understand that."

"I've met Mr. Aguila," Davenport said. "The Mexican detective, Roberto Salinas, is a friend of his daughter, Claire. Detective

Salinas and I attended the same conference in Orlando, but I returned early to join you at the Vogel murder scene. He's a very bright detective with a bias toward his countrymen wherever they live."

"Which makes him an unreliable witness," Malloy said, leaning back in his chair.

"Which makes him knowledgeable on both the lawful and lawless characteristics of people from his own culture," Stokes countered.

Davenport leaned back in his chair. "Malloy, how did it go with Mr. Vogel?"

"Horrible," Malloy said. "I've never had to tell a husband that his wife was either raped or having an affair, and, oh, by the way, I need a DNA sample."

"How did he take it?" Davenport asked.

"Better than I expected. He seemed more willing to accept the rape scenario than the affair, yet I think he suspected something along those lines—an affair, I mean. He identified the jewelry and the gun."

"What did you learn about Mrs. Vogel's activities on Saturday?" Stokes asked Malloy.

"I checked the country club and The Ashram yoga studio where she would likely go." Malloy rolled his eyes. "She didn't have a tee time, but she had gone to The Ashram. Perhaps Stokes could follow up on that?" he said, smiling.

"Does it seem odd that, when her husband is out of town, she sits home most of the day and then cancels dinner with friends in the evening?" Stokes asked, doodling on her pad.

"Perhaps the strange silver car that drove into the garage is a clue," Powers suggested.

Malloy furrowed his brow. "Did the crime scene techs find a planner or date book?"

Stokes rummaged through the papers on the desk and pulled

out an inventory of items taken from the house. "No planner or date book. Why?"

Malloy said, "Vogel couldn't find hers. He thought we had taken it."

"So, we're missing a planner," Stokes said. "Her phone should help with appointments."

"She might have left it at work," Malloy suggested. "Has any-one gone to the dealership yet?"

"Next stop for you," Davenport said to Malloy.

Davenport shuffled through his papers and produced the list of friends Todd had brought to the office. He handed it to Stokes. "Check with her friends and find out if they have any idea who might want to hurt her. You were right on Mrs. Davis. There's something there."

Stokes frowned but nodded. "Yes, sir."

"There's a break there," Powers interrupted. "Mr. and Mrs. Davis came in to sign their statements while I was checking on Mr. Vogel's conference friends. Jordan Davis repeated his story about a white car in the Vogels' driveway around ten-thirty."

Stokes furrowed her brow. "But, they described it as gray or light-colored at first. Now it's white?"

"That's what they said. Mr. Davis seemed a little blustery, like his wife had pressured him to come."

"Good job, Powers," Davenport said, jotting notes. "What did you learn about the convention?"

Powers checked his notes. "The hotel manager confirmed that Mr. Vogel checked in on Thursday and checked out early Sunday morning as he reported. One manager is on vacation. I'm still working on the complete names and phone numbers of the people on Mr. Vogel's list. It seems he socialized with a lot of people, but he didn't know their last names."

"That's not unusual," Davenport said. "I learned that the calls received on Barbara's phone confirm Todd's statement—one long call Saturday around six, a missed call around ten-thirty, and a missed call early Sunday morning. She also got a call Saturday afternoon from her son, Drew. All calls came from the Orlando area."

"Drew was in Orlando also?" Malloy asked.

"So it seems," Davenport said, "and Barbara made a call after she talked to her husband. We don't have the name yet." Davenport shuffled his papers together and stuffed them into his briefcase. "That's it for tonight. Good job, everyone." He looked out the squad room window. The rain had stopped. "Now go home... or wherever you go when you leave work."

He watched his team collect their raincoats and leave the office. He envied their lives, full of hope and ambition, not to mention the ability to go home when he still had work to do. Since his divorce he lived in an apartment in Garland, a nice apartment with a pool and rec center, but lonely just the same. He wondered how different it might have been if he had children. He hoped that the young people working with him didn't face the same future. Heaving a sigh, he collected his briefcase, grabbed his raincoat, and left the department. Back to Orchard... one more visit...and an important one.

CHAPTER 28

Davenport turned onto the Gonzalez family's gravel driveway for the second time. He compared the modest home and cluttered neighborhood with The Havens, where immaculate flower beds and palm trees adorned every home. How ironic, he thought, that workers who lived in this neighborhood, devoid of lawns, carefully manicured those in The Havens.

He exited his car, dodging the puddles that hadn't soaked into the gravel. The air felt fresh after the rain and the moon peeked out from behind the clouds. In the dark, Davenport could see Paula Gonzalez through the living room window, talking to someone on the phone. He rang the doorbell, and Carlos opened the door.

"Mr. Chavez, I didn't expect to see you here."

Carlos fidgeted, shifting from foot to foot. "Paula asked me to come."

Davenport wiped his feet on the mat, followed Carlos into the now-familiar room, and sat in the same chair he had used before. Paula ended her call and sat on the sofa. Her daughter, who had been playing with a doll in the corner, toddled awkwardly to her mother.

Carlos picked her up. "I'll take Mary to Billy's room."

When they had left, Davenport said, "Carlos tells me that you have information you held back earlier…about your husband?"

"My sister is coming…she's on her way."

"Why is she coming?"

"To show you what I found."

"Which is…?"

"Things…that Julio shouldn't have."

Davenport leaned forward. "Why does your sister have these things?"

Paula sniffled and blinked back tears. "Because I didn't want the police to find them…I'm so sorry." She burst into tears. "I know it was wrong, but I was afraid. Carlos convinced me to tell you so maybe you can find who killed my husband."

The doorbell rang as Carlos emerged from the bedroom. He opened the door to a thin woman with thick curly hair.

"Help me," the woman said to Carlos.

Carlos left with her, and within moments they reentered carrying a large cardboard box. They placed it on the floor between Paula and the detective.

Paula introduced her sister, Martha. She was older than Paula, with deep-set eyes that darted defiantly between her sister and the detective.

Carlos reached over to open the box, but Davenport put his hand out to stop him. "How many people have touched this box?" He looked from Martha to Paula.

Martha, who remained standing, arms akimbo, said in a terse voice, "Paula opened it so I could look inside, but I didn't touch anything. My husband helped me load it into the car. He looked inside too, but didn't touch anything but the box itself." She spoke quickly, with no hint of an accent.

Davenport turned to Paula. "Mrs. Gonzalez, did anyone else handle the box?"

"Not that I know of."

"But you suspected something odd about the contents," Davenport pressed. When Paula nodded, he leaned over and peered inside. "Tell me how you found it."

"I found it in the bedroom closet, way in the back, about a week ago. It's the box I use for Billy's out-grown clothes. I pulled it out to find clothes for Mary." She sighed. "I found things at the bottom I didn't know were there."

"Did you ask Julio about the contents?"

Her eyes misted. "I knew what it meant—that he'd been steal-ing—but I didn't want him to be deported." She rubbed her eyes on her shirt sleeve. "I knew he did it for Mary."

"So, you put the box back, and didn't mention it to him, but you thought about it after he died?"

"Yes, but before, when Mrs. Vogel was murdered, and the officers questioned Carlos...I thought they might be involved in something together." She sobbed again and brought her sleeve to her face. "I'm sorry, Carlos. I shouldn't have suspected you."

Carlos frowned but said nothing.

"So, you gave the box to your sister?" Davenport asked.

"Not right away. I planned to talk with Julio first, but then he was killed—murdered," she said, covering her face with her hands.

Martha went into the bathroom and came out with a wad of toilet paper. Paula blew her nose and wadded the paper in her hands.

"Can't you leave her alone?" Martha hissed. "Can't you see she's suffering? She's given you the box, she has apologized, what else do you want?" She sat next to her sister, putting her arm around her.

Davenport turned to Martha. "Perhaps you can finish the story?"

Paula whispered, "Please, Martha, tell him the rest."

Martha held her sister's hand as she spoke. "When Paula woke up and realized that Julio hadn't come home, she called her boss, then me. I came over, and she told me about the box." Martha gave the detective a stern look. "No one contacted her for hours. She didn't know if he was dead, injured, or just...gone somewhere. I told her I would take the box for awhile, until we knew what happened. It's my fault, too."

Davenport sat on the floor in front of the box. "Are you sure this is everything? You didn't keep anything back?"

"This is everything," Martha said, and Paula nodded.

Davenport took plastic gloves from his pocket, stretched them onto his hands and reached inside. He extracted an odd assortment of items, from Hummel statues to Precious Moments angels, and jewelry, both costume and valuable. The cache had been accumulated by someone who didn't know the value of items, an amateur. Finally, he pulled out a locked metal cash box.

"Do you have the key?" Davenport asked Paula.

Paula sighed and reached into the pocket of her shorts. "I just found it today…when I was cleaning out Julio's drawers." She began to sob and brought the soggy toilet paper back to her nose. "I didn't have it when I found the box…I promise."

Davenport opened the box with the key, looked inside and showed it to Paula. "There's a lot of money in here. You didn't know about it?"

"I didn't know. Why would he hide it from me?" Paula sobbed.

Martha scoffed. "Because he was saving it for his family."

"We're his family," Paula said in desperation.

"His brother," Martha said with bitterness in her voice.

"No!" Paula said. "It can't be."

"Is there anything else, Mrs. Gonzalez?" Davenport asked. "What made you suspicious of Julio?"

"Tell him," Martha said, her voice hard.

Paula bit her lip. "It was the lying," she finally said, between sobs, "about where he went when he should have been working…" She looked at Martha who nodded in encouragement. "I saw a flip phone—not his regular cellphone—in his jeans one day. It had one number in it. When I asked him about it, he got angry and snatched it from me. He said it was for work…but he'd been acting strange…"

"Do you know where the phone is? The phone number?"

Davenport asked.

Paula shook her head, tears flowing again. Martha disappeared and returned with a bigger wad of toilet paper.

"Mrs. Gonzalez, your husband must have planned to sell these items. In fact, he had probably been doing this for awhile. Do you know who might buy stolen goods from him?"

Paula wiped her eyes. "He has a distant cousin from his hometown—Henry Garza. He lives in Garland."

Billy came into the room with Mary toddling behind. Davenport quickly returned the items and the metal box to the carton and closed the lid. "Do you remember what your husband wore Saturday night?" he asked.

Paula turned to Martha. "Watch the kids?"

Martha nodded, and Paula led Davenport into the bedroom. She reached into a tub of clothes and pulled out a pair of jeans.

"You washed them?"

"I…I do laundry Sundays," she said.

"What about the shirt? We suspect it has blood stains."

"I…I threw it out. It was ruined." Paula leaned against the dresser, her hands shaking. "He cut himself at work."

Davenport waited quietly as her entire body shook and tears welled in her eyes. She turned and left the bedroom. When she returned, she handed him a T-shirt streaked with blood.

CHAPTER 29

Todd parked his Lexus and stormed into the side entrance of the Glen Haven Country Club. He pushed through the glass door of the Pro Shop, feeling the full force of the air-conditioning. He gave a slight wave to the golf pro, Ben Stevens, who was assisting a Mexican man wearing black slacks and a polo shirt. Three women, none of whom looked Hispanic, moved along the clothing racks, inspecting the women's golf shirts and hats.

Impatient, Todd hovered over the customer, watching as he handed Ben a premier credit card. After returning the card to his wallet, the customer joined the women, and they left the shop.

"Who's that?" Todd asked, following Ben into a side office. "He looks familiar."

Ben sat at his cluttered desk and motioned for Todd to sit across from him. "Martín Aguila, the part-time groundskeeper."

"What did he buy?"

Ben gave Todd a level stare. "He's staying at the Carsons' and just paid their annual membership dues. Nice of him."

"That's a lot of money for someone who's mowing golf courses," Todd grumbled. "Speaking of which, what the hell is this about?" He extracted a letter from his pocket and dropped it onto the desk between them. "Should I be mowing lawns? How can you do this to me now, of all days?"

Ben took the letter but didn't read it. He knew the contents. "I'm sorry, Todd. It went out before...I would have waited, but you know the problem. You didn't pay your membership dues last year, and this year's dues are late...that's..."

"I know how much I owe."

"And there's the tab. We can't let you charge anymore."

"Ben, my friend, can you hold off until my wife's estate is settled? Business has been slow."

Ben watched as Todd's hands shook. He, and everyone else, knew it wasn't only the business. It was the lifestyle, the new Lexus, the expensive gambling trips, exclusive vacations, and the alcohol.

"I can give you a month, Todd, but corporate won't let me go beyond."

"Do I still have my locker?"

"Sure, but you have to pay for each round of golf—non-member fees. I'm sorry."

Todd took the letter, folded it into a square and stuffed it back into his pocket. He rose and left Ben's office, slamming the door behind him. He stomped down the long hallway separating the country club from The Oasis restaurant and bar. He had directed his children to meet him in the bar to spare them the humiliation of watching their father beg a nobody from Georgia for a reprieve on his membership dues.

As Todd approached the restaurant, he saw Martín Aguila again, standing at the hostess podium with the three women. They were chatting with Suzie, the divorced daughter of one of Todd's golf partners, who had recently moved in with her parents.

Frustrated that he once again had to wait for the same group, Todd studied the foursome: Martín and the tall thin woman he assumed was his wife, a younger woman who resembled the wife, and the third woman who looked like an escapee from Woodstock. As he watched, a middle-aged Hispanic couple appeared from the bar with a waitress. The couple joined the others and, together, they followed the waitress to their table.

Todd sidled up to the podium. "Hey, Suzie," he said, smiling and showing his whitened teeth. "How's it going, darlin'?"

"Fine, Mr. Vogel. I'm sorry to hear about your wife." She looked around and lowered her voice. "It must give you some peace, knowing the killer is dead."

"Thanks, Suzie. It does but, you know, they're still asking questions, tying up threads, whatever that means. It's nonsense, but it should be over soon." He tapped the plastic reservation sheet Suzie was perusing.

"Did you have a reservation?" she asked, her fingers scanning the sheet.

"Diana Thurman, my daughter, made the reservation."

Suzie smiled. "Of course. I'm sorry I didn't recognize them. They're at the bar. Your table will be ready in a few minutes. Please give them my condolences."

Todd leaned in toward Suzie. "That man, Mr. Aguila, does he come here often? I thought he worked here."

"I've only seen him here a few times."

"Who's the other Mexican with them?"

She turned to look at the group as they disappeared into the restaurant. "He must be the cop or lawyer I heard about."

"What?"

"Well," Suzie said, fingering her blonde hair, "my dad golfed with Phil Barnaby—Judy's husband—and they were here for drinks a little while ago. Phil told my dad that Mr. Aguila took Carlos and that Mexican guy to the DPS today. He called himself a detective, but Judy told Phil he looked like a lawyer…too fancy for a cop, she thought. Anyway, they met with that detective from Garland—Davenport, I think."

Todd forced a smile and winked at the petite divorcee. "Probably the Mexican Mafia."

Suzie scrunched her nose. "Does Mexico have a Mafia?"

"Cartels, whatever," he said as he tapped her hand lightly, winked again, and entered the bar, where friends stopped him along the way to offer condolences. He regretted choosing to eat out. It would have been better to stay home, but no one wanted to cook in Barbara's kitchen.

At the bar, he leaned toward the bartender. "Deb, can you bring a vodka tonic to my table?" He pointed to his children seated on leather chairs on either side of a low table. "Also, another of whatever they ordered." He pulled a fifty-dollar bill from his wallet.

"I can put it on your tab," Deb said.

"It's okay, I'll pay now."

"Sure, Todd," Deb said, taking the bill. "I'm very sorry about Barbara."

Todd nodded, took his change, left a tip, and joined his family.

"What kept you?" Drew asked as Todd sat down.

"It's nothing," Todd answered. "We should have stayed home. It's too much, all this attention."

"You have to face it eventually, Dad," Diana said.

"I wonder if they'll make any changes around here," Drew said. "The security is awful."

"The place is like a playground. Anyone can get in." Todd felt his hands shake. *Where was that drink?*

"What do you think they'll do about the guy who killed her?" Drew asked. "I mean, do they close the case?"

"They're sure taking their time," Todd said as Deb brought their drinks on a tray.

"Your dinner table is ready," she said.

"It's about time," Todd said, shoving his chair back.

CHAPTER 30

Claire and Roberto sat at a small high table on the outdoor patio of The Oasis, awaiting the arrival of Claire's family and Madge, who had reluctantly offered to give them some private time, their first opportunity to be alone together.

"I'm sorry about Madge," Roberto said, shaking his head. "She caught me after my talk. When she learned I was coming here, she became determined to come with me—she wanted to surprise you." He sipped his drink. "It was a coincidence when Detective Davenport and his colleagues asked us to join them. I had no idea that Davenport would be here, in The Havens."

Claire smiled. "I admit I'm a bit disappointed that I have to share you with Madge. Her persuasive powers are legendary."

"Let's not waste what time we have," Roberto said. He reached over and touched her hair, gently taking strands from behind her ear. "I'm glad you haven't cut your hair."

"I'm not sixty yet," she laughed, remembering their conversation in Merida. "But it's more salt than pepper this year."

"I love it," he said. "I have missed it…and you too, of course."

The afternoon rain had left a cool evening breeze in its wake, and Claire remembered similar evenings spent with Roberto in Merida the year before. So many emotions ran through her, so many things still unsaid.

"I'm sure your parents are happy to see you and Cristina," Roberto observed.

Claire smiled. "That's true, but we expected a relaxing vacation, not a murder investigation—especially one where my father is involved." She studied her wine glass. "Then, Mom, Cristina and I almost had a head-on collision before you even got here." She raised her eyebrows as he reacted.

"What happened?" Roberto put his glass down, giving her his full attention.

"We nearly got rammed head-on by a car careening around the corner of the back entrance to The Havens, where that grocery store is."

"When was this?"

"Sunday night, around midnight."

"What kind of car?"

"I don't know," Claire said. "Silver, I think. Why?"

"*Nada*," he said.

"I know that look."

Roberto smiled and took her left hand in his, gently caressing her now-bare ring finger. "I feel badly about your father, being questioned and having his car examined yesterday. And then today…"

"What happened?"

"When your father and I brought Carlos to the DPS, the Public Safety officers were rude to him."

Claire frowned. "What about the detective?"

"He was embarrassed. He invited me into the interview as a professional courtesy, but he wouldn't let your father go in. I understand why, but I'd hoped he would let him in, for Carlos's sake."

"My father's sensitive to stereotypes. He has dealt with them his whole life. When his family moved out of the migrant stream—those were early days, before the Civil Rights movement—teachers criticized him, and students teased him because he didn't speak English well. When he owned his own business, he tried to help others along the way, providing training and jobs to Hispanic workers. I'm very proud of him."

"Your father's a good man," Roberto said. "I understand why

Carlos has attached himself to him." He looked into his glass, then returned his gaze to Claire. "Detective Davenport has invited me for breakfast tomorrow morning. Do you mind?"

"You're here for four hours and are already involved in a murder investigation?" She tried to hide the disappointment in her voice, but she immediately regretted her words.

"You're right," he said. "I'll tell him I'd rather spend my few days with you—which is true."

Claire shook her head. "No, I'm being selfish. I want you to go." She took his hand. "Now can we talk about something else?"

"Absolutely," Roberto said. "Like how you missed me so much you changed your travel plans to be here at the same time I came?"

Claire flushed, bringing a soft glow to her skin. "No, how I accommodated your schedule so that I could involve you in a murder investigation."

"Hah," he laughed. Roberto reached over and took Claire's other hand. "I have missed you. And I'm happy to meet your parents and your daughter."

Too soon, a waitress motioned to Roberto and Claire, and they joined Martín's group at the restaurant podium. They followed the waitress to a quiet table facing an outside dining area and small garden with a fountain and benches.

Roberto and Claire nursed their own drinks while the others awaited theirs. When the drinks arrived and they had all ordered, the conversation meandered from Cristina's Malawi research trip and the mysterious friend, Kyle, to Claire's new position as chairperson of the Keene College Anthropology Department.

"Tell me again how that happened," Roberto asked Claire. "Last year you seemed ready to retire, leave academia behind."

Claire grimaced. "Don't remind me."

Madge snorted and gulped her gin and tonic. "This will be interesting," she said.

"My story, Madge," Claire said smiling. "I agreed to the chair position because the department disintegrated after the disastrous conference last spring. When the dean came to me, I couldn't refuse. It wouldn't have been fair."

Claire paused as the waiter returned with their food. She poked her salmon with a fork and continued, "After our Mayanist program recovers from the damages incurred when our director nearly destroyed it before it started, I'll be free and clear. I might retire and become a novelist."

"No way," Madge said, a chunk of steak dangling from her fork. "You can't retire until George and I do. Remember, George postponed his retirement, and I came out of retirement to curate the new museum…we need you to stay with the program."

"Jamal is more than ready to take over the program when you both retire," Claire said, "and there are plenty of senior faculty qualified to be department chair."

"So, where does a retired anthropologist-novelist live?" Cristina teased.

"Wherever she wants," Claire quipped.

Theresa watched a man enter the restaurant with a young couple. The waitress who led them to their table paused often as diners stopped them to speak in muted, serious tones. "We saw that man in the golf store," she observed.

Claire followed Theresa's gaze. She thought him tall and handsome, with penetrating eyes. These features were replicated in the younger couple following uncertainly behind him. The hostess led them to a nearby table, and they settled into their chairs.

"That's Mr. Vogel," Martín said. "I didn't recognize him in the store."

"Those must be his twin children," Theresa said.

After the waitress left Todd's table, he nodded to his children, who then looked toward the Aguilas, the woman's eyes locking with Claire's.

"Oh, no," Theresa whispered. She turned away from the Vogels and toward Martín. "He's probably telling them about Carlos and you being friends."

"There's nothing we can do about it, *esposa*," Martín said to Theresa. "He's grieving and looking for answers."

Claire's thoughts wandered to the conversations she heard at The Lodge, the rumors about both Todd and his wife having affairs.

As if reading her mind, Theresa said, "You wonder about people."

"In what way?" asked Roberto.

"You think that rich people have everything they need," Theresa said. "They look young regardless of their age, they have everything, but they don't seem happy."

"Why does that surprise you?" Madge asked.

Theresa shrugged. "I guess, living in the city, in the neighborhood, I saw how people struggled to make ends meet. I guess I thought that if I had this and that, I'd be happier."

"Unfortunately, a lot of people think that," Roberto said. He looked at Theresa curiously. "What makes you say this?"

"It's something we heard at our book group today," Theresa said. She looked at her daughter and granddaughter. "I hate to gossip."

"Well, I don't," said Madge. "It might be important. We should tell them."

In turns, whispering, the women related the rumors of affairs on both sides of the Vogel family.

"Both of them were having affairs?" Martín asked. "And Mrs. Vogel with two men? That seems unlikely."

"I didn't say we believe it, *Papa*," Cristina whispered, "but, what if Carlos is right, and Julio didn't kill Mrs. Vogel? Someone had a motive."

"And if Julio didn't commit suicide, someone killed him," Claire added.

Their attention was diverted as a middle-aged man wearing a sports coat approached the Vogels.

The man leaned close to Todd and said, "Mr. Vogel? You've been served."

Diners stared as Todd turned white and shoved the document into his pocket. "It's nothing important," he whispered to his children. But everyone around them heard.

At the Aguila table, Madge finished her drink in one gulp. "I love this place."

CHAPTER 31

Tuesday Morning

The morning sun beat into the lanai where Diana and Drew sat, ignoring their coffee as they listened to Todd scream into the phone.

"What do you mean, he's not in the office?" Todd's voice shook. "Where is he?" A short pause. "Does he even know that Barbara's been murdered?" Silence. "Condolences are one thing…having my attorney here with me is another, dammit!" Another silence. "Tell him he's got a helluva lot of explaining to do!" Todd punched the end-call button.

"Calm down, Dad, or you'll have a heart attack," Diana said.

Todd stood over his children, his face red. "How can I calm down when I was served divorce papers in a crowded restaurant two days after my wife's murder?"

Diana stood to refill her coffee from the carafe on the table. Todd did the same, then stomped to the lanai portable bar and added a shot of whiskey.

"We don't know when she signed the papers," Diana reasoned. "It would take time, especially if Ronnie had to coordinate with a local attorney."

"He's licensed in Florida, too. It had to be him." Todd gulped the spiked coffee, choking on his words.

"He'll get back with you, I'm sure," Drew assured him.

Todd glared at his children. "I suppose you two knew all about this?" His voice reverberated in the small space.

"Quiet, Dad," Diana urged. "The neighbors will hear you."

"I don't care," Todd said.

"I didn't know anything," Drew said, glancing at his sister.

Todd clenched his jaw and slammed the mug heavily on the glass table. "I'm going to the office."

After Todd stormed off, Diana reclined in her chair. Drew strode to the bar and splashed more whiskey into his half-empty coffee mug.

"You knew about the divorce, right, Diana?" Drew asked, adding coffee to the alcohol before returning to his chair.

"I didn't know she filed, Drew," Diana said. "She told me they were having problems, and she was considering divorce."

"Mom always confided in you."

"It wasn't a secret. I thought she told you, too."

"She didn't. What kind of problems?"

Diana shrugged. "They argued about the business, but I think it went deeper than that—more personal."

"Dad seemed surprised," Drew said. "It seems if they had problems, the topic might have been broached at some point."

"Mom's pretty private. Perhaps she knew something about him, and he didn't know she knew." Diana stood and looked through the birdcage at the lake. "She said that if they divorced, there would be some changes in management of the businesses. She promised she would tell us if she filed, and she asked that I not mention it to Dad. Again, I thought you knew."

"Changes?" Drew said, standing to join her. "To be clear, because they weren't divorced, the original trust agreement stands. You and I inherit the Chicago store and Dad inherits the Florida business. Right?"

"That's how I understand it," Diana said.

"So, what happens now?"

"We meet with Ronnie," Diana said. "He'll have to talk to us about the trust soon. What's important now is for you and I to seriously discuss the Chicago store. We'll be joint owners."

"I hadn't thought about it," Drew said.

"It seems to me it's a good time to take control of the finances. Mom and I handled the finances of both stores, with Annette being the business manager. Now, I'll be handling the finances alone. I'll need help."

"You mean, you want to hire an accountant who thinks like you and Mom?"

"Exactly," Diana said. "Mom, Annette, and I controlled Dad's expenses, and yours. I need an Annette. I doubt that Dad would allow her to manage both stores. He might even fire her." Diana shuddered to think of that possibility.

"You don't need anyone else," Drew said. "We can do it together." He retrieved his mug from the table and finished his drink.

"Neither you nor Dad understand the finances," Diana said. "I doubt you know anything about our sales, and how they've dropped because you two are never around to sell anything."

Drew's eyes narrowed. "Don't compare us," he said, his jaw tightening. "It has nothing to do with the businesses. We're recovering from the recession, that's all."

"The recession ended years ago." Diana furrowed her brow. "Are you sure you and Dad didn't discuss this at the convention? He didn't mention any problems?"

"It's not something we would discuss with hundreds of people around."

Diana studied him carefully. "You didn't go to the convention, did you?"

"Of course, I did!" Drew said, his voice rising as his face reddened. "I just stayed at a different hotel—ask Dad. We played golf." He evened his tone, saying, "I went to the snow and farm machine events, but I'm a businessman. I get more results at the golf course with clients. That's where the deals are made, dear sister, not in meetings."

"That's where alcohol is served, dear brother," she said, crossing her arms. "And you stayed until Monday, a workday."

Drew shrugged. "I had clients to meet with. Besides, if I had flown home, we both would've had to fly back the next day."

"Penny expected you home Sunday."

Drew clenched his jaw in anger, a habit he had inherited from his father. "It's none of your business."

They both jumped when a figure appeared around the back of the house. An elderly woman approached the birdcage, wielding a baking dish.

"Hi, there. Remember me?" the lady said through the screen door.

"Yes, Alice," Diana said, opening the door. "It's nice to see you."

"I'm so sorry to hear about your mother," she said, as she stomped into the lanai. "Hello, Drew. Did you bring the kids?"

"Of course not, under the circumstances," Drew said, standing next to Diana. "This is a private backyard."

"Oh, I know, but Todd doesn't care. I rang the doorbell and no one answered, then I heard voices back here."

"Dad's not here," Diana said.

"I made a casserole." Alice held out the dish.

"Thank you very much," Diana said, taking it from her. "That's very nice of you."

Alice stood for a moment, shuffling her feet. "You know I saw the guy...right here...at the birdcage...then I saw him leave. I told that Black cop everything."

"You saw the Mexican's car?" Drew asked.

"It must have been him, don't you think?" Alice said.

"It must have been," Drew agreed.

"You were very helpful, I'm sure," Diana said. "We'll tell Dad you were here. Thank you for the casserole."

They watched Alice leave the lanai and retreat toward the hedge that separated the houses. "Does Dad know she saw Julio Gonzalez?" Diana asked. "He didn't mention it."

"It should settle the case, though," Drew said. "Don't you agree?"

CHAPTER 32

Scott Malloy parked in front of Denton's Equipment and Sales in Garland. His Mustang was dwarfed by huge front loaders, backhoes, and other machinery that marred the Florida landscape year-round.

Inside, mid-sized equipment—professional lawn mowers, small tractors and forklifts—lined the central aisle. He stopped at the information desk, identified himself, and followed directions to the business office at the back of the store.

Don Johansen, assistant manager for sales, was a tall, lean man in his mid-fifties. He introduced Malloy to the purchasing and promotion agent, Skip Waters, a round, balding man of about the same age. Johansen also introduced Annette Fulton, Barbara's administrative assistant, a stately woman with intelligent eyes and gray hair.

"Todd's a good man," Skip Waters said, leaning back on his chair at such an angle Malloy thought he might either tip it over or break it. "He's friendly and treats us well."

Johansen sat stiffly in his chair, nearest Malloy. "I'm in charge when Todd isn't here. Everyone will say this is a great place to work."

Malloy, who hadn't asked about morale, looked at Annette's impassive face.

"Weren't the Vogels co-owners?" Malloy asked. "Wouldn't they each be in charge if the other were away?"

"Well, sure," said Johansen, "but Barbara didn't know about sales. She left that to the men, thank God." Don winked at Annette, who dabbed her eyes but remained mute.

"And what was Mrs. Vogel's role in the company?"

"She did the books," Johansen said.

Malloy turned to Annette. "And you were Mrs. Vogel's assistant?"

Annette wiped her eyes with a tissue she had wadded in her fist. "Barbara *was* the owner," Annette said with a quick glance at the men, "and financial director. I'm the business manager. I'm an accountant."

Malloy scribbled in his notebook and asked, "How is the business doing?"

Johansen answered, "Depends on who you ask, I guess."

"What do you mean?"

"Sales are good," Johansen said, "but equipment costs keep rising, so our numbers girls…" he pointed to Annette, "…are always complaining about the expenses." He threw her an air kiss. "No offense, Annie."

"Are you laying people off?" Malloy asked. He looked at Annette, thinking this might be her domain, but Johansen replied, "No, no…it's mainly a thing between Todd and Barbara. She doesn't…didn't…understand that to make money, you have to spend money."

"You mean advertising?"

"Well, that, and promotion," Johansen said, prompting a heavy sigh from Annette's side of the table.

"Ms. Fulton, was promotion a problem?" Malloy asked, turning to her.

Annette dabbed at her eyes. "Promotion is fine, but when it means taking contractors to casinos and country clubs, Barbara and I disagreed with Todd." Her voice came out forcefully. Malloy imagined that she and Mrs. Vogel had been allies.

"See what we mean?" Waters said, nodding at Malloy as if he would understand.

"Can any of you think of anyone who might be unhappy

working here, or anyone fired recently who might bear a grudge against Mrs. Vogel?" Malloy asked.

"No, sir," Annette spoke up. "Everybody loved Barbara."

"That's true," agreed Johansen, and Waters nodded.

"Is there anything you can tell me that might shed light on who would want to hurt her?"

"Nothing," said Johansen, and the other two shook their heads.

"Mr. Johansen and Mr. Waters, thank you for your time. You may go," Malloy said. He turned to Annette. "Could I have a few minutes with you, Ms. Fulton?"

Malloy shook hands with the men and followed Annette into her office.

They entered a room as large as the conference room they had just left, with two desks, one facing a window into the store and another facing the back wall. Annette sat at this desk, offering Malloy a chair next to it. He presumed the window desk had belonged to Mrs. Vogel.

"It must be hard for you working two jobs now," Malloy said.

"We had different responsibilities, but we knew each other's jobs, for vacations and sickness."

"You knew her well?"

"We've known each other for years."

"How did you come to work here?"

"Barbara's parents, Charles and Susan, owned Denton's Equipment in Chicago. I was the assistant accountant to Barbara's mother," Annette explained. Mrs. Denton taught Barbara the business end of the company. Later, Barbara and I worked together in the office—her parents called us their 'numbers girls,' and these guys here do the same." She frowned. "Eventually, the Dentons bought this property and moved here. After they passed away, Barbara and Todd took over this dealership, and Drew and Diana took over the Chicago store."

After a thoughtful pause, Annette continued, "About that time, my husband had just died, and Barbara asked me to come down and work with her here. My husband and I had no children. I knew the change of scenery would be good for me…not to mention the climate. I was excited to work with Barbara again."

"You both share the same philosophy of business, and work well together?"

"Yes," Annette said, "and Barbara and I continued to be the financial managers of the Chicago store with Diana and Drew managing the day-to-day operations."

"Did Mr. and Mrs. Vogel argue about the finances at the store?" Malloy asked.

Annette sighed and pulled a tissue from a box on her desk. "Mr. Vogel is a good salesman, and I know that sales are what we're here for—what pays my salary—but he and Barbara often discussed the finances and expenditures, yes."

"Is there any reason to believe company money might have been used for non-business purposes? Do you think the Vogels might be in debt, for example?"

"The business, or their personal finances?"

"Either? Both?"

"I can't really say, but Mr. Vogel spent a lot of money. For him, appearances are important—the right car, fancy clothes, country club, etcetera. Appearances didn't interest Barbara. She liked The Havens, but it was Mr. Vogel's idea to live there."

"And the company?"

"We're doing okay," Annette said. "But, despite my coworkers' complaints, Barbara and I were usually unsuccessful in our attempts to control expenses incurred to impress potential customers."

"Could you show me your books or computer programs?"

Annette sat upright. "Not without a warrant."

"Of course," Malloy conceded, turning a page in his notebook.

"Perhaps you can help me in another way. Is there anyone else in the dealership who was close to Mrs. Vogel, besides you? Anyone she socialized with?"

"Not really. Barbara kept business and friendship separate. Most of us live near Garland. I really don't know much about her life in The Havens."

"You and Barbara didn't socialize even though you came here to work for her?"

"We'd go out about once a month for lunch or dinner. I've made my own friends, and we have different interests outside of the business."

"Can you tell me about Todd and Barbara's personal relation-ship?"

Annette looked back at Barbara's desk as if she were there, lis-tening. "There seemed to be tension between them in the office."

"Did she mention divorce?"

"No, but I worried about that, what would happen if they divorced."

"Would divorce have an impact on the business?" Malloy asked.

"She owned both dealerships," Annette said, glancing at the clock on the wall. "I don't know how they would be divided, if that's what you're asking."

"Do you see their children often? Do they come to Florida?"

Annette nodded. "Diana and Drew come here once or twice a year with their families, usually separately so the Chicago store is covered. Drew comes down for conventions when they're held in Orlando, and Todd travels to conventions in the Chicago area from time to time."

Malloy blinked. "Did Drew attend the Orlando convention last weekend?"

"I have no idea. He didn't come to the store, and Todd didn't say anything about meeting him there." Annette began to shuffle papers on her desk. "Is that all? I have a lot of work to do."

"Just one more thing," Malloy said. "Did Mrs. Vogel have a planner or an appointment book?"

"She had a planner that she took back and forth." She rose and went to the other desk, opened the side drawer, and pulled out a black appointment book. "Oh, she left it here."

Annette passed it to Malloy and sat down again. He flipped through the most recent pages, then handed the appointment book back to her.

"Can you identify any appointments in the last month that might be out of the ordinary?" he asked as she took the book.

Ms. Fulton scanned the names and identified business meetings with contractors and other customers.

"I saw several notations for RM," Malloy said. "Reminders about phone calls and sending documents. Do you know who it is?"

"That's Ronald Murphy, her lawyer."

"Thank you for your time, Ms. Fulton," Malloy said.

Malloy felt all eyes upon him as he made his way back through the store. He unlocked and got into his car. As he backed out of his parking space, a silver Lexus screeched into the owner's parking space. Todd Vogel slammed his car door and stormed into the building.

There goes an angry man, Malloy thought as he pulled out of the parking lot.

CHAPTER 33

Roberto entered Betty's Café, locating Davenport in a booth near the back, drinking coffee. Roberto slipped into the seat across from him. When the waitress left with Roberto's order, Davenport said, "Thank you for accepting my invitation and last night's phone call regarding the Vogels' affairs. I'm meeting both Julie Barnes and Bruce Cook after breakfast."

"I feel like a spy," Roberto admitted, "but I thought it might be important."

"I must confess I have an ulterior motive in speaking to you away from my office," Davenport said. "Tensions are a bit high there now."

"I sensed that yesterday, with the local DPS staff."

"And within my team as well," Davenport admitted. "I hoped you might help me learn more about the workers and their families. I don't understand why they are reluctant to talk to us, and when they do, they lie."

Roberto smiled and leaned back as the waitress returned with their food. "I'm sure the residents of The Havens also lie," Roberto countered, "you just don't understand Mexican motives." Roberto paused as he took a few bites of egg. "In Mexican culture family is most important, especially among the poor. Everyone is expected to protect their family, even when it might be unwise."

"That happened here," Davenport said. He told Roberto about the box of items Paula Gonzalez had turned over to him, and his suspicion that Carlos had covered for Julio. "They don't lie, so much as omit important details."

"It's why Carlos helped Julio get a job even though he feared

194

his cousin might be a thief," Roberto added. "In my job, I learned that this is common in Mayan villages."

"You're not Mayan?" Davenport asked.

"My family moved to Merida from Mexico City when I was in *prepa*—high school. Claire and I met thirty years ago when I was a police recruit and she was a graduate student teaching English in Merida. We met again last year when Claire assisted in my murder and smuggling case. She knows Mayan culture and language."

"So, you're meeting her family for the first time?"

Roberto smiled. "Yes, and bad timing, I think."

Davenport finished his coffee. "One member of my team is concerned about your connection with the Aguila family and their relationship with Carlos and the workers."

"I understand their concern," Roberto smiled, "but there's no Mexican plot here." Both men paused as the waitress refilled their coffee cups and took their plates.

"In fact," Roberto said, "I have another possible piece of evidence." He told Davenport about Claire's almost-accident at the back entrance to The Havens, near the G&G. "It happened Sunday night about midnight and might fit the timeline for the death of Mr. Gonzalez—of course I don't know your theory about his death, but I thought it might be important. Would you like to speak to Claire?"

"Yes, thank you," Davenport said. "It's probably unrelated, but she should make a report."

"Carlos said you consider Julio's death a suicide. Is that true?"

"We suspect remorse," Davenport explained. "Killing himself with the murder weapon and jewelry was an admission of guilt."

Roberto leaned forward, his elbows on the table, index fingers tented at his mouth. "But Julio could have gotten rid of all of it. Doesn't that seem strange? Why bring attention to himself?"

"That's why I'm still investigating," Davenport admitted.

"Something is wrong with this scenario."

"I agree," Roberto said.

The waitress approached with the check, but Davenport took it as Roberto reached for it. "My invitation," Davenport said, glancing at his watch.

Roberto sat quietly as Davenport called Julie Barnes. He tried to control the adrenaline rush he felt inside himself as Davenport prepared for his day in the hunt for the truth.

"Would you like to go with me," Davenport asked as he ended the call, "or do you have plans with Claire?" He smiled slightly, noting how Roberto's face lit up at the offer.

"I'd love to," he said, jumping up from the table. "When the women learned I had a breakfast date with you, they went shopping, and Martín is mowing the golf course. I feel like a fifth wheel—is that what you say in English?"

Davenport smiled. "Yes, that's it."

"In fact," Roberto said, "I hoped you would offer." He followed Davenport from the restaurant. "You can teach me about wealthy American culture, like Claire taught me about the Maya. So far I find it all baffling; I think she called it culture shock."

◆ ◆ ◆ ◆ ◆

Detectives Salinas and Davenport pulled into the driveway at the end of Sea Horse Lane, several blocks from the Vogel house. The home of Julie and Steve Barnes dwarfed all others in the neighborhood, taking up two lots of perfectly manicured St. Augustine grass. Tall windows with decorative etching dominated the front of the house, and an attached three-stall garage hinted at an RV or boat.

Roberto whistled. "Five Mexican families could live in this house, and two more in the garage," he said. "Are you sure the husband isn't home?"

"She asked us to come in the morning because her husband plays golf—I think she suspects the reason for our visit."

"Don't you think it's risky for Mr. Vogel and Mrs. Barnes to live so close?"

"It's no different from any small town," Davenport laughed. "Besides, we don't know for sure that they're having an affair. Your source is a bunch of ladies."

"Fair enough," Roberto said as they approached the front door.

The woman who answered the ring was of medium height with black hair tied back in a ponytail. She wore a black capri leotard, yoga shirt, and no makeup. "I didn't expect two of you," she said as she let them in. She cast a careful look at the Mexican man. "I hope this won't take long. I have a yoga session soon."

"We won't be long," Davenport promised. "Detective Salinas is in the United States for a conference and is visiting friends in The Havens for a few days. He asked if he could shadow me to see how we do things here." He gave Salinas an apologetic smile.

Roberto reached out to shake her hand. "I hope you don't mind."

"Since I am not sure what this is about, I guess I can't complain," she said, offering them chairs in her living room. High vaulted ceilings and tall windows gave the room a cathedral feel. Julie sat on the leather sofa and crossed one leg under her. "How can I help you?"

"We're investigating the death of Barbara Vogel," Davenport said, "and talking to people who might have known the Vogel family."

"It's awful," Julie said without emotion, "but I didn't know her very well."

"Can you tell me *how* you knew her?" Davenport asked.

"We're both members of the country club. I golf regularly, but I don't think she particularly enjoyed golf—she golfed with Todd in charity outings."

"Did you know her from any other activities?" Davenport pressed.

"We didn't socialize," Julie said, shrugging. "She used to play bridge at The Lodge, but not lately. She goes to The Ashram and the New You Fitness Center."

Julie wrinkled her nose as she rearranged her legs on the sofa. "I go to a private gym in Garland. The facility here is so full, it's hard to get a class, and there aren't any private sessions. Classes are full of people who aren't really serious. They start in January, take up slots, but by March they are done with it and back to eating donuts, and then in April, before the warmer pool weather, they're at it again."

Roberto leaned back, struggling to maintain a neutral façade. He wondered if English had a word like *narcisista*.

Davenport leaned forward. "I've heard that you and Mr. Vogel are involved. Is that true?"

Julie sat upright, returning her feet to the floor. "Who told you that?"

"It's just a rumor, but we have to check it out."

"I don't understand what this is all about. I thought you had your killer. Why are you bothering me? My relationship with Todd is none of your business."

"We still have to look at all the angles," Davenport said. "Since Mr. Gonzalez is dead, we can't interview him, nor can he go on trial. We need to ascertain he was the one responsible."

"This is ridiculous—and harassment." She threw a quick glance at Roberto. "Did the Mexican government send someone here to get involved?"

"Involved in what?" asked Davenport.

"Exonerating their citizens." She glanced at Roberto again. "Sorry, but why was Julio here anyway—a thief and murderer?"

Roberto shook his head. "I didn't know Mr. Gonzalez, and

I'm not here to speak on his behalf. I understand he had been here awhile, and that his wife and children are U.S. citizens."

Julie returned his gaze, touching her face with her fingers. "Isn't that what they all do?"

Davenport saw Roberto raise his eyebrows and lean back in his chair. "You're evading the question," Davenport said.

Julie sat back and crossed her arms. "Barbara manipulated Todd. She held it over him every day that she had the money." She smiled then, a smile that chilled Roberto. "Besides, she had affairs too…and I mean affairs, in the plural."

"Do you know with whom?" Davenport asked.

Julie reached up and pulled her hair out of her ponytail, letting it fall seductively around her face. "Bruce Cook, for one."

"And the others?"

"I know of one other, an older man. I don't think he lives here, but my friends have seen them. He looks rich, I hear."

"Do you know if Mr. Vogel planned to divorce his wife?"

"I don't know. Maybe, but I don't think he could afford to leave her. She owned the business."

"But they had problems?" Roberto asked.

Julie shrugged. "We all do, don't we?"

"Are you in love with Mr. Vogel?" Davenport asked.

"I thought I loved him," she said slowly, biting her lip, "but now I'm not sure."

"What changed?" Davenport asked.

"He's been more distant in the past few weeks," she said, reclining on the sofa again. "He said things would be better for us soon, but when he suspected that Barbara might divorce him, he acted like he wasn't happy about it."

"Money aside, isn't that what you both wanted?" Davenport asked. "For him to get divorced, I mean."

She shrugged. "At one time, but now I hear the police are questioning him. Do you think he killed Barbara?"

"What do you think?" Roberto asked.

"He couldn't even stand up to her, let alone kill her."

"Does your husband know about your affair?"

"He's even weaker than Todd. He would pout if he knew. And he wouldn't kill anyone, if that's what you're wondering."

CHAPTER 34

"Whew," Davenport said as they got into his car. "That was ugly."

Roberto fastened his seat belt. "What do you think?"

"I don't see her as a murderer, do you?"

They drove in silence toward The Hub. Roberto agreed with his companion, but he wondered about the American rich and their reluctance to think outside the comfortable boxes they constructed, with people like Julio Gonzalez safely excluded.

"We're meeting Mr. Cook at the DPS," Davenport said as they pulled into the parking lot. He noticed a silver Audi parked in the guest lot. Inside, Patsy scrutinized Roberto as he followed Davenport into the reception area. She pointed toward a lean man with gray-streaked black hair, who sat on one of the plastic chairs lining the wall, his leg bouncing uncontrollably.

"Mr. Cook?" Davenport asked. "Thank you for coming in. This is Detective Salinas, who is here as an observer. That is, if you don't mind."

Bruce Cook stood and shook hands with both men. "It's okay. I'm not sure how I can help you, though."

Cook followed Davenport and Roberto into the office, Davenport clearing off a section of his desk before sitting down. "I apologize for the untidiness. My team is sharing an office here. You probably know I'm here from the Gardenia County Sheriff's Department to investigate the murders of Barbara Vogel and Julio Gonzalez." He directed the two men to sit.

Davenport pulled a digital recorder from under a stack of papers. "Do you mind if I tape our conversation?"

Cook stared at the device and cleared his throat. "No, it's

okay." He rested his right ankle on his left knee, which did not still the tremor in his legs. "Though, I thought the cases were already solved."

"We still have some ends to tie up," Davenport said as he started the recorder. "This is just for our records." Cook didn't look convinced. His dark eyes, narrow and deep-set into a narrow face, moved from one detective to the other.

"Mr. Cook, what do you do for a living?" Davenport asked.

"I'm a retired chef," he said, then smiled slightly. "Yes, I'm a chef named Cook. It does happen."

"Do chefs actually retire?" Roberto asked. "It seems it would be hard to stop if you enjoy it."

"You're right," Cook said. "I'm often hired to cater events here, much to the chagrin of Chef Pierre at The Oasis. But I do it less expensively and have a more—how do I say—mainstream clientele. The more status-conscious hire Chef Pierre." He sighed heavily, his hands pressed on his jittery legs.

Roberto, noting Mr. Cook's nervousness, said, "In Mexico, it would be Chef Pedro. It doesn't have the same—how do you say—sophistication?"

Cook smirked. "It's all pretension—his name is Pete."

Davenport appreciated how Roberto had calmed Mr. Cook. He smiled and asked, "How well did you know Barbara Vogel?"

The directness of the question startled Cook, and to the surprise of both detectives, his eyes filled with tears.

"Sir?" asked Davenport. "I am sorry to have to ask you about this."

Cook wiped his eyes with the sleeve of his Hawaiian shirt. "I loved her."

"Did she love you?" Davenport asked.

"I think so."

"Does your wife know?" Davenport asked.

"I don't think so," he said.

Roberto doubted that. This was clearly an emotional man. "Did Mr. Vogel know?" he asked.

"I don't know."

"How did you meet?" Davenport asked.

"Barbara chaired the hospitality committee for The Lodge. She planned community or private parties and dinners." He sniffled again, and Davenport reached for a tissue from a box on the opposite desk. "We met when she was planning a wedding reception that I catered for two widowed people in their 70s. Barbara loved planning it. She had so many ideas for celebrating the event—the decorations and music."

Roberto asked, "How long had you been having an affair with Mrs. Vogel?"

Cook thought about this. "About two years, off and on. From time to time, one of us would break it off to work on our marriages, but we always came back to each other."

Davenport asked, "And recently?"

Cook shrugged and placed his hands on his knees to control his trembling legs. "Barbara had finally decided to file for divorce. She was sick of his drinking and neglect of their business." He sniffled again and wadded the tissue. "Her accountant learned that Todd—and their son—had been using expense accounts for non-business trips and had falsified vouchers. That was the end of it for her."

"Barbara wanted a divorce so she would have more control of the business?" Davenport asked.

Cook smiled a crooked smile. "I'd like to think she wanted a divorce so she could marry me. Besides, she already owned both businesses. Couldn't she just fire her husband?"

Davenport smiled. "That would be an interesting scenario, Mr. Cook."

"If she divorced Todd, would you divorce your wife?" Roberto asked.

Cook turned somber and his knee moved up and down. "If Barbara would have me, I would."

"What would you say if you learned that Barbara had another lover?" Davenport asked.

Cook leaned back. "It's not true. My wife heard the rumor from her bridge group, about this older man, and I let the story ride—sorry to say—because it took attention away from me."

"How do you know it's not true?" Davenport asked.

Cook stroked his nose, thinking, and his legs became still. "I confronted Barbara about it. She laughed and told me he was her attorney who flew down from time to time to meet with her and Todd about the business. She had been consulting him about a divorce."

"Do you know his name?" Davenport asked.

"She called him Ronnie. I don't know his last name."

"Is that your silver Audi in the parking lot?" Davenport asked.

"Yes."

"Were you at Barbara's house between seven o'clock and midnight Saturday night?" The detectives watched Cook collapse back into his chair. "I need to ask," Davenport said.

"Are you asking if I killed the woman I love?" His hands shook. "That's insane!"

"I didn't ask that. I asked where you were."

"At the Garland Holiday Inn. My wife and I had a horrible argument, and I needed to get away."

"Did you argue about Barbara?" Davenport asked.

Davenport had trapped him. Having stated his wife did not know anything, what else could they have argued about that would send him to a hotel?

"I'd rather not say," he said.

Davenport fiddled with the recorder. "Perhaps we need to check with the hotel…or ask your wife where she was during those times?"

"Are you joking?" Cook's voice raised an entire octave. He stood unsteadily, his hands resting on the desk for support, then slumped back into the chair. "I stayed at the hotel, but I visited Barbara around seven and stayed about two hours. She got a phone call and said I had to leave. I thought maybe she learned Todd was coming home early."

"Thank you for your honesty," Davenport said. "But for now, we do need your fingerprints and a DNA swab...for comparison."

"Comparison with what?"

"Evidence found at the scene."

Cook sat back heavily and pressed his lips together as he stared at Davenport. "Please don't tell my wife."

CHAPTER 35

"Okay, girls, I need your help." Amanda Davis returned from the kitchen, tapping the end-call button on her cellphone. She took her place at the bridge table and pushed her cards to the side.

"Who was that?" Harriet, Amanda's partner, asked, placing her pink glasses on top of her mass of chemically enhanced auburn curls.

Marianne frowned, working her fingers through short gray hair. "I thought we had a rule, no phone calls during our games."

"Hush, Marianne. This must be important," Harriet said, returning her gaze to Amanda.

Amanda sat back in her chair, studying her friends. "It's about Barbara," she said.

Marianne's partner, Fran, peered into her empty teacup. "Tell us."

"A Deputy Stokes is coming, again, to ask me questions. I told her my bridge group was here, and she asked if she could talk to all of us."

Harriet leaned back. "Poor Barbara," she said, her shoulders sagging. "I didn't know her as well as you all did, but it's terrible what happened."

"But we all knew her," insisted Amanda, her gaze moving from woman to woman.

"What do the police want to know?" Fran asked. "I thought it was solved."

"We've been interviewed twice and made a statement, but they still aren't satisfied," Amanda said in frustration.

"What have you told them?" asked Marianne.

Amanda frowned as she tasted her tepid tea. "That she canceled dinner to wait for Carlos, and for Todd's phone call."

"Was that the truth?" Harriet asked as the teakettle in the kitchen whistled.

Amanda followed the whistling into the kitchen. "More or less," she answered, returning to the table with a box of tea bags and the kettle. She passed the box around and refilled cups. "Jordan thinks he saw Bruce's car pull into her garage, but we didn't tell the police."

"You lied?" Fran asked sharply.

"Don't say that!" Amanda snapped then blushed and hurried to the kitchen to return the kettle and tea bags.

"I'm sorry," Amanda said when she returned to the table. She bit her lip as she saw Fran's mouth pucker in anger. "It's just been so stressful...Barbara and I, we were friends." She sat and reached for Fran's hand. "We didn't exactly lie, Fran. We didn't actually see Bruce, just his car." Amanda's guests, afraid to speak, simultaneously dipped their tea bags into the boiling liquid.

"Besides," Amanda said, after a heavy sigh, "the other car we saw showed up much later...we decided not to involve Bruce."

"What do we say if the officer asks about Bruce?" Marianne asked, breaking their silence.

"Say nothing," Amanda said. "Barbara's dead, what does it matter?"

"But shouldn't we help the police?" Harriet asked. "I mean, really, what's to hide?"

"What's to hide?" Marianne shook her head, unbelieving.

"Please, ladies, just answer the questions," Amanda pleaded. "Don't offer anything." She jumped up when the doorbell rang, and the labradoodle followed her to the door. "Remember, it's none of our business."

Amanda invited Detective Stokes in, introduced her to the group, and offered her a chair. The dog returned to its bed.

"Thank you for letting me interrupt your game. I'll only take a few minutes." Stokes sat and opened her notebook. "I'm hoping that Barbara's friends can provide some insight into her personality and tell me anything that might help us understand her death."

Marianne said, "We thought the murder was solved."

"It's always more complicated than it seems from the outside," Stokes said, smiling.

"No one would want to hurt Barbara," Harriet said.

Stokes considered these women, playing cards here instead of with the bridge club. "Is there a reason your group doesn't meet at The Lodge?" she asked.

A shuffling of feet and movement of eyes around the table ensued before Amanda spoke. "Several of us broke off from the group—we didn't like the noise and atmosphere—and Barbara preferred more intimate settings. If we're short a person, we find a substitute."

Harriet fiddled with her glasses, pushing them further back on her head. "I'm not usually in the group," she said, her lips quivering. "I guess I'm her substitute."

"But you all knew Barbara, correct?" Stokes coaxed.

Amanda folded her manicured hands on the table. "I knew her best. We've been neighbors since Jordan and I moved in four years ago. Unlike most of us, Barbara worked full-time and wasn't involved in social life."

"But she volunteered for special committees," Marianne said. "She liked to organize events."

Stokes turned to Amanda. "Have you or your husband spoken to Todd since Sunday?"

Amanda's hands pressed together on the table. "Not me, but Jordan talked to Todd Sunday night. He was worried about him and wanted to give his condolences. We were both concerned."

"It would be a natural thing to do," Stokes said, encouraging her. "Did your husband call Todd?"

Amanda nodded. "He called Todd and left a message. Todd called him back later from The Havens Inn. It was a private conversation."

Stokes looked over the ladies at the table, all sitting at rapt attention. "You're right, Mrs. Davis. It's totally understandable."

Stokes watched the ladies sit back in their chairs with obvious disappointment, collectively sipping their tea.

Stokes took a few moments to check her notes. Her gaze landed on a copy of the morning edition of *The Havens Gazette* lying on a lamp table next to her chair. The paper had been opened to a photograph of Julio's car at the scene of his death. She caught Amanda looking at her.

"I understand that Barbara and Todd worked together at the business," Stokes said, turning away from the *Gazette*. "That can be challenging. I'm not married, but I think it would be very hard for me to work with my husband if we were both cops," she said, her mind racing back to her failed relationship with Malloy.

"Barbara didn't talk much about their business," Fran offered.

Stokes looked at Amanda, who began to click her nails on the table and bite her cheek. "Amanda, did she talk to you about their business?"

Amanda surveyed her audience, their eyes wide, awaiting her response. "Jordan and I owned a business together, and sometimes Barbara and I talked about the challenges. She complained that Todd spent too much time away from the business, entertaining customers, and Todd complained to Jordan that Barbara didn't understand the sales side of the business—nothing unusual. Jordan and I had the same issues."

Marianne, who had been sitting quietly, her elbows on the table, nibbling a pinkie, broke her silence. "I hate to gossip, but my nephew works at the dealership part time—he's a college student—and he told me Barbara and Todd argued a lot. I guess her office has a window into the store, and it's a running joke with the employees that she'd give him a time-out, because he'd retreat to his office and wouldn't come out for hours."

"There's more to it than that," Fran persisted. "It's her business, not his. I heard that her parents only hired him into the company because he married Barbara. She has…had the brains."

"Did she talk to any of you about her marriage?" Stokes asked. "About divorce, for example? I'm sure you all complain among yourselves about your spouses."

"Well, yes," Fran offered, "but it doesn't mean anything."

Amanda's face reddened, and her eyes teared up. "We're all upset about Barbara. She was my friend, and I'm sad she's gone. But I feel numb, and I hate having to talk to the police all the time. I haven't had time to grieve…and probably won't until this is all over."

Stokes sat quietly through this exchange, regretting her intrusive questions. "I do understand your feelings," she said. "But it's important that we determine what happened to her. Please be patient with the process." She paused before asking the most intrusive question. "I heard that there may have been other people in their lives…is it true?"

Substantial shuffling occurred, and Fran blurted, "He had several affairs before she did."

"Is this why Barbara didn't want to play bridge at The Lodge?" Stokes asked. "Did life became a little complicated for her?"

Stokes looked at the women, one by one, and each nodded.

"She told me privately that she was thinking of divorce," Amanda admitted.

"Did she see any hope for reconciliation?" Stokes asked.

Amanda snorted. "She wanted Todd out of her business and out of her life."

CHAPTER 36

Madge and the Aguila women entered Maria's Mercado in the small community of Orchard. The pungent aroma of Mexican spices and baskets displaying colorful peppers—sweet and potent—immediately took Claire back to Merida. She closed her eyes and breathed deeply, absorbing the rich smells and recreating the memories of her last visit, when she and Roberto had become reacquainted.

Cristina also took a deep breath, but her expression was less blissful. "Wow, this is strong!"

"I've failed as a mother," Claire said.

Theresa pulled a shopping list from her purse. "I'm glad you suggested shopping here," she said to her companions. "It's a great idea to treat Roberto to a Mexican meal."

Claire took her mother's arm. "Just passing the small shops and bakery as we drove through Orchard made me nostalgic for Merida," she said.

Each woman grabbed a small basket before heading into the store. Claire had been assigned beans and spices for *pollo pibil,* a Yucatecan specialty of chicken wrapped in corn husks. Theresa chose the chicken thighs from the meat counter and wandered to the back of the store where a young salesclerk, with large dark eyes and a single braid down her back, disappeared into a back room. She emerged moments later with husks, cleaned of silk.

Her basket filled, Theresa found Cristina at the beer cooler, extracting two six-packs of Mexican beer. Claire joined them.

"See? You know your Mexican food," Claire teased as they joined the checkout line.

Madge emerged from the back of the store with tortilla chips, salsa, and spicy nuts. "You people have no snacks. That's why you're all so skinny." She joined them in line.

As they loaded the groceries in the car, Claire's phone rang. "Roberto's with Detective Davenport," she announced when she hung up. "He wants us to go to the DPS and give a report to Deputy Stokes on the near collision."

"Do they think it's important?" Theresa asked, getting into the passenger seat.

"It might mean something," Cristina said, settling next to Madge in the back seat.

As they drove along the same road they had traveled Sunday night, Claire asked, "Do you all remember what happened? I'm hoping you two had a better look at the car or driver than I did."

"It happened so fast," Cristina said, "and I was in the back seat."

"I had my eyes closed," Theresa admitted.

"Oh, great," Claire said, as she turned onto Brook Haven Road. "You two are a lot of help. I remember the car's color and the white man behind the wheel, and I was swerving."

Cristina snorted. "A white man in The Havens with a nice silver car? And you claim to be a trained observer?"

"Not when I'm trying to keep us alive." Claire smiled, glancing in her rearview mirror at Madge. "It's too bad Madge wasn't with us. She would have remembered."

"Hah," Madge said. "That's not what you thought when I rode shot-gun on our great murderer-chase."

"Look!" Cristina yelled from the back seat. "That vanity plate!"

"I ❤ The Havens?" Claire asked, reading the plate on an approaching car.

"No, not that, but I remember the car had an unusual plate, five capital letters with a hyphen. I think the first letter was an M."

♦ ♦ ♦ ♦ ♦

Pamela Stokes grimaced as she entered the shared office at The Havens DPS, carrying a copy of the *Gazette*. It wouldn't take a detective to see that Malloy had been there. She bristled as she scooped up a disposable coffee cup, empty sugar and creamer packets, and a take-out bag from Betty's Café. She threw the trash into the wastebasket, then settled into a chair, glancing at her watch. Davenport had asked her to come in to meet with the Aguila women—something about a near collision Sunday night around the time Julio died. *Why is this family so intertwined with the investigation?*

Underneath a small mound of crumbs, Stokes discovered a grease-stained note from Malloy. She slouched into her chair and read: "Hey, Pam, can you check on a Ronald Murphy—attorney from Chicago—and don't forget to check the yoga studio and the country club—your favorite places, I'm sure—for Mrs. Vogel's movements on Saturday. Have fun!"

Stokes wadded up the note and tossed it on the table. *Jerk,* she thought. As she waited for the Aguilas, she typed up her report from her own interview with the unofficial bridge club and from The Ashram, which she had already visited. She learned that Barbara took classes there and had come in that morning. However, no one knew her well; she went there to practice her yoga and kept to herself.

Having completed her report, Stokes placed a call to Glen Haven Country Club, setting up an interview with the manager and golf pro, Ben Stevens. As she sat back to make a note, Judy Barnaby knocked on the office door and stepped inside.

"There's a Claire Aguila Carson here, with her family and a hippy-lady," Judy snorted. "Can I send Ms. LaDiDa and Ms. Woodstock in?"

"I'll come out to greet them," Stokes said, curious about the hippy-lady. In the reception area, she was brought up short at the sight of Madge. *Hippy indeed!*

"This is Doctor Madge Carmichael, my colleague and friend," Claire explained. "She's staying with my family for a few days." Stokes shook hands with Claire, Cristina, Theresa, and Madge.

"I hope you don't mind me tagging along," Madge said, turning on her sweet-old-lady charm. "Claire has been showing me around. I'm looking for a retirement community for my husband, George, and myself."

Claire stared at her friend, attempting a straight face. First, although Madge and George had been married and divorced many years ago, they had not, to her knowledge, remarried. Second, she couldn't see Madge and George living in The Havens any more than she could envision her father living here. Strangely, however, she could imagine Madge careening around town in a golf cart.

"Thank you all for coming," Stokes said cautiously, "but it's a small office, and I need to talk to those involved in the incident."

"That's okay," Madge said, disappointed. She plopped into a molded plastic chair that barely fit her frame. "I'll just read the *Gazette*." She picked up a copy from the end table, and settled in.

◆ ◆ ◆ ◆ ◆

Back in the office, Stokes motioned for the ladies to sit. "It's nice to see you again," Stokes said, remembering their first meeting in the DPS parking lot. "Detective Davenport said that you might have some information about a car incident?"

Claire recounted the story as she remembered it, Cristina filling in details.

"Do you know what time this happened?" Stokes asked.

"Near midnight," Claire said. She described the car as well as she could. "I don't know cars, sorry to say, but it looked new, perhaps a Toyota? I remember a large grill coming at me."

"And Cristina saw a front vanity plate," Theresa said.

Cristina described the plate, apologizing for not seeing it more clearly. The women watched as Stokes wrote the information down.

"Do you remember anything about the gas and grocery store on the corner? Was it open or closed? Any cars in the parking lot?" Stokes asked.

Claire looked at her companions. "I remember that a car came up behind me when I pulled over. I motioned for it to pass. I needed to calm myself."

Cristina closed her eyes, as if to remember the scene. "When the car passed us, the headlights shone on the parking lot. The store was closed, but I remember a light-colored car parked in the lot."

"I remember," Theresa said. "It was white and kind of beat up."

"You saw no other cars there?" Stokes asked.

"No," Cristina said.

"Can you remember anything else?"

Theresa remembered the book group and turned to Claire. "Should we tell her about Elena?"

"Elena?" Stokes asked.

Theresa folded her hands on her lap. "Elena Huerta works for The Havens. She also does housekeeping for residents, including Mrs. Vogel. We talked to her Monday, and she seemed very upset about Mrs. Vogel's death."

"She also knew Mr. Gonzalez, who died," Claire added.

Stokes wrote her name down. "Thank you very much, ladies."

"Well, she didn't lie and tell us we were helpful to the investigation," Cristina laughed as they returned to the reception area.

"But she did seem interested in Elena," Theresa said as they joined Madge, who was still perusing the local newspaper.

"Guess what?" Madge said when she saw them enter. "There's a big dance in the plaza Thursday night. They call it 'Fiesta Night.' We have to go and meet the natives!"

CHAPTER 37

After the Aguila entourage left, Stokes jotted a note to herself to check on Elena Huerta. The office door opened again, and Malloy strolled in, carrying a food container and soft drink.

"So, you're back," Stokes said, "and you've brought more food…great. I don't suppose it's too much to ask you to clean up before you leave the office?"

"Hello to you, too," Malloy said as Stokes collected her notebook and stood to leave. "Where are you going?"

"To Glen Haven, per your orders. Did Davenport get run over by a golf cart and leave you in charge?"

Malloy placed his food on the desk and looked at Stokes. "What's the matter, Pam?" He saw the crumpled note on the table. "Come on, we're a team. It was a request, not an order."

Stokes sighed heavily as she moved past him and out the door. "Just clean up your garbage, okay?"

Malloy sat at the desk Stokes had vacated and moved her papers aside, making room for his own notebook and lunch. He glanced at the reminder Stokes had written to herself and left on the desk, "Claire Aguila—follow up on Elena Huerta."

Malloy picked up the note, sat back in the chair, and brought the note up to his face, brushing it across the stubble on his cheek. Despite his bravado, he understood her anger. Stokes should have gotten the interim position. She worked harder than he did, and was, he admitted, a smarter cop. He wondered, if she had gotten the position, if they would still be together. How would he have reacted? He returned the note and began typing up the report from his meeting at Denton Sales.

Before he had finished the first paragraph, the office door flew open and Judy stampeded in, closing the door behind her. "Scott...er...Detective Malloy...it's getting crazy here." She threw herself into the chair opposite his desk.

"What is it, Judy?" Malloy grunted. "Can't you knock?"

While Malloy shared the view of the others that Judy was a busybody, he had come to appreciate the tidbits of information she shared with him concerning the—often salacious—behavior of the local baby boomers.

"I gotta tell ya, it's like collusion." She separated two fistfuls of hair from her ponytail and pulled to tighten it. "Did you know Davenport took that Mexican detective—if he is one—on his interviews today? Shouldn't you be working with him?"

Judy had hit a nerve and knew it. She sat back and raised her eyebrows, waiting for a response. Malloy didn't understand it either, but he knew better than to express his concerns with her. "I'm sure there's nothing going on. Davenport sent me to Denton's Sales Office, and he likely invited him along as a courtesy."

Judy huffed. "And what about that Mrs....Doctor....what's her name? I hate these two-last-name women."

"What about her?" asked Malloy, picking up Stokes's note and rereading it.

"Well, she's the daughter of a suspect, she parades in here with a crazy lady, and she leaves, smiling at me as if we're best friends...I don't get it."

"Maybe they had some information."

Judy sat back in the chair and crossed her arms. "I don't know why Davenport doesn't just close the case."

The door banged open again, and Todd Vogel stormed in. Patsy followed behind, her stride no match for her prey.

"I'm sorry, I couldn't get him to wait," Patsy said, breathing heavily.

Judy stood and offered Todd her chair. She and Patsy lingered in the doorway until Malloy gave them a wave, and they reluctantly closed the door behind them.

Todd placed his hands on the desk and leaned toward Malloy.

"Please sit down, Mr. Vogel."

"Where's Davenport?"

"He's in Garland at the Sheriff's Department. Can I help you?"

"I need to know what's going on," Todd said, ignoring the offered chair.

"Detective Davenport is meeting with the coroner and crime scene team today. Our team is meeting tonight, and we should have more information for you tomorrow."

Todd's jaw clenched. "Not that…on how the investigation is being handled."

Malloy blinked. "You better sit down."

Todd sat, but leaned forward, his hands pressing against his thighs. "It's about this Mexican conspiracy," he said.

"Conspiracy?" Malloy felt a quiver of *déjà vu*.

"First, I see this Martín Aguila guy with Carlos, a suspect; then I see him at dinner with a Mexican they say is a cop, and then I hear that this so-called cop is doing interviews with Davenport."

"Who told you he conducted interviews?" Malloy asked.

"A friend…it doesn't matter," Todd said. "Don't you think it's strange? It looks like a conspiracy…or crime syndicate."

"Crime syndicate?" Malloy said.

"Aguila's got money." Todd told Malloy about the gold card and the dinner at the country club.

Malloy fiddled with the papers on his desk. "Just because he has a deluxe credit card and eats out doesn't mean he's a mobster."

"But he's only been here a short time. When did the robberies start? Wasn't it about the same time?"

Malloy thought about this. "He's staying at a friend's house. I don't think there's anything strange there." But Malloy scribbled a note to check on the dates. "Is there anything else, Mr. Vogel?"

"I want *you* to check them out," Todd said, his voice hard.

"The detective *and* Mr. Aguila?"

"Of course."

"I can't do that on your word," Malloy said, "but I'll pass your concerns on to Detective Davenport."

Todd thought about this. "What if Davenport's compromised? Can't you handle it?"

Malloy considered. "I'll see what I can do." He studied Todd's face, haggard and worried. "We'll have more information on your wife's murder tomorrow."

Todd looked confused. "Oh, yes, I'd appreciate that."

CHAPTER 38

Late Afternoon

Davenport sat with Malloy and Stokes around the oval conference table at the Gardenia County Sheriff's Department, shuffling documents and photographs. The air-conditioning no longer gave relief as the late afternoon sun blazed through the windows. Stokes had unbuttoned the top button of her uniform and let her hair out of its bun, allowing it to cascade over her shoulders. This action had not been lost on Malloy, who had partially untied his tie and undone his top button. Only the detective-sergeant left his clothing intact, except his sports coat.

"Where's Powers?" asked Stokes. "I haven't seen him since yesterday."

Davenport laughed. "He called in sick. He blames dumpster diving in the rain, but he's still checking Vogel's contacts in Orlando. He'll be back tomorrow."

"Working from home," Malloy said, raising his eyebrows. "Brilliant."

Davenport sorted his papers into piles. "Let's get this done so you two can get home before dark tonight."

"That would be great, sir," said Malloy, "I have a date." He shot a quick glance at Stokes and winked at her.

"Is it prom already?" Stokes chided, tucking her hair behind her ears.

"What? You don't have a date?" Malloy quipped.

"We have a lot to discuss, if you don't mind," Davenport said, raising his eyebrows.

Davenport shuffled through his notes. "Yesterday, I asked

Carlos Chavez to come to the DPS. I wanted to ask him about the jewelry in the book bag. I was surprised when Detective Salinas and Mr. Aguila brought him into the office—they had spoken to Carlos at The Barn.

Malloy bristled. "They interviewed Carlos?"

Davenport stared at Malloy as he adjusted his glasses. "They were visiting with Carlos when Powers called him into the DPS. Carlos had told Martín and Salinas that Paula Gonzalez knows something about her husband's actions lately—things she hadn't disclosed to me." He folded his hands on the table, keeping his focus on Malloy, whose gaze flitted from his boss to Stokes. "Detective Salinas told Carlos that Paula should talk to me— what any officer would say—to tell me what she knows, and they brought him in."

"What did Paula know?" Stokes asked, to break the tension.

Davenport turned his attention to Stokes. "Carlos denied knowing anything about the jewelry in the book bag, but he arranged for me to visit Paula. He was right. She had found a box filled with miscellaneous items, jewelry, and knick-knacks that more or less prove Julio was stealing. Inside the larger box, Julio had hidden a metal cash box that contained more than five thousand dollars." He paused for effect. "What does that tell us?"

"It proves he was a thief," Malloy said. "Why did Carlos and Paula think it would exonerate Julio?"

"Paula pleaded with us that Julio would not kill anyone, but she thinks he became involved in something illegal. She found a phone with one number on it, and he had been acting strangely and lying to her."

"Where's the phone?" Malloy asked.

"She never saw it again…something to look for."

"But Barbara's jewelry wasn't in the box," Stokes said. "Why was it in the book bag alongside the jewelry she wore that night?"

"Maybe he didn't have time," Malloy argued. "That's why he

threw it in the bag."

"That still makes no sense to me," Stokes argued.

"It doesn't prove he killed Barbara," Davenport agreed. "Let's move on."

Davenport picked up a thin, stapled report. "We now have swabs from Mrs. Vogel, Julio, Mr. Vogel, and Mr. Cook. They're rushing the lab comparisons on the linen, but it'll take time."

"Did we learn anything new from fingerprints?" Malloy asked.

"Mostly the Vogels' prints." Davenport skimmed the report. "They found several partials on the master bathroom doors and front door handle, but no hits back on the database, so whoever was there isn't in our system." He skimmed down a few lines. "Actually, they did find something unexpected—an index fingerprint on the refrigerator, above the dispenser panel. It seems that Drew Vogel had visited recently."

"Drew?" asked Malloy.

"It could've been there awhile," Stokes considered.

"That's what we need to find out. It seems he has a police record for impaired driving." He read on. "Mrs. Vogel's phone shows a call from Drew in the early evening. It didn't last long—several minutes."

"To see if she was home?" Stokes suggested.

"Perhaps," Davenport said. "Or just a brief conversation."

"What about the footprints?" Malloy asked.

Davenport flipped a page. "The lab techs are confident that the footprints among the plants lining the birdcage are consistent with the size and pattern of Julio's shoes. The splotch of blood—that Ryan claimed was from a box cutter at work— is likely from Julio's fresh wound, and there's no evidence he entered the Vogel house."

When Davenport's phone rang, Stokes and Malloy waited, silent tension between them, until they heard Davenport say, "You need to come in and change your statement." He punched the end button. "Well," he said, "Jordan Davis now says that the photograph of Julio's car, published in the *Gazette*, resembles the car they saw in the driveway around ten o'clock Saturday night."

"I saw that photograph at Amanda Davis's house. The *Gazette* was open on a table. She saw me look at it." Stokes grabbed her copy of the *Gazette* and turned to the page in question. "Is that their third statement?" she asked.

"Yes, and I wonder what's going on," Davenport said.

"I don't think it's so odd," Malloy said. "They didn't get a good look the first time. Now, it registered with them."

"Very convenient, I think," said Stokes.

Davenport sighed and turned a page in his report. "We need to move on to the gun or we'll never finish." He read, "The only prints on the gun are those of Mr. Gonzalez."

"Why is that unusual?" Malloy asked. "He killed Mrs. Vogel, then killed himself."

Stokes pursed her lips. "Think about it, Scott. How did Julio know about the gun? He came to rob a house, not kill someone. It wasn't his gun. The only prints on the sideboard, where they kept the gun, belonged to the Vogels. Their prints should also be on the gun."

Malloy shrugged. "The obvious answer," he said, "is that she went to the drawer for the gun, and he took it from her. He wiped the gun clean after killing her."

Stokes sat back and crossed her arms. "So, you say that he didn't plan to take it at first, wiped it clean, but got nervous, or heard something, and took it. Then later, he decided to kill himself with it?" Stokes bit her lower lip. "There's something I don't like about the robbery/murder/suicide scenario floating around."

"What are you thinking?" Davenport asked.

"The murderer tied her up. Why shoot her? She couldn't take the gun from the drawer if she's tied up. Why not rob her and leave?"

"She could identify him," Malloy said.

"We don't know if he wore a mask," Stokes admitted, "but from what we know about Julio, he was a petty thief, not a murderer."

Malloy tapped his fingers on the table in irritation. "She surprised him," Malloy suggested. "She pulled out the gun, he took it, tied her up, stole the jewelry, then got scared that she would identify him, and killed her. Later, he felt remorse and killed himself. Let it go."

"So, when did he rape her?" Stokes asked, sarcasm in her voice. "I'm not convinced..." She looked to Davenport, who waved her to proceed. "Julio wants citizenship. He's not a smart man, because he takes to stealing, but all the thefts take place when homes are empty. Why does he choose this house? If he stood outside he would have seen her, and we have no evidence he entered. Could he go into a house and not leave a trace?" Stokes paused to think. "If he did go in, why toss the jewelry into the bag Carlos gave him and then kill himself? Why leave his wife in a terrible situation of holding stolen items? It doesn't make sense."

"He was a liar," Malloy persisted. "He lied to Ryan about switching his hours. He lied to his wife, his boss, and his friends. He stole, and he had opportunity." He glared at Stokes. "Why are we bending over backwards to defend this guy?"

Davenport listened to the debate. When they had stopped for air, he said, "Indeed, he did lie about stealing, but I agree with Stokes that it's doubtful he would kill himself." He paused to flip through his notebook. "I think we've been looking at this all wrong."

"What now?" Malloy said testily.

"Are we looking at a frame-up?" Stokes asked. "That would explain the jewelry in the bag, and the lack of evidence that Julio entered the Vogel house...but it would also mean Julio was murdered."

"Exactly," said Davenport. "That puts us back to square one."

CHAPTER 39

"Back to Mrs. Vogel, you mean?" Stokes asked. "Now that both deaths are likely murders, are we looking for the person who killed them both?"

"For now," Davenport said, "we can say the deaths are connected, and Julio's death unlikely a suicide." He turned to Malloy. "What did you find out at the dealership?"

"I talked to the assistant sales manager, the purchasing agent, and the accountant," Malloy reported. "The sales and purchasing agents are men who worked closely with Mr. Vogel; the accountant, Annette Fulton, worked with Mrs. Vogel in the office. Annette and Mrs. Vogel knew each other from Chicago. There's tension between sales and accounting. Both Annette and Barbara felt the salesmen spent too much money schmoozing construction executives with golf and casino incentives."

"Did you ask about Todd and Barbara's relationship within the company?" Stokes asked. "Any sign of troubles in the family?"

"Ms. Fulton was protective of Barbara and had little to say about their marriage. She worried about what would happen to the business if they divorced."

Malloy pulled something from his satchel. "I did manage to get Mrs. Vogel's planner. Most entries are business-related, but the most intriguing is Ronald Murphy, her attorney."

"Anything else?" Davenport asked.

"Something interesting," Malloy said. "Mr. Vogel arrived at Denton's just as I pulled out. He stormed out of his car and into the store. I didn't attempt to talk to him, and I don't think he noticed me."

"He seemed angry, not grieved?" Stokes asked. "Isn't that odd?"

"I'm not sure, but I wouldn't want to be on the other side of that door," Malloy said. "Maybe an employee called and warned him about me, and he thought he might catch me interviewing his employees."

"Interesting," Davenport said, adjusting his glasses. "Who looked into Mr. Murphy?"

"I checked him out," Stokes said. "He's been the personal and business attorney for the Denton family for years. He gave me the 'attorney-client' spiel. I gave him the 'murder exemption to the attorney-client' spiel, and he said he would contact us in the next few days, after he talked to his clients."

Davenport skimmed through the planner as Stokes gave her report. When she finished, he asked, "What did you learn from Amanda Davis?"

"Besides Amanda's interest in Julio's car," Stokes said, "I learned that Barbara's bridge group doesn't meet at The Lodge with the other players. I'm afraid I didn't learn much more than we've already surmised—that both Mr. and Mrs. Vogel were having affairs. Not surprisingly, her friends supported Barbara's motives for infidelity and cursed her husband's."

"You learned nothing new?" Malloy asked, raising his eyebrows.

"I learned that they avoid The Lodge because both Julie Barnes and Bruce Cook's wife play bridge there—very awkward," Stokes said. "They also confirmed tension between Barbara and Todd about the business. Apparently, Barbara wanted her husband out of her business and out of her life…and that's a quote." She gave Malloy a quick wink.

"Go on," Davenport said.

"As for her day," Stokes continued, "she attended her yoga class Saturday morning, but the receptionist didn't know her well enough to add anything else." She thumbed through her notes. "Ben Stevens, the golf pro at the Glen Haven Country Club, hasn't seen Mrs. Vogel for awhile and admitted that the Vogels' membership was suspended for unpaid dues. So, we might want to look into their finances."

Davenport nodded. "Especially considering what Malloy learned at the dealership. But that reminds me," he said, scanning the report, "there's something about golf and golf bags in the crime scene report. Here it is—the team found Mrs. Vogel's golf bag in the hall closet, but didn't find Mr. Vogel's bag anywhere on the premises."

"How do you tell a man's golf bag from a woman's?" asked Malloy.

Stokes rolled her eyes. "A preponderance of the color pink, breast-cancer club covers, stuffed animals, and probably every club in its proper place…"

Davenport gave her a quick glance, and Stokes bit her lip. "Sorry, sir," she said.

"His clubs are likely in his locker at Glen Haven," Davenport said. "He golfs often, she doesn't. But we should ask Mr. Vogel about them."

"We haven't checked his car," Stokes said, suddenly remembering something else. "Didn't Alice tell Powers something about a golf bag in the car?"

"She did! Damn!" Davenport said, shuffling through the reports.

"Here we go again," Malloy said, sitting back and crossing his arms.

"Still a suspect," Davenport reminded him. "Let's find out if he took them to Orlando."

Davenport found Powers's report from the first day. "Yes, Alice told Powers that Todd struggled to get his suitcase out of his trunk because of the golf bag. Good job, Stokes."

"Kudos to Powers," Stokes said, giving the absent deputy credit for his report. "Can't we get a search warrant? If we ask him about his clubs, he can get rid of the evidence."

"That's a risk we'll have to take," Davenport said. "As of now, we don't have enough to get a warrant. We have the gun, but we need more."

Davenport gave Malloy a quick glance. "I asked Detective Salinas to join me for breakfast to discuss Mexican culture and help me understand Carlos's behavior. As a courtesy, and because he had given me the heads-up, I invited him to accompany me on my interviews with Julie Barnes and Bruce Cook."

He noted the look of curiosity on Stokes's face and disgust on Malloy's.

"At first," Davenport continued, "Julie denied an affair, but ended up arguing that Barbara made Todd's life miserable by holding the business and the money over his head. It seems Todd suspected his wife was planning a divorce. However, Julie implied that her relationship with Todd was waning. She might have been losing interest in him since she learned that his financial prospects were not up to her expectations. It'll be important to talk to that lawyer about the Vogels' finances. For the record, Julie's not a pleasant person. She even made sure we knew Barbara also had a lover. She named Bruce Cook."

Davenport sat back in his chair. "Detective Salinas asked me if I knew what 'narcisista'—or something like that—meant, which says it all about Mrs. Barnes. She implied some sort of conspiracy in which Detective Salinas had become involved to protect Mexican workers." Davenport sighed. "Salinas took it well, but it wasn't pretty."

"But it does seem like the workers are the most likely suspects," Malloy reasoned, "and we appear to be eliminating them from the investigation."

Davenport frowned. "We aren't eliminating anyone, which

brings us to Bruce Cook, who didn't deny the affair. He admitted he would have liked to marry Mrs. Vogel and that he was at her house between seven and nine. Unfortunately for him, he didn't have an alibi for the time between nine o'clock p.m. and midnight. He admitted he spent the night in a hotel, but when we requested fingerprints and the DNA test, he begged for discretion. It seems he owns that silver car Mrs. Van Dee saw enter the garage."

"And perhaps he owns the fingerprints on the doors and the DNA on the sheets," Stokes mused.

"A distinct possibility," Davenport said. "Is there anything else?"

Malloy cleared his throat. "There is something else," he admitted. "It's about Martín Aguila and Detective Salinas."

Davenport sighed. "Go on."

"Mr. Vogel came in today. He's suspicious of Mr. Aguila because he moved here about the same time as the robberies, and he seems to have a lot of money."

"And?" Davenport asked.

"Vogel saw Aguila at the pro shop where he paid the Carsons' membership dues. The Aguilas drive a nice car and live in a nice house. It seemed strange to him. And then Aguila is a friend of Carlos, who is still a suspect...or should be."

Stokes glared at him. "A Mexican-American man shouldn't have money?"

"It's the whole family," Malloy said, turning to face Stokes. "They're pushing themselves into the investigation. Judy told me you spoke to the daughter at the DPS today, and that you both acted friendly."

"No," Stokes said, her voice terse. "You're wrong. She came in with her mother and daughter to report a near accident at the G&G Sunday night, around midnight." She gave Malloy a defiant look. "Detective Davenport told me to expect her."

Davenport nodded, and Malloy paled. "What about this?" Malloy accused, holding up the note with Elena Huerta's name.

"They gave us a lead on a witness." Stokes sat back and crossed her arms. "Mrs. Huerta is an employee of The Havens who cleaned house for Mrs. Vogel—which I forgot to report—sorry sir," she said to Davenport. "Doctor Aguila is not a friend, but she is involved peripherally because her parents live here, and Mr. Aguila knows the workers. That's not a crime."

"So, she and her family are interviewing witnesses now?" Malloy said.

"*I* will be interviewing Elena Huerta tomorrow," Stokes said stiffly. "I invited Doctor Aguila because I felt Elena might be more comfortable with a Spanish speaker."

"But *Doctor* Aguila brought this Mexican cop into town," Malloy stammered, turning to Davenport again. "I know you worked with him today, sir, but he shows up and suddenly he's part of the investigation."

"Are you questioning my judgment?" Davenport asked, leveling his eyes on Malloy.

"No, sir, I'm only reporting what Mr. Vogel said."

"Which mirrors what Julie Barnes said today, with less subtlety," Davenport said.

"Even Judy talked about it," Malloy said, wincing at this acknowledgment.

Davenport leaned forward. "What did Mr. Vogel want you to do?"

"He wanted me to check up on Mr. Aguila and Detective Salinas."

"And did you?" Malloy nodded.

"Without my authority?"

"I told him I couldn't—without your permission—but he thought that…"

"That I might be compromised?" Davenport asked.

"I'm sorry, sir."

Davenport sat back. "What did you find out?"

Malloy looked at his pad, avoiding eye contact. "That Salinas is a Mexican detective who came to Orlando for a conference…"

"Which you already knew," Davenport interrupted.

Malloy continued, his voice shaky from the reprimand. "Mr. Aguila is a retired business owner from Michigan."

Davenport stood, taking a deep breath. "This is a warning, Malloy. From now on, you take orders from me, not members of the public—and certainly not from a murder suspect."

CHAPTER 40

That evening after dinner, Theresa invited Madge to her euchre group, so the remaining Aguilas and Roberto walked to the Sand Bar, the Sea Haven pool and bar. A soft breeze brought relief from the hot and rainless day, causing ripples in the kidney-shaped neighborhood pool. Claire and Cristina dropped their beach bags and eased themselves into the tepid water.

"I like him, Mom," Cristina said. "It's okay, you know. It's been a long time since Dad died. You're still young."

Claire looked to where Roberto sat with Martín, as if they had been friends for years. "Well, I'm old enough to have a daughter in graduate school," she said, "but I'm afraid."

"Of what?"

Claire tightened the scrunchie that kept her hair dry. "He hasn't given me any sign that he's interested."

"You've got to be kidding!" her daughter said through a stifled laugh. "Why would he tell you he was coming to Florida for a conference if he wasn't interested? Besides, I've seen the signs. He follows you with his eyes—nice eyes by the way—wherever you go."

Claire smiled. "Maybe he's drawn to my crime-solving ability. He needs a Watson."

"He needs someone—and so do you."

Claire changed the subject. "And your medical student, Kyle?"

"We're serious, but I'm not ready to commit yet, and I don't think he is either."

"But I am?" Claire teased.

"If you and he are ready, I'm happy for you."

They swam to the steps and climbed out of the pool. Claire felt self-conscious in her bathing suit and quickly donned her bathing suit cover. Well-shaped for a 50-something woman, she *was* still a 50-something woman. She grabbed her beach bag from a lounge chair. "I'm going in to change," she announced to her family. Cristina followed with a wave.

"What would you two like to drink?" Roberto asked.

"Chardonnay," said Claire.

"Make that two."

They returned to find two glasses of wine added to the assortment of beverages already on the patio table. Martín sat, watching Roberto write into his ever-present notebook.

Claire remembered when that notebook terrified her. Whenever she and Roberto met in Merida during his murder investigation, it sat between them, causing her heart to race in fear and guilt that, once again, she would be asked to betray her colleagues.

Claire sat next to Roberto, conscious of their closeness. She peered at his cryptic notes, written in Spanish.

"We're putting together a timeline for Barbara's last evening," Martín said, as if he solved crimes every day.

Claire smiled. "We?"

Roberto winked at Claire. "This crime-solving is definitely in your family bloodline." He poured himself another glass of beer from the pitcher. "I can't tell you details, of course. Doug—Detective Davenport—is meeting with his team now."

"We went in to see Deputy Stokes after our trip to Orchard," Claire said. "We reported the near collision."

"Did she seem interested in your report?" Martín asked.

"Not particularly," Claire said, "but she patiently took notes."

"We also told her about Elena Huerta, a potential witness," Cristina said.

"Who?" Roberto asked.

"She's an employee of The Havens who cleans houses," Claire said. "We spoke with her at The Lodge, before Mom's book group. She worked for the Vogels and knew Julio Gonzalez."

"You've had a busy day," Roberto said.

"There's nothing you can tell us?" Cristina asked Roberto.

Roberto looked over the top of his glass. "They still suspect Julio killed himself, but they're waiting for forensic evidence—blood at the scene and fingerprints."

"What if someone killed him?" Claire asked. "Have they thought about that?"

"I'm not involved in their meetings," Roberto said, shrugging his shoulders. "But he did have the murder weapon and Barbara's stolen jewelry in his car."

"Maybe he had an accomplice," Cristina suggested. "Perhaps they met in Julio's car and argued?"

"Who would that accomplice be?" Martín asked, fearing the answer.

Roberto sighed. "I suspect that would be Carlos, in their minds."

Martín ran his hands through his hair. "I refuse to believe Carlos was involved!"

"But what about the jewelry in the bag of books?" Claire asked. "Carlos knows the neighborhood. Maybe you're too close to him to be objective."

"And Julio *was* a thief," Roberto said. "His wife admitted it, and Davenport saw the goods."

"No!" Martín said. "Absolutely not!"

"What about a murder-for-hire?" Claire suggested.

"No one really does that, do they?" asked Cristina.

Roberto shrugged. "It happens."

"Who would hire him?" asked Cristina.

"What about their lovers?" Claire suggested. "You talked to

them today."

Roberto shook his head. "I don't see either one as a serious suspect. Bruce loved her too much, and Julie cared too little."

"What about Mr. Vogel?" asked Claire.

They sat quietly as they considered this possibility. The silence was broken by the sound of laughter coming from the small parking spaces behind the bar, followed by the appearance of Theresa and Madge. They swayed a bit as they made their way to the table.

Martín stared as the newcomers pulled up chairs to join them. "I'd offer you two a drink," he said, "but it appears you've had enough already. Where did you drive from?"

"We're fine," said Theresa, waving her hand and giggling. "We went to The Palms with the euchre group."

"You didn't play cards?" Claire asked, watching as Madge struggled to fit into the patio chair.

"There were too many of us," Theresa said, "so we decided to skip cards."

Madge laughed and said, "This place is amazing! I had no idea. All these cute little communities with their own bars...customized golf carts...who thought this up?"

"What have you been drinking?" asked Claire. "Or smoking?"

"Piña coladas!" Theresa said. "They're great." She smiled sheepishly at Roberto. "We really didn't drink too much."

Roberto smiled back. "I'm sure your friends liked meeting Madge."

"They *love* Madge," Theresa said, patting Madge on the arm.

Claire couldn't remember when she had last seen her mother intoxicated. She blamed Madge.

"So, what did you talk about?" Claire asked. "Do you remember?"

"This and that," Theresa said, "but Madge got them talking about Barbara."

Claire looked at her friend, who gave a mischievous wink. "What did they say?" Claire asked.

Theresa blushed and turned to Madge. "You tell her, Madge."

Madge leaned forward, pulling her sweater around her shoulders. "Louise—you remember her from the book group—seemed to know Barbara best. She and Barbara both volunteered for the Friends of The Havens Library. One day they both volunteered to sort books for the annual book sale, and they had a nice conversation. Louise thought something was bothering Barbara. She asked Louise about retirement, and said she wanted to be free of the business. She seemed stressed about how the business was doing."

"The group wondered if it had anything to do with Todd's affair," Theresa interjected.

"Or Barbara's," suggested Madge.

"Anyway, it seemed to me that he's the one who likes the country club life," Theresa said. "Barbara enjoyed community service." The fresh air had had a sobering effect on her; she settled in her chair and seemed suddenly embarrassed. "They all agreed that Barbara wanted a change in her life."

"Sounds like she felt trapped," Cristina said.

"What else did the ladies tell you?" Roberto asked, his interest piqued.

Madge smiled at Claire. "Well, I learned that she goes to The Ashram and has her hair done at Pauline's Salon. Donna is her stylist...so, which of us is up for yoga and who needs a new hairdo?"

Claire's phone rang. When she ended the call she said, "Deputy Stokes has asked me to go with her tomorrow when she interviews Elena Huerta."

CHAPTER 41

Wednesday morning

Malloy and Stokes sat across from each other at a desk in the Department of Public Safety, the silence between them as tepid as their neglected coffees. They had divided the crime scene reports and were concentrating on the evidence.

Finally, Malloy broke the silence. "I still can't believe you invited that Aguila woman to go to the interview with you."

Stokes looked up from a diagram of the Vogel living room, marred by a computer-generated body in the center of the floor. "She's Doctor Aguila to you, and, as I said yesterday, I invited her because she speaks Spanish—and because I trust her judgment. If Davenport objected, he would have said so."

"What about her father's connection with Carlos? And the fact that he was at the victim's house Saturday night? You have to admit that's suspicious."

"There's nothing suspicious about a man dropping off mulch when it's his job," Stokes said, as she examined photographs of the robe Mrs. Vogel was wearing when she died.

"I suppose the crazy lady's going too?"

"Not invited," Stokes said as her phone rang. She answered and listened. "I'll be right there," she said, and disconnected.

She piled her reports and handed them to Malloy. "Doctor Aguila's here. I'll ask her if her father killed Mrs. Vogel—and Julio too—you never know." She winked and left the room.

Malloy scowled and returned to his chore. He wondered why Julio's prints had not shown up inside the house. *Could he have removed all of them? Did he wear gloves? He must have.*

His cellphone rang. He listened to the caller as Davenport entered the office. "We suspected that," Malloy said. "What time?"

"Who was that?" Davenport asked as he placed his briefcase and take-out coffee on his desk.

"Jonah Jackson from the Orchard bar," Malloy said, gazing longingly at the detective's coffee cup. "Julio's friends admitted to him that they weren't totally truthful with Powers the other night. They want to talk to him again tonight."

"Good," Davenport said, as he removed the cover from his coffee cup. "You should go with him. Find out everything you can about Julio's actions in the days prior to the Vogel murder—and his own death."

"Carlos too?" Malloy asked. "Isn't he still part of our investigation?"

Davenport shrugged. "If there's anything new. I think he's conflicted between a desire to help us and an obligation to protect Julio."

"So, we focus on Julio," Malloy pressed.

"On his death," Davenport said, distracted. "Do you have the reports?"

Malloy handed them to Davenport. "Are you staying?"

Davenport stuffed the reports in his briefcase. "No, I have a meeting. Why?"

"No reason," Malloy said, fiddling with his tie. "Sir, don't you think it's irregular for Stokes to take Doctor Aguila on her interview with Elena Huerta?"

"This whole case is irregular," Davenport said, resealing the lid on his cup. "I'll be back in a few hours. Tell Stokes I want an update when I get back."

Malloy waited a few minutes, then made a call. "That's great!" He jotted in his pad. "Hey, thanks. I owe you one."

Malloy hung up and sat back in his chair, gazing out the window at the sports field behind The Lodge.

◆ ◆ ◆ ◆ ◆

From their bench at the rear of The Lodge, Claire and Stokes watched a pickleball game in progress on the courts. Two couples lobbed the ball back and forth, laughing as it consistently bounced between them.

"Remember," Stokes said as she stood and arranged her uniform, "don't ask questions, only translate if she needs it."

"Agreed," said Claire, a little disappointed. She opened one side of the double door, allowing Stokes to enter first.

The community room had clearly been the site of a bingo game the night before. The bingo machine still stood at the head table. Empty beer and wine bottles, plastic cups, and family-sized potato chip bags covered the long tables. Some trash had miraculously made it into a waste bin, along with disposable bingo sheets and dried daubers.

Elena Huerta entered from the kitchen, hauling a wheeled trash bin nearly as tall as she. "Deputy Stokes?" she asked in heavily accented English.

"Thank you for talking with us," Stokes said. "Do you remember Doctor Aguila?"

"*Si,* you're Mrs. Aguila's daughter," Elena said.

"It's Claire," she said. "Deputy Stokes asked me to come in case you need to explain something in Spanish."

"Okay," Elena nodded. "My English is good…*mas o menos.*" She smiled apologetically.

Stokes directed Elena to a metal folding chair.

"Will it take long?" Elena asked. "I have much to do here, and I still have to clean a house this morning."

Claire looked at Stokes, who sighed and offered, "If we help you clean up, can you answer some questions?"

Elena smiled. "*Muchas gracias.*"

Within ten minutes the tables had been cleared, the trash

bagged, the bottles and cans thrown into a recycle bin, and the bags and bins hauled out the back door. All that remained for Elena was mopping.

"That's enough," Elena said, smiling again. "I can talk now."

They sat at one of the long tables, Claire next to Elena and Stokes across from them. Elena seemed nervous as Stokes asked her how she knew Mrs. Vogel.

"I met Mrs. V a few years ago. Every year, The Havens gives a Christmas party for the families of the workers. That year, Mrs. V took over the group that gives the party. It was the best party. Mr. Cook made a very good meal and the committee ladies helped Mrs. V decorate this room." She motioned with her hand. "It looked so pretty. Mrs. V handed out books and gifts and was so friendly to the children."

Elena smiled at the memory. "Before Mrs. V, the committee ladies left after the party and the families cleaned up, but Mrs. V and Mr. Cook, they cleaned up. I stayed to help her. She asked if I knew anyone who could clean her house once a week, because she still worked, not like most of them. I told her I could do it, and now, I clean…cleaned…for her every Friday." She paused. "Sometimes I worked other days, like if she had a party or if her family was coming to visit."

Stokes wrote quickly in her notebook, and asked, "Was Mr. Vogel ever home when you cleaned for them?"

"Sometimes," she said. "Sometimes he put on those funny golf clothes and left in the cart."

"How did he treat you?" Stokes asked.

Elena clasped her hands in her lap. "Okay. Sometimes he asked me to do work that Mrs. V didn't ask me to do. Sometimes he complained that I didn't do something right, but, not so bad. Mrs. V paid me, and she never complained."

"Did they argue?" Stokes asked. She noticed Elena lean back in the metal chair and glance quickly at Claire before responding.

"Sometimes," she said. "Sometimes, in the morning I could tell they argued. Mrs. V left the house first on those days. Sometimes he stayed home and acted angry, sometimes he yelled at me. Sometimes when I worked in the afternoon instead of the morning Mrs. V would come home, and she seemed worried. She just paid me and sent me home."

"Did he ever hurt her?" Stokes asked.

"I don't think so," Elena said. "She had a temper too. She was *muy fuerte*. One time, when I arrived, Mr. V wasn't there, but then he came home and looked very—how do you say—*desaliñado*— like he had been gone all night. She was *muy enojada* and left the house without him. He told me not to clean until after he left for work."

Stokes looked to Claire.

"Very strong, messy, and very angry," Claire translated.

Stokes turned back to Elena. "Were you afraid of Mr. Vogel?"

"Sometimes, but he was never mean, just angry."

Stokes noticed that as the questions became more difficult for Elena, the more she spoke in Spanish. "Have you met their children?"

"*Los gemelos*," Elena said, "yes, they come sometimes, with their families, but usually not at the same time, except for holidays. When they come, I clean for Mrs. V."

"What do you think of the families?" Stokes asked.

Elena shrugged. "They are okay. I like Miss Diana, but Mr. Drew…he is like Mr. V."

"In what way?" Claire asked without thinking, quickly covering her mouth with her hand.

"Mr. V and his son, they both drink…*mucho*."

CHAPTER 42

"I'm sorry," Claire said as she and Stokes left The Lodge. "I promised I wouldn't ask questions."

"Never mind," Stokes said as she and Claire climbed into the squad car. "I'm glad you were there. It calmed her. I don't think she would have opened up otherwise."

They drove the short distance to the DPS parking lot.

"That's my dad's car," Claire said as she exited the cruiser. "What's he doing here?"

"I don't know," Stokes said, suspecting it had something to do with Scott Malloy.

"I'm going in," Claire said.

Stokes had no choice but to follow her into the building, where Judy gave Stokes a warning glance.

"I'm here to see my father," Claire said. She turned to Stokes. "Please?"

Claire followed Stokes to the office and stood back as Stokes peeked into the room. "Doctor Aguila is here."

Claire heard a muffled response from within as Stokes ushered her in. Her father winced when he saw Claire enter.

"What's going on?" Claire asked Malloy.

"You should wait outside," Malloy said. "We'll be done shortly."

"Why is he here?" She turned to Martín. "Why are you here?"

Martín turned to his daughter. "They're asking about my finances. They invaded my bank accounts without a warrant. I'm explaining to them that I sold my business, and that I'm not a member of a cartel that steals jewelry and commits murder."

"What?" Claire gaped at her father.

"They seem to think that I'm using The Barn to recruit work-ers to commit crimes," Martín said, his sarcasm rising. "In fact, it seems the only crime committed has been by either the bank employee who violated my privacy or the police who seized my records without a warrant." He stared at Malloy. "Someone is in trouble, and it's not me."

Malloy cleared his throat. "I'm not accusing you of anything, Mr. Aguila. We followed proper channels, and we're doing our job in checking leads. You were at the Vogel house at the crucial time. It would be remiss of us not to do so. In a case of theft and murder, we must follow the money."

"We?" Claire looked at Stokes. "Are you placating me while you investigate my family?"

Stokes glared at Malloy, then turned to Claire. "No, that's not what's happening."

"What *is* happening?" Claire asked, putting her hand on her father's shoulder.

The door opened and Davenport entered the room. He looked at Stokes, whose face reddened in embarrassment, then Malloy, whose face had suddenly turned white. Claire stepped away to allow Davenport to enter, her hands shaking. Martín stood, holding onto the chair he had vacated.

"What's going on here?" Davenport said, struggling to digest the scene.

"That's what we are trying to find out," Martín said. "I'm wondering why my finances are being investigated without a warrant."

Claire took Martín's arm. "Is my father done here?"

Davenport stood still, his jaw clenched. "You both may go," he said. The detective stood stiffly at the table until the Aguilas had departed. "What's going on here?" he repeated. "Stokes?"

"I don't know, sir. Doctor Aguila and I just returned from our interview with Elena Huerta."

Detective Davenport stared at his deputy detective. "Malloy?"

"I checked his finances—loose ends," Malloy said.

"Under whose authorization?" Davenport said, his fists clenched. He turned to Stokes. "Did you know about this?"

Stokes glanced at Malloy, who gave her a pleading look. "No, sir," she said.

"You may leave, Stokes. Call Powers. We'll meet here at one o'clock for assignments."

"Yes, sir." Stokes left, closing the door behind her.

"What the hell, Malloy?" Davenport said, as the sound of Stokes's footsteps diminished. "What did you do?"

Malloy fingered his tie with shaking hands. "I have a friend of a friend who works for the same bank where Mr. Aguila has his accounts…" Malloy looked at the detective, who stared at him, unblinking.

"And?"

Malloy handed a bank statement to Davenport. "My friend emailed this to me. Aguila has a lot of cash and CDs, almost two million in his account."

"You had a friend go into a private citizen's finances without a warrant?" Davenport towered over him, the bank statement tight in his fist.

"Don't you think that's a lot of money for a man who mows lawns?" Malloy's face paled as Davenport's reddened.

"It's not against the law to have money, even for a Mexican-American." Davenport took a deep breath and squinted at Malloy. "Did you wonder why a man with two million dollars would be running a petty theft ring in The Havens and working as a maintenance man?"

Malloy fiddled with his tie, loosening it; the office seemed to get hotter the more Davenport stared at him. "It was informal…just a favor, really. If we want information on his business account, we can get a warrant for that."

"A favor? For Vogel? Is this because of his racist assumptions about Hispanics?"

"No, it's other things."

"Like what?"

"Judy told me he arrived here about the same time the robberies started, and immediately he's hanging around with Carlos."

"Judy?" Davenport's voice rose. "You're still taking orders from a suspect and local security? Are you kidding me?"

"No, I'm just listening to what they say."

"Where did you get the idea that it's okay to do this?" Davenport threw the crumpled statement on the table. "Being an Interim Deputy Detective does *not* give you the authority to conduct your own investigation."

Malloy's face blanched further at the derision in Davenport's voice as he stretched out the title of his temporary rank.

"Am I fired, sir?"

"You damn well should be, deputy," Davenport said. He sat down in his chair. "This is what is going to happen. Are you listening?"

"Yes, sir."

"First, I want the name and phone number of the idiot who broke the law to get you this information—and the president of that bank. Your friend may, in fact, lose his job. Understand?"

Malloy nodded.

"Second, just so we are crystal clear, if I hear of you pulling anything like this again, you'll be working security alongside your friend, Judy, the rest of your career."

"Thank you, sir."

"I'm not done yet. You're no longer an active member of this team. You will not be conducting interviews or attending meetings unless I request your presence. Stokes will take over your assignments and Powers will be her second, understand?"

Malloy nodded, trying to control his breathing.

"From now on," Davenport continued, "you will report to the Garland office and get your orders from me personally. Your responsibilities will be limited to telephone calls and whatever other assignments I decide you should handle."

"And after this case?" Malloy said, his voice shaking.

"We'll see. Don't screw up. If I hear you're sharing gossip with Judy or Mr. Vogel, you're done. Understand?"

"Yes, sir."

"And we are through with Mr. Aguila," Davenport said, his voice low and intransigent. "We'll be lucky if we're not sued." He glared at Malloy. "Go home."

◆ ◆ ◆ ◆ ◆

Claire leaned against her car and called Madge. She hadn't seen her since breakfast and felt badly that she had been ignoring her friend, uninvited though she had been.

"Where are you?" Claire asked when Madge answered.

"In the golf cart, dammit. I just had a run-in with the DPS Nazi—she calls herself Officer Barnaby."

"Huh?"

"I'll tell you later. Where are you?"

"At the DPS," Claire said. "I just had a run-in with Detective Malloy, but let's compare stories."

"I just left The Ashram, near that plaza," Madge said. "I've learned a few things."

Oh, no, thought Claire. "I'll meet you in the plaza." she said.

Claire turned right out of the DPS parking lot onto Deer Haven and drove a quarter mile to the deli that sat on the west end of Founder's Plaza, a community square with access by a one-way avenue that circles it for golf-cart and emergency use only.

Claire parked at the deli and walked into the plaza where Madge sat on a bench, the Aguila's golf cart parked askew in front of her.

She forced herself to walk slowly, breathe in, breathe out, thinking she was the one who needed yoga. She gazed up at the lush live oak trees, netted with Spanish moss, that lined the plaza and shaded the interior of the park. Colorful bougainvillea surrounded a center gazebo and white wrought iron benches were scattered throughout the area.

No longer able to stall, Claire approached Madge's bench and stared at her friend, who wore a psychedelic yoga leotard and a Jefferson Airplane T-shirt, an outfit outrageous even by Madge standards. Before Claire could comment, Madge slapped a traffic ticket on the bench between them.

"What happened?" Claire asked, trying not to laugh. "And why are you dressed like that?"

"That local rent-a-cop, Judy Barnaby, gave me a ticket in the golf cart. Can you believe it? Evidently, cart paths become sidewalks in The Hub. You have to drive carts in the street—who knew?" She asked if I was a registered guest. Is this a hotel?"

Claire smiled. "If that's your problem, I win." Claire told her about Malloy's unauthorized investigation and the interview with Elena Huerta.

"Shit," Madge said. "What is this place?"

"Not sure, but when Davenport arrived and heard about it, he told Dad and me to leave. Stokes was so shocked she couldn't even speak. I think fur is flying over there—at least I hope so."

"Reminds me of the Maya at their worst—sacrificing outsiders to maintain the political hierarchy and the kings," Madge mused. "Where's your dad now?"

"I think he went home to pack. He's had it with The Havens." She sat against the bench. "What have you been doing?"

"Ha, while you hung out with the cops, I did research."

"Oh, no. Please, Madge, don't get involved."

Madge smiled. "I went to The Ashram and took a yoga class."

"Thus, the outfit."

"They told me I couldn't wear my skirt in class, so I bought this leotard. Can you believe they sell clothes like this in yoga studios—it's really my style. The T-shirt is mine. I just happened to wear it today, but I think it really goes together. Anyway, who knew you aren't supposed to talk in yoga class? I kept getting shushed when I asked questions. All I got out of it was a dislocated hip from something called dog facing downward...have you ever heard of anything so ridiculous?"

Claire laughed. "I don't believe you've never done yoga...you of all people."

"I did once, years ago," Madge said, "but it stressed me out. Now I'm too old to start again."

"Not true," Claire reassured her friend. "So, you learned nothing at The Ashram?"

"Not in class, but I learned something while shopping for my leotard."

"Tell me," Claire said.

"Another lady and I were shopping in the big girl section. It turns out she's in Barbara's bridge group—Fran. When I told her I was visiting the Aguilas, she wanted to know what I knew about the murder. Of course, I didn't say anything, except that I heard Barbara was unhappy in her life. Fran giggled at that, saying that Barbara wanted to go to culinary school. I asked why that was funny. She said that Barbara was tired of tractors."

CHAPTER 43

Wednesday Afternoon

"Where's Malloy?" Powers asked as he and Stokes waited for
Davenport to arrive at the DPS.

Stokes wondered the same thing. She hadn't seen or heard
from him since she was dismissed from the office that morning.
"Don't know," she said. "Maybe he caught your cold."

"Don't wish that on anyone," Powers said as Davenport
entered the room.

"So, how is everyone doing?" Davenport asked, taking his
chair. "Feeling better, Powers?"

"Yes, sir," Powers responded. "Where's Malloy?"

Davenport stalled as he opened his briefcase. "On special
assignment," he said, avoiding eye contact with Stokes. "I think
we're through with Mr. Aguila," the detective continued, his voice
low and even, "unless something comes up that puts him back in
the picture."

"What about Julio Gonzalez?" Powers asked.

Davenport sat back in his chair. "We still have a problem with
Mr. Gonzalez. There's no evidence he entered the house, only his
footprints outdoors." He skimmed a document sitting on his
desk. "The lab tests show no stippling—gun powder residue—or
clear prints on Julio's right hand. That might not be important,
but it does challenge our suicide theory. Also, the techs noted a
possible void of blood spatter on the passenger seat and window.
That might mean someone blocked the spatter exploding away
from the gun."

Stokes drew geometric designs on a legal pad, her way of

thinking ideas through. "What makes a petty thief a murderer?"

"And a rapist?" Powers added.

"Carlisle found no evidence of rape," Davenport said. "But Barbara did have sex with someone, probably our Mr. Cook." He looked at his team. "So, what's our motive?"

"Greed?" suggested Powers.

"Desperation," suggested Stokes. She stopped doodling and looked at Davenport. "Do you have the photographs of Mrs. Vogel and her kimono, sir?"

Davenport opened his briefcase and pulled out the packet of photographs, sorting through until he identified two photos, one of Mrs. Vogel lying on the floor, blood covering the front of her kimono, her hands tied in front of her with the sash. The other photograph showed the entire length of the sash, blood soaked at both ends.

Stokes moved them closer to Powers and Davenport. "When I saw these," she said, "I remembered that Doctor Carlisle and the lab techs alerted us to the sash, but we hadn't looked carefully at it. We assumed that her hands had been tied before she was murdered." Powers examined the photographs as Davenport sat back and assessed Stokes.

Stokes pointed to the photographs. "It looks like Barbara fell forward and bled through the wound. But the back of the sash, that wraps around the robe, has only traces of blood."

Powers whistled. "So, her hands weren't tied when she was shot," he said.

Exactly," Stokes said. "Someone repositioned the body, removed the sash, and tied her hands with it later, presumably after the blood had nearly dried."

"Did the murderer want it to look like a robbery?" Powers asked.

"That's reasonable," Stokes said, "but he would have to stick around for the blood to dry."

"Why wait around?" Powers asked. "He could have tied them right afterwards."

Stokes paused. "If he did it right away, he'd risk leaving bloody prints around the body." She turned to Davenport. "How long would that take?"

Davenport considered. "It would probably dry in about an hour—too long to stick around."

"So maybe he did drink that scotch," Powers said, half in jest.

"Or, someone else came later and interfered with the crime scene," Stokes mused.

"Good work, Stokes," Davenport said. "It's curious that there's no evidence that she was tied to a chair. Was she walking around?"

"Maybe she went for the gun, and that's when she was shot," Stokes suggested.

"How many people were in the house that night?" Powers asked.

"Good question," Davenport responded. He returned the photographs to the others in the pile. "Powers, did you bring that list of pawn shops?"

Powers pulled several sheets of paper from his backpack and handed them to Davenport. "Are we still interested in the stolen property?"

"Julio's thefts still need to be explained," Davenport said, "and Stokes's theory doesn't eliminate him from consideration." He reached into his briefcase and pulled out several stapled sheets. "The department's team working on the local robberies put together a summary of recent thefts and local pawn shops. It includes some photographs, but most are descriptions."

Davenport handed the lists to Powers. "I'd like you and Stokes to meet with Deputy Delaney in Garland for an update. I've circled Henry's *Casa de Empeños,* a shop that Mrs. Gonzalez suggested— Detective Salinas helped me with the pronunciation. It's owned by a distant relative of Julio and Carlos. Let's see if any of these shops dealt with Mr. Gonzalez. We may even uncover more than one thief."

Davenport stood to leave. "I'm taking Griffin with me to update Mr. Vogel. I want to ask about his golf clubs. And, if his son is there, I might ask him when he last touched the refrigerator at his parents' house prior to the murder."

"Anything else for us, sir?" Stokes asked.

Davenport considered. "Yes. Julio's friends at Jonah's Bar want to talk to us again. They'll be there at eight o'clock tonight. Stokes, I want you and Powers to find out what they didn't tell us the first time."

"What about Malloy?" Powers asked. "He and I could go, and Stokes can go home."

"Malloy is finishing up your calls, checking out the night and weekend shift employees at the Orlando convention hotel," Davenport said.

Powers shot a quick glance at Stokes, who gave him a brief shake of her head. "Okay then, Stokes. Let's tour the pawnshops."

◆ ◆ ◆ ◆ ◆

"So, Pam, what's up?" Powers started the engine of the squad car while Stokes hooked her seat belt.

"What do you mean?" Stokes asked as she struggled to think of an answer.

"Why is the Golden Boy suddenly making phone calls?" Powers said, pulling out of the parking lot. "I'm not complaining, mind you."

"It had something to do with Mr. Aguila," Stokes confessed.

"How so?"

"He threatened to sue the department—you promise not to say anything?"

"Sure," Powers said, his eyes widened.

"I think Malloy was conducting his own investigation into Mr. Aguila's finances without a warrant."

"I'd say 'welcome to my world,' but it probably wouldn't go over very well. Whenever Blacks are successful, it's assumed they're into something illegal."

Stokes nodded sympathetically, skimming the pawnshop addresses. "Prejudices only muddy the water when it comes to detective work. At any rate, it looks like you and I got promoted."

CHAPTER 44

"Who the hell do you think you are, Ron?" Todd yelled into the phone, his face contorted in rage. "Don't tell me you're just the messenger! I know who your real clients are!"

Todd slammed his phone on the patio bar. He glared at Diana, who sat anxiously at the nearby table. "So, when were you going to tell me that your mother filed for divorce?" Getting no response, Todd made himself a fresh gin and tonic.

Drew stared through the birdcage at Clam Lake, watching an egret perched on the shoreline. "Are there really alligators in there?" he asked, turning back toward his father and sister and swirling ice cubes in his glass.

"The alligators are here, eating their father alive," Todd said, taking a huge gulp from his glass.

Drew joined Todd at the bar, and freshened his own drink. "We just heard your side of the conversation, Dad."

"Ron made it more than clear that he represents your mother's interests, not mine." He took another gulp and swirled his glass. "And you both knew all about the divorce."

"We didn't know she filed," Diane cajoled as Drew and Todd joined her at the table. "We found out the same way you did, when you were served papers Monday night."

"Mom told Diana weeks ago," Drew said, sidling his chair closer to his father, their alliance sealed with alcohol. "You and I just found out."

"So, I'm the bad guy?" Diana asked, her eyes boring into Todd's. "Mom told me she was considering divorce and asked me not to say anything until we heard from both of you. When you didn't mention it, I thought perhaps you had settled your differences. It didn't seem like something to discuss under the circumstances."

"What did Ronnie say about the trust?" Drew asked.

"I'll tell you how it is," Todd spat. "Under the original terms of the trust—that your grandparents set up—if your mother died, you and Drew would have inherited the Chicago store, and I would have inherited the Garland store."

"We knew that," said Drew.

Diana looked at her father. "What changed?"

"Hah, you two don't know the rest." Todd taunted them. "You'll love this part."

"Just tell us," Drew said, his jaw tight. "What the hell!"

Todd glared at Drew. "When your grandparents bought the Florida store and your mother and I took over the Chicago store, they revised the trust, adding a stipulation that, if your mother filed for divorce, I would lose my rights to both businesses. After forty years of slaving, I'd get nothing!" He gulped his drink. "And your mother didn't even bother to tell me she had filed. Incredible!"

"Did she know about the stipulation?" Drew asked, his hands unsteady. "I can't believe she'd file without telling you what she meant to do…give you a warning."

"She didn't plan on being murdered," Diana argued. "I'm sure she would have talked to all of us when you returned from Orlando."

"Why wait until she had already filed? When it was a done deal? And I was away?"

"Perhaps she knew you would try to talk her out of it," Diana reasoned.

"We could have talked about it…I could have reasoned with her. I had no idea she had filed, and I certainly didn't know what that meant for me."

"You're sure that filing for divorce initiated the stipulation?" Drew asked, thinking. "Is that what Ronnie said?"

"Damn right," Todd said. "Her family always hated me. How the hell can a mere filing for divorce nullify the trust?" His eyes flashed anger. "There's more. The stipulation regarding a divorce filing not only disinherited me, but you two also."

"What?" Diana asked, as Drew gulped the last of his drink.

Todd gave them a cruel smile. "According to the stipulation, if your mother hadn't died, she would have continued to own both stores. She planned to retire and expected you two to each manage one store with the option to buy at a family price. According to Ronnie, she needed the income to support herself in retirement."

Drew placed his glass on the table and gripped it with shaking hands. "What happens now that she's dead? What does the trust say?"

"You each inherit a store." Todd glared at his son. "Your mother didn't tell you this?"

Drew's face blanched. "No! I knew nothing about this." He turned to Diana. "Did you know?"

"No, I did not!" Diana insisted. She turned to Todd who stood like a statue, his hands clenched around his glass. "But everything will work out, Dad," she pleaded. "The horrible truth is that Mom is dead. Even if one of us inherits the Garland store, we'll need you, Dad. Right, Drew?" She gave her brother a desperate look.

Todd stared at his children. "I bet she and your grandparents had a great time scheming, and I bet old Ronnie got a nice chunk of money for putting this together. By the way, he's flying down tomorrow to talk to Annette. That'll be interesting."

The argument ceased suddenly when the doorbell rang. Diana jogged through the house to the front door, opening it to two officers, one a middle-aged man wearing a suit, the other a younger man in uniform.

"Miss Vogel?"

"Diana Thurman. May I help you?"

"I'm Detective Davenport, and this is Deputy Griffin from the Gardenia County Sheriff's Department. Is your father here?"

Diana nodded and allowed them in. Drew and Todd entered from the lanai, with halting steps, both still gripping their drink glasses.

"I hope you're here to give me an update," Todd said, his voice sightly slurred. He waved his free hand with feigned casualness. "This is my son, Drew, and my daughter, Diana."

Davenport shook hands with the siblings. Drew's face was flushed, perhaps with anger, perhaps embarrassment or inebriation, maybe a combination of all three.

"Can we sit?" Davenport asked. "We have information, but also some questions."

Todd led them into the living room. Davenport noticed that Todd and Diana avoided the central area, moving along the edge of the room to take their seats. Drew paused, then crossed to sit in an upholstered chair by the window. Griffin and Davenport sat on the sofa facing the family.

Griffin took a notepad from his pocket as Davenport addressed the twins. "I'd like to extend my condolences for the death of your mother. I know this is difficult for you."

Drew nodded and Diana said, "Thank you. We're still in shock."

"What news do you have?" Todd asked, his eyes darting between the two officers.

"We haven't received all the forensic results yet," Davenport said. "We should have them soon."

Drew frowned. "You know who killed her, right? That guy who killed himself?"

"We're still investigating," Davenport said, "but we do suspect that Julio Gonzalez was responsible for the local thefts."

"Hah!" Drew said, too loudly. "That proves he's guilty."

"I don't care about the jewelry," Todd said, his hands shaking in his lap.

Davenport leaned forward, placing his elbows on his knees and folding his hands. "Mr. Vogel, we do know that Mr. Gonzalez stood outside your house, but we have no evidence that he entered—no footprints or fingerprints in the house or on the jewelry."

"Maybe he wore gloves," Drew said. "Why are you still looking for suspects?"

"We have some unexplained evidence," Davenport said. He turned to Drew. "Mr. Vogel, when did you last visit this house?"

Drew shrugged. "Spring break, with the kids."

"We have a problem, then," Davenport said. "Our team found your partial fingerprint on the refrigerator. I wonder how it got there."

"That's ridiculous," Drew insisted. "How often do people clean stainless-steel refrigerators? And they're partials? Doesn't that mean other prints are on top of it?"

"There are surprisingly few fingerprints on the refrigerator," Davenport said. "We found other partial prints, as yet unidentified."

Diana looked at her brother, frowned, and addressed Davenport. "If Drew was here recently, there would be more prints. This doesn't make sense."

Davenport kept his gaze on Drew, who placed his empty glass on an end table with shaking hands. "Some surfaces had been wiped clean," Davenport continued. "You're sure you weren't here in the past week?"

"I was at the convention," Drew snapped.

"We've been checking with your father's contacts at the convention hotel and with hotel personnel. No one remembers seeing you there," Davenport pressed.

"I stayed at a Marriott nearby," he said defiantly and turned to Todd. "Tell him, Dad."

"He was there," Todd confirmed, glancing at Drew. "What's this all about?"

"Why did you stay at a different hotel?" Davenport asked.

Drew scoffed. "I have clients associated with several northern equipment companies. We stay at the hotels our clients prefer—generally with a nice golf course and close to a casino. The old guys stay at the convention hotel." He looked at Todd. "Right, Dad?"

Todd forced a smile. "Yes, I guess so."

"Besides," Drew said, suddenly talkative, "it's a huge convention, and we attend different sessions. Florida machinery is different from Chicago's. Dad's not interested in the latest in snow removal—I am."

"Did you meet up?" Davenport asked, glancing from father to son.

"Sure," Todd answered. "We had lunch and played golf at Drew's hotel Saturday afternoon. Right, Drew?"

Drew nodded assent.

"What did you do after golf?"

"I went back to my hotel," Todd said. "I don't understand these questions."

"It's my job," Davenport assured him. "Drew?"

Drew shrugged. "I went to a casino and card club with clients."

"You didn't drive to The Havens to visit your mother while in Florida?" Davenport asked.

"No, I didn't have a lot of spare time."

"But you called her," Davenport confirmed. "We have her phone."

"I called to tell her I couldn't come. It's a long drive."

"Not so long," Davenport said, catching a quick glance

between Diana and her brother. "A witness saw a light-colored car, gray or white, in your parents' driveway late Saturday night. That wasn't your rental car?"

Drew's head jerked in surprise. "No, of course not."

Todd stood as if to dismiss the officers. "Is that it, then?"

"One more thing," Davenport said, turning to Todd. "Did you take your golf clubs to Orlando?"

"No," Todd said. "Why is that important?"

"We're not sure it is," Davenport said. "When the team went through your house, they found your wife's clubs and not yours. Just another loose end."

"They're in my locker at Glen Haven."

"Do you mind if we look at them?" Davenport asked.

Todd sighed heavily. "If you have to."

"Good. Deputy Griffin will take you to the country club."

Todd laughed uneasily, looking at Diana and Drew. "See what I told you?"

"Yeah," Drew said, throwing his dad a confused look. "I don't understand this."

"Just loose ends," Davenport said.

◆ ◆ ◆ ◆ ◆

"Can I at least take my own car?" Todd asked Griffin when they left the house. "I don't want to be seen in a squad car."

"Suit yourself," Griffin said. "I'll follow you to Glen Haven."

At the country club, Todd led Griffin to the men's locker room. It was mid-afternoon, in the heat of the day, after the morning golfers had finished their rounds and eaten lunch but before the late afternoon golfers emerged from their air-conditioned homes. It distressed Todd to find a few dedicated golfers gathered around their lockers. He grimaced as he passed by, Griffin following on his heels. Todd wished the less conspicuous

Malloy had come with him, not a uniformed deputy. He could feel the curious stares of his friends.

"Todd, we're so sorry about Barbara," one man said, patting Todd on the shoulder as he walked by. "Let us know if there's anything we can do."

"Thanks, Bob," Todd said, "I will." He turned to the others and said, "This is Deputy Griffin. He's tying up loose ends."

"Hey, deputy," said another man. "Clear this up soon, okay? We miss our star."

Uncomfortable laughter passed among the golfers as Todd fumbled with the lock.

Griffin smiled. "We're doing our best."

As the group moved on, another man said, "Heard you had a good round in Orlando."

When the men had left, Griffin said, "I thought you didn't take your clubs."

"I rented clubs there." Todd spun the lock and swung the locker open, exposing a collection of golfing gloves and several boxes of balls piled up on the top shelf. A light-weight jacket and cap hung on a hook. He pulled out his golf bag. "I don't know what you're looking for, but go for it."

Griffin took a pair of gloves from his pocket and stretched them on. He didn't golf, so he had no idea what to look for. Without a warrant, he supposed Davenport just wanted to know that the clubs were there and not dripping with blood, but he did notice something odd about them.

"I need to take some photographs," Griffin said apologetically, as he pulled his phone from his pocket. He did so, then motioned for Todd to replace the clubs in the locker. "Have you been to your locker since you returned from Orlando?" Griffin asked.

"Davenport allowed me to shower and change while the evidence team tore up my house. You were there, I remember, taking photos."

While Todd set the lock, Griffin took a photograph of the locker. "How did your friend know you had a good game in Orlando?"

Todd's jaw set. "I might have told Jordan about it," he said.

"Jordan Davis? You've talked to him?"

"Briefly, he's my neighbor."

"When?"

"Once or twice."

"Did he tell you he saw a car in your driveway?"

"He wanted me to know someone had been there. In fact, he thinks it looked like the car in the *Gazette,* Julio Gonzalez's car. But your boss won't believe him, I'm sure."

CHAPTER 45

Wearing street clothes, Stokes and Powers entered Jonah's, a dilap-idated bar located just outside Orchard. The faded blue-wooden framed building had no square corners, and yellow lopsided shutters dangled by no more than two nails each over dirty glass windows. Inside, the dominant decor consisted of blinking beer signs and low-hanging lights that camouflaged the dingy tables and countertops. Their feet stuck to the floor as they entered and examined the scene. Stokes scanned the patrons, mostly men, though she observed several couples deep in conversation.

"These are my people," Powers said. "I grew up around here, so don't worry, I'll protect you."

"Thanks," Stokes smiled. "It's good to know you have my back."

Stokes followed Powers to the bar, studying the local patrons—primarily Hispanic and Black men with weathered faces and laborers' hands. She tried to imagine Powers as a young Black man from this area, with ambitions to be a police officer. She wondered what it was like for him, getting accepted into deputy training, moving up and away from his roots.

Jonah Jackson, the bar's owner, stood wiping down the counter. He watched them approach, dark eyes under gray bushy eyebrows.

"Mr. Jackson, I'm Deputy Mike Powers and this is Deputy Pamela Stokes."

"Yes, I remember you, Deputy Powers." Jonah nodded to Stokes and motioned toward a round table, where three men had congregated near a makeshift stage in the far corner of the bar. The deputies weaved through the room, past two pool tables where a small group of men hovered, encouraging players and waiting their turn, quarters placed on worn felt-covered tables. They all turned to look at the newcomers. The lack of uniforms didn't fool anyone.

The men greeted them with nearly imperceptible nods. Powers remembered Fred, an elderly Hispanic man with gray hair and piercing blue eyes, and Willie, a Black man in his fifties with calloused hands. He introduced them to Stokes. Willie introduced the third man, Luis, who sat hesitantly on the edge of his seat. Stokes let Powers take the lead.

"Jonah said you guys had more information for us?" Powers asked, receiving three nods in return.

Willie and Luis turned to Fred, who spoke. "It's about Julio being sick Saturday night," Fred said. He looked to his friends, who nodded encouragement. "That's what he told us and what we told you—he came for a beer but didn't stay long."

"Go on," Powers said.

"Well," Fred continued, "it's true he came, but his hand was bandaged, and he had blood on his shirt. We asked him what happened, and he said he cut himself at work."

"When did he first call to say he wasn't coming?" Powers asked.

Willie frowned. "That's the thing," he said. "He called us early in his shift, said he couldn't come, then he comes in around eleven, his hand bandaged, and tells a crazy story about going to the ER."

"Crazy?" asked Stokes.

Fred shook his head. "You see, we all knew he didn't go to the ER. Illegals don't go to the ER. Besides, it looked like he bandaged it himself."

Stokes studied the men, clearly struggling with the implications. "So, you wondered why he said he wasn't coming, then turned up later with a wound?"

"Yes, ma'am," Willie said.

"Why didn't you tell us about this before?" Powers asked.

"Because Missus Vogel had just been killed," Willie said, as if talking to a child. "We knew he'd never hurt that lady."

"Why do you think he came in that night?" Stokes asked.

"We've been talkin' 'bout that, too," Willie said. "We think he needed an alibi." Willie turned to Luis. "Luis wasn't here when you came by before. He's scared to talk to cops, you know, but I told him it might be important, what he knows."

"We're not interested in your status, Luis," Stokes said. "We just want to know how Mrs. Vogel and Julio died."

Luis looked to his companions, then to the deputies. "I know y'all think Julio killed himself, but he didn't." Luis licked his lips and picked up his beer. "Someone was scarin' him."

"Threatening him?" Powers asked. "About what?"

"*No sé*—I don't know. Someone wanted Julio to do something he didn't want to do. I think whoever it was knew something about him."

"Do you mean blackmail?" Stokes prodded. "What do you think the person knew?"

Luis gave a pleading look to his companions. Fred took over the story.

"We think Julio was robbing houses," the elderly man said, "but we don't know for sure. He worried about his sick kid and was getting a lot of pressure from his mama in Mexico to help his brother. Carlos tried to help him, but I think Julio just went the wrong way…he got desperate, you know?"

Luis leaned in and lowered his voice. "One night, Julio told me his troubles would be over soon, that he'd have help for his *niña* and *hermanito*. I asked him who was going to help him, but he got quiet-like, said he couldn't talk about it, said he didn't have a choice, but he had a plan…or something like that."

"Do you think someone was paying Julio to do something illegal?" Stokes asked.

Luis nodded. "Maybe."

Willie took over the story. "When Julio came here Saturday night, we thought he needed an alibi for stealing, figuring he got himself hurt at someone's house. But he wasn't worried about the cut, and seemed more like his old self. He said things had worked out better than he thought. He had a beer and left. When we heard about poor Missus Vogel, we didn't think nothin' of it. Julio said nothin' about it and didn't act scared. But then, when he was killed, Luis told us what Julio told him, and we figured we better tell y'all about it."

"Thank you for coming forward," Stokes said. "You've been very helpful."

◆ ◆ ◆ ◆ ◆

In her apartment, Stokes settled into her favorite chair, a large leather recliner in the corner of her living room. Her cat, Romeo, settled next to her. She allowed herself a glass of wine as she typed her report on her laptop. When her doorbell rang, she swore and put her laptop aside. She peeked out the window and opened the door. Malloy.

"What's up, Scott?"

"Can I come in? I finished my calls, and I'm on my way home."

"I'm working on my report," Stokes responded, "and I'm tired."

"Please, Pam? I need to talk." His voice had an edge, shaky and uncertain.

Stokes closed her eyes, trying to still her conflicting emotions. "A working meeting, right?"

"Sure, if it means I can have a beer."

Malloy slid onto the sofa, like old times. Stokes felt frustration rise in her as she recalled how their relationship had soured and eventually rotted. When she returned from the kitchen with his beer, Romeo had abandoned his place on the chair and cuddled next to Malloy. *Traitor*, she thought. She handed Malloy his beer, returned to her chair, and waited for him to speak.

Malloy stared at his bottle, the arrogant self-assurance gone. "I'm in trouble, Pam," he said, finally looking directly at her. "I screwed up, and everybody knows about it."

"Not everybody...yet," Stokes said. "Davenport didn't say anything at the meeting. Powers knows something is amiss, but he hasn't pushed for information." She sipped her wine, hoping her lie wouldn't come back to bite her. "No one wants you to fail, not even me, believe it or not."

"The Aguila family knows."

"They would know anyway," Stokes said.

Malloy took a gulp of beer. "I was stupid to let Judy and Todd get into my head."

"What happened?"

"Todd questioned me about Martín Aguila, wondering how he could afford to live here and why a Mexican cop was hanging around. Then Judy's been nagging about how you and Claire Aguila seem to be good buddies..."

"And how Salinas has been conducting interviews with Davenport instead of you?" she asked. "So, you investigated his finances?"

"Not me. I have a friend...dammit, it's not right," he blurted. "I don't know why Davenport's overlooking the workers. I still think the whole case revolves around them. I can't see it any other way."

"But still, you need a warrant to go into someone's bank accounts."

"Thanks for letting me know," he said sharply. "At least he didn't suspend me, but he might as well have. I've been relegated to office work. Powers should have finished these calls. He started them."

"You're lucky, Scott. It could be worse."

"Easy for you to say," Malloy huffed. "It means I'm not getting promoted to permanent detective anytime soon."

"This position is temporary anyway," Stokes reasoned. "You'll get another chance."

"You'll get there before me," Malloy snipped.

Stokes squinted in irritation. "What did you learn from your calls?" she asked.

"Todd was at his conference until Sunday morning like he said, but there is something," Malloy admitted. "No one I spoke with saw him between ten Saturday night and two o'clock Sunday morning, damn him. But that's not enough time for him to return home to kill his wife."

"That's four hours. Plenty of time—about an hour to get home, two to kill his wife, and one hour to return. It was late at night, light traffic. Come on, Scott."

"It could be coincidence, just bad luck for him."

Stokes shook her head and sighed. "Mike and I learned something at the bar," she offered, to change the subject. "Julio's friends agreed not to tell Powers about the bandage and the bloody shirt because they had heard about Mrs. Vogel's murder."

"They saw him with bloody clothes and a bandage, and lied about it?" Malloy asked.

"A lie by omission," Stokes said. "But they did come forward with another man, Luis, who's a closer friend to Julio. He thinks someone threatened or blackmailed Julio into doing something illegal."

"They would say that," Malloy argued. "It could have been one of his friends behind it, then something went wrong, and Julio killed Mrs. Vogel. They could be lying now, to cover their own involvement." He rolled his eyes. "I wouldn't have been taken in by that crap."

"But Julio seemed relieved when he went to the bar that night," Stokes said, "and he told his friends things looked better for him. Does that sound like someone who just killed a lady?" She sipped her wine. "I keep thinking about the money in Julio's box—just over five thousand dollars. What if someone paid him to kill Mrs. Vogel?"

"Then that proves Julio killed her." Malloy tipped his beer toward Stokes. "Also, Julio had Barbara's jewelry in his car...and killed himself with the victim's gun. Case solved."

"Suicide hasn't been established yet," Stokes said. "He might have been murdered and framed. There's also that near collision between a silver car and Claire Aguila's car Sunday night near the G&G."

"You're accusing Vogel of killing Julio too? That's rich, Pam. How many silver cars are there in The Havens, I wonder?" Malloy chided. "You and Davenport are putting too much credence in the Aguilas and Salinas—this is what Todd and Judy are talking about."

Stokes glared at Malloy who placed his empty bottle on her table. "The sooner you separate yourself from Vogel and Judy, the better you'll be," she warned. "I think you have a problem with your anybody-but-the-husband theory."

Malloy patted the sofa, and motioned Stokes to sit next to him. "Let's not argue, Pam."

"We're debating the evidence," Stokes countered. "Besides, I thought you had a girlfriend."

"Didn't work out," Malloy said. "Can't we put all this department stuff behind us?"

Stokes sat back and frowned. "You mean the stuff where you are an already-suspended interim deputy detective, and I'm an over-qualified uniformed sheriff's deputy?"

"So, it's a no?" Malloy pressed.

"Definitely a no."

CHAPTER 46

Thursday morning

Stokes, Powers, and Griffin huddled around a small conference table in the county Sheriff's Department, waiting for their boss to get off the phone. Malloy, who had been summoned to the meeting by Davenport, sat off to the side, unusually quiet. They'd all had a late night, and were focused on the coffee and sweet rolls Davenport had offered in return for their early start. Stokes studied the three authorized warrants Davenport had laid out for them: one for Todd Vogel's car, one for his phone, and one for his golf bag and locker. It was six-thirty in the morning.

"I might just arrest the Davises," Davenport said after he hung up, reaching for a custard-filled Danish. "That was Amanda Davis. She and her husband are coming in to change their statement on the mystery car…again."

"It must be contagious," Stokes said, pulling a small corner from a chocolate croissant. "Powers and I had the same experience last night."

"You start then, Stokes," Davenport said.

"In short, Julio's friends admitted that he arrived at the bar with a bandaged hand and bloody shirt, but they kept quiet to protect him. The new information came from Luis, who wasn't there for the first interview. He thinks someone pressured or blackmailed Julio into doing something illegal. And since we know Julio was at the Vogel house, I think it had something to do with her death…I just don't know what."

"The men said something interesting," Powers added. "They thought Julio went to the bar to give himself an alibi."

"Maybe he did," Malloy said.

"But why was he at the Vogels?" Stokes asked. "Why is there no evidence he entered the house? Why did he go to the bar if he had just killed a woman? Why did he have more than five thousand dollars in his house?"

"What do you think?" Davenport asked Stokes.

Stokes sat back. "I think there were two men at the Vogel house, one watching and the other inside with the victim. What if Julio saw the killer and blackmailed him?"

"So, again, why was Julio there?" Malloy asked. "He didn't just happen to be in the neighborhood."

"I think someone hired him to kill her," Stokes said. "That's the only explanation for going to the Vogels after hurting himself at work. Why not just go home, or to the bar early to commiserate with friends?" She answered her own question. "Because, he *had* to go there to do something that had been planned by someone else. He saw someone in the house…perhaps the murderer, and he left…glad not to have to fulfill his contract."

"Julio went to the bar wearing bloody clothes, and with a wounded hand," Malloy noted. "Not much of an alibi."

Davenport considered for a moment before speaking. "If Julio killed Mrs. Vogel, he would have had a lot of blood on his clothes and shoes. He wouldn't have gone to the bar for an alibi—not without changing his clothes. Besides, his shoes were clean except for the dirt from along the birdcage."

Stokes scanned her notes. "That bothers me," she said. "The techs didn't find any evidence of a blood trail on the carpeting, furniture, or sinks that would indicate cleanup. It's almost like the murderer flew away."

Davenport assessed Stokes and nodded. "That bothers me, too." He turned to Malloy. "Scott, what did you learn from your Orlando phone calls?"

Malloy shuffled his notes. "The general manager of the

convention hotel confirmed that Todd had registered there. Both he and the Sunday manager confirmed that he checked out around six Sunday morning. They couldn't confirm golf clubs, agreeing that guests who drive usually keep their clubs in their cars."

"Todd told me he rented clubs," Griffin interjected.

Malloy narrowed his eyes at Griffin. "Anyway," he said, "to continue, the manager knew Drew, but he hadn't seen him. He thought Drew stayed at another hotel, which Drew already confirmed."

"Did you confirm that with the hotel?" Davenport asked.

"Um, not yet, but I will," Malloy answered, blushing. "Today."

"What about Todd's timeline?" Davenport moved on, without comment.

"The Saturday night bartender saw Todd with a group of people at the bar. She confirmed that he left the table around ten o'clock, announcing to the group that he had to call his wife. Both the night manager and the bartender noticed a woman in the group, Lisa Monroe. This is only interesting because Todd didn't list any women in his statement. I called *Mrs.* Monroe, and she told me that she had arranged to meet Todd for a drink after he called his wife, but he didn't show up."

"So, no alibi there either," Stokes said.

"The Saturday night manager didn't see Todd leave the hotel that night, but he saw him reenter the hotel around two in the morning with a bulky pharmacy bag," Malloy reported, throwing a quick glance at Stokes. "Another thing...when the bartender left the hotel at two a.m., she saw Todd getting out of his car, carrying that bag. When she asked where he'd been, he laughed and said he had a headache."

"Anything else?" Davenport asked.

"Sir?" Stokes said, returning Malloy's glance. "Malloy and I talked about the timeline, and I think Todd had plenty of time to make the round-trip from Orlando to his home Saturday night into Sunday morning."

"Go on."

"What if Mr. Vogel paid Julio to kill his wife?"

The room stilled as the group took this in. Griffin busied himself reading his notes, Powers raised his eyebrows, Malloy made a snorting sound, and Davenport adjusted his glasses.

Malloy cleared his throat. "Stokes's idea doesn't make sense. If Vogel paid Julio to kill her, he had no reason to drive all the way back to The Havens," he said. "In fact, that supports his alibi."

"Murder-for-hire is a crime," Stokes said. "Besides, we have no evidence Julio entered the house. He's a petty thief with five thousand dollars in a cardboard box, and he shows up at a bar in bloody clothes. Would a murderer do that?"

"We have no proof Todd made the round-trip," Malloy countered.

"It's the five thousand dollars," Stokes said. "Powers and I visited the pawn shops. Only one owner admitted doing business with Julio—his distant cousin, Henry Garza. However, instead of pawning his items and reselling them, Garza and his wife bought them and gave Julio the money. They gave us a box of stolen items. We should be able to clear these up relatively easily. I think they're hoping for leniency. They felt sorry for Julio and his family." Stokes paused. "The thing is, nothing he stole was worth five thousand dollars. He got that money from somewhere else."

"And because we have no evidence of Julio being in the Vogel house, we don't know how the jewelry got into the book bag," Davenport said.

"We still don't know that he didn't enter the house," Malloy persisted. "Lack of evidence doesn't mean he didn't cover his tracks."

"We're waiting for results on the blood on Julio's shirt," Davenport said. "If it's hers, we have a case." He turned to Griffin.

"Tell us about the clubs, Ken."

Griffin leaned forward, his own ideas having been confirmed by Stokes. "One of Todd's friends at the country club congratulated him on his golf game in Orlando—Todd claimed he mentioned the game to his neighbor, Jordan Davis, who probably told others. Anyway, when I pressed Vogel on this, he insisted he had rented clubs there." He paused to look at Malloy. "But Mrs. Van Dee saw them in his trunk. I don't know why he lied about it."

"What evidence do we have for a warrant on the clubs, besides his lie?" Stokes asked, looking at the warrant.

"Well," Griffin stammered nervously, "I had a hunch. The bag looked too clean. I couldn't legally look inside the pockets of the bag, but each club had a cover, the towel was clean, and the bottom of the bag was spotless. I looked at the other men's bags, and they were scuffed and dirty." He shrugged. "Luckily the judge thought that, altogether, it was enough."

Griffin then paused, checking his notes. "Something else," he added. "Speaking of Jordan Davis, Todd admitted he's had several conversations with his neighbor, which might explain the Davises' schizophrenic witness statements."

"Thanks, Griffin," Davenport said. He sat quietly for a moment, appraising his team, his gaze pausing a moment on Stokes. "If Stokes's blackmail scenario is correct, we now have a motive for Julio to be murdered. We have a suspicious-looking suicide and blood spatter, and a car seen racing away from the scene near the time of death."

Davenport then threw a quick glance in Malloy's direction. "It looks to me like these deaths are linked, but not in the way we had suspected. Based on my suspicions and Doctor Aguila's statement, I requested deputies to check the roadway and trash bins at the strip malls along the county road. They found nothing suspicious in the G&G dumpster, so, if Julio was murdered, someone shot him at close range and needed to get rid of bloody clothes away from the scene."

"Where do we go from here?" Powers asked.

Davenport flipped through his notes. "Powers, I want you to go with me to the Vogel house with the first warrants. The car hauler will be there soon. I want us there at the same time."

"Yes, sir."

"Stokes," Davenport said, "go to The Havens DPS. Call the Davises about their latest statement and have them come in to sign. Later, I may need you to take Doctor Aguila to the police garage to identify Vogel's car up close."

Davenport handed Griffin the warrant for the golf bag. "I want you to meet Craig Hughes at Glen Haven. He'll examine the locker and take the clubs for evidence. Then I want you to hook up with the team searching for the discarded clothes."

"Yes, sir," Griffin said, his eyes shining with the exuberance of a young cop on his first big case.

Davenport turned to Malloy, his voice stern. "I think Drew and Todd are lying to us. I want you to go to Orlando and see if you can learn anything more from the people you called regarding Todd's movements. Then I want you to check on Drew's movements. Find his hotel, the car rental agency, and the golf course where he and Todd played golf. I want to know their movements every minute on Saturday and Sunday. Check in with Detective Burns at the Orlando Police Department before you ask a single question." Davenport paused. "Understand?"

"Yes, sir. Thank you." Malloy turned and left the room, straightening his tie.

Davenport turned to the group, each deputy glued in place. "What are you waiting for? Let's go."

CHAPTER 47

Todd sat on a kitchen stool, drinking his first cup of coffee and skimming the *Gazette* for any new articles on Barbara's or Julio's death. He looked out the window, recognizing a familiar SUV in his driveway alongside a car hauler in the street. *What the hell?*

"Good morning, Mr. Vogel," Davenport said when Todd opened the door. "This is Deputy Powers. Can we come in?"

"I remember," Vogel said, standing aside. "What's going on? What's with the truck?"

The deputies entered the foyer, and Davenport extracted documents from his suit pocket.

"What's that?"

"A warrant for your car," Davenport said. "Please open your garage door."

"Why do you need my car?"

"And your phone," Davenport said, offering him two warrants. Vogel ignored the gesture. "We have permission to examine your car for evidence linking it with the deaths of Mr. Gonzalez and your wife."

"This is ridiculous!" He backed up as the officers moved into the living room.

Davenport opened the other warrant. "This is a copy of the warrant being executed this minute at Glen Haven for your golf bag and your locker."

"I don't believe this!" Todd protested, his face ashen. He turned quickly as Drew and Diana emerged from their bedrooms.

"What's going on?" Drew asked.

"They're taking my car and phone!" Todd blustered. "And my golf bag!"

Drew looked at his father in disbelief, then turned to Davenport. "What's this about?"

"Nothing," Todd said, his hands clenched at his sides. "Open the garage door before everyone in the neighborhood sees this."

But it was too late. When Drew opened the garage door, neighbors were already peeking out of windows and standing on porches in robes or pajamas. Todd followed Drew into the garage and handed his keys to the truck driver.

Father and son returned to the kitchen, where Davenport and Powers watched Diana pour herself a cup of coffee, trying to control her shaking hands. She stood mute at the counter.

"What do I do without a car?" Todd demanded.

"We'll let you know when you can pick it up. In fact, we've finished with your wife's car. Drew can drive you to Garland to pick it up."

Todd crossed his arms and sat on a stool. "What about my wife's body? We plan to take her ashes to Chicago for burial."

Davenport frowned. "Your wife's body will be released to the mortuary today or tomorrow. However, I'm afraid I'm going to ask you to stick around until our investigation is completed."

"What about Diana and me?" Drew asked.

"I request that you all stay here for a few days," Davenport said. "We still have questions, and some of them pertain to you as well, Drew."

"Me?" Drew said. "I…we can't stay here indefinitely. We have tickets to fly home tomorrow… we have families…jobs."

"You might be able to leave tomorrow," Davenport said, shrugging.

"Do we need a lawyer?" Drew asked.

"If you would like to consult your lawyer, we can talk at the station instead."

Todd and Drew exchanged glances. "What do you need to know?" Todd asked.

"I need to ask both of you, again, if either of you came to the house Saturday night or early Sunday morning."

"Why are you still asking these questions?" Diana demanded, her voice shaking.

"This is ridiculous," Todd said. "How many times do we have to tell you we weren't here?"

"Can you account for each other's movements Saturday night?" Davenport asked them. "Were you together?"

"I already told you," Drew said, "I went to a nearby casino."

"And I was at my hotel," Todd declared, his arms still crossed. He stood as if to dismiss the deputies. "Is that it?"

"For now," Davenport said evenly.

Todd led them to the door. Resigned, he said, "We had planned to attend the event in the plaza tonight, but, with all the drama, I doubt it's possible now."

"You are free to move around the community, Mr. Vogel," Davenport said, motioning Powers to follow him to the door. "I'll let you know when I hear from the police garage and the funeral home."

Todd opened the door as Amanda and Jordan Davis paused their Mercedes momentarily in front of Todd's house. They glanced briefly at Todd before proceeding into their driveway.

"Great," Todd said. "And he's my friend."

Davenport and Powers gave their apologies and left, following the car hauler up Marlin Lane.

◆ ◆ ◆ ◆ ◆

"Damn it, Drew!" Todd screamed, as he stood at the sideboard and poured a generous shot of scotch into a Waterford glass. "Were you here?"

Drew left his coffee on the end table, joined his father at the sideboard, and poured himself a drink. "I was in Orlando with you, remember?"

"It's still morning," Diana observed from her place on the sofa.

"Be quiet," her brother snorted. "So self-righteous. Just like her."

"Like Mother?" Diana's hands clenched in her lap. "How dare you!"

Drew gulped his drink. "I'm sorry. I didn't mean it, but damn, Diana, I don't know how you can be so calm."

"I'm not calm. I'm furious. I'm sick of your bullshit!" Diana said.

"Leave me alone," Drew said, his face contorted. He sat in a chair and emptied his glass.

Todd collapsed onto the sofa and gulped his drink. Diana sighed heavily as she rose and began pacing the floor. "Dad, were you having an affair?"

"Why do you ask?" He sighed, exasperated.

"Because Mom seemed upset about more than business issues."

"We had managerial differences—nothing to cause a divorce," Todd retorted. "And just so you know, your wonderful mother was having an affair. I've known for awhile. I even guessed he'd been here when the police told me about the sheets and her clothing. If it wasn't the Mexican, it had to be him. It wasn't me."

"Who's the man?" Drew asked.

"What does it matter?" Diana said. "He didn't kill her. If he did, the cops wouldn't be bothering you two."

"Don't let that detective get under your skin," Todd said. "It has to be that Mexican cop. He's got them feeling sorry for the illegals. I think they want to make it look like they're doing their job. I'm not worried."

"You're sure?" Drew asked. "They seemed pretty determined to give both of us a hard time. It didn't feel like they were just checking off boxes."

"I just want it to be over," Todd said.

Diana retrieved her coffee cup and took it to the kitchen. "I can't take this anymore. Drew, can I borrow your rental?"

"Sure. Just don't crash it."

CHAPTER 48

Detective Davenport greeted officers and staff as he passed through the Sheriff's Department squad room, alive with the cacophony of overlapping conversations. His cubicle, which he called his office because it was larger than the others, was located at the rear of the squad room. He settled into his chair, checked his emails and reviewed the full reports submitted by his team.

He studied Malloy's report on the participants at the Orlando convention. Malloy had minimized the importance of the nearly four-hour gap between when Vogel left the bar and reappeared in the hotel parking lot. *Where did he go?* The trip to the pharmacy was a poor alibi. Davenport could drive from Orlando to Garland in an hour during the day. It would take another half-hour to get to The Havens. In the middle of the night, the round trip would take two or two-and-a-half hours, tops. Why hadn't Malloy highlighted this detail? He knew Stokes would have jumped on it.

He had been hard on Malloy, he knew, but not as hard as he should have been. He hoped Malloy's trip to Orlando would fill in the time gaps, and perhaps broaden his perspective. In the meantime, he felt lucky not to get a call from Aguila's lawyer.

Davenport also thought about Drew. It seemed odd that he and Todd stayed at different hotels. Wouldn't they take the opportunity to stay at the same hotel—have dinner, talk about the businesses, grandkids, whatever? Maybe lunch and golf were enough for them. Or was something else going on?

His mind wandered to the Aguila women's account of the car nearly hitting them Sunday night. It fit the general description of Todd's car, but so did hundreds of cars in The Havens. What kind of connection could there be between the Vogels and Julio Gonzalez? He was missing something, though he could sense the answer lurking just below the surface.

His phone rang. "Sir," the desk sergeant said, "there's a lawyer here to see you, Ronald Murphy."

"Take him to the conference room."

◆ ◆ ◆ ◆ ◆

Davenport studied the tall, elderly man with sparse gray hair and black-rimmed glasses. "I appreciate your willingness to fly down and meet with me," Davenport said.

"I was coming down today anyway, to meet with the family. I'm staying here in Garland."

"This is a terrible time for the Vogel family," Davenport said.

Murphy adjusted his glasses. "I'm not sure why you requested this meeting and these documents." He indicated his briefcase.

Davenport leaned forward. "We have learned from various sources that there might have been confusion within the family about the disposition of the family businesses, and how ownership might have been complicated by a divorce between Barbara and Todd. I believe you might be able to help us understand the financial arrangements of Denton Sales."

"Are you saying that family members are being investigated in regard to Barbara's murder?" Murphy's eyes narrowed behind his slipping glasses, and he adjusted them again. "Todd said Barbara had been murdered by a thief. If you suspect otherwise, any conversations I have with the family are covered by attorney-client privilege."

"Would you serve as defense attorney for any member of the Vogel family?"

"I represent the family business, but I normally worked with

Barbara, as I had with her parents. I handle personal matters with the family from time to time."

"We are still investigating several scenarios, but since Mr. Gonzalez is dead, we can't interview him. You should know that we are looking carefully at Todd Vogel. If he is charged with a crime, would you serve as his defense attorney?"

"No, I'd help him find representation."

"Then, let's talk about the trust," Davenport said. "Do you have a copy for me?"

Murphy nodded and pulled a document from his briefcase. "I'm not sure how this will help you," he said, resigned. "Barbara's parents, Charles and Susan Denton, opened Denton Equipment and Supply in Chicago. Both Barbara and her brother, Brian, worked in the store growing up, learning the business. When Brian died in Vietnam, Barbara became more involved in the business, working in the office while completing her MBA. She met Todd in graduate school, and when they married, he became part of the family business. The business did very well, and Charlie and Susan decided to open a second store in central Florida and eventually retire here."

When Murphy hesitated, Davenport nodded for him to continue. "After Charlie and Susan passed away, Barbara and Todd took over the Florida store, and Diana and Drew ran the Chicago business."

"When did the elder Dentons establish the trust?" Davenport asked.

"When Barbara and Todd married. Then, when Charlie and Susan procured the space for the Florida business, they asked me to update it, designating Barbara as the beneficiary of both stores at their death. Under the terms, Barbara would be authorized to assign the management of the stores using her judgment. If Barbara died, Todd would be the beneficiary of the Florida business, and her children would become joint beneficiaries of the Chicago store. That's fairly standard, but there was one very specific stipulation. If either of them, Barbara or Todd, filed for divorce, Todd would have no claim whatsoever in either business."

"What does this mean for the twins?" Davenport asked.

"Once either Todd or Barbara filed—filing was the trigger, not finalization of the divorce—Barbara would own both businesses. The twins could buy her out of one or both businesses, or continue to work as managers."

Davenport placed his elbows on the desk, his chin resting on his fist. "That seems unusual. Isn't it more common for business assets to be divided or determined in the process of divorce? Why did they make this stipulation?"

Murphy sat back, his hands on his knees. "Again, I'm not sure how much of this is covered by attorney-client privilege."

"Mr. Murphy," Davenport pressed, "you are the attorney for a business whose owner has been murdered. If you want to fulfill your obligation to the trust, help me find Barbara's killer."

Murphy's gray eyes skittered around the room before focusing on the detective. "Barbara's parents didn't like Todd. In fact, I think they were surprised the marriage lasted. Barbara graduated *summa cum laude* in her program. Todd barely earned his degree. Before they married, Barbara worked at Denton's, as I said. Todd worked at the same firm where his father worked, but he lost the job. According to Charlie, the Dentons brought him into the business, assuming they could keep an eye on him. Unfortunately, it soon became clear that Todd...lacked discipline."

"In what way?"

"Both Denton businesses depend on large construction contracts—backhoes, earth movers, trucks. The Garland store is located in the heart of agricultural Florida. Their major customers are owners or investors in large-scale agriculture, horse farms, and expanding retail. Those contracts are worth a lot of money, and Todd relishes his role as promoter, courting executives with entertainment."

"Isn't that an important part of sales?"

"Yes, but in Todd's case, the promotion budget often exceeded the income earned."

"Is there any indication that either of the businesses might be in trouble?" Davenport asked. "Ms. Fulton, Barbara's accountant, seemed concerned about the issues you have just raised."

"I'm licensed in both Illinois and Florida, and I represent both businesses. As trustee, I file a report every year along with financial statements. Barbara and Diana provide me with the annual reports from each business. It appears that both businesses are in trouble. I suspect Drew takes after his father."

"Was there a divorce pending when she died?" Davenport asked.

Murphy paused and pulled a document from his folder. "She signed the papers Friday while Todd was in Orlando."

"The day before she died?" Davenport said, leaning back. "Did Todd or the twins know about the filing?"

"They know now. Todd was served yesterday. He called me, accusing me of conspiring with Barbara's family to cut him out of the business. He's furious. Said he'd see me in court."

Davenport leaned in again. "Are you sure he didn't know about this stipulation before Barbara died?"

Murphy's eyes roamed the room again. "He called me about a month ago, asking general questions about the trust. He had never called me before, and it seemed odd. He asked about how the businesses would be divided in case of a divorce. I asked him if there was something wrong, and he said no, but Barbara called me soon after and directed me to start divorce proceedings."

"When he called, did you tell him he'd be out of the trust if she filed for divorce?"

"Yes, but he seemed agitated, and I'm not sure he really

listened or even understood that the divorce filing initiated the change." He paused, considering his words. "Todd isn't a good businessman. He tends to hear what he wants to hear, and not read the small print."

"When did he learn he had already lost his interest in the businesses?"

"As I said, he called me yesterday, after he was served—at a restaurant unfortunately. That's when I explained again about the stipulation."

"And did he act like he already knew this?" Davenport asked.

"No, he acted surprised. Said he didn't believe it."

"So, when Barbara died, he may have thought he would inherit the Florida business?"

"Yes, and the twins thought they would inherit the Chicago store."

Davenport furrowed his brow. "And you didn't consider bringing these details to our attention?"

"It was a robbery-murder," Murphy replied, "and I understood it was solved. I never considered it. Besides, if Todd knew she filed, it wouldn't matter. It was already done. Her death would change nothing."

"Do you think Barbara told him? Perhaps threatened him in anger? Perhaps she thought it might change his behavior?" Davenport looked at his watch. "You do see that if Todd believed he would be cut out of the trust if Barbara filed, he would have an interest in her dying before that happened?"

CHAPTER 49

Thursday afternoon

The Aguila household had been unusually quiet since Martín's confrontation with Detective Malloy on Wednesday. Martín had been furious, contacting his lawyer as soon as he left the interview. Everyone gave him space, as he was in what Theresa called his "slow-burn mode." Claire knew what that meant—her father trying to control his temper. The household retreated into their own worlds. Cristina worked on her doctoral thesis in Claire's room, while Madge, strangely subdued, worked in the bedroom she shared with Cristina, perusing documents that George had forwarded to her from the university lab. Claire and Roberto took walks through the Sky and Sun Havens and relaxed at the Sand Bar pool. On Wednesday evening they drove into Garland for dinner away from The Havens.

The subdued mood had continued into Thursday. While Claire, Theresa, and Cristina prepared their Mexican lunch, Roberto helped Madge make her airline reservations to coincide with his own flights. Martín mowed the front nine at the golf course and returned home in time for lunch, feeling calmer and ready to socialize again. Now, the revived group sat around the table on the lanai, surrounded by plates covered with discarded corn husks and the remnants of Yucatecan chicken and rice.

"I've missed real Mexican food," Roberto said. "Thank you."

"I wish your mother and daughter were here," Cristina said. "I'd love to meet them."

Claire smiled. "I haven't met Mrs. Salinas yet," she said, "but you'd love Marta."

"I want you all to meet them," Roberto said, throwing Claire a brief look.

Martín took a sip of his iced tea. "Roberto, I'm sorry your trip hasn't been more enjoyable. I feel like we embroiled you unnecessarily in our drama."

"I am not at all sorry, Martín," Roberto assured him. "I've enjoyed meeting you, your lovely wife, and amazing granddaughter."

"What about me?" Claire quipped, "and Madge."

Roberto smiled. "I learned about your qualities last year…"

"And yet you still came," Claire laughed. "I'm glad you did." She turned to Madge. "I'm glad you came too, Madge."

"Me too," Madge said, "I loved meeting your family." She gathered up the dishes and carried them to the kitchen while Cristina collected silverware and platters.

"We wish you could stay longer," Theresa said to Roberto.

"I would love to stay, but…do you have the phrase about fish smelling after three days?"

Martín laughed. "We do, but we wish you could stay longer, so we can find out."

"As much as I would love to test the theory, I'm a lowly Mexican police officer on vacation. My commander suggested I extend my stay, since I haven't taken a vacation in years." Roberto smiled. "I suspect he expected Miami Beach, not a retirement community."

"And for that, I am grateful," Claire said.

When Madge and Cristina returned to the lanai, Theresa said, "And we're also glad to finally meet the famous Madge Carmichael, navigator supreme, so I hear."

Madge smiled. "That's not what Claire said as we sped through Mayan villages." She winked at her friend. "In fact, you would be embarrassed at the language your daughter used, in English, Spanish, *and* Mayan."

Claire laughed. "Only because I had Roberto and homeland security agents yelling at me through the phone while we chased a murderer."

"I'm also very glad to meet you," Cristina said to Madge. "I love listening to your stories. Now I know who encouraged Mom to finish her doctorate in anthropology."

"She didn't need much encouragement," Madge said. "She persisted despite getting pregnant with you a little earlier than she and your father anticipated."

"Still, I'm glad you were her mentor," Martín said.

The Mexican national anthem emanated from somewhere, and everyone looked at Roberto as he pulled his phone from his jeans pocket. He spoke for a few minutes and hung up, looking at Claire. "Deputy Stokes. You missed her call. She wants to meet you at the DPS. She'll take you to the police garage to look at Mr. Vogel's car."

Cristina jumped up. "Can I go?"

Claire looked at Roberto, reluctant to leave him behind.

"Don't worry about me," he said. "I'm happy to hang out with your family—is that what you say?"

Martín smiled. "Yes, we have things to talk about."

"We'll be back in time for *Fiesta* Night," Claire promised.

"As an anthropologist, I'm sure you'll love it," Theresa said, smiling.

Madge stood suddenly. "Do you mind if I borrow the golf cart? I have things to do," she announced. "I'll meet you all at the plaza."

◆ ◆ ◆ ◆ ◆

While Davenport waited for Stokes to arrive at the police garage with Claire Aguila, he studied Julio Gonzalez's car, an older white Ford Fiesta with numerous dents. Jordan Davis had described the car as a gray-white sedan with no identifiable features. It would be impossible for the Davises to mistake Julio's car for the one they described. Yet, after seeing Julio's car in the newspaper, they had changed their statement. *Why?* he thought.

Deputy Paul Clark of the evidence team approached with a clipboard and handed it to Davenport. "Mrs. Vogel's car is still here."

"Mr. Vogel hasn't picked it up?" Davenport asked. "What about this car?" He indicated Julio's car.

"We're done with it," Clark said. "There are two items of interest—a cellphone that we sent to the lab, and this." He took an evidence bag from the front seat. "We found this under the driver's seat—a parking ticket from The Havens DPS."

Davenport looked at the ticket. "Dick Broden, the night security, issued it the night of Mrs. Vogel's murder," he said. "And the phone?"

"Still dumping the data," Clark said. "Also, Mrs. Gonzalez has called every day. She wants her car back."

Davenport looked through the window at the blood spatter pattern on the passenger seat. "Tell her we're very sorry," Davenport said, "and, when you get the phone records, take them to Mrs. Gonzalez to identify any unusual phone numbers."

"Yes, sir."

Davenport turned when he heard footsteps entering the garage. He greeted Stokes, Claire, and Cristina, then directed them to the silver Lexus. The doors and trunk were open, and fingerprint dust covered everything. A plastic tub, piled with evidence bags, sat on a table next to the car. Davenport stood aside as Claire and Cristina walked around the Lexus. "What do you think?"

"Could you turn on the headlights?" Claire asked.

Stokes reached into the car and flicked them on.

Cristina nodded, pointing to the front fender where a license plate would go. "The car we saw had a vanity plate here—it had capital letters and no numbers."

Stokes knelt to examine the area she had indicated. "It looks cleaner than the rest of the fender, and a bit scratched."

Cristina circled the car again. "It looks like the car," she said. "Could the plate have been removed?"

"It's possible," Davenport said. "I'll give you a few minutes to look it over."

While Claire and Cristina circled the car, Davenport turned to Stokes. "Have the Davises come in yet?"

"Later this afternoon, sir," she said.

He handed her the parking ticket. "When you go back to the DPS, give this to Judy and find out where it was issued."

"Yes, sir."

"Detective?"

Davenport turned to see Cristina staring into the evidence tub.

"What's this?" she asked.

Davenport joined her at the tub. Cristina pointed at something near the bottom of the bin. He extracted the evidence bag she indicated. They all stared at a vanity plate: MBA-UC.

Stokes picked up a clipboard from the table and skimmed the list with her fingernail. "They found it under the padding in the trunk."

Davenport moved away as his phone rang. He called to Stokes, who joined him away from the others. "It's Griffin," he said. "He found discarded clothing with blood-like stains and a damaged flip phone in a convenience store dumpster along the county road."

CHAPTER 50

Madge sat in the chair at Pauline's Salon while Donna, her stylist, pulled foils from her hair. She had succumbed to the suggestion of "highlights" and had spent the last hour enduring the process.

"Are you new to The Havens?" Donna asked, her similarly tinted waves falling over the rims of her glasses.

"Just visiting," Madge said. "Wow, there's a lot going on here...a murder and everything?" At the next chair, the salon owner, Pauline, snipped away at the tinted blonde curls of a thin fifty-something woman. "Who are you visiting?" the client asked.

"The Aguilas," Madge said, and several short gasps erupted around her.

Another stylist, Becky, put her hands on either side of her client's head. "Hold still, Shirley, or I'll have to shave your head." She glanced at Madge. "I hope your friends aren't associated with that Mexican who killed Barbara."

Before Madge could respond, Donna said, "It's dreadful. All those workers...coming and going, stealing from us."

"I heard there's a Mexican cop or lawyer going around with that detective," Shirley said, her head still swaying from side to side. "What's that all about?"

Madge heard an intake of breath coming from Pauline's client.

"Ladies, come on," Pauline said. "Barbara and Amanda were friends. Let it rest."

Shirley turned toward Pauline's chair, where Amanda Davis sat stiffly, blinking back tears. "I'm sorry, hon," Shirley said. "It must be horrible, living across the street. It could have been you."

Donna moved Madge to the sink as the women discussed the unreliability of the workers, so Madge restrained from inserting her comments.

Back in her chair, Madge held her breath as Becky sprayed a heavy dose of hairspray on Shirley's somewhat jagged haircut.

"Gwen Estes came in yesterday," Becky said. "She saw a blue car at the Vogels around midnight on Saturday. She was walking Precious—that spoiled dog—all it has to do is whine and she'll put her robe over her pajamas and take it for a walk, bless her heart. Anyway, she saw this car, and then she saw it again in front of The Barn. Judy told her they brought the guy in."

"Wait," Becky said, her scissors paused mid-snip. "Isn't that the Mexican who's living here?"

All heads turned toward Madge, who bit her lip before she could respond with her usual sarcasm. Instead, she said, "I like the color, Donna. Can you trim a few inches?"

Pauline stood back a step to assess her work. "Amanda, you should know what's going on. You saw Julio's car, right?"

Amanda sniffled and looked at Pauline through the mirror. "I'm not sure." Hair blowers stopped, scissors paused, and all the women waiting for their appointments lifted their heads from their magazines.

Pauline said, "That's what we heard…come on, hon, tell us."

"I don't know anything," Amanda snapped. "Jordan saw the car, I didn't."

"What's going to happen with Todd and Julie?" Becky asked the group.

"Who cares about Julie?" Pauline said. "She's a gold digger… this is, what? Her third husband? I don't think Steve has to worry. Todd has nothing to offer her."

"It's all about poor Barbara," Shirley said. "What about Bruce?" All eyes turned to Amanda.

"Bruce might have been there," Amanda confessed.

"Maybe he and Barbara had a fight?" Donna said, taking up the fresh topic.

"Perhaps it's something worse?" Becky suggested as Shirley rose from her chair, hanging back so as not to miss any gossip. "I heard her driveway was a regular parking lot that night–and with Todd out of town…"

"Maybe Barbara was into something," Donna suggested. "She's so goody-goody, who knows? She might've been the local drug dealer."

Becky chuckled. "Well, who knows?"

Donna removed Madge's cape and set her free. "Come on, ladies," Donna said, "we all know Barbara. Can you see her dealing drugs from her house?"

"You never know about people," Shirley said, frowning at her hair before stomping to the checkout.

Madge avoided checking out by skimming the shelves of hair products that took up an entire wall in the salon. *What's hair refresher?* When Amanda approached the cash register, Madge grabbed a bottle of organic conditioner and stood behind Amanda in line. Madge paid her bill, gulped at the price, and hurried out the door. Amanda stood nearby, wiping her eyes with a tissue.

"Amanda?" Madge took her arm. "I'm sorry about what happened in there. I'm a stranger here, but I can tell how close you and Barbara were."

"All that Southern 'hon' stuff…it's bullshit…accusing her of dealing drugs?" Amanda paused and looked at Madge. "Listen, my husband and I have to talk to the police now. We made a terrible mistake." She seemed about to say more, but something caught her attention, and instead her face fell. "Oh, no."

Madge followed her gaze to the window of Betty's Café. "Isn't that Todd's daughter?" Madge asked.

"I have to go," Amanda said, and walked quickly away.

Madge entered the café. Diana sat at a window, speaking on her cellphone while wiping tears from her eyes. Madge stood uncertainly nearby until Diana finished her call.

"Ms. Vogel? I'm Madge Carmichael. May I join you?"

"Diana Thurman," Diana said. "This isn't a good time." She looked up at Madge. "Do I know you?"

"I'm visiting my friend—Claire Aguila. I recognize you from the restaurant a few nights ago."

"Oh, great," Diana said, her face flushed, remembering her embarrassment when her father had been served divorce papers in front of everyone. She sighed and motioned Madge to sit.

"I'm sorry to impose," Madge said, "but I want to extend my condolences."

"My father thinks the Aguilas are intruding on our lives and our grief."

"I understand how you feel, but I assure you that the Aguilas aren't like that."

"Dad is convinced that a Mexican worker killed my mother," Diana said. "He can't understand why the officers haven't interrogated Carlos or Mr. Aguila."

"But they did," Madge said, "twice." She sighed. "I don't know who killed your mother, but I know you are hurting and looking for answers."

Diana sniffled into her tissue. "Is your friend Claire the one who's with the Mexican cop?"

"Yes, they're friends."

"Do you think I could talk to them?"

Madge sat back. "I'm sure you could. Why?"

"I can't say, but I need to talk to someone who's not official… if you know what I mean. I…I just found something, and I need advice."

"We'll be at *Fiesta* Night tonight. Will you be there?" Madge asked.

"Dad mentioned something about it. Drew and I were scheduled to leave tomorrow, but the detective asked us to stay—like we could refuse." She pulled a small pad from her purse, wrote on it, and tore a sheet off for Madge. "My number," she said. Madge accepted it, then asked for the pad and wrote down Claire's phone number in turn.

"I'll give them the message," Madge said, standing to leave.

"I...I just don't know what to do," Diana said, stifling tears.

CHAPTER 51

A hot and exhausted team gathered again at the Gardenia County Sheriff's Department. It was late afternoon, and their day had started at six-thirty a.m. Davenport, tie askew, and Stokes, hair hanging in strands from her bun, were frazzled. Powers slumped in his chair, a lab report clasped in his hands. Griffin, however, could hardly contain his excitement. His green eyes shone with anticipation.

Davenport had sorted papers into two piles. "I now consider Julio's death a murder, and the two murders connected. I'd like to start with the evidence we've collected today, so we're all on the same page." He looked at the youngest member of the team. "Griffin," he said, "tell us what you have."

Griffin leaned forward in his chair. "I met Craig Hughes at the Glen Haven locker room with the warrant. The manager wasn't happy, but he cleared the golfers out. Hughes took the golf bag to the lab. He's rushing the analysis, but it might be a few days."

"Thanks to our Mrs. Van Dee, we have strong evidence that he took his clubs to Orlando," Davenport said and turned to Powers. "Good detail on your report, Mike."

Powers sat back, straightening his uniform tie. "Thank you, sir."

"Now, Griffin," Davenport said, "show us what you found in the trash."

Griffin extracted a small stack of photographs from an envelope and spread them in front of the team: blood-covered slacks, an expensive golf jacket, running shoes, and a crushed flip phone. "We found these stashed in a dumpster at a convenience store along the county road between The Havens and Garland. Lucky for us, the trash collectors arrived as we started. They actually helped go through it. Not a fun job, by the way…"

"Tell me about it," Powers grimaced. "Finally, someone lower on the totem pole than me."

But Griffin's enthusiasm hadn't waned. "My question is, who wears a Columbia jacket to commit a murder?"

"Who indeed," Davenport agreed. "The lab has the clothes, and the tech team has the smashed phone. Lucky for us—unlucky for the suspect—the SIM card was damaged but readable. Hughes will report on it as soon as he can."

"We still don't know whose clothes these are," Stokes noted.

"Let's hope the phone helps us out," Davenport said. He turned to Stokes. "Can you report the findings on Todd's car?"

Stokes stood and pulled a clear plastic tub toward the table. "Doctor Aguila and her daughter weren't positive about Todd's car until they recognized the vanity plate—MBA-UC—which was found hidden under the trunk carpeting."

Stokes extracted several golf balls that immediately rolled around the table. "These were in Todd's trunk. Loose golf balls also corroborate Mrs. Van Dee's statement." She then pulled out items most cars contain: maps, a handful of store and gas receipts, disposable coffee cups and water bottles, placing them all on the table.

"Did we ever get a final statement from the Davises on the car they saw?" Powers asked.

"I hope so," Stokes said. "Mr. and Mrs. Davis came in to change their statement…again. They originally reported a light-colored car at the Vogel house, with a very vague description. Then, when the photograph of Julio's car appeared in the *Gazette*, they came in to—let's say enhance—their story, claiming the photograph of Julio's car resembled the car they saw, scrapes and all. Today, they changed their story again. I think Amanda's friendship with Barbara trumped Jordan's friendship with Todd. Amanda seemed determined to get the description right this time. Now they say that Drew's rental car resembles the car they saw."

"Drew's car?" asked Powers. "So, he was here after all?"

"He still denies it," Davenport said, "but that might change with Malloy's findings."

"Has Malloy learned anything in Orlando?" Stokes asked.

"Malloy called today," Davenport reported. "He hasn't found anyone who saw Todd between ten-thirty Saturday night and two o'clock Sunday morning. He wants more time to check up on Drew. I think he's beginning to see a larger picture. He confirmed that Todd and Drew had lunch and golfed together Saturday, but went separate ways afterwards. Todd returned to the conference hotel for dinner in the evening, as we know. Drew spent the early evening at a casino with clients but cashed out at eight o'clock. Malloy's trying to trace Drew's actions after that time, because he, too, has a four-hour gap between cashing out and returning to his hotel room around midnight. He could easily have traveled the distance to and from The Havens."

"You mean they both could have gone to see Barbara that night?" Griffin asked. "Was it planned or coincidence?"

"We don't know for sure that either of them drove to The Havens," Davenport said, "but Malloy wants a warrant for Drew's rental car. This is particularly interesting since Mr. Davis finally admitted the car they saw later Saturday night resembled Drew's rental, which is a light gray."

Powers extracted several documents from his envelope. "Besides Drew's print on the refrigerator, they found Drew's and Bruce Cook's prints along the door frame and knobs of the kitchen door to the garage."

"And Drew still denies being there," Davenport said. "Thanks again to Mrs. Van Dee, we can assume it was Bruce's silver car that pulled into the garage around seven, but that's probably not the car she saw leave at ten."

Powers smiled slightly and continued, "Bruce Cook wins the DNA test for the bedsheets. His prints were also found in the master bathroom, though whoever washed or wiped the drink glasses clean likely erased his prints."

"So, Cook's going to have to tell his wife, after all," Davenport said. "Anything else?"

Powers skimmed the report, then shook his head. "I don't believe this," he said. "Todd's fingerprints are on the hundred-dollar bill found under Barbara's body."

"Todd touched the bloody money?" Griffin blinked. "How did it get there?"

Davenport shrugged. "The lab tech thinks it was dropped there and she fell on it when she was shot. It strongly suggests that Todd was there."

"Is it possible the prints were made before the murder?" Stokes asked. "Todd must have handled the money when he put it in the security box."

"According to Hughes, he touched the money sometime before the blood dried," Powers said.

The team sat silently for several seconds, taking the information in.

"So perhaps they were both there?" Stokes asked. "How can that be?"

Davenport, who had been quiet during this revelation, adjusted his glasses and crossed his hands on the desk. "I don't know what the hell it means." He stared out the window to the darkened sky. "Anything new on the gun, Powers?" he asked after a long pause.

"According to Hughes, Todd's gun killed both Barbara and Julio," Powers reported. "There was no gun powder residue or back spatter on Julio's right hand—his left was still bandaged. If he had killed himself, there would be both." Powers pulled another photo from the folder and placed it in the middle of the table. "In this photograph, you can see the large void area on the passenger seat where someone sat, blocking the blood spatter."

"Someone was in the car with him?" Griffin asked.

"Let's look at that jacket again," Davenport said.

Griffin placed the photo in the middle of the table. Blood spatter covered the front and left side of the jacket.

"That means the murderer leaned over from the passenger seat to shoot Julio?" Powers asked, shaking his head. "Todd?"

"What about the blood on Julio's clothes Saturday night?" Stokes asked.

Powers skimmed again. "It was all Julio's blood. None from Barbara. He wasn't there."

Leaning back, Davenport said, "The evidence we now have connects the two crimes, and the common denominator seems to be Todd Vogel. There are too many connections between these two murders: the gun, the identification of his car, his golf clubs, and his lies. And if the blood on the dumpster clothes is Julio's, we have a strong case."

"We still have no evidence that Todd returned home that night," Powers said.

"But we do have a witness sighting of his car around midnight at the G&G," Stokes mused, "and his appearance in the hotel parking lot Sunday at two a.m."

The door opened, and Deputy Hughes entered. "You guys are going to love me." Hughes held up two evidence bags. "We don't have your lab results for the dumpster clothes, but we found two items I knew you'd want to see."

He handed one bag to Davenport. "Your missing earring."

"Where was it?" Davenport asked.

"In a crease in the bottom of the golf bag," Hughes said, smiling. He held up the second bag, which contained the damaged flip phone and SIM card.

"The SIM card holds only one number. It's also the only number that Mrs. Gonzalez couldn't identify on Julio's smart phone, and it was called twice."

"Wait!" Stokes said. "What about those receipts in Todd's car?" She rummaged through the pile of items found in Vogel's glove compartment. "Here's something," she said, extracting a receipt. "Walmart, dated three weeks ago, for two flip phones."

"Did you call the mystery number?" Davenport asked Hughes.

"That's your job," Hughes said, handing him a phone with the installed SIM card.

Davenport called the number. They all leaned in, listening.

"Hello?" came the response.

"Who's this?" asked Davenport.

"Ryan. Who's this?"

CHAPTER 52

Streetlamps illuminated the trees and flowers in Founder's Plaza. The narrow avenue surrounding it was closed to car traffic, so the Aguilas, crammed into Martín's car, parked in the public lot and walked the distance to the plaza. They crossed the avenue, dodging golf carts that were competing for parking spots along the curb. They joined the growing crowd of people congregating at the beverage and food kiosks, but the Aguilas directed their attention to the unofficial parade of customized carts driving around the block, lights flashing and music blasting from CD players.

Cristina stared at the drivers, mostly senior men wearing Hawaiian shirts and sunglasses— despite the darkened skies— cruising alone. In other carts, couples called out to friends and waved, the men a little less flashy, but the women dressed to display their best assets.

"Oh my," Claire laughed. "This is like high school. We did this on Friday nights in the summer, honking our horns and playing music. My friend, Karen, had the nicest car—her brother's Volkswagen convertible. If my mother knew what I was doing, she would have killed me."

"Did you know about it, Nana?" Cristina asked Theresa.

Theresa laughed. "That's in the parental category of 'you don't want to know.'"

Theresa's friend, Rose, rode by with her husband, waving at the Aguilas. Claire recognized her by her bright blue hair, now adorned with a flashing pink tiara.

"Where's Madge?" Theresa asked, reminded of her absence.

"She left in the golf cart this afternoon."

"She'll be here," Claire assured her. "She wouldn't miss this for the world." As she spoke, she heard a honk, and turned to see Madge pulling the golf cart into one of the empty parking spots.

"This is awesome!" Madge exclaimed as she joined them at the curb, adjusting the bodice of her ankle-length lavender and pink Hawaiian muumuu. "This place is an anthropological mecca. It has the whole package…conspicuous consumption, baby boomers acting like teenagers—cliques and bullying—not to mention the climate."

"We were discussing the same thing," Cristina said, studying Madge. "You got your hair done."

"Can you believe they charge $180 for this—plus tip?" She pulled at her curls, now a lighter shade of gray. "I could fly to Guatemala for less." Madge looked around. "Where's Roberto? He's missing the show!"

"He's being very mysterious," Theresa said. "He got a call and left the house awhile ago. He said he'd meet us here."

"There he is," Cristina said, pointing toward Roberto, who was maneuvering between two customized carts, a Mercedes blaring "Light My Fire" and a red roadster competing with "Bohemian Rhapsody."

"*¡Ay caramba!*" Roberto said, as he joined them. "This is some *fiesta!*"

They walked together along the sidewalk that lined the plaza, stopping at the beer kiosk, where Martín offered to buy drinks.

"None for me," said Roberto, and the others also declined.

"What's going on?" Martín asked.

"I can't say," Roberto answered, "but this is not going to be a festive evening for everyone."

A loud screech drew their attention to a sky-blue Mustang golf cart with a fringe along the top.

"There's Louise," Theresa said as they approached her friend from the euchre and book clubs. Madge waved wildly.

Louise introduced her husband, then addressed Madge, saying, "We all hope you move here!"

"I like Louise," Madge said as they moved on. "I might even like euchre."

They turned away from the cart parade, and Theresa led them into the plaza, where the largest crowd converged from all directions around a raised gazebo. A dance floor had been laid in front of it, rows of folding chairs on three sides. A band was setting up. A fifty-something woman wearing a tight, gold, sequined tunic over red spandex set up microphones as the band members hung a banner—Rita and her Rockin' Rollers. Claire's group wandered through the park as they waited for the music to start.

Roberto's attention turned to a copse of trees at the far corner of the plaza. "Stop," he said.

In the ambient light of a streetlamp, the group watched Diana and Drew, huddled together as Deputy Powers and another officer led Todd away from the park. Judy Barnaby stood to the side, next to a heavy-set man with a gray fringe of hair, wearing a short-sleeved shirt and bow tie.

"Who's that man with Judy Barnaby?" Madge asked.

"That's her husband, Phil," Theresa replied, softly. "I hear he was a high-powered attorney in Chicago."

A crowd had started to meander toward the scene, as Phil Barnaby, his face reddened, stormed up to the deputies. "Don't talk without an attorney, Todd…" Phil's voice reverberated in the night air, only to be drowned out when the Rockin' Rollers erupted with a deafening blare of electric guitars. Todd stood quietly between the deputies as Barnaby took a belligerent stance and spoke again, Rita's falsetto failing to mask his final words: "Don't worry, Todd. I'll be right there!"

As the deputies led Todd toward the squad car parked just

beyond the plaza, Roberto directed the group's attention to a young man standing nearby, wearing jeans and a Grateful Dead T-shirt. "That's Deputy Griffin. He's on duty. If anything happens, find him. He'll know what to do."

"What could happen?" Claire asked.

"I hope nothing," Roberto answered. They watched Drew and Diana stand in shocked silence as the deputies took their father away.

"Oh, I almost forgot," Madge said, taking a note from her bag. "I saw Diana at the diner. She asked me to give this to you, Claire, but she wants to talk to Roberto." She handed the note to Claire. "She's worried about something."

"Should I call her?" Claire asked Roberto.

"She needs to talk to Detective Davenport," Roberto warned. "Don't get involved."

The music, its volume not compensating for its quality, pulled them back toward the gazebo. The Righteous Brothers, covered poorly by one of the Rockin' Rollers, drew Martín and Theresa to the dance floor, followed by Roberto and Claire, representing the only people of color in the crowd.

Claire tried to push the arrest scene from her mind. She wanted to concentrate on the man she knew she loved—the man she was dancing with for the first time.

After a few songs, Roberto and Claire withdrew to the chairs to observe others. Claire rested her head on Roberto's shoulder. They laughed as they watched Martín and Cristina dance to "Old Time Rock and Roll." Many couples, of various gendered combinations—due to the obvious numerical discrepancy of females to males—now crowded the dance floor, doing a mishmash from the sixties—a jerk-like Mashed Potato and a very dangerous and painful-looking Twist. For a reason that Claire could not fathom, a group of middle-aged people dressed in square-dance costumes danced a do-si-do in a circle off to the side.

Claire left Roberto to find the restroom located along one edge of the plaza. The trash bins stood along the building, nearly filled with plastic beer glasses and trash from the food kiosks. Approaching the restroom, she noticed Diana and Drew seated on one of the benches at the curb. Diana sobbed while Drew sat straight, looking ahead, not touching her.

◆ ◆ ◆ ◆ ◆

Roberto sat alone on the bench, watching the Aguila entourage. Theresa and Martín danced, Martín's style hampered by his damaged leg. Madge sat on a nearby bench, surrounded by a group of ladies who listened intently to whatever she said. He was simultaneously disturbed and amazed at Claire's unlikely friend.

"So, what do you think?"

Roberto turned and smiled at Cristina, who joined him on the bench.

Roberto smiled. "At our *fiestas*, the young people dance in the plaza while the elders look on, watching their children and grandchildren for the smallest indiscretion." He turned to her. "What do you think of The Havens?"

"In our neighborhood, there's a shared history. Everyone knows everyone's life story, good and bad," Cristina said. "There's no history here. Instead, people are recreating themselves, but they're also leaving families behind—or perhaps their kids have left them behind." She paused as she watched the people laughing and singing along with the band. "But I understand this place better now than when I arrived."

Roberto thought about this. "In my neighborhood, it's all kids...and at least three generations per household." He appraised Cristina, thinking. "Do you think your grandparents will decide to stay in a place like this?"

"I doubt it," Cristina sighed.

"What about your mother?" he asked.

A twinkle entered Cristina's eye. "Not at all. She's torn between the tranquility of Northern Michigan and the intellectual stimulation of cities. She loves Merida."

Roberto looked toward the direction of the restroom to see if Claire was nearby, then looked intently at her daughter. "What do you think about your mother and me?"

Cristina smiled. "This is the happiest I've seen her in years, though she's trying to hide it, for my sake."

"I wish I knew how she feels."

"I don't think she knows how you feel about her."

"I'm passionate—my feelings are always on my sleeve, as you say."

Cristina scrunched her face. "I'm afraid I see you as reserved, even mysterious."

"That's my police training," Roberto said, smiling. "Underneath, I'm a passionate man trying to show your mother that I have another side."

Cristina frowned. "I don't want my mother to sit in Westport, Michigan, for the rest of her life. I want her to do something outrageous."

Roberto tipped his head and lowered his voice. "If I asked your mother to marry me, would we have your blessing?"

"Absolutely!"

As Claire left the restroom, Diana appeared from the side of the building. "Claire Aguila?"

Her nerves on edge, Claire jumped. "Diana!" she said.

Diana's eyes were reddened from crying. "I'm sorry. I didn't mean to scare you," she said. "Did Madge give you the message?"

"She said you wanted to talk to me," Claire said, trying to slow her breathing. "I'm sorry…I saw them take your father away."

Diana wiped at her eyes. "I don't understand why they took him, and why Mr. Barnaby made such a fuss about it. It was awful."

"I really don't know," Claire said, leading Diana to a bench away from the music. "Where's Drew?"

Diana glanced behind herself. "I don't know, and I don't care," she said, sniffling. "I hoped you could ask your detective friend to speak with me before I go to Detective Davenport. I don't know if he can help me, but…I found something…can he call me?"

"Madge gave me your number. When can you meet?"

"Tonight, if possible—away from Drew."

"You two talking about me?" Diana and Claire both jumped as Drew appeared from behind them. Diana gave Claire a desperate look as Drew came around the bench and faced them.

"Please accept my condolences," Claire said when Diana introduced them. Drew held his hand out to shake hers.

"That's a bad scratch," Claire said, as he pulled his hand back.

Drew laughed. "No good deed goes unpunished. That's what I get for working in Mom's garden."

Claire smiled, but she saw Diana frown.

"It's time to go," Drew said, motioning his sister to leave. Diana sat back against the bench as Drew reached for her arm. "Come on, Di. We have to go home then to Garland." He pulled her up from the bench. "Hurry." Diana gave Claire a quick glance, her lip trembling, as Drew led her away.

Claire looked around for Deputy Griffin, who was nowhere in sight. She grabbed her phone. "Roberto, come quick. I think Diana's in trouble."

Griffin emerged from the restroom and Claire ran to him. She pointed to the street where Drew's car sat at the curb, the emergency lights flashing. Drew was urging a reluctant Diana into the car.

"I think they're going to Todd's house," Claire said.

"Damn," Griffin said. He pulled out his phone as Roberto

joined them. "I'm calling for backup, but they're coming from Garland, and Powers took the squad car."

"My car's close," Roberto said. "I'll take you."

Roberto pulled Claire aside. "Stay here or go home. Promise?"

Claire knew he was referring to the last time he had issued such an order and she had disobeyed. "I promise," she said, then returned to the gazebo, where her family and Madge waited anxiously.

Madge spoke first. "What do we do now?"

CHAPTER 53

Deputy Powers brought Barnaby into the interview room where Todd sat nervously, watching Stokes set up the digital recorder. Powers handed Davenport a document and left the room. Todd introduced Barnaby to Davenport and Stokes. Davenport nodded to Stokes to start the recorder.

"Mr. Barnaby, are you acting as Mr. Vogel's defense attorney?" Davenport asked, studying the stocky man with the fringe of gray hair.

"I am his local representative until he hires a criminal attorney," Barnaby answered.

Davenport frowned. "Are you related to Judy Barnaby at the DPS?"

"She's my wife."

"I see," Davenport said. "Has Judy informed you about the cases?"

"She didn't have to. It's all in the *Gazette.*"

"Exactly," Davenport said, leaning forward. "You're not a defense attorney?"

Mr. Barnaby adjusted horn-rimmed glasses. "I was senior partner in a corporate law firm in Chicago, and I'm also licensed in Florida." He fingered his bow tie. "I saw how your Black deputy escorted Mr. Vogel from the plaza in front of the whole town. It was a disgrace!"

Stokes glared at Barnaby, the recorder preventing her from saying something detrimental to the interview.

"Mr. Barnaby," Davenport said, slowly and deliberately. "Deputy Powers—that's the name of the officer, by the way—has already informed me that you made the public disturbance."

"The whole town watched him being dragged away," Barnaby blustered.

"It's my understanding that the arrest occurred away from the crowds," Davenport reasoned.

"By now, the whole town knows I was arrested," Todd spat.

"These are serious crimes," Davenport said. "Let's begin, shall we?" He turned to Todd. "For the record, did Deputy Powers read you your Miranda Rights?"

"Yes," Todd said.

Davenport showed Todd the document Powers had given him. "This is your signature?"

"Yes."

"Do you know why you're here?"

Todd leaned back in his chair, his arms crossed. "I assume it's about my wife's murder, but it's harassment. I didn't do it."

"We do have a question about your alibi," Davenport said. "Where were you between ten-o'clock Saturday night and two o'clock Sunday morning?"

"At the convention hotel."

"Can you prove that?"

"This is ridiculous!" Barnaby blurted.

His face white, hands clutching his knees, Todd said, "I...met someone."

"Who?" Davenport asked.

"A friend, Lisa Monroe."

Davenport shrugged. "She claims you stood her up. Apparently, you left your group at the bar after ten o'clock and weren't seen again until two o'clock Sunday morning in the hotel parking lot. Where had you been?"

"To the pharmacy. I needed a pain reliever."

"For almost four hours?" Davenport said. "You can't walk a block in Orlando without finding a pharmacy."

"After I called my wife, I stayed in my room, but couldn't sleep. Around one o'clock I decided to look for a 24-hour pharmacy."

"Witnesses said the bag you carried was bulky. Could it have held your gun?" Stokes asked.

"Why would I have my gun?" Todd demanded.

"You tell me," Davenport said.

"Your deputy said the gun was in Julio's car with the jewelry. How could I have it?"

"That was Sunday night, when Julio was murdered," Davenport said.

"Murdered?" Todd said. "Not suicide?"

"It was murder," Davenport said, his voice terse.

"This is ludicrous," Barnaby said, his face reddening.

"Did you take your golf clubs to Orlando?" Davenport asked, changing the subject.

"No!" Todd protested. "I told you, I didn't take my golf clubs."

"Then why didn't you rent clubs when you golfed with your son?" Davenport asked. "We found a receipt in your car. You paid for two rounds of eighteen-hole golf and a cart, but only one set of clubs. Unless Drew brought his clubs on the plane, I suspect that the rental was for him."

"That doesn't matter," Todd said, his hands folded together.

"Perhaps not," Davenport said, "but it means you have lied to us, and it makes me want to know why." He leaned back. "We also have sufficient evidence that you and Mr. Gonzalez had some kind of relationship."

Barnaby sat back, teeth clenched, arms crossed as Davenport motioned to Stokes, who retrieved a bagged phone from the evidence tub. Todd's eyes widened.

"This is Julio's flip phone," Stokes said. "He hid it in the G&G."

"I never saw that before," Todd protested.

"That's interesting," Davenport said, "because we found a

receipt in your car for two such phones."

"Do you know where the second phone is?" Stokes asked.

"I have no idea about either phone," Todd said, his voice cracking. He watched as Stokes took two evidence bags from the tub, one containing a smart phone, the other a damaged flip phone.

"This phone is yours," Davenport said, holding up the smart phone he had seized with the warrant.

"Can I have it back?"

"No."

"That's not my phone," Todd said, indicating the damaged phone.

"Actually, it's the second phone you purchased."

"Where did you find that?" Barnaby asked.

"We'll get to that later," Davenport said. "For now, it's the SIM card that's important. Unfortunately, Mr. Vogel, you attempted to destroy the phone but didn't take the time to extract the SIM card. It was found with evidence of another crime."

Davenport watched Todd as he deflated in front of them, taking his head in his hands and pressing his eyes shut.

"Several calls were made between these two flip phones in the days before your wife's murder, several more between eleven and just after midnight Saturday night and early Sunday morning."

"I don't know what you're talking about," Todd's voice weakened with each denial.

Davenport leaned forward, his hands on the edge of the table. "I'm talking about a murder-for-hire," he said, his voice raised. "You hired Julio to kill your wife, but, for some reason, you came home late Saturday night. It's unlikely anyone would see you drive into your own garage that late."

Davenport paused to catch Todd's reaction. "We believe you found your wife dead. In a panic, you altered the scene. You repositioned her body and tied her hands with the sash. You took the watch and earrings from her body, and took the gun used to kill her. You also took the jewelry from your security box and hid the items in your golf bag until you could plant them in Julio's car, except for one earring you missed—we found that in a deep fold of your golf bag. I can't think of anything colder and more calculating than that."

Stokes interjected, "For reasons unknown, you touched, but did not take, a one-hundred-dollar bill you found under her body." She sat back and crossed her arms. "You did all that, then returned to Orlando."

"Wait a minute," Barnaby said, leaning forward. "You've just proved he didn't kill her."

"A criminal attorney would tell you, Mr. Barnaby, that hiring someone to kill his wife is the same thing." Davenport sighed and turned to Todd. "I think you hired Julio to kill her, and you tampered with a crime scene to incriminate Julio. But he didn't kill her."

"He must have!" Todd pleaded.

"You also pressured Mr. Davis to lie for you about the description of the car he saw," Stokes inserted.

"That's not true!" Todd exploded and looked to Barnaby, who sat stone still. "Say something, Barnaby."

"Maybe you should stop talking, Todd," Barnaby said.

Davenport turned to Stokes to continue. She folded her hands on the table, speaking softly, "Why did you hire Julio to kill your lovely, innocent wife?"

"We're done!" Barnaby declared, pushing on the table as if to stand.

Todd's face contorted and his eyes blazed. "Loving?! Innocent?! She was destroying me! She and her family contrived to get rid of me, kick me out of the business. She was going to divorce me, but I didn't kill her!"

Stokes considered Todd, whose arrogance had been reduced to self-pity. "We obtained a warrant for your bank records—two withdrawals of five thousand dollars—one down-payment that we found at Julio's house and an additional five thousand dollars which is still missing."

"Julio killed her, took the money from the box, then black-mailed me," Todd blustered. "He said he saw me kill her...but I didn't kill her!"

Powers knocked on the interview room door and stuck his head in. "Sir, there's a call."

Davenport nodded and turned off the recorder, leaving Stokes with the frantic suspect and the confused attorney.

"It's Griffin," Powers said when Davenport joined him in the hallway. "He and Salinas are on their way to Todd's house. There's something going on there between Drew and Diana— some kind of altercation that started at the plaza."

"Where's Malloy?" Davenport asked.

"He just returned from Orlando."

"Get Stokes," Davenport barked.

Moments later, Powers and Stokes rushed from the interrogation room. "What's up?" she asked Davenport.

"I need you and Powers to go to the Vogel house. Salinas and Griffin are there with Drew and Diana. Get backup."

"Do we have the wrong person, sir?" Stokes asked.

"I think we have a damn mess," Davenport said.

"Powers told me Malloy's here," Stokes said. "Perhaps it's time to release him from Purgatory?"

"You think so?"

Stokes nodded.

"Send him to the interview room—with water. It's going to be a long night."

CHAPTER 54

"What do we do now?" Claire asked.

"We need to follow them," Madge said, excitedly. "We can take the golf cart."

"Roberto wants us to go home," Claire said, "but he didn't see how Drew grabbed her."

"That's their job, Claire," Martín said. "We can't interfere."

"It's going to take Roberto and Deputy Griffin forever to get to Sea Haven by car," Claire argued. "Someone needs to help Diana."

"The golf cart is no match for a car," Martín said. "It's dark. I'll take the golf cart home. You ride home with the others."

Madge stood off to one side, her feet shuffling, her fingers fidgeting with her clothing. "I'd like to take the cart back to the house," she said. "You'll come with me, won't you, Claire? In case I get lost?"

Claire knew Madge's mannerisms as well as she knew her mother's. Madge was in her mischievous mode. "Sure," Claire said. *Better than letting her loose alone.*

Madge and Claire watched as the others walked toward their car.

"Let's go!" Madge said. "We gotta hurry!"

"Where're we going?"

"To the Vogels' house!"

"Madge!" Claire said hoarsely over the din of the music, but she followed her friend, who was stumbling toward the cart as quickly as her short legs could go.

Madge jumped into the driver's seat of the cart, inserted the key and started up the electric motor.

"Do you know how to get out of here?" Claire asked, jumping on the cart, clutching hers and Madge's purses as Madge jerked out of the parking spot.

"Of course, I've been exploring this place all week. I know a short cut."

Madge maneuvered around the parked carts and turned right onto a new service road that ran north of the plaza, through an open field, the future home of the new executive golf course. Far to the east stood the administrative buildings for The Havens and the DPS; to the west, Brook Haven Road led to the G&G and the county road.

"This is the wrong way!" Claire yelled as she grabbed onto the roof of the cart. "It's construction!"

Madge had picked up as much speed as possible in an electric cart, hurtling past huge construction equipment and bouncing over future tee boxes and dirt banks. "I came through here today," Madge said. "We just have to watch for the new ponds and sand traps."

The rising moon slipped behind a cloud, darkening their way. They maneuvered around large tree stumps and scattered holes.

"Damn! Madge! Be careful!" yelled Claire, her voice reverberating in the night air.

"I saw it," Madge said as they bounced along, then ran into a sand trap. "Shit!"

They jumped out of the cart, maneuvering it out of the sand trap and back onto the still-ungraded fairway, where newly planted palm trees provided a miniature corridor. They bumped along and nearly tipped over when they careened around a raised tee box. They could now see car headlights coming from the county road, on Brook Haven Road toward The Havens. The moon emerged from the cloud and lit their path, distant lights gleaming from houses in Sea Haven.

"There's a pond around here somewhere," Madge said as she and Claire both watched left and right.

"There!" yelled Claire. She grabbed the steering wheel from Madge and pulled it toward herself as a large pond loomed just ahead. They skirted the pond and stopped so Madge could get her bearings.

"Damn it, Madge," Claire said. "That better be an artificial alligator!"

Madge pressed on the pedal and veered sharply to the right, past the three-foot log lying on the edge of the pond. The log moved, its mouth opened, then it slithered into the water.

"Shit!" said Claire as Madge continued forward until they came onto a graded path. The path took them to another unpaved entrance onto Brook Haven Road, north of the Sea Haven gate. They crossed Brook Haven, where Madge pulled into a narrow skirting along the fence that separated the road from Sea Haven. A key-coded gate was built into the fence.

Madge smiled and pushed a button on the code box. "It's a service gate," she said as the gate swung open, and they entered Sea Haven.

"You're kidding me," Claire said. "But you can't see this from the road."

"Not unless you know where it is," Madge said. "I happened to see a maintenance truck enter through here—he pushed the 'enter' button—great security. I couldn't resist trying it out."

"This is Marlin Lane," Claire exclaimed as they passed into Sea Haven. Streetlights illuminated the first few residences. At the third home, Drew was throwing suitcases into the trunk of his car, while Diana tried to pull something out.

"Roberto and Griffin aren't here yet," Claire said as Madge pressed on the pedal again, rushing through the T in the road where Manatee ended at Marlin. Claire found her phone and called Roberto. "Where are you?"

"We're almost there...traffic and pedestrians..." Roberto said, irritation evident in his voice. "Where are you?"

"We're at Todd's house!" Claire lowered her voice as Madge approached. "You better come quick! Something's happening!" She clicked off the phone as she heard the familiar Spanish expletives echo from the receiver.

Madge turned off the lights on the cart as they pulled closer to the house. The twins stood in the dim glow cast from the porch light. They were arguing, but their words were muffled. Diana had tossed a duffel to the pavement, opened it, and was throwing fistfuls of something that looked like money onto the ground.

"What have you done?" Diana's words became clearer as her voice raised in pitch.

"I did nothing!" Drew said. "I gambled...I won...nothing wrong with that." He pushed Diana so hard she fell to the driveway, then hauled her up from the cement and pushed her against the car.

"Go! Go!" Claire said, too loudly. Madge pulled the cart into the driveway behind Drew's car. She took the key and they both jumped from the cart and ran toward Diana.

"What the hell!" Drew said. "Move that damn cart!" He ran down the driveway and jumped into the cart. "Where's the damn key?"

He leapt from the cart and grabbed at Madge's hand, but she pushed him aside and tossed the key into Alice's bougainvillea.

"Fuck," Drew said. He pushed the cart down the drive, but stopped short as another vehicle pulled in behind.

Roberto looked to Griffin. "I suggest you arrest that man."

Griffin paused before opening the door. "I've never made an arrest."

"It's your first one, then."

CHAPTER 55

Diana stood like a statue as she watched the deputies drive off in a squad car with her brother. Powers and Griffin followed in a second backup vehicle while Stokes stayed behind with the third cruiser. Madge and Claire faced the stern gaze of Detective Salinas—again.

"I'm so sorry," Claire said. "I did it again, didn't I?"

Roberto raised his eyebrows. "I expected nothing less from you and your *compañera*." He looked to Madge. "Can you make it home from here, Madge? I'd like Claire to stay with Diana."

Madge started to protest, but the look on Roberto's face deterred her. She eased down to her knees and pulled the key from the hedge. Struggling to stand, she held up the key. "I guess I'll be first to tell the others." She pouted as she pulled out of the driveway.

Stokes approached Diana. "Let's go inside?"

Diana roused herself, tears streaming down her face. "I need a drink," she said unexpectedly.

The four entered the house. Inside, it looked like a teenage party had been interrupted by unsuspecting parents. An opened suitcase lay on the floor with items tossed into it. Assorted alcohol bottles testified to a pre-*fiesta* binge, and a lamp had fallen onto the floor.

"Was there an argument here?" Stokes asked.

"Drew said we had to leave town…I thought we were going to Garland to see our father." She bent down to pick up the lamp, miraculously unbroken. "He'd been drinking."

"Leave it, Diana," Stokes said. "Let's go to the lanai."

322

Diana led Stokes, Roberto, and Claire to the lanai, where they sat down in the darkness. The moon shone on Clam Lake, producing an eerie reflection. Roberto and Claire declined the offer of drinks, watching as Diana poured herself a scotch and sat on a patio sofa.

Claire struggled to put the puzzle pieces together. She had been obsessed with Todd, his car, and what Madge had learned about him from her mother's friends…but Drew? She watched Roberto take his notebook from his pocket.

"The money in the duffel," Diana said, "what does it mean? Why did he have it?"

Reluctant to speculate, Stokes said, "He may have taken it from your mother—or she gave it to him."

Diana stared at Roberto, then Stokes. "Are you saying that Drew killed our mother? For money? That can't be true!" Her hands trembled, sloshing the scotch in her glass.

"It's not proof," Stokes said, "but it's important when combined with other evidence we have—that and the fact Drew lied about coming to your parents' house."

"What about Dad?"

"Detective Davenport is interviewing him," Stokes said quietly. "We believe your father contracted Julio to kill your mother, but Julio didn't kill her."

"Julio didn't kill her?" Diana whispered as if to herself. "Alice told us she saw someone in the yard—she thought it was the Mexican man—and saw him leave in a car!"

"She saw Julio," Stokes explained. "Julio thought he saw your father commit the murder and tried to blackmail him."

"I don't understand any of this!" Diana said. She sat back, sobbing. A meow and scratching sound drew Diana's attention to the door that led outside the birdcage.

"That's Alice's cat," Diana said.

The others turned to look at the cat pawing at the screen door.

"That's Alice's cat?" Roberto asked. "Is that her house next door?"

Diana nodded. "Puffy scratched our daughter over Christmas. Alice tries to keep her indoors, but she always gets out."

Claire opened the door, allowing the cat to wander in, fur ruffled and paws dirty.

"She's been outside for awhile," Claire said. "Do you think we should check on Alice?"

Stokes turned to Diana. "Have you seen Mrs. Van Dee lately?"

Diana shook her head. "Not since she brought over the casserole and told us about seeing Julio."

"It's dark over there, Roberto," Claire said. "Can I go check on her?"

Roberto joined her at the door facing Alice's house. "I'll go with you."

"I'll stay with Diana," Stokes said. "We need to talk."

"Something's wrong," Claire said to Roberto after they left the house. "Drew has a bad scratch on his arm."

They climbed through the hedge dividing the two houses and knocked on the lanai door. Hearing nothing, they followed the narrow lawn toward the front of the house, looking in the windows as they did so. Ringing the front doorbell got no response. Roberto then tried the knob, and the door opened.

"Alice?" Claire called out.

She started to enter, but Roberto held her back. "Let me go first." He took his phone from his pocket and punched a number. "Detective Davenport?"

"Oh, no," Claire said.

"I wanted him to know we were entering," Roberto explained when he ended the call.

They walked through the darkness, the air cold as the air-conditioning had not been lowered for the evening. Claire called out again but got no response. They peered into each spotless room.

The bedroom door was ajar; Claire followed behind Roberto. It took a few moments for their eyes to adjust. Roberto nearly tripped over Alice, who lay sprawled on the floor, blood seeping from a wound on her head. Roberto knelt to examine her eyes, then called Davenport again.

◆ ◆ ◆ ◆ ◆

Diana stood transfixed at the birdcage door, staring at Alice's house. She cradled Puffy in her arms. Once dark, Alice's house was now lit brightly, shadowy figures moving from room to room. Deputy Stokes had joined Roberto and Claire at Alice's house, and an ambulance had taken Alice away. *Something horrible must have happened*, she thought.

Diana had followed Stokes's advice and called her husband, giving sketchy details in between choking sobs. Carl promised to find a lawyer for her father and her brother. She freshened her drink before calling her sister-in-law. This conversation would require it.

"Drew and Todd arrested?" Penny screamed into the phone when Diana had summarized what she knew. "That's impossible!"

"I can't believe it either, Penny," Diana said, sniffling, "but it's true. It has something to do with Mom's murder."

"What?" Penny said, her voice rising. "They were both at the convention…weren't they?"

Diana gulped her drink. "They both deny coming here Saturday night, but the police know something that I don't."

Diana heard Penny struggling for breath. "Should I come down?"

"Not yet, but make arrangements for the kids—call Carl. He can help. He's looking for a lawyer. If your family has an attorney, let Carl know. I'll have more information tomorrow."

The more she thought about her father and brother, the more the pieces began to fit together. Her family had been steeped in tension for years. Between Dad's and Drew's drinking, Dad's behavior, the businesses, and Mom's frustration with the men in her life, it was inevitable something would give. Diana didn't know what had happened, but she had a horrible sense that her father or brother—or both—had done something terrible.

A dark figure crossed through the hedge towards her. She put Puffy down and opened the lanai door to Claire.

"What happened?" Diana asked as Claire entered.

"Alice is badly injured," Claire said, her hands shaking, her knees weak. "I need to sit down."

"Oh, no!" Diana led Claire to the same chair she had left earlier.

"Was it an accident? Heart attack?" Diana asked, sitting down again.

"I can't say," Claire sighed. She would never forget the image of Alice's white face and all the blood. "I guess she could have fallen, but I think the deputies suspect an assault."

"But who would…could do that?" Fresh tears streamed down Diana's face as she tore a tissue from a box on a small lamp table. "I don't understand," she repeated.

Claire's hands trembled as the puzzle pieces began to fall into place. "I'm sure the police will sort it all out," she said as she watched Diana sink back into her chair.

Puffy jumped onto Diana's lap, and Diana began to sob, gasping for air, engulfed in grief.

CHAPTER 56

Davenport reentered the interview room. Todd looked haggard, and Barnaby had moved his chair further from his temporary client. Malloy rushed into the room behind his superior, cradling four water bottles and his typed notes. He settled into the chair Stokes had abandoned, straightened his tie, and handed his notes to Davenport, who introduced him to Mr. Barnaby and then started the recorder.

"Detective Malloy has just returned from Orlando," Davenport explained. "He'll be sitting in for this session."

Malloy sighed quietly, noting that Davenport had introduced him with his title. Maybe this was his chance. *Thank you, Pam!*

Davenport quickly skimmed the notes Malloy had handed him. "Mr. Vogel, you have just confessed to hiring Julio Gonzalez to murder your wife—a crime that could result in a life prison sentence or the death penalty, depending on circumstances. It might have been a good idea to research Florida laws before committing such an offense. It makes losing your job at the dealership seem like a minor setback."

Vogel confessed to murder-for-hire? Molloy thought, astonished. *Damn!*

Todd's hands shook as he drank from his water bottle. "But you said Julio didn't kill her, so, someone else did. I'm not guilty."

"Don't say anything," Barnaby warned.

"It might be better if you did," Davenport said. "The more you cooperate, the better it might be for you in the end."

No one spoke while Todd composed himself. "Barbara and I had an argument several weeks ago about a lot of things brewing between us—business and personal finances—the same old stuff. Then it turned to mutual accusations of infidelity. She said she was divorcing me, that I would no longer have the business—she would own both, and she and the twins would take them over. I slaved forty years for her family, and she threatened to leave me...with nothing."

Todd ran his fingers through his hair. "I knew about Julio's sick daughter from gossip at Glen Haven. I also guessed he was involved with the local thefts. I made a deal with him. I wouldn't turn him in if he would do me a favor for ten thousand dollars. He accepted the deal, but afterwards, he denied killing her. But he must have!"

"Let me understand..." Malloy said, his own voice quivering, "...the favor was to kill your wife before she could divorce you?"

Todd covered his mouth with his hands. "He agreed to do it while I attended my conference."

"You gave him the down payment," Davenport said. "Did you pay him the final five thousand?"

"I told him to take it from the security box," Todd said, his voice breaking. "When my wife didn't answer my ten-thirty call, I called Julio to confirm it was done. He didn't answer, so I panicked and came home around midnight, and...and found her. The money wasn't in the box, so I thought he took it...but the scene was wrong." He gulped air. "I didn't kill her."

Todd put his head in his trembling hands. "Later, Julio called and tried to blackmail me. He said he saw me commit the murder, but it wasn't me!"

Davenport sat back in his chair. "When did you learn that the terms of the trust went into effect when she filed, and not when the divorce was final?"

Todd's face turned red. "She didn't tell me that detail," he spat. "I found out after, from her lawyer."

"So, you killed Julio because he blackmailed you?" Malloy

accused. "And after you paid him to kill your wife, you pointed your finger everywhere…Julio, Martín Aguila, Carlos…to protect yourself." Malloy's voice shook, his own role in denying Todd's culpability crashing down on him.

"Wait a damn minute!" Barnaby exploded, the veins in his neck bulging. "Now you're accusing Todd of killing Julio, too? What's your evidence?"

Davenport ignored Barnaby's outburst. "You were unlucky in several respects," he explained to Todd. "First, you nearly collided with another car as you left the G&G parking lot—after you killed Julio. Passengers in the other car identified your vehicle."

"I stayed at The Havens Inn Sunday night."

"You may have ended up there, but you detoured to a convenience store where you disposed of the evidence. We have it." Davenport pointed to a bin on the floor at his feet.

Todd leaned forward and started to speak.

"Be quiet," Barnaby ordered.

Davenport continued, "Witnesses saw a vanity plate on the car that nearly hit them. We found that same plate stashed under the padding in your trunk—MBA-UC—your degree at the University of Chicago. Did you hide it?"

Todd looked at Barnaby, whose face had turned white, and then glanced quickly at Malloy, as if hoping he would come to his defense. Malloy didn't look at him.

"It fell off, and I threw it in the trunk so I could put it back on later. I don't know how it got under the padding."

"Fair enough," Davenport said. He motioned to Malloy, who extracted the bag from the bin. "These are the bloody clothes we found with your smashed flip phone. We're quite sure they're yours. It's unlikely that a minor crook would wear a Columbia golf windbreaker to a murder. The blood coverage on the jacket indicates that the person who wore it sat in Julio's passenger seat."

"My client will say nothing more until he hires a criminal

attorney," Barnaby said, straightening his tie.

"That's a good idea," Davenport agreed. "We have one troubling gap in our evidence. We know you hired Julio to kill your wife, and we have evidence you killed Julio. We also know that you altered the murder scene. But we lack direct evidence that either you or Julio actually killed your wife."

Davenport paused. "However, we do have one interesting piece of information from Detective Malloy's visit to Orlando." He nodded to Malloy.

Malloy sat straight. "I learned you weren't the only person with opportunity to make the round-trip between Orlando and The Havens. Drew also cannot account for his movements Saturday night."

"What are you saying?" Todd glared at Malloy, then Davenport. "This is preposterous!"

Davenport's phone rang. He left Malloy behind to absorb the shocked looks of Todd and Barnaby.

"What do you want, Judy?" Davenport sighed impatiently, answering the call in the hallway. He'd had it with the Barnabys.

"It's about the parking ticket," Judy said. "We haven't been able to record the tickets lately—too busy helping you with your investigation—anyway, Dick Broden issued the ticket to Julio at ten-twenty Saturday night. His vehicle was parked at the service entrance to Sea Haven."

"So, Julio didn't park in the Vogels' driveway," Davenport said. "And we're just finding this out?"

"We just found out," Judy said, in a huff. "Now you know."

Davenport hung up and returned to the interview room. "Are you covering for someone, Mr. Vogel?"

CHAPTER 57

Friday morning

Claire pulled into the Sheriff's Department parking lot, Diana sitting motionless in the passenger seat. "We're here," Claire said, reaching over to touch Diana's hand. They exited the car, Claire removing Diana's luggage from the trunk and placing it on the ground.

"Are you sure you don't need a ride to the airport?" Claire asked. "I'd be glad to drive you."

Diana shook her head. "Ronnie and I are taking Mom's car to his hotel—after he, Drew, and Dad meet with the criminal attorney. We'll fly out tomorrow with Mom's ashes." She reached out to shake Claire's hand, but Claire pulled her in for a brief hug instead.

"Thank you for your help," Diana continued. "I'm so sorry my family dragged your father into this."

"My father doesn't blame you, and my family shares my sympathy for what you're going through."

Diana took an envelope from her purse and handed it to Claire. "Please give this to Mrs. Gonzalez. I want to do something for her family. They've been through so much."

Claire took the envelope. "I wish the best for you, Diana. Please keep in touch."

"Thank you. I will." Diana wiped at her eyes. "Well, I should go. I can't keep Deputy Stokes waiting."

◆ ◆ ◆ ◆ ◆

Inside the station, Stokes led Diana, pulling her wheeled suit-case behind her, through a maze of desks. Deputies looked up as Stokes directed her to a small desk near the back of the squad room. Stokes's desk was cluttered with papers but decorated with only two photographs, one of Stokes with several siblings and parents, the other a picture of a gray tabby cat.

"I guess I'm cat-sitting for Alice," Stokes said, noticing Diana's interest in the photo. "My cat, Romeo, is not happy with the threats to his territory, but they won't have to tolerate each other for long."

"How is Alice?" Diana asked.

"She'll be all right, but she lost a lot of blood. She regained consciousness and told deputies that Drew attacked her. She remembers falling, but nothing after that. Drew accused her of telling deputies she saw him at your parents' house. She didn't see Drew in the yard, but she saw him leaving in the rental car. She didn't know it was him."

"Poor Alice," Diana said, sobbing. She pulled a tissue from her purse and blew her nose. "What happens to Drew and my father now?"

"Prosecutors will likely charge your father with first degree murder for killing Julio, and he may also be charged with con-spiracy to murder your mother."

"I can't believe it's true," Diana said weakly. "What about Drew?"

Stokes met Diana's eyes. "It's up to the prosecutor," she said. "Drew could be charged with first degree murder, though he claims your mother's death was accidental."

Diana latched onto that idea. "An accident…of course…it had to be…"

"The money you found in the duffel came from your parents' cash box. He ditched the clothes, but the blood found in the car and on the money matches your mother's."

"But why?" Diana asked, her eyes pleading. "Was it the divorce? The trust? I thought he'd been gambling…I never thought he could kill anyone, let alone our mother. The whole scenario still feels so unreal to me."

Stokes sat back and sighed. Perhaps she wasn't ready to be a detective. She doubted she would ever become accustomed to these kinds of conversations. "I don't know what the prosecutor will charge Drew for his assault on Alice, but, in any case, your father and brother are looking at long prison sentences."

Stokes reached out as Diana slouched and began to slide from the chair. Ken Griffin, sitting at the next desk, rushed over and caught her before she hit the floor.

"I'll get you some water," Griffin offered as he helped her sit back up.

"Thank you," Diana said weakly, color returning to her face.

Stokes sat quietly, waiting for Diana to catch her breath and absorb the tragic news.

After Griffin returned with water and Diana had taken a few sips, Stokes put the pieces together for her. "We think Alice saw Julio at the birdcage the night your mother was killed. Julio saw the murderer, but he thought it was your father, who had hired him to rob and kill your mother. Julio never entered the house. Instead, he tried to blackmail your father, which is why your father killed him."

Stokes paused to collect her thoughts. "Julio actually saw Drew, who is being interviewed this morning. That's all I can tell you now."

"I can't stand to hear any more." Diana gasped for air and took a gulp of water, trying to control her shaking hands. "May I see them?"

"Detective Davenport will call when he is through with the interview."

Diana took a deep breath. "Annette Fulton has planned a

memorial lunch for Mother at her favorite restaurant today. How do I tell her employees that Drew and Dad are in jail?"

"Annette will know what to say. Your mother's employees need some closure and an opportunity to mourn."

"I'm taking her ashes back to Chicago for a memorial. It will be awful, under the circumstances, but my mother's life deserves to be celebrated where she worked and lived for so many years."

Stokes's phone rang, and she answered. After a brief conversation she hung up and said, "You can meet with your brother and father in a few minutes." Stokes interlaced her fingers on the desk. "What do you think you'll do with the businesses?"

The question calmed Diana, allowing her to focus on something that she had control over. "I haven't digested the fact that I have two businesses to run," she admitted. "I'll know more about my options once I talk to Ronnie and the employees. I may have to sell the Florida business, but, until then, I plan to put Annette in charge. I trust her. There will be a lot of financial issues to work through…debts to pay…I don't think I can do this alone."

"If you're like your mother, you'll manage, Diana."

CHAPTER 58

Davenport and Malloy entered the interview room where Drew, disheveled and unshaven, sat with Ronald Murphy, who looked as if he had not slept either.

"I hope you both had a comfortable night," Davenport said to the men.

"What do you think?" Drew said. He turned to Murphy. "What's the matter, Ronnie? Your bed at the Holiday Inn not firm enough?"

Murphy settled his glasses on his face and scowled. "I spent all night trying to find a criminal lawyer for you two. You're lucky you got me today and not Mr. Barnaby, who, like both of you, was in way over his head."

Drew slouched in his chair as Davenport shuffled papers on the table. "Mr. Vogel, your sister is here. She wants to talk with you and your father. She can meet with you both later, if you wish."

Drew shrugged.

"Are we ready then?" asked Davenport. Drew nodded, and Malloy started the recorder.

"Mr. Vogel," Davenport said, "do you still claim you weren't at your mother's home Saturday night?"

"Yes."

Davenport looked at Malloy. "What have you found, detective?"

Malloy straightened his tie. "We've confirmed that you and your father were together Saturday afternoon, but, like your father, your whereabouts at night are suspect."

"I went to the casino," Drew repeated. "I gambled and bought drinks."

"But you cashed out at eight o'clock and didn't return to your hotel until midnight," Malloy said, extracting a photo from his folder. "Unfortunately for you, many tourists get confused on the expressways and accidentally go through the SunPass lanes and, as a result, supplement Florida's coffers." He showed Drew the security-cam photo of his car passing through the gate. The timestamp read eleven-thirty-five p.m. "You were driving east-bound near Orlando. It's your rental car plate."

Drew blanched.

"We contacted the rental agency and compared your beginning mileage to the current mileage on your car, which is in the police garage," Malloy continued. "The mileage difference is consistent with the miles driven from the airport to your hotel to the casino, plus a round-trip to The Havens."

"Of course," Davenport added, "we have enough evidence without this to charge you with the murder of your mother, not to mention charges of aggravated assault with intent to commit murder against Alice Van Dee."

"The old lady accused me of killing my mother. I barely hit her…she tripped over that damn cat and fell."

"Alice regained consciousness this morning and tells a different story." Malloy pointed to Drew's arm. "And it looks like perhaps her cat attacked you when you threw it outside."

Drew shrugged.

"But you *did* kill your mother," Davenport said, leaning forward.

"You don't have to say anything," Murphy said sternly.

Drew looked at Murphy, then Davenport. "I called Mom. I wanted to talk to her. She told me to come at ten, but I got there early and saw a car leaving from the garage, a man driving. I waited for him to leave, then pulled into the driveway. It was obvious she had a lover…two glasses on the counter…and she wore this negligee and her kimono. I confronted her about having an affair." He wiped his hands on his pants. "I fixed myself a drink, and she told me she was divorcing Dad. We argued…"

"You argued about the divorce?" Davenport asked.

"And other things. You don't know how it was, working with her. She had a temper."

"So, you argued about more than the divorce," Davenport suggested.

"She held the purse-strings for both businesses. She had Diana and Annette Fulton under her thumb, always complaining about expenses."

"You killed her because she questioned your expenses?" Davenport asked.

"No!" Drew raised his voice. "It's the trust! She told me that Diana and I would have to buy her out in order to own the Chicago business. It wasn't fair! We counted on that as our inheritance!"

"So, you killed her before she could get that divorce?" Malloy asked.

"I didn't know it was already a done deal…that she had filed…and it was done." Drew's eyes were wide in terror. "When she told me…I couldn't believe it…I told her we…expected to get the businesses when she and Dad retired. I told her to ignore the trust, but she said she needed to keep control of the businesses after the divorce…that we had to wait to inherit them… or buy her out. So, I told her I needed money now…I asked for money because I had over-spent my expense account. She yelled, calling me a lazy drunk, like my father. 'I'm not made of money,' she said. 'I have to pay for your fun.' It was horrible, but finally she went into the bedroom…"

Drew wiped sweat from his brow. His eyes darted wildly from the detectives to Murphy, who put his hand out to stop Drew, but his client was spiraling out of control.

"...When she came out of the bedroom, she looked confused...she said, 'Where did this come from?' like she didn't know there was a wad of money in the cash box...then she threw it at me and pushed me. I pushed her against the sideboard. I think she remembered the gun...she reached into the drawer and pulled it out...I was scared...I took it from her...she kept yelling at me—'Drunk!...Drunk!'—and the gun went off." Drew collapsed back against the chair, tears flowing freely.

Davenport leaned forward. "Did you know that you and Diana would inherit the stores if she died? Did that occur to you as you were fighting for the gun?"

"She was using us...I couldn't live with her controlling me any more...I was so angry!"

"My God," Murphy said, "I think you've said enough."

"Your mother didn't die right away," Davenport said. "You knew that she had filed, and the deal was done. You could have saved her. Did you think of calling 911?"

Drew looked stunned, like the idea had never occurred to him. "Not dead?"

"It took her awhile to die," Davenport said evenly.

Drew fell forward, dropping his head onto his arms on the table.

"So, you cleaned the gun, washed the glasses and bottle," Davenport continued. "You pulled your car—which fits the original description given to us—into the garage, changed your clothes, and disposed of the incriminating clothes later. However, the forensic team found your mother's blood in the garage, in your car, on the duffel, and on the money. We know you tried to wipe it up with your clothes, but we have enough evidence without them to prove your guilt."

"But you forgot about the fridge," Malloy said.

"Ironically," Davenport added, "the stray prints and the series of lies you and your father told us turned our attention your way. You didn't know at first that your father had hired Julio Gonzalez to kill your mother that night. But you knew right away that something was wrong—the scene was wrong and your father was lying."

"Did you suspect that your father killed Julio?" Malloy asked, his anger rising. "It seems you both had the same motives—greed and a need to be rid of your mother."

"And then, there's Alice," Davenport said. "When Alice told you she saw someone pull out of the driveway, you thought she recognized you. She didn't, but her indiscretion led you to attempt murder. You have a long time in prison ahead of you. Lots of time to think about what you have done and consider that you will never inherit either store."

"What's amazing," Malloy said, "is that you and your father didn't meet up at the house—you were both there. What would have happened then, I wonder?"

Davenport sat back in his chair. "You must have wondered why your father's description of the scene differed from what you left behind, including the jewelry your mother wore. But you said nothing. It benefited you, and ultimately, he covered for you."

"I...I didn't understand it...but I couldn't do anything or say anything...I just hoped it would all go away when everyone thought Julio did it."

"You also knew your father used his own clubs in Florida," Malloy scowled. "You and your father consistently lied to us, unconcerned, and you both would have let an innocent man be punished for your actions."

Drew shrugged. "We had more to lose than any of those people."

♦ ♦ ♦ ♦ ♦

Pam Stokes led Diana down a long hallway. The closer they got to the jail side of the building, the straighter Diana walked, as if drawing on some inner strength. They shook hands at the security door.

"Thank you," Diana said.

"Good luck," Stokes said.

Inside, a deputy delivered Diana to a small meeting room, where her father, brother, and Ron Murphy all glared at each other. The deputy led her in and positioned himself outside the room.

Diana sat in a faded plastic molded chair facing Drew and Todd. "Well, this is special."

"We can always count on you for sarcasm," Drew said.

"It's the only response I have when I learn my father paid a man to kill my mother, and his own son—my brother—did it for him."

"It's not what you think," Todd said.

"I think it's worse," Diana retorted, suddenly exhausted.

"You need to help us," Todd said, reaching for her arm. "We're meeting our criminal attorney this afternoon, before our arraignments. You need to raise our bail money."

"Sorry," Diana said, pulling her arm away. "You're on your own."

"What about the businesses?" Todd asked, desperately. "You have to keep them open for us."

"If I could, I'd sell the Florida business tomorrow, but I have the employees to think about." She looked at Murphy, who gave her a slight nod. "I'll act on Ronnie's advice, not yours. For now, Annette will handle Mom's store."

"And the house?" Todd pleaded, as the horror of his predicament sank in.

"The house is yours, Dad. You have to decide if you can afford to keep it after you pay for bail—if you get bail—and attorney fees."

"What about me?" Drew whined. "You have to come up with the money from the Chicago business for me."

"I'll do no such thing," Diana said, "and I have no idea what Penny will do."

"Does she know?"

"The outline, not the details. You haven't called her?"

Drew shook his head. "But I still own half the Chicago business," he commanded.

"You killed our mother. I don't think the trust owes you anything." She turned to Ronnie. "But, of course, Ronnie represents the trust. He'll make those decisions."

All heads turned toward Ron Murphy, who had sat quietly during the exchange. "It'll take awhile to sort everything out," he said, "but since the divorce papers had been filed, Todd inherits nothing."

Diana stood to leave. "When our grandparents wrote up the trust, I doubt they considered what might happen if their grandson murdered their daughter, or if their son-in-law conspired to kill his wife." She paused in the doorway. "On second thought, that was probably exactly what they *were* afraid of."

CHAPTER 59

Davenport stood with his team under a jacaranda tree at the edge of a small cemetery behind the Orchard Community Church. The names of the gravestones represented the diversity in this small town. The deputies watched the gathering of friends and family at Julio's grave, united to mourn a flawed member of their community. Stokes thought of Diana, traveling alone with her mother's ashes and facing family and friends who knew what Todd and Drew had done. How would she explain this to her children? To Drew's family?

The graveside service had ended, and the mourners began to gather around Paula Gonzalez. Behind Paula, her sister Martha stood quietly with Billy and little Mary, who held onto her big brother's hand. Carlos and Sofia took turns hugging Paula as she wept silently. Elena Huerta followed them, then Amanda Davis appeared from behind a nearby tree.

Claire waited for Amanda to express condolences to Paula, then approached the widow, hugged her, and gave her the envelope. "Mr. Vogel's daughter, Diana Thurman, wants you to have this."

Paula opened it and peeked at the check, breaking into tears. "It's so much!" she said. "You'll give me her address?"

"Of course."

Davenport motioned for his team to join the Aguila family, which had congregated near the church. Malloy stood back, reluctant to face Martín, but Davenport patted him on the shoulder.

"Come on," he said.

The Aguilas met the deputies halfway. Claire joined them, introducing Madge to those who hadn't had the pleasure of her company.

Roberto stepped forward. "It has been a pleasure meeting your team," he said, shaking hands with the deputies, holding Malloy's hand a second longer than the others. "And I apologize for imposing on your investigation. I appreciate your willingness to include me. I have learned much from you."

"And I from you," Davenport said.

Stokes reached out to shake Claire's hand. "Thank you for your assistance with Mrs. Huerta." Stokes glanced at Malloy, back in uniform, his eyes not meeting hers.

"I'm glad this is over," Claire said, "but miserable about all the pain and suffering."

"I hated this case," Stokes admitted. "So many victims. Too much death."

"How is Alice?" Claire asked.

"Better. Her son is here, and she'll be home soon. She told me to thank you for saving her life."

Claire smiled. "I didn't do anything."

"It was your idea to check on her."

"How does she know that?"

"I might have mentioned it," Stokes admitted, smiling.

Malloy approached Martín, who also stood away from the group. "Mr. Aguila, I'm sorry for how I treated you. It was unprofessional."

Martín reached out to shake his hand. "I accept your apology, but, please, apologize to Carlos."

"I promise," Malloy said.

When the Aguilas and the deputies departed for their vehicles, Malloy and Stokes stayed back.

Stokes nudged Malloy. "How does it feel to be back in uniform?"

Malloy took her elbow. "I know that Davenport brought me into the interview because you suggested it."

"He was ready to give you that second chance," Stokes smiled. "Too bad it didn't last."

"I knew Sara wouldn't take a long maternity leave, but I didn't think she'd return quite so soon," Malloy said, shrugging.

Stokes laughed. "I talked to her. She and Marcos love the baby to death, but she was going crazy. Both her mother and mother-in-law were competing for primary caregiver status, so she gave in and set up a schedule. I think she's ecstatic to be back."

"Coffee?" Malloy asked.

"Coffee."

◆ ◆ ◆ ◆ ◆

On their way back to The Havens, Roberto and Claire met the family and Madge at a steak house in Garland. They ordered lunch, exhaustion evident on every face.

"I can't imagine the pain that Paula must feel. She's lost her husband, and her children have lost their father," Theresa said after a silence.

"He wasn't perfect," Roberto noted. "It was likely only a matter of time before he was caught stealing, and possibly deported."

"Always the cop," Claire said. "I'm sure you're right, but still, I can't help thinking it would have worked out for them. Paula has a strong family, and Carlos tried to help him."

"But the true villains were Todd and Drew," Madge said. "Julio stole for his family; they murdered for greed. There's no comparison."

"But he might have killed Barbara," Roberto reminded them. "He accepted the down payment."

After a thoughtful silence, Martín asked Roberto, "When did Todd realize that Drew might have killed Barbara?"

Roberto shrugged. "I suspect Todd began to suspect Drew when he continued to lie about being at the house. The stray fingerprint, the scotch, the three glasses…all led him to believe his son had been there."

"What about the gun?" Claire asked.

"Julio was supposed to get rid of it. Todd panicked when he saw it. He took it back to Orlando, hiding it in a pharmacy bag. I'm not sure why, but Davenport thinks he didn't want it at the scene. So, accidentally, he might have removed Drew's prints—if Drew hadn't already cleaned them off."

Roberto pushed his empty plate aside. "When his friend, Jordan Davis, met him at The Havens Inn Sunday night and told him he saw a light-colored car in the driveway, Todd assumed it had been Julio's, but Julio denied going into the house. Then the photograph of Julio's dented car appeared in the newspaper, and Jordan told Todd it wasn't Julio's car he saw, but a newer one, more like Drew's rental. Then Todd knew. Even so, he pressured Jordan to identify Julio's car as the one he saw. Eventually, Amanda convinced Jordan to tell the truth. Then, the local police found a parking ticket which had been issued to Julio that night at the security gate on Brook Haven Road."

"I wonder when Todd and Drew realized this about the other," Claire said.

Theresa frowned. "It must have been a horrible moment for them both."

Martín shook his head. "Welcome to The Havens. I think I'll go back to my city, where it's safe."

CHAPTER 60

"Do you *really* think your family and Madge wanted to stay in Garland to see a super-hero movie?" Roberto asked Claire as he folded a pair of slacks into his suitcase. He had been sleeping on a sofa bed in a tiny room that the Carsons used as a home office.

"Ha! They're probably drinking margaritas at The Oasis." Claire sat in the swivel chair at the desk and watched Roberto pack, the air heavy between them. "It's nice of you to offer to drive Madge to the airport tomorrow."

"*No hay problema*," Roberto laughed. "I wanted to make sure she left before she bought a house." Reaching over, he pulled Claire from the chair and kissed her.

"So you still want to be with me even though, once again, I'm embroiled in murder?" she asked, leaning into him.

"That makes the possibility of life with you all the more intriguing." Roberto kissed her again and smiled. "You know, they're not going to stay away all night."

"Now what?"

"Whose room, yours or mine?"

"Mine, or you'll have to repack," Claire said, taking his hand.

◆ ◆ ◆ ◆ ◆

Later, in Claire's bed, sleepy and contented, they listened as Claire's family quietly entered the house. Claire expected Madge to barge into the room, but she heard only whispers as her parents, Cristina, and Madge retreated to their rooms.

In the early morning, Claire awoke, startled to feel someone sleeping next to her. It had been a long time. She touched Roberto's face, then tiptoed to the bathroom. She dressed and padded into the kitchen, following the aroma of brewed coffee, a sense of discomfort rising as she wondered what her family would say to her. *My God, I'm fifty-five years old,* she thought. But the house was empty. A note sat on a bakery box of croissants—gone to breakfast.

She took a cup of coffee and a croissant out to the lanai, gazing out at the lake that ended just past the Carsons' home. Less than a week ago, Drew Vogel had killed his own mother. It seemed unreal, and tears came to her eyes when she thought of Julio, murdered because of his dreams, and poor Alice, punished for her curiosity.

She turned when she heard the slider open. Roberto entered, wearing shorts and a T-shirt, carrying his own coffee and croissant. "We've been abandoned," he said as he sat next to her.

"I can't believe you're leaving today, Roberto."

"I wish I could take you with me."

Claire reached over and took his hand. "How long does it last?"

Roberto brushed her disheveled hair from her face. "How long does what last?"

"The guilty feeling that I'm being unfaithful to my husband. You understand, don't you?"

"I do understand. I felt the same…for a long time."

"So, how long does it last?"

"As long as you let it," he said, bringing his face close to hers and kissing her. "But there's an option," he said softly. "You could come with me. I could kick my mother and daughter out of my house."

Claire laughed. "Don't you dare!" She studied him over her coffee cup. "I haven't given you an answer yet. I still have a job. I have obligations. Besides, I refuse to displace your family. I already love Marta, and I know I'll love your mother, too, though I don't know what they'll think of me."

"Marta idolizes you—she wants to follow in your footsteps as an anthropologist. And Mother can't believe anyone would want to marry me, so she'll welcome you with open arms."

"But what will I do there?" Claire teased. "I certainly don't want to assist you in any more murder investigations. I've had enough of that."

Roberto laughed. "Don't worry, I don't want you meddling in my job anymore, but you have options."

"Like being Eduardo Ramirez's curator?" Claire referred to the murderer who had offered her a job in Merida the year before.

"Well, not unless you work via video chat to his prison cell," Roberto said, brushing croissant crumbs off his University of Yucatán T-shirt. He pointed to the shirt. "You could teach anthropology at UADY, give English lessons—or write that novel."

"What about my family?"

"They're one day away, and they'd visit." The slider opened, and Claire's family joined them on the lanai, each with a coffee cup in hand. "Let's ask them," Roberto said, as they settled themselves at the patio table.

"What?" asked Theresa.

Roberto smiled. "Would you visit us if Claire moved to Merida?"

"Only if you marry her," Cristina said, smiling.

"That's up to your mother," Roberto said. "I've made her an offer."

"So, Dad," Claire said, her eyes teasing, "would you visit us?"

Martín sipped his coffee, considering. "No, never. I hate Mexico."

Theresa slapped her husband lightly. "Martín!"

Martín laughed. "Of course, I'd come."

Theresa placed her cup on the table. "What's your answer,

Claire?"

Claire sighed. "It's complicated."

Martín shook his head. "No, it's not. It's yes or no."

Claire took Roberto's hand and looked into his eyes. "Of course, I want to marry you, Roberto."

"So, it's settled," Martín said, winking at Roberto.

"And you thought your family wouldn't like me," Roberto said, smiling.

"Evidently I was wrong," Claire replied through a laugh.

Cristina clapped her hands. "I have an idea! I think a Mexican wedding would be perfect!"

Martín's eyes teared up. "I've never visited my family's homeland. To see my daughter married in a Merida cathedral would bring our family full circle."

Madge entered the lanai, dropping her huge cloth bags at the sliding door. "You said yes?" she asked, smiling. "You're getting married? In Merida? I can't wait to be a bridesmaid!"

"Me too," said Cristina. "You and me, Madge!"

"We just need a date," Theresa said. "I'll email Roberto's mother...does she email, Roberto?"

"Yes, she does."

"It's settled," Martín said again.

Claire sat stunned. "You all planned this ahead of time, didn't you?"

Roberto smiled. "Any respectable Mexican man asks a father's permission to marry his daughter."

END

ACKNOWLEDGEMENTS

In *Culture Shock*, as in *Human Sacrifice*, I am grateful to my husband, LaVail, who read multiple versions of the manuscript and whose critique was instrumental in bringing life to my wayward characters. Again, thanks to our son, Nathan, who has been a patient reader and consultant on crime scene and police procedures.

Special thanks to friends and family who have continuously encouraged me to keep writing, and who have read and commented on early versions of *Culture Shock*: Sandy Seppala Gyr, Susan Grant, and our children, Sarah Mulder and David Hull. Thank you to Robert Downes and Cari Noga, brilliant writers who were willing to read my final version. I am grateful to Sandy Seppala Gyr for her patience and diligence in copy editing, and to my longtime friend, Jim DeWildt, for his artwork.

A special award is due to the Old Town Writer's Group members who both challenged and encouraged me through the late drafts of *Human Sacrifice* and the entire manuscript of *Culture Shock*. Thank you for offering a comfortable space for all of us to discuss our work and share ideas.

Thank you to Mission Point Press editors and staff: Doug Weaver, Sarah Meiers, Darlene Short, and especially Scott Couturier, who has guided me through both *Human Sacrifice* and *Culture Shock*.

A note on the locations described in the novel: My husband and I have visited and toured numerous retirement communities in our search for our ideal retirement. We have friends and relatives who live in all types of communities from mobile home parks to exclusive McMansion communities. The Havens is a fictitious community, and all characters are fictitious. Yet our travels and experiences have given me an insight into the lifestyle and cultures that evolve in these communities, often replicating those in the larger society. I hope that my friends and acquaintances are not offended, but understand that my characters have lives of their own, and I had no choice but to report on them.

ABOUT THE AUTHOR

Dr. Cindy L. Hull is an anthropologist and Professor Emeritus from Grand Valley State University. Her research interests have taken her to Mexico, Micronesia, and rural Michigan. She has published two ethnographies: *Katun: A Twenty-Year Journey with the Maya*; and *Chippewa Lake: A Community in Search of an Identity*. Her first mystery novel, *Human Sacrifice*, took place in the Yucatán Peninsula and introduced her protagonist, Dr. Claire Aguila. Her newest mystery, *Culture Shock*, takes Dr. Aguila and her family to the mysterious world of the Florida retirement community. Alas, Cindy has not succumbed to the allure of life in a retirement community. Instead, she happily resides with her husband in Traverse City, Michigan.